W9-BAV-784

Also by Alix Kates Shulman

Memoirs of an Ex-Prom Queen (novel)

To the Barricades
The Anarchist Life of Emma Goldman

Red Emma Speaks
Selected Writings and Speeches (editor)

JUVENILES

Bosley on the Number Line

Awake or Asleep

Finders Keepers

Burning Questions

Burning Questions

A NOVEL

Alix
Kates
Shulman

ALFRED A. KNOPF NEW YORK 1978

I wish to thank the MacDowell Colony for privacy and my friends, family, and women's group for the support and stimulation that enabled fiction to flow. Except for those of historical record, all characters and events in this book are fictional, drawn solely from the imagination, and any resemblance to real persons or events is unintentional.

THIS IS A BORZOI BOOK
PUBLISHED BY ALFRED A. KNOPF, INC.

 Published in the United States by Alfred A. Knopf, Inc., New York, and simultaneously in Canada by Random House of Canada Limited, Toronto. Distributed by Random House, Inc., New York.

Library of Congress Cataloging in Publication Data

Shulman, Alix Kates. Burning questions.

I. Title.
PZ4.S56314BU [PS3569.H77] 813'.5'4 77-21534
ISBN 0-394-40021-6

Manufactured in the United States of America
FIRST EDITION

Grateful acknowledgment is made to the following for permission to reprint previously published material:

Encyclopaedia Britannica: excerpt from the article "Club" in *Encyclopaedia Britannica*, 14th edition (1968), 5:955.

The Feminist Press: excerpts from *The Woman and the Myth: Margaret Fuller's Life and Writings*. Copyright © 1976 by Bell

Gale Chevigny. Published by the Feminist Press, Box 334, Old Westbury, New York 11568.

Harcourt Brace Jovanovich, Inc.: excerpt from "To Posterity" by Bertolt Brecht, translated by H. R. Hays.

Harper & Row, Inc.: excerpt from *My Life as a Rebel* by Angelica Balabanoff, 1938.

Harvard University Press and Little, Brown and Company: excerpts from *Poem #174* by Emily Dickinson, from *The Complete Poems,* Little, Brown and Company, 1960.

Houghton Mifflin Company and the Sterling Lord Agency, Inc.: excerpt from the poem "Rapunzel" from *Transformations* by Anne Sexton. Copyright © 1971 by Anne Sexton. Reprinted by permission of the publisher and the Sterling Lord Agency, Inc., agent for the Estate of Anne Sexton.

International Publishers Co., Inc.: excerpt from *They Shall Not Pass: The Autobiography of La Pasionaria* by Delores Ibarruri, International Publishers, New York, 1966; and excerpts from *We Are Many* by Mother Bloor, International Publishers, New York, 1940.

Robin Morgan: excerpts from "Principles by the New York Radical Women" reprinted from *Sisterhood Is Powerful,* Robin Morgan, editor, Random House, 1970.

To DD and SS

At last, to be identified!
At last, the lamps upon thy side
The rest of Life to see!

Past Midnight! Past the Morning Star!
Past Sunrise!
Ah, what leagues there were
Between our feet, and Day!

—EMILY DICKINSON

Burning Questions

MY LIFE AS A REBEL

—by—

Zane

New Space Press   New York   1977

For the Third Street Circle

To rebel is justified.

—Mao Tse-Tung

Contents

Preface

With joy and envy I read the lives of those great revolutionary women of the past—the "Moscow Amazons" of the eighteen sixties, seventies, and eighties who helped assassinate the Tsar, the "Pétroleuses" who mounted the barricades of Paris to defend the Commune, and all the other brave, single-minded women who devoted their lives to the revolution: Rosa Luxemburg, Emma Goldman, Louise Michel, La Pasionaria.

Their lives are so direct, their stories high drama. They begin with the stations of their birth, skip quickly to the crucial incident of childhood—the one riveting moment when the sight of some unspeakable cruelty or the touching kindness of a concerned elder (an aunt, a teacher) awakens them from their slumbering innocence to pose their destiny. They brood, then plunge directly into reading the book that will change their lives by its stunning revelations or wrestling with the idea that will launch them on lives of implacable commitment. Nothing will keep them now from leaving the provinces for St. Petersburg, for Zurich, Geneva, or Paris, where "the new ideas fill the air." Studying medicine at a university or philosophy in a workers' study group, they stay awake every night, sometimes till dawn, passionately debating the new ideas with their "little circle" or reading the forbidden books that pass secretly from hand to hand, until at last they take the irrevocable step by which they merge their lives with those of their "comrades" in "the Great Cause" of "our generation." (Sometimes they speak of love, but men are by no means the important element in their lives.) Long before they die, which they are prepared to do at any time, each one knows the very words she wishes to pass on to the future:

Sofia Bardina: "Persecute us—you have material strength for a while, gentlemen, but we have moral strength, the strength of ideas; and ideas, alas, you cannot pierce with bayonets."

La Pasionaria: "It is better to die on your feet than live on your knees."

Marie Schmitt, Communarde: "I am only sorry that I did not do everything I am accused of."

Louise Michel: "Why should I defend myself? . . . You are men who are going to judge me. You are before me; your faces are revealed. You are men, and I am only a woman; yet I look you in the eye. . . . If you let me live, I shall never cease to cry for vengeance; . . . I have finished. If you are not cowards, kill me."

It was not like that for us. For my generation nothing was ever so clear. Perhaps I shouldn't even speak of "us" and "my generation"; nowadays, generations succeed each other so quickly. In Babylon, Indiana, where I grew up, my "generation" seemed to consist of jocks, grinds, and the contented, whom I rejected by leaving at the first opportunity; then, in New York City, where I rushed to find myself, there were the people who rejected me. We were called the Silent Generation because some of us felt we had nothing to say and the rest had no one to say it to. But I was fortunate enough and young enough to pass from one generation to another at the appropriate moment by a timely change of style. From Silent to Beat to Revolutionary.

But I am also uneasy with words like "revolutionary." It is true that I am privileged to teach the course in Revolutionary Women at the New School for Social Research in New York City, and here I am setting down *My Life as a Rebel*. But it is with grave reservation that I invoke those revolutionary greats. Even at the height of the sixties, when the word "revolutionary" was as debased as it was fashionable, applying to scanty clothing, flowing hair, manufacturers of certain plastics, and busy fornicators, as well as to a handful of civilian bombers and thousands of compassionate partisans of a new world order, to me there was something pretentious in the word. I would never have called myself an "artist," either, among the beats on MacDougal Street, though I too kept a journal and took life classes at the Art Students League. It always seemed to me that an "artist," a "revolutionary," had to earn the names by performing significant and heroic acts. Tokens, good intentions, were not enough. Even as a child I thought it shamefully dishonest to boast of exploits one had yet to perform; when Adlai Stevenson let us down by losing the election to Eisenhower after boasting all over the country that he could win, I wondered how he would ever be able to stand up in public again. I felt sorry for him (he was my father's candidate); but mostly I felt contempt. Decades later I had similar reservations about movement people who said they were going to change the world but had no idea how, and without winning their titles by acts of courage or suffering went around arrogantly declaring themselves avatars of a New Society. If they didn't know how to bring it off, then at least, I thought, instead of bluffing and boasting they ought to have proven their sincerity: actively, like Rosa or Che or the Lincoln Brigade who fought in Spain, or the visionary souls who were with Mao on the Long March, or those Buddhist monks who burned themselves before heads of state; or else passively by being persecuted like Sacco and Vanzetti and the poor Rosenbergs who gave their lives or those New Haven lesbians who went to jail rather than rat on one of their sisters.

(Though as a child I kept a picture of Joan of Arc, most defiant of all, above my bed, and years later, caught up in our own movement, I too spent a night in jail, I never imagined that such fancied or impure acts as mine could make me a "revolutionary.")

Yet, despite my qualms, I choose to begin my book by invoking those heroic women of the past. No matter how far short of their achievements mine may fall, our lives are intimately connected by history. Though the 1960s are not the 1860s, though our suburbs are hardly peasant villages or Greenwich Village Moscow, still, for one glorious moment some of us did manage to find each other and launch our rebellion.

Of course it didn't last; a new generation with a different style replaced us soon enough. But then, the Paris Commune failed as well, wiped out in a matter of weeks; Rosa Luxemburg was murdered and her party smashed; La Pasionaria saw Franco conquer Spain; Emma Goldman was forced into permanent exile; and even the Moscow Amazons, whose revolution ostensibly triumphed, would probably rise from their graves if they knew what happened to their precious Russia under the tyrant Stalin. Still, as Angelica Balabanoff wrote half a century ago in her own account of *My Life as a Rebel*, ". . . the experience of the individual in relation to historic events does not belong to oneself alone. It should be put at the disposal of those who can make use of it. . . . History has been falsified without shame. . . . The truth was never more necessary than it is today."

Despite our setbacks, then, I write my book. History isn't over yet. When and where you are born are strictly matters of luck. "The historical ebb and flow are governed by their own laws," wrote Trotsky, "mere impatience will not expedite their change." If you choose to join up with history, you have to take what circumstances are dealt you.

If, now, before setting down my own modest *Life as a Rebel,* I begin by citing the greats, it is not to glorify myself. Rather, it is to show how important are circumstances, in hopes that history may conclude we did the best we could, given ours.

Zane IndiAnna
New Space Cafe
New York City
1977

PART I

Babylon

1 · DIGGING TO CHINA

What makes a rebel?

If you had seen the flags waving in front of each frame house set on its neat carpet of lawn on Endicott Road or any of the surrounding streets in Babylon, Indiana, on a Flag Day, Memorial Day, Veterans Day, V-J Day, or even a particularly fine Sunday after the War (World War II), you would never have guessed it possible that a fanatical radical was incubating there.

And yet, while the other kids were riding their tricycles and bicycles across the hills of Babylon, learning to spot the new models of every make of car that began appearing in 1946 and would come out once a year forever now that the War was over, I was out in our back yard sitting in a certain spot safe from the menacing bees in my mother's hollyhocks but within the magical scented circle of her yellow tea roses, digging to China.

China!—an inconceivably distant place where people walked around upside down, wrote in pictographs, ate with chopsticks, sang their words, sailed on junks, rode in rickshaws, and hid their treasures in caves guarded by terrifying silent dogs with eyes as big as saucers—accessible through my back yard. I'd begun digging as soon as I learned it was there, dreaming, longing, hungering to see, though after a while people laughed at me. I knew that getting through was a staggering task, China being some eight thousand miles away; but unlike the skeptics I lived among, who doubted the existence of other states, much less other worlds, I didn't think it impossible. Time, distance—my entire world was made up of unknown mysteries that gradually yielded to the accretions of steady effort and the slow erosion of experience. Learning when to take the long route to school around the treacherous snowdrifts on Silverbrook Boulevard; combining three completely different tunes into the glorious harmony of a single Christmas carol (walking slowly down the aisle in white dresses carrying lighted candles, every mouth a perfect O); mastering written language; knowing when to multiply and when to divide; diving through the surface of a pool into an entirely different medium and rising up again; the miraculous healing of a wound—digging to China. In Miss Peterson's "transportation unit" the other kids made locomotives and cabooses, hansoms and kayaks; but I made cardboard and toothpick models of a sedan chair, a rickshaw, and a junk, bringing China to life. After that I thought about it each night and dug a bit every day. Five whole summers I dug, half believing I would get there, a born fanatic.

Maybe it was a little weird, like jumping off the garage roof with an umbrella hoping to fly, but so what? It was worth it to see the hole get deeper every day. If my parents fretted, they didn't let on. Even after my Aunt Louise used psychology, trying to "inject the Reality Principle" with children's books about the Chinese people and play-by-plays of the struggle of the courageous peasants against the terrible Chiang Kai-shek, I wouldn't give up. My goal was audacious enough to sweep away the difficulties: imagine tunneling straight through the earth to the very opposite of everything you started from. China! Limitless difference: men in pigtails, hats like lampshades, mincing steps, emperors! Each day (which was naturally night in China) as I dug a little deeper into the earth with the hand cultivator that had replaced my sandbox shovel, I saw a bit more clearly where I was going. My dreams and desires fed each other. If it was possible for my friend Eleanor (with her mother) to sit on the opposite side of the front row of the vast Movie Palace from me (with my mother) and both of us somehow still manage to see the same amazing pictures flashing across a single centered screen, then if I dug diligently long enough I might emerge in China. No expert in the possible had ruled it out; indeed, no one even discouraged me: "Else, would you please call Zane to wash up for dinner? She's out in back, digging to China."

Maybe my grandiose ambitions were my parents' fault, naming me Zane, marking me for life as "different." They probably didn't realize what they were starting. A combination of Zeke and Anna (Daddy and Mama), Zane meant "God's gracious gift."

Plain and special at once, a version of John and Jane, it was a distinctive name (there were Zane Grey and me), promising, a name to live up to, announcing my specialness in a single syllable. Even as a small child I'd recognized its value as I chalked fancy Z's up and down the sidewalks of Babylon. The last letter of the alphabet, my initial occupied the place of treasures, like dessert, like nighttime, like the final wish that could reverse all others, like the tastiest morsel one saved up for the end, like China at the end of the tunnel. "Zane: What an unusual name," teachers would say. "Is it short for something?" And I would swell with pride replying no. As certain parents bought their children growth stocks, my parents, smart but not rich, gave me a special name, probably unique in Indiana, knowing it would distinguish me before I raised a finger.

Distinction, however, was not the best thing to have in Babylon. God's gracious gift: a blessing, but a mixed one. The Best was less acceptable than the Same. My parents had considered withholding their permission for the school to skip me over 3A and afterward often wondered if they hadn't harmed me by granting it, making me younger than the rest. Even if you excelled, you'd better not be different. Daddy almost said as much, trying to prepare me for life, arming me with accomplishments and cunning but warning me not to use them, perhaps already uneasy about my name. My Uncle Herman learned the hard way that Different was wrong. The wrong attitude, the wrong amount of hair (like that contradiction in terms, Grace Gross, whose legs hung with hair and whose eyebrows met between her eyes as indelicately as a boy's), the wrong color skin ("God made the little niggers,/Made them in the night,/Made them in a hurry,/ And forgot to paint them white," wrote Barbie Pratt in my autograph book), the wrong clothes from the wrong stores, made you unfit for Babylon—a place which, of all the places in the world, was right: by definition.

True, an outsider driving through our town might think Babylon indistinguishable from a thousand other postwar residential communities with houses sporting windows and gables like smiling faces, two-car garages, neatly tended flower borders, and uniform treelawns within a twenty-mile radius of a manufacturing center of approx. 80,000 pop. The same winding roads, grandly named boulevards but as yet imperfectly drained; the same scattering of vacant lots; the same bowling alley, dry cleaner, gift shop, chop suey house, record store clustered at Tompkins Corners; the same lending library with its Thursday night Great Literature discussion group; the same two-story high school with its regular Friday night basketball game and Tuesday night samba lessons to paying couples in the gym. But anyone born there knew immediately that Babylon, though seemingly insignificant, was quite simply the standard by which the rest of the world was to be judged and by which "different" was to be defined. Not only did the poorer suburbs stand condemned by comparison, but even the reputedly richer ones, with their higher per capita income and teacher-to-pupil ratios, were despised (though less so) for their difference from us.

But generally such indelicacies as poverty or dark skin didn't apply to us. To start with, you didn't move to Babylon unless you were white and rich enough for a down payment on a house. Then once safely up there you could easily prove the rest of the world didn't count. Rest of the world? We ignored even Middletown, that belching metropolis in the valley below of which we were supposedly only a small suburb, referring to it disparagingly as "the city," tarnished by industry and grime. The #32 express bus that took Babylon fathers downtown to their offices whizzed past the streets that housed the poor so fast that nothing could be seen. (Later, in high school, we sometimes cut classes and went down to Middletown to shop or sit in Walgreen's and flirt with soldiers—by then we had the Korean War; but we knew what would happen to us if our parents ever found out.) It was as impolite to notice the black or poor as it was to notice a harelip. "Don't stare." If you did happen to see, you were to hold in your observations like a belch until you were safely back in the privacy of Babylon, where you could once again breathe easily and then promptly forget.

But some people, the bane of their teachers, noticed the worst and couldn't forget; I, it seemed, was one of them. Long before I ever ventured down to Middletown I had evidence of God's grand scheme of injustice. "Whenever I am asked," wrote Angelica Balabanoff, Lenin's sometime collaborator, "how I came to turn my back upon my family, upon the comfort and luxury of my home in southern Russia, and to become a revolutionist, I am at a loss for an answer. All the years of my childhood, as far back as I can remember, seem to have been years of rebellion. . . . Once when I saw some peasant on our estate kiss the border of my father's coat when he returned from a long journey, I cringed with shame. My first realization of inequality and injustice grew out of these experiences in my early childhood." We saw no peasants flogged, knew no poor. The daily humiliation we witnessed at school of the queer, fat, slow, orphaned, and small by the big and loud was the worst cruelty we could imagine. Unlike the fabled Old Country schoolmasters whose abuses inspired rebellion, our teachers were not permitted to hit us, and in fact the best endeared themselves by permitting us to paint murals on the walls of the cafeteria. Still, somehow, I knew.

It wasn't that I doubted that ours was the best place on earth; it was just that now and then the curtains parted for a minute to reveal a world beyond. China lay buried deep under our house, though most people weren't interested. Just so, behind Mama's lovely smile were the anxious questions I overheard her ask my Aunt Louise when I was supposedly asleep. Behind the starched shirts of the charity kids delivered to our school each morning in a panel station wagon were the sad hearts of orphans. And there on the third floor of our own white colonial on Endicott Road I sometimes heard our Polish maid Else cry her poor self to sleep.

As Sleeping Beauty, doomed to prick her finger on a spindle, found the fateful needle in the tower of her very own castle though her parents had banished all spindles from the land, I found all the injustice of the world lurking on our property.

2 · ELSE

There were maids before Else and at least one more after, for Mama worked in an office till sometime after the War. But Else is the one I remember with her sad blue eyes and silver cross and two limp blond braids she wore wrapped around her head like the maidens in distress pictured in my giant illustrated Grimm. She lived in the attic under our very roof, breathing the same air and eating the same food as the rest of us; but like the family of raccoons who nested in our chimney one winter, whining an unnerving song that kept us all awake until Daddy found them and smoked them out, she lived with us but not among us.

Once I stole up the steep stairs to the attic on my hands and knees to find her kneeling at the foot of her narrow bed, praying to Jesus. She held her silver cross in her hand and murmured words in a foreign tongue, with her sad eyes rolled toward the ceiling till all that showed were the whites. I was uneasy to be witness to such an intimate scene, but I was afraid to withdraw, knowing the stairs might creak. Mama had always insisted I be polite and considerate to Else. "No, darling," she said sternly, "don't go up there now, that's Else's private room, she needs her privacy too." I remembered the interview in which Mama had promised Else two hours each afternoon to rest up before beginning dinner, besides Sundays and Thursday nights off, a cash retainer, and four white uniforms. But still, it disturbed me to think of her up there all alone; I always knew it was wicked to keep a maid in the attic. As I sat on the stairs listening to her pray in words I couldn't understand, I had no doubt she was praying for release from some onerous burden—possibly me.

I often thought about her up there by herself. During the days, with Mama and Daddy away at work, everything seemed happy enough. After school I trailed her up and down the stairs through her daily chores—cleaning, ironing, mending, telephoning for the groceries, cooking, doing the laundry, and "thorough cleaning" once a week—and sometimes heard her sing strange songs in her high, thin voice. But when my parents were home, speaking to her in their special voice, she was morose and obedient. When I sat on the porch learning chess openings from Daddy on Saturdays, she slipped around the house pretending to be invisible. And at night I sometimes thought I heard her cry.

Living alone in an attic like serving girls in fairy tales—what was it like? Into Else's room went furniture no one wanted. Her bathtub was rusty. The lightbulb in her ceiling had a chain instead of a neat switch like all of ours.

Not that anyone mistreated her. Daddy called her "Miss Else" and Mama, assuring me that Else was grateful to have a clean room and bath in a nice place like Babylon, took pains to see that she was comfortable. "Now, Else," she would say, "you be sure to order whatever brand of tea you like best." "Yes, Mrs. Bentwood."

But I still knew it was wrong. While we used any door we chose, she used only the back door; and while we ate together every night exchanging mind-stumping riddles and intimate stories, she ate alone in the kitchen. First she served us, emerging through the swinging door in her fresh uniform to refill our glasses with ice water or pass the serving dishes a second time (serve from the left, clear from the right) whenever my mother sat up tall, smiled, and rang the little silver dinner bell; then, after the dishes were cleared away and the dining table reduced to its minimum size, restoring the dining area to its original living room state, Else would assemble a meal from among the leftovers and serve herself in the kitchen.

Wrong. My Aunt Louise, who'd awakened my compassion when I was very young by weeping beside our radio while the war news blared, had taught me about injustice. And though I ignored it when I could, after a certain winter night I knew Else's situation precisely fit the description.

The dinner dishes had been cleared away and my parents were settled before the fire in the living room. I was in my Daddy's lap waiting to hear the next installment of one of his long, fanciful stories that eventually wound up to bed like a circular staircase, when he handed me his coffee cup and sent me off to the kitchen for a refill. I slid down from his lap and pushed through the swinging door, cup in hand—to find Else seated at the kitchen table eating by herself, her eyes red from crying.

Though I'd suspected often enough that she cried, I'd never before caught her at it.

"What's the matter, Else?" I asked.

"It's nothing, darling, nothing."

Nevertheless, tears fell from her eyes.

"Don't cry, Else," I said. "Please don't." Then, applying Mama's comforting remedy, I walked over to Else, patted her arm, and said in Mama's voice, "There, there."

Suddenly Else grabbed my waist with one arm, and pulling me to her, pressed me violently to her white starched breast. I heard her heart thumping amid muffled sobs, felt the silver cross pressing against my cheek. Quickly my own heart thumped back.

From the living room I distinctly heard my parents' voices, knew they'd be sitting in the facing green wing chairs beside the fire, my father's feet up on the hassock, my lovely mother, knees crossed, sipping her coffee, both waiting for me to return with Daddy's cup in time to have my story before their evening radio programs began. My mother's melodious voice drifted across the air sweet as a lullaby.

The silver cross, cold and sharp, began to gnaw my cheek as I waited inside the vise of Else's bony embrace.

"It's because you have to eat alone in the kitchen, isn't it?" I ventured, naming our crime. The worst sentence my parents had ever passed on me was banishment to a corner for an agonizing number of solitary minutes.

Another violent squeeze, and then at last she spoke through her tears.

"No, no, no. It's your father. The way he plays with you and talks to you. He sets you on his lap and tells you such stories." She sniffled loudly without releasing me.

Her answer was as perplexing as her tears. I adored my father; he adored me. It was natural; I had never thought about it. Yet somehow, now, it was making Else cry. "Won't your daddy tell you stories?" I asked. But she only clutched me tighter and continued to sob.

Perhaps she had no father. Perhaps she was an orphan, like the kids from the Welfare Center where Aunt Louise worked who came to our school in a station wagon and joined our classes. There had been two of them in my kindergarten class, a boy and a girl, whom everyone called brother and sister though we all knew they were unrelated. I had watched them, trying to put myself in their place. Then one day the station wagon stopped coming and we never saw them again.

"Don't you have a Daddy, Else?" I whispered.

As abruptly as she had captured me, she now released me and dried her tears on her apron. I rubbed my cheek where I still felt the silver cross pressing and stared fixedly at the red-and-white checked oilcloth on the kitchen table. Else stirred her tea, which by then must have been quite cold, and stared out through her sad eyes and the kitchen window toward the lighted windows of the houses beyond and never answered me.

After a few moments I filled Daddy's cup and slipped awkwardly out of the kitchen back to the cozy living room. Guiltily I rejoiced that I had a father, a mother, a piano, a dog, everything.

Daddy gave the fire a congenial poke and then, lifting me once again to his knee, resting his head on one of the wings of his high-backed chair, closed his eyes (of which mine were said to be exact replicas) and resumed his impossibly beautiful story.

3 · UNCLE HERMAN

When Else left us the following spring, I wasn't sorry. Her sadness seemed to increase every day, no matter what I did, and I somehow felt responsible. Once she was gone I moved up to the mysterious, forbidden attic until Mama, who had to take a few days of vacation time in order to conduct her interviews, had found Else's replacement. In that strange room where strange women had lived so near yet so far, I pretended to lead another life—sleeping in a narrow cot, exploring the angles of the slanted eaves, delving into forbidden closets.

I don't remember who replaced Else. Once the ground thawed out I started tunneling again toward China (in real China, whispered Aunt Louise, the People's Army was gaining ground) until the end of the summer when Mama took the rest of her vacation and we all drove up to the Indiana Dunes—those high mountains of clear white sand that got us listed among the world's lesser wonders. Indeed, from that summer I would probably have remembered only the Dunes if it hadn't also been the summer Uncle Herman was called before the Board of Education and his name was in the papers, the summer he got sick.

It started innocently enough. Mama suggested that while we were away he and Aunt Louise should move into our house, which was cooler and more comfortable than their tiny apartment in Middletown and had a piano in need of Herman's attention.

We got home to find that a protest had been entered by some of our neighbors the night before our return. Daddy stepped out of the car and gave such a cry that before I could get out myself I was trembling. Daddy never raised his voice; I knew something terrible must have happened.

I opened the door. Destruction surrounded me. Mama's precious rose bushes, in perfect flower when we'd left, had been hacked to the ground, their delicate yellow blossoms and buds strewn carelessly across the yard. The young buckeye tree behind the porch which Daddy had planted for the future had been ringed with a knife and my tunnel heaped with trash. Two windows of the garage from which I had sometimes jumped, attempting to fly, were broken, and across a third like a signature was soaped, *Go back to Russia.*

All at once Uncle Herman and Aunt Louise were standing beside us, wringing their hands and carrying on. Uncle Herman, who always needed a haircut and something more, shook his rumpled head sadly while Mama held Louise, who cried as she had during the War. I watched them from a safe distance.

"We don't even live here," moaned Louise. "Herman never set foot inside Russia. He despises Stalin. There's no justice. What shall we do?"

"There, there," said Mama, bringing comfort to me if to no one else.

Normally, Mama would be the one in need of help, Louise the one to give it. Louise was a psychiatric social worker and, on important matters particularly, we all consulted her. Not only because of her vast store of arcane knowledge—even greater than Daddy's, and he taught mathematics—but because she held an opinion on every question. She was, in Daddy's words, a "tough cookie," or, as Mama put it, a "woman of views." From my private listening post at the top of the stairs I had heard her explain to Mama everything from the causes of poverty, suicide, stuttering, and juvenile delinquency, to matters of such crucial interest to me as the meaning of dreams, the reasons for nail-biting, and the strange significance of digging tunnels. With Daddy, of course, she discussed union and world politics, speaking for herself and Herman, whose English was poor. To me she explained the nuances of injustice and how to make invisible ink from ordinary lemon juice and doll beds from matchboxes. Years later, when the great St. Lawrence Inland Waterway finally connected the dry towns of the Midwest with the fabulous sea (and Louise was a hefty widow of forty-five), she became the first woman in America to sign on to a freighter and ship out around the world from an inland port. But now, with destruction surrounding us, Louise was brought low. Drooping and silent as the ruined roses, she was bereft of explanations.

Daddy rose to the occasion. "What shall we do?" he shouted, sounding angrier than I'd ever heard him. His face was as red as his freckles. "Do! I'm going to set in some more!" And although like Herman he was one of those who taught rather than one of those who "do," he backed the car straight out of the drive without unpacking and announced he was off to Tompkins Corners Garden Supply.

The next day I helped Daddy rake the yard and try to restore the roses, but when I finally looked down into my violated tunnel I decided to table my China project. Who was I to defy our neighbors? The truth was, I suspected that the whole ugly back yard business was somehow my fault. It happened that during the brief interlude between maids two men had come to our house asking questions, and though they were the sort of men I'd been warned not to speak to under any circumstances, by the time I'd opened the door and seen their mean faces it had been too late to keep them out. Now I had the uneasy feeling that their visit and the derangement of our yard were connected—both had something to do with Uncle Herman; and while not quite abandoning my dream of China (no dream is ever abandoned), I decided for the time being to stop digging.

The men had walked in without waiting, removed their hats, and taken seats on the rose sofa while I went for Mama.

"We'd just like to ask you a few questions, Mrs. Bentwood," they said, getting out little black notebooks.

I watched from the doorway. Mama lit a cigarette and sat down. I could tell she was not happy, though the men wouldn't have known it from the way she smiled and sweetly asked, "What exactly is it you'd like to know?"

They asked several questions about my uncle and someone else. I knew it was trouble. Kids at school taunted me about my uncle who was reported to be a "commie" though he led the Glee Club. He was a small kindly man whom no one liked, I believed, because of his German name (though he was two parts Hungarian, one part Czech, and only one scant part German, Mama assured me) and because, with his masterly command of the universal language of music, he barely used English. As for his being a "commie," a word I never heard until my classmates' accusations, I adamantly denied it. Still, the strangers were asking questions;

and I, having opened the door to them, felt responsible for the whole confusing predicament that made poor Mama have to use her hostess voice and keep on smoking cigarettes.

Then one of the men noticed me. His face pursed to a frown. With his hand pressed to the place he kept his badge, he caught Mama's eye and tilted his head toward me.

I was afraid to move. But sweet Mama rescued me. "Why don't you go out back, Zane dear, and work on your tunnel?" she said, enabling me to slip out the back door. (If they'd only known where I was digging to!)

That night, and for several nights afterward, there was frantic telephoning and late-night soul-searching.

"Louise?" Mama said grimly into the phone, unaware that I was listening. "Two FBI men just visited me. They were asking about Herman. I stalled them off, but they're coming back. Tell me, Louise, has Herman done anything I ought to know about? . . . Well, of course I didn't. You know I wouldn't. But they gave me a fright, I can tell you that. Now what do you think I ought to say when they come back?"

I don't know what Aunt Louise told Mama to say, but later, when it was all over, I heard Mama tell Louise over coffee that she was really quite pleased with herself for the way she'd handled the affair.

"You would have been proud of me, I think. I told them I didn't really like Herman, even if he was my brother-in-law. Wasn't that smart? I said Herman had always seemed to me a bit spineless, not bothering about English, and a trifle peculiar; but though I disliked him, I had no reason to believe he was a communist. He didn't act like one. He never talked about Russia or tried to get me to join anything. And you know, I think it worked. I think I probably helped him. Because if I didn't even like him, why would I have gone out of my way to defend him?"

"They came snooping around our building too," said Louise, "asking all the neighbors. You know Ida Prichett—that retired woman from Georgia who's lived on our floor for thirteen years? She told me that when they asked her if she had anything to say against our character, she turned on them and said in that thick accent of hers, 'Why, how *day*-ah you come into my home and ask me a question like that! How *day*-ah you!' and pushed them right out the door. But of course, she doesn't have a job to lose, she doesn't teach in the public schools."

If only I'd thought of pushing the men out the door, I mused with sudden remorse.

"Oh, I don't know, Anna," Aunt Louise continued. "Sometimes I wonder why they're not after me instead, because of the union."

When winter came again, Mama and Herman were both out of jobs. Mama left hers to be a full-time mother now that the country was, as she put it, "back to normal"; but Herman's left him, trailing ugly headlines behind. Not only was he stripped of the school Glee Club; now he couldn't even teach as a substitute. Rapidly failing, without a job, he took to his bed. "Why get up?" he said to Mama when we went to visit. And except to cook small meals and practice his violin while Louise dressed to go to work, he didn't. As Mama explained, Herman was a very sick man.

The last time I saw him was when we went to Middletown to visit him after the Rosenbergs died, burned as spies like Joan of Arc, leaving two more orphans in the world. Amid a clutter of books, newspapers, magazines, and ashtrays piled on the radiator tops and in the corners of the tiny living room, Louise railed against evil, sobbing, shaking her fists in the air, then wringing her hands, while once again Mama tried to calm her—"For Herman's sake, darling. He's sleeping. Shh."

When he died Louise didn't cry at all; she seemed angrier than sad. She read a short fiery sermon by Herman's favorite writer, Trotsky (whom I would read myself years later). But I was too disturbed to listen. Instead I watched Louise standing before the open grave in her heavy space shoes, like a black candle in a black veiled hat, her eyes aflame, staring strangely down. As I told my diary, "she looked noble," particularly when they lowered Herman's coffin into a hole that seemed no deeper than my once active tunnel to China, which now existed, like Uncle Herman himself, on another plane.

My China—that single busy street bustling with rickshaws and rice merchants in one particular unnamed Chinese city where I would one day emerge—depended on nothing but my imagination. Whether China was our great suffering ally who'd fought the brutal Japanese, or the heroic champion of the people my Aunt

Louise had described, or the dangerous communist horde moving down the winding wall to overrun the world I learned about in school, I didn't care. To me China was an idea under my dreams, the mysterious shadow that lay on the other side of my burgeoning life, representing all that might be possible.

Like the small jar full of precious black sand given to my teacher Miss Peterson by a soldier friend who had carried it all the way back from the shores of the South Seas during the War and which Miss P. had distributed, teaspoon by teaspoon, to her class, my tunnel to China could challenge the limits of the thinkable. Through it I could connect myself to the farthest spot on earth from Babylon.

4 · THE RUMMAGE SALE

But the education of a rebel begins at home, and one Saturday I found myself in a place as astonishing as I'd ever imagined China —a place all the more surprising for being situated only a few miles down the hill from my back yard in the forbidden section of Middletown known as Brownsville.

There we were at dawn on that third Saturday before Christmas 1953--seventeen Babylon ninth graders in Brownsville in two station wagons and a rented truck filled with merchandise. Though chaperoned by two mothers and one dad, we were still totally off-limits.

The store owner was twenty minutes late. "I don't know where that man can be," said Barbie Pratt's mother, checking her watch again. "What a place to leave us stranded at seven o'clock in the morning!"

Ostensibly our purpose was fund-raising. To finance the graduation party and our class gift to the school with whatever was left over, the junior high school graduating class was holding a rummage sale. But as Mrs. Pratt later revealed, there was also the matter of character building.

"Barbie," said Mrs. Pratt, looking up and down ugly St. James Avenue with its dilapidated three-story buildings, "will you lock that door?" Snowflakes fell slowly onto the windshield, melting instantly to slush. A sign rattled in the wind. The only indications of habitation were a few smoking chimneys and several flashing neon lights, but no sign of Mr. Lord, the owner of the storefront we had rented for the day.

From the other station wagon parked behind us muffled boy-sounds were soon replaced by Babylon marching songs. "Come on," said Barbie eagerly, pressing her nose against the back window of the Pratt car that had carried the girls down into the city, "let's outsing them!" And suddenly the familiar sounds of Babylon sailed from the Harding wagon to ours and back again, filling the alien Brownsville air.

As usual, I was out of it. I'd become an orator, not a singer; these were not my friends, not my songs. I seemed to be the only one who knew we were in for something. My luck, I'd signed up for the rummage sale in the first place only because you had to sign up for something and it had been billed as "charity." But like every other class event, this too was dominated by the popular crowd. Neither of my two defenses against their snickers—aloofness and nuttiness—could serve me now, locked in partnership with them for the day. I attempted to sing along—but softly.

When a long blue car commanding instant respect pulled up alongside us I tensed with fear (how many times had we been told Brownsville was dangerous?), but everyone else seemed relieved.

"Ah! Mr. Lord at last," said Mrs. Pratt; "A cadillac," said her daughter.

Mr. Lord parked his car, then returned to us with a grin and withdrew a heavy key ring from the depths of his overcoat pocket. "Come on," he said, and while he chewed on an unlit cigar, he began systematically opening a series of locks on the empty storefront named Saint's Hall.

It was a cold, dirty place: one large room and one small one, each with a single inadequate light, peeling paint, cracked plaster walls. I wondered if its name were a corruption of St. James Avenue on which it crouched or if somewhere in its dark past it had housed a church or an actual saint. Now, both name and condition contrasted eerily with the message on the fading sign the window still bore of the hall's last defeated incarnation dedicated to cleanliness and modernity: SPOTLESS CLEANING 24-HOUR PROMPT SERVICE.

When we were all inside, Mr. Lord gathered us around the

small electric heater he had taken from a closet and plugged into the wall, raised his hands to silence the giggling, and issued his warnings and advice.

"You've got a good day for a rummage sale," he began encouragingly. "It's close to Christmas and they're gonna splurge. Any of you ever done this before?"

Several hands went up, but not mine. I'd sold lemonade near the bus stop on Silverbrook Boulevard to the daddies coming home from work, but nothing more.

"Never mind. You'll get the hang of it. One thing you've got to understand is, these people don't know nothing. *You* know the difference between quality and junk, but they don't. A cashmere coat from Tyson's, a rag from Bailey's basement, don't make no difference to them. So make sure you tell them it's all quality and you'll make yourself a pile." He lit his cigar, took several puffs, and continued. "Keep your eyes open. Believe me, I know these people like the back of my hand, they're animals. They'll steal you blind if you let 'em. You gotta keep 'em moving, watch 'em like a hawk. If one of 'em acts suspicious or gives you any trouble, don't fool around, just send over your man or get a boy to find a cop."

While Barbie's boyfriend Jim Eagle waved his hand to volunteer his services, I winced at the word "animals." Sense as well as decency forbade such speech. Among the earliest rules I'd learned upon joining the debating team was not to be demagogic; in fact, "resorting to name-calling and loaded words" was the fourth sin of delivery listed in my precious *Debater's Manual*. But this was Mr. Lord's territory, not ours.

"You got your tables, your racks folded up in back. There's a broom and a box of hangers in the closet. Don't keep too much money in the cash box. It don't matter you've dragged all this stuff down here for them, they'll still steal you blind. Why look for trouble? I'll stop back in an hour or so when you're getting ready to open."

While Mr. Lord and his car disappeared down St. James Avenue, we unloaded the truck in the gloomy light of the street lamp, and by nine o'clock we had everything ready. Despite attacks of giggles and much horsing around, despite squabbles over prices and insults over donations, we had managed to arrange in a systematic fashion the discarded contents of a hundred Babylon lives—sized, sorted, and priced on a half-dozen folding tables. Though the clothes were old, the shoes worn, the crockery chipped, the toys broken, the appliances obsolete, the silverware bent, the knives rusted, the handkerchiefs frayed, the records scratched, the sets incomplete, the knickknacks damaged, the books false, it was hoped that someone would want everything, even inscribed family photographs and a butterfly collection.

"Ready?" said Barbie, beside the door. "Remember what Mr. Lord said: keep your eyes open." Outside people were already peering through the streaked window of Saint's Hall, leaving little circles of steam on the glass proving they were not phantoms but real customers. Behind Barbie, tall Jim Eagle leaned vigilantly against the door. "Any questions before we let them in?" asked Barbie.

I was burning with questions, but that day I had no trouble keeping my mouth shut.

Barbie flashed a signal to Jim, who promptly unfastened the lock and pulled open the door.

In Babylon certain color combinations were forbidden. Such combinations as green with blue, orange with red (or red with pink or pink with orange), brown with black, or purple with anything were considered quite untenable. Such breaches of taste, variously called loud, gauche, stupid, Italian, Jew, were simply prohibited without anyone's ever questioning why. And now gradually the room was filling up with people who so consistently violated these simple, basic rules that one could only conclude they were unaware of them. In they came, people of another race, crossing our threshold guardedly, viewing us with caution and something else. No white dickies under uniform sweaters, no skirts to the prescribed length of thirteen inches from the floor, no medium-wale corduroy pants with crew-necked pullovers, but reckless combinations of tops and bottoms in rash collisions of color. Their very skin and hair violated Babylon's minimal rules of decorum.

Barbie Pratt sent Jim Eagle, manning the next table, a delighted smile, while the customers fanned through the room surveying the goods with practiced eyes, searching for the remaining life in each abandoned object. (Charity, this was called in Babylon

—a generous service for the less fortunate.) As the customers pushed their feet into worn-out shoes, snapped open and closed discarded handbags, estimated the exact damage done to appliances, searched skeptically through boxes of broken toys, preparing to make their forced compromises and strike their bargains, the elated, giggling children of Babylon named their prices and opened their palms.

"Not eating?" asked Mrs. Harding solicitously at lunch break. Suspicious of the facilities in that forlorn neighborhood, she had thoughtfully set up a tray of Cokes, sandwiches, and cookies in the small back room where we went in shifts.

I couldn't eat.

"I know it's not the most appetizing place," she said comfortingly, holding out a cookie, "but we'll only be here a few more hours. Take a little something for energy. I think all of you are just wonderful to give up your Saturday to do this work."

She said "all of you," but I knew she meant me, for the others, chomping their sandwiches, were bursting with delighted observations.

"Did you see the fat one in the red sox and pink slippers? She really thought she was something!"

"Better yet, the one in the purple turban!"

"That's nothing. I just had one with no teeth. I couldn't understand a word she said."

"Even with teeth I can't understand them."

"Can you believe people would really dress like this?"

"They think they're Cab Calloway."

The boys ate so well that Mrs. Harding, a mother of girls, had to limit them to two sandwiches each with a cautionary lecture on sharing. They ate more and spoke less than the girls, but between sandwiches, in Babylon style, they did incisive on-the-spot imitations of the customers, their specialty.

The smell of peanut butter and the imitations reminded me of the awful summer I'd been sent to Girl Scout camp, where I languished in homesickness for two agonizing weeks while everyone else raced around swimming, playing Red Rover, roasting wieners and marshmallows, guzzling peanut butter with a spoon, singing campfire songs, and endlessly discussing one another in the bunks. I'd tried not to cry or make a fuss, but we saw the world differently, they and I, and I wondered how they could fool themselves into thinking it was "fun." Then, too, it had seemed simpler not to eat anything at all (or to wash myself, either) until I could get back home where it was safe; then, too, I had tricked myself through the endless ordeal by manipulating time and space: patiently breaking hours into minutes and seconds to prove their finitude, reducing complex actions to simple, discrete, insubstantial images projected on a tiny mental screen. Like the Girl Scout softball team, the customers at my housewares table moved in predictable motions in black and white, which I could shut off when I chose by throwing a small switch.

By three thirty almost everything had been sold, and we voted unanimously to close up early. I melted with gratitude toward my merciful classmates, agents of today's salvation. We hid our money and cleaned up dutifully, and by the time Mr. Lord returned we were restlessly waiting to leave.

"Finished?" he said, nodding with appreciation. "Not bad."

Everyone smiled smugly.

"How much did you take in?"

Mrs. Harding, coloring, whispered a figure in Mr. Lord's ear. His eyebrows went up as he removed the cold cigar from between his lips and announced that we had probably broken a record.

"And I think it was probably a good character lesson, too," said Mrs. Pratt the moralist.

"See how the other half lives," said Mr. Lord.

"And the work," added Mrs. Harding. "A little hard work is good for the character. Believe me," she sighed, "I know."

Instead of splitting again into two groups for the station wagons, all the kids piled into the now-empty truck. The predictable couples, led by Barbie Pratt and Jim Eagle, paired off on the floor; the rest, dividing as usual into girls and boys (with me in the balance), lined up against the sides.

It was a cold ride up the icy hill, but we sang all the way to Babylon. Even I sang, so happy was I to be leaving Brownsville at last.

That night, however, in a fit of remorse, I laid out for the following day my cherry-red sweater with my pink pleated skirt and vowed to the picture over my bed of Joan of Arc (eye on the future, sword in hand, refusing to dress as her judges demanded even if she had to burn for it) to wear the forbidden combination to school.

5 · MIDDLETOWN

How I wish I could report here that the misery of poor Else, the persecution of Uncle Herman, the bleeding of the people of Brownsville, not to mention a dozen other blatant humiliations of the blameless in which, to my shame, I found myself murkily entangled, had been eloquent enough to send me out into the world fighting. They were more than wicked enough. When, years later, strangers in the movement exchanged tales of their political awakenings as routinely as boys boast of their sexual scores, I came to know a number of radicals who proudly attributed their conversions to as impersonal an experience as a movie or a novel or the sight of a distant shantytown viewed from an uncle's car; and there were others, "birthright radicals" or "red diaper babies," as the daughters and sons of the Old Left were called, who traced their enlightenment back to the womb. But in our town, where Marx was banned and Roosevelt was considered quite red enough, where the daughters of the revolution meant the descendents of the *Mayflower*, sentiment, compassion, even horror, were not enough. To awaken one had to have an Idea.

Not that I wasn't disturbed by those sorry Babylon affairs in which I found myself quite as implicated as any spectator to an accident who notes her own reactions. But my response stopped several crucial steps short of rebellion. It stopped precisely at Guilt. There I was, stuck, cringing, tossing in my sleep, bolting upright at dawn in my little decorated room (a new pair of day-beds in case I should want to invite a sleepover; a three-way mirror on my vanity table; unopened bottles of popular perfumes), disturbed by secret sins that repeated themselves in exasperating variation till even my waking dreams were haunted by vague plans of escape, as unpleasant as they were impractical. Not escape into action or purpose or even some more Utopian town—for at that time any other town was inconceivable to a child of Babylon—but escape into silliness, silence, excellence, eccentricity. A tweed workman's cap worn jauntily low over the left eyebrow, a unique amble, all A's, elocution, red with pink, shorn hair, Zanity.

When the Idea that would transform me finally did arrive, I didn't even recognize it, though it came wrapped in dotted yellow gift paper as a birthday present from Aunt Louise, and I was by then in desperate need of it.

To realize just how badly I needed it, I have only to remember the candles on my cake burning away, dripping tasteless green wax all over the chocolate cream frosting as I hesitated to commit myself to a single wish.

"Come on now, make it snappy," urged Daddy; "you've taken long enough for three wishes."

But it seemed to me that the longer I waited (as the older I grew), the harder it was to know what precisely I wanted. Time made it worse, not better. These birthdays had been going on for fifteen years—long enough for me to have learned the uselessness of a superwish, which only postponed indefinitely the moment of choice, but not long enough to learn much else.

Under family pressure I settled for less than perfect and blew out my candles for another year, not guessing that in the pile of presents on the hall table—the material expressions of my various relations' wishes for me, mainly clothes and more perfumes—lay a partial solution to my quandary. A book, inscribed on the flyleaf: *Jan. 29, 1955. For my beloved niece Zane. Understanding is the first step. Aunt Louise.*

Anyone who studies the lives of the revolutionaries discovers early on that for each one, there is always at least one significant book that points them on their way. ("Don't think the press is any less necessary and valuable to the party's work than throwing bombs," cautioned the ferocious but prudent Perovskaia.) Less often than you might guess does it turn out to be a political tract. For the thirteen-year-old future Bolshevik Vera Figner, the Bible did it, where she read, "Leave thy father and thy mother and follow me." For the assassin Zasulich it was poetry (though, she slyly confessed, "sometimes I found what I wanted in poems that the author might have meant differently"). For Emma Goldman it was the novel *What Is to Be Done?* And for me it was *Middletown,* that long, sociological study by a pair of New York professors of Muncie, Indiana, a city eighty miles from Babylon which the authors, for disguise, had carelessly given the same name as the city seven miles from my own birthplace where some of my poorer relations, including Aunt Louise, continued to live.

It was so dry and unlikely a book for a fifteen-year-old that if it hadn't come from Aunt Louise, who'd always selected the perfect birthday gifts for me, I would probably never have read it. I looked at it lying on the dotted yellow paper I had opened without tearing. ("Save it," said Louise, "it'll make perfect wallpaper for a shadow box room.") It was not forbidden like the books my parents had removed from a downstairs shelf and secreted in a carton I'd found hidden in the attic. (*Progress and Poverty* by Henry George, the dangerous *Communist Manifesto*, a giant illustrated *Encyclopedia of Sex*, and a stack of old issues of *The New Masses*.) Nor was it gay like the charming tales of the haves and have-nots lovingly translated from the Russian that my aunt had brought me in former years. It had only its donor to recommend it.

"Thank you," I said, bending to kiss her cheek, for that winter I had suddenly shot up taller than all of them. Secretly planning to shelve the book, I tried to hide my disappointment.

"Don't thank me yet," she said. "First read the book. See what you think. Then you can thank me."

When I finally opened the book after six months of stalling, at once I began to understand. "The first step" of Louise's inscription was more like a first leap. At the tender age of fifteen I sat on my elm-shaded back porch chewing on my fingernails during the three most humid weeks of the summer (for that year the last polio scare in history kept us all out of the water) and sailed over the horizon into historical consciousness, as my aunt had probably planned for me all along.

The coincidence of the title with the place I lived was only a symbol of the coincidence of the contents with the contents of our lives. Though our Middletown was no more *the* Middletown than our Babylon was *the* Babylon, I quickly forgot the difference. For there, in plodding chapters on The Family, Getting a Living, Training the Young, Using Leisure, etc., etc., as frank as a diary, was a veritable portrait of us.

Us! A whole book (and a sequel, too, promised Aunt Louise, and after that a multitude of essays and reviews which she had clipped from national periodicals), not about the English or the French, the Indians or the Eskimos, the Russians or the Chinese, but about us!

The message I drew from the book was complicated. By singling us out as sufficiently interesting—one might even say fascinating—to merit a serious two-volume study, the Professors Lynd revealed us at the same time to be anything but the universal standard we all blithely considered ourselves. From the point of view of New Yorkers, we were curiosities. Indeed, from the point of view of history—the new idea which began to grow in my mind as breasts were growing on my body—we were no more than a tiny collection of the most transient and insignificant drops of protoplasm, the more ridiculous for our universal pretensions.

"Every people tends to regard its own culture as superior; not perfect perhaps, but essentially admirable," wrote the Lynds. "The commonplace assumptions of the student of comparative culture—such assumptions as that no cultural form is ultimate, inevitable, divinely or otherwise ordained . . . lie in the main over the horizon from everyday Middletown thought."

Encased in the same rolled-up jeans and baggy shirt worn by every other slightly confused, boy-crazy Babylon High School girl that year—a uniform which I'm ashamed to confess I like everyone had until that very moment indeed considered inevitable!—I watched amazed as the Lynds revealed the hidden meanings of our lives, just as surely as Mr. Aldrich, the geometry teacher, had revealed to us the properties of a circle. Oh, it was rich! While the foolish people of Indiana had proceeded about their ordinary dirty business, Mr. and Mrs. Clever Lynd of New York had quietly watched and recorded.

Seeing us through the eyes of others for the first time was a shocking revelation. A single set of facts suddenly took on two opposite interpretations. As soon as I saw us one way, the other way popped out at me like those pictures of a profile or a vase, depending on whether you focus on foreground or background; or the drawings of stairs that alternately protrude and recede; or those magical hidden pictures from *Highlights* magazine that Louise herself supplied me with, in which twenty-seven puppies' faces were concealed among the fine lines of scenic drawings. In *Middletown* all our hidden faces were revealed.

Once over the rim into self-consciousness, there was no going back. Now it was clear that we of Babylon were neither unique, as I had always tenaciously believed, nor universal, as I had also lazily assumed, but *historical:* products of our quirky time and place, decipherable and predictable by men and women of knowledge.

"What *Middletown* reveals is a man of almost unbelievable stupidities," wrote the Eastern critic H. L. Mencken in a review Aunt Louise kindly produced for me. "Well-fed, well-dressed, complacent and cocksure, he yet remains almost destitute of ideas. The things he admires are mainly mean things and the things he thinks he knows are nearly all untrue."

(Untrue? Another new idea!)

"His principal effort in this world," continued Mencken, describing *Middletown* man, "is to appear as much as possible like his fellows—to act like them in all situations and to think like them whenever his powers of thought are challenged. What the people of Middletown fear above all things is oddness. To do anything that is not commonly done is to risk social ostracism; to think anything that is not commonly thought is to be set down as criminal or insane."

If at first I was embarrassed by the revelations in *Middletown* of our stupendous shortcomings, in the next moment I was vindicated. After all, I had never really belonged. I'd been branded weird for nothing more errant than playing chess, a passion I'd innocently developed at home with Daddy and hadn't had the sense to hide; then, for my haircuts, my sox, my attitudes. Belonging was for older kids with fancier parents and perfect teeth. (Years later, it was for younger ones.) True, I had sometimes hoped to win their admiration for my unpredictable stands, but for the most part, I would have been content simply to slip unobtrusively past the inarticulate lanky varsity boys who shuffled their feet a certain way and slumped their shoulders inside their letter jackets, and the laughing Go-Club girls with their long-lashed flashing eyes and flashing teeth and flipped hair that grazed their shoulders when they tossed their heads. I made way for them as they dashed up the stairs and tripped through the halls to mid-day rendezvous; I followed behind them as they walked arm in arm to Charlie's after school where I sometimes sat at the counter pretending to be engrossed in a soda or a thought and watched them. Playing the latest Elvis Presley, I watched them through seven glass windows stealing kisses and more in the listening booths of the record store. I drew their portraits in study hall, observed them pass notes at the drinking fountain and thus betray each other (but not me). And though I denounced them to my friend Dee-Dee, I was flattered whenever one of them, in an act of daring, befriended me.

It was interesting to observe them at close quarters performing their little skits, flashing their teeth, trading sweaters, pronouncing with unctuous intimacy those names that echoed through the school corridors: Barbie, Marlene, Stephanie, Pam. But watching them fritter away their precious youth without developing what Daddy called character, seeing them rely on advantages of birth rather than earned virtues, I knew they were bound to end badly, as my reading of *Middletown* confirmed.

Still, if one night I could have closed my diary and gone to sleep as always to awaken the next morning to find them all waiting for me in the front hall—the girls pressing their blue signature-covered notebooks to their breasts like precious babies, scarves framing their faces; the boys punching fists to palms, saying: "C'mon, forget about Zane, we'll be late." And the girls responding: "No, we've got to wait for her. Hurry up, Zane, the bell rings in five minutes!" And I: "I'm coming, I'm coming, I'm just pinning on my Go-Club pin!"—if it could have happened suddenly like that, I might have considered giving it a brief fling, strictly for the experience. Even though I had Daddy's word that power and riches don't bring happiness, and Louise's assurance that anyway some things mean more than happiness, and had figured out myself that the pretty laughing girls would soon be growing old in identical houses at the edge of town and the boys would shortly be men, stuck for life behind windows of insurance offices or haberdashery shops or used-car lots where neon lights flashed the names of their uncles or fathers-in-law; while I like Joan of Arc might be called to do something unheard-of or exemplary—I might have joined the Go-Club for a little while to get the feel of it.

But of course I never did wake up to find them waiting for me. Occasionally one of them was there, asking me please to sneak her records out of the school office since I had a system, or to let her sit next to me in math, or wondering if I would cut afternoon classes and go downtown with her because she was having a test she wasn't prepared to take and if she cut with me she was sure to get away with it. But I remained unacceptably "different."

Or, rather, acceptably so. In the new light of *Middletown*, I saw that "different" was good or bad depending on who was watching. If playing chess turned me freaky, that was Babylon's failing, not mine. The Lynds would surely have taken my side if they'd heard about it.

Not that finding one's predicament described in print made life any easier in practice. But it was at least reassuring. ("The first step.") Even with those who hardly read, the written word carried authority: Senator Joe McCarthy had merely had to wave a written list of names, false or not, to make people believe he knew who was red and who wasn't.

But while the Lynds, Mencken, and the rest could write about us and go away, for those of us who had to stay, understanding, though comforting, was not enough. I had committed indiscretions well beyond chess. On the debating team I'd got carried away defending whatever was forbidden, making one smartass speech after another. ("You should be a lawyer," said my friend Dee-Dee.) When the Italian movie *The Miracle*, about a woman who thinks she's the Virgin Mary, was banned by the Catholic Church, I delivered an impassioned defense of free speech to the Saturday matinee audience at the Movie Palace. When girls were forced to wear bathing caps in the swimming pool because hair clogged the drains, I had mine shorn, becoming the first girl with a DA in Babylon High. I still had to wear a bathing cap, of course, but the stir I caused was so elating that I bought myself a rep tie, buttondown shirt, and black gaberdine suit in Bailey's boy's department (where I worked on Saturdays and got a discount) and flaunted my contempt for the rest by dressing in my private version of Marlene Dietrich and Joan of Arc. And when the principal of Babylon High canceled the entire school's free seventh period lunch in favor of study hall for the rest of the year, because a few people (not I) had been caught smoking and necking behind the backstop, I stood on the front steps at noontime and tried to organize a seventh period boycott. Unfortunately, it earned me an "incorrigible" on my permanent record, I later learned, as well as a phone call to Daddy, but at the time all I was aware of was the delicious admiration of a few classmates and a growing reputation for acting on principle.

The main effect of *Middletown* was this: at last I understood that there was nothing inevitable about the life we led. For Tahitians, white sand, not black, must seem the rarity. For the Chinese—or even for people like the Lynds of New York, who from their elevated vantage point could see right through us—Babylon must seem the "other side" of the world.

Though the book actually told me very little I didn't already know from experience (and was not listed on any subversive index), it changed me forever. The idea I needed to guide me was now in my head. Aunt Louise, bless her, had done it again. By the time of my sixteenth birthday, I knew what I wanted. No green wax would mar my next year's cake. I had only one wish, which I began to pursue with the same single-mindedness that had once sent me fanatically digging to China.

To get out.

6 · PREPARATION AND DEPARTURE

Russian Vera Figner, bomber of the Tsar's Winter Palace, wrote in her memoirs that even as a child, "I found it unthinkable that I might live without making some mark upon the world."

My ambitions were far more modest, inspired by a maxim of Oliver Wendell Holmes, Jr., repeated to me by my Aunt Louise: "It is required of a man that he should share the passion and action of his time at peril of being judged not to have lived."

Which meant: I must break for New York, the one place where, if I couldn't make a mark, at least I could be around where marks were being made.

"If you want to go to New York, why don't you apply to Barnard?" Aunt Louise suggested sensibly at the start of my turbulent senior year. She thought I ought to go to the University of Chicago, but Barnard would do.

I, however, knew Barnard was out of the question. Going East was much too expensive; besides, no one from Babylon ever went East to college. Not even Chicago, though close enough, was a real possibility. Even if I could somehow manage to pass the College Boards, with my deportment record I'd probably never get in. The last time I'd sneaked a look at my records in the school office I'd been obliged to trim my ambitions. The "inquisitive turn of mind" was heartening, but the "rebellious streak," documented and underlined, and that old "incorrigible," though they boosted my ego, limited my options. The counselor too had doubts. "You've got debating to your credit for extracurricular, but you know, Zane . . ." She said Barnard had "very high standards" and wasn't for "our kind"; as for the University of Chicago, frankly, she counseled, it was riddled with communists.

For a while I toyed with skipping college altogether, running straight to New York after commencement. But I wasn't sure. For all my big talk, I was nuts about learning and terrified of New York. Not one soul from Babylon was going there, and if I did go running off I wouldn't have a dorm or money or a friend. (I'd had a Saturday job at Bailey's for a year and a half, but I'd spent all my money on books and records.)

Then Daddy came to my rescue with a compromise offer I was happy to snap up. "Here's what we've decided to do," he said. We were playing chess; it was his move. "If you go to Middletown Junior College for two years, then after you graduate, if you still want to, we'll help you go to New York." He brought it out gleefully like a discovered check. "Of course, you might want to continue school."

I pretended disappointment. "Two years? Why wait? Why not send me to New York right now?"

"No," said Daddy.

"Why not?"

"First of all, you'll be very sorry if you don't go to college. But besides that, frankly, we think sixteen is a bit too young to go away. Don't you? In two years we feel you'll be considerably more mature."

Sheldon Aldrich, a boy in my class who had suddenly thrust himself into my life, had said he loved me precisely because I was "so mature," though naturally I couldn't mention that to Daddy.

I could have pursued the line that Daddy was bribing me and made some easy points. But instead I said I'd think it over. Daddy's offer was as reassuring as it was generous; though I'd never have admitted it, I was relieved to have a little time to bone up for my future before I was on my own.

In the fall I became a freshman commuter to Middletown Junior. Only the most esoteric courses in the catalogue attracted me. I cut my hair shorter than anyone thought possible, shorter than Saint Joan's; and though I quickly let it grow back in, it had its effect. Between classes I brooded in the library and read little magazines. Naturally I joined the debating team and went all out for chess. I walked barefoot on campus (weather permitting), wore only black, defied regulations in the spring by wearing shorts to classes (if they don't like it, I told my advisor, let them kick me out!), and enjoyed creating a campus scandal by drinking beer in the Keller with the boys on Friday afternoons (TGIF). But none of those acts could be considered episodes of principled dissent. Rather, they were individual statements, lonely and daft, designed to prove that unlike other girls at Middletown State Junior College, in training to be nursery school teachers, wives, secretaries, or dental assistants, I would not waste my life in smiling acquiescence.

My true major was New York City. In my second year I discovered Middletown's only coffee house; after that I dragged my reluctant friend Dee-Dee downtown on Saturday nights to mingle with a handful of malcontents in turtlenecks, rumored to be mostly fairies. There, in thrall to bohemia, I practiced hurling harsh judgments against the local arts while Dee-Dee sat in awe, and each night I fiddled with my radio dial until the short skip got me New York. Broadway, the Jean Shepard Show, and on my lucky nights, Birdland.

My spirit flew East, except on Sundays. All my life Sundays had been our family day; now, knowing they were numbered, I felt their poignant music. We had always spoken a secret language, my family. We three together, like a run in rummy: reading aloud to each other *Green Mansions* and *As You Like It* and other books unread in Babylon or taking turns at the piano while the others harmonized. We three: who buried two family dogs, who all studied music, who tried to get up to the Indiana Dunes every other year, who settled every argument by looking it up, and who, even after my graduation, pranced about the house in our underwear without the slightest shame like no other family in town!

But now that our Sundays were running out we observed them passionately: lavish brunches at noon, speculative flights in the afternoon, a hard game of chess, a fire in the evening, music. And while I tried to toughen myself up during the week, I softened in the heat of Sunday. Until at last the time came for me to go: Autumn 1958.

"I've forgotten something!" I suddenly panicked as we all walked into the Middletown station lugging my new matched Amelia Earhart luggage (graduation present from Mama). "Something important."

"Think," said Mama.

I ran over my important assets. An A.A. (Associate of Arts) degree from Middletown State Junior College, a *Claire de Lune* proficiency on the piano, a long Dunhill cigarette holder (the latest addition to my Dietrich look), my *Debater's Manual* and *Middletown*, my train ticket, and, courtesy Daddy, a checkbook, to be used until I found a job, and the small leather-bound notebook marked *New York*, bestowed and begun by Aunt Louise, containing a few addresses, beginner tourist tips, and that inspiring inscription from Oliver Wendell Holmes, Jr., about sharing the passion and action of your time, which I had already committed to memory. I liked a motto which made a virtue, even a duty, of the very course I had chosen to follow. Not that I had any idea of what passions or actions awaited me, but I did want to be on hand in the right place for such time as they appeared. The rest was clothes and personals, packed away in the suitcases.

"Put everything down and wait right here," said Daddy. "I'll go find us a porter. Don't try to lift those heavy ones."

"Eventually I'll have to lift them," I said as he walked off.

No matter. Ten more minutes and I'd be free. I'd promised Daddy to try to get a room at the Barbizon or the Y, but actually I intended to heigh-ho it right down to Greenwich Village.

"Now you be sure to let us know if you need anything," said my sweet smiling Mama, hugging me. "And write to us."

"You too, Mama."

"Bye, my baby. Take good care of our precious."

"Bye, my sweet Mama."

We allowed ourselves to talk that way—just us. Down her

cheeks streamed special family tears. Even Daddy's eyes shone suspiciously on his return. We followed the bags to the platform where the train was waiting. After tipping the porter, Daddy cleared his throat, adjusted his necktie, and gave me the grave look that said: remember to bundle up in the cold, watch that king's pawn opening, don't sign anything you haven't read all the way through, try not to make a spectacle of yourself, and be circumspect about your virginity.

I let him off with a dirty look. A sweet man, but he knew nothing about sex. Like most dads, mine was as square as a coffin peg and had a thing about virginity.

"I just know I forgot something important," I said again.

"Don't worry. Whatever it is, I can send it later," said Mama.

"Your alarm clock?" suggested Daddy. "You'll need that clock, Zane. You certainly don't want to be one of those people who sleeps her life away. It's important to have a regular schedule if you want to get ahead."

"Schedule! Really, Daddy!" I said, unable to resist taking a stand on each little thing, though if the truth were known, I intended to stay up all night and work all day and not waste one precious New York minute sleeping. Life is short for what I had to do. But bohemians didn't wear watches, so I said: "Anyway, why should my life be regulated by some arbitrary time?"

"The time of day, my dear, is hardly arbitrary. Why, do you realize that each second is calibrated to the—"

Mama yanked at his sleeve in mediation. A yank meaning, Now Zeke, this is no time to get into one of your father-daughter imbroglios. Aloud she said: "You have to realize that nowadays the youngsters are interested in other things than just getting ahead. Art, music, ideas, the better things . . ."

She waved her arm vaguely in a graceful gesture set off by the new fox-trimmed coat she'd induced my dad to buy her for Christmas despite the limitations of his teacher's salary. Because even though she had abandoned her job and maid years before, in Babylon not even a teacher's family can be expected to walk around in rags.

If only the train hadn't been already in the station waiting for the passengers to finish with their drawn-out goodbyes, I would have leaped straight into the discussion (as on other Sundays) to explain that art, music, ideas, were not merely "the better things." A recent article in a little magazine made it very clear that Art and Ideas were revolutionary forces, not amusements for the idle. Times had changed. Oh, if only we could sit down to one more hot family brunch and put Art first on the agenda I could make them understand everything! But suddenly eighteen years together were about to end for no better reason than that I had announced to everyone I was going to New York and when I say something I stick to it! ("Zane's leaving." "Her parents promised her, but they didn't really think she'd go." "You know her." "I always knew she'd do something with her life." "I always said if anyone got out of here it would be that nut Zane.")

And now it is time. The train is waiting.

"Maybe you better get on the train darling and find a seat," says Mama. "I guess it's really goodbye."

I stop midkiss. Goodbye? I want her to pull me off the step, shake her finger and forbid me to go away. There is still time to please them and register at State Teachers College, marry Sheldon Aldrich, buy one of the new houses going up on the edge of town (his parents will offer the down payment for a wedding present), and go to my Mama's for dinner every Sunday for the rest of my life.

But one thing I'm not is a quitter. (Said Joan of Arc to her accusers: "Since God had commanded me to go, I must do it. And since God had commanded it, had I had a hundred fathers and a hundred mothers, and had I been a king's daughter, I would have gone.")

"Now, you have a wonderful time. Call us collect whenever you need to."

"Oh, Mama, Mama."

"Study hard, Zane. Behave yourself."

"Daddy, Daddy."

"And if you change your mind, or, uh, need any money . . ."

"Goodbye."

The train moves and I begin my amazing balancing act on two thin rails that stretch on for a thousand miles.

My parents will wave till I'm long gone. Then slowly they'll turn around, walk to the parking lot, and get into the car. ("One of these days we'll really have to think about getting a new car,

Zeke, this one isn't going to last forever," my mother will say, brushing off the front seat for her fox-trimmed coat.) This time they'll drive home in silence, except at Tompkins Corners where Mama will say, "Zeke! For heaven's sakes! Don't turn till the light changes." I know the route with my eyes closed. When I was little I slept on Mama's lap in the back seat driving home feeling each curve and turn as Daddy guided us jerkily up the hill. "Wake up Zane darling, we're home," Mama would croon when Daddy stopped at the back porch path to let us off before pulling the car past the myrtle patch into the garage. "Careful of the myrtle," Mama will say, even though I have left them.

This time she'll get out alone. After Daddy parks the car he'll walk up the steps, wipe off his shoes, go inside, kiss her, and turn out the porch light. (No need to leave the porch light on for me.)

And then?

Then I don't know. Anything can happen, because from now on I won't be there. Already I'm streaking off through the air like a Sputnik in space, across the midland plains, over the Appalachian Mountains, toward the ocean (and China?), eager and terrified, never to return. Already I'm sitting in the club car with a gin and tonic (Wrong drink? Too late to change it) waiting to see what will happen next. Already I'm prepared to switch drinks, alter my accent, change my shoes, and harden my heart for the tough exciting bohemian life ahead. In wicked Greenwich Village.

Thank you Daddy for teaching me chess. And all the sneaky tricky gambits.

Thank you Aunt Louise for a point of view.

Thank you Mama for always defending me.

Thanks for everything.

Forgive me.

PART II

MacDougal Street

I wasn't trying to create any kind of new consciousness or anything like that. We didn't have a whole lot of heavy abstract thoughts. We were just a bunch of guys who were out trying to get laid.

—JACK KEROUAC
on the Beat Generation

1 · ARRIVAL

Now I wonder where I ever found the nerve to follow that confused cacophony of voices—the Lynds, Jean Shepard, Charlie Parker, Justice Holmes—to the big city without the slightest notion of what to do next.

My A.A. from Middletown State Junior College had prepared me for nothing but running away—a temporary aspiration at best. And after escape? Then? The voices I followed gave only the vaguest hints: Passion! Action! History! Dangerous notions to plant in the mind of an impressionable eighteen-year-old who has never been away from her Mama; a particularly hard tune to carry in 1958, a year history was as firmly under the baton of the Philistines as any in the century. Even in New York City, that grand exception, five years after the execution of the Rosenbergs the U.S. branch of world revolution was so well camouflaged that the Red Squad's Manhattan confiscations south of Fourteenth Street were at a rate of ten stashes of pot to one pile of pamphlets. The artists considered most "revolutionary" at that time would dare sign their names to nothing more subversive than their own frequently incomprehensible works. In 1958 a rebel man was one who could survive his nightly boozing, and a rebel woman was one who could sleep around and pretend to enjoy it. If I'd boarded a train a decade later, I might have found the revolution recruiting on every street corner of the Village, but in 1958 it was still in hiding. Even the most ardent newcomer with the best will in the world could hardly know what to look for, much less where to look. So much for revolution.

As purposeless as I was determined, as confused as I was ardent, like any adolescent I'd neglected to think about what awaited me. To say I was seeking adventure is too cynical; I was more vaguely seeking. Coming wide-eyed from Babylon, fleeing the Philistines, hoping to be an apprentice dancer, actress, scholar, poet, editor, reporter, advocate (because of my experience, respectively, in the drama club, newspaper, and debating team of Middletown State Junior College), I thought I would make my way on enthusiasm backed up by talent. Sure, there might be a glut of talent in the city when I arrived—but that wouldn't discourage me. I was set for the worst. Hadn't I spent interminable summer afternoons in high school on back porches in that elm-shaded town debating with my friends precisely the relative merits of frog size to pond size? No great rewards without great risks—something I learned in the minuscule bohemia that flourished in the Flats just off-campus all over America, even in Middletown, Indiana. Maybe ten years later I'd be dutifully home with a family, but ten years was almost forever; meanwhile, the search was on. I was prepared to go the clerk-typist route and collect my happiness after working hours.

No one in Babylon understood. To them, New York was Sin City, the Village its septic tank, less a neighborhood than a floating orgy where people fucked like Latins or Bennington girls, taking dangerous drugs in illegal lofts with the bearded hipsters pictured in magazines. Even if I too got my ideas from magazines, the mere thought of those folks back home with their eyes bugging and tongues clucking spurred me on. Let them think!—I knew that in New York I'd find not the fifth-rate bohemia available in Middletown with its tiny colony of misfits, its one "art theater," its bitter professors, its loyalty oaths and hounded homosexuals, but the original, where it was only a matter of time until you heard the poem or smoked the pot or found the crowd that would enable you to move the world. New York—a world of pace-setters, a whole neighborhood of tolerators, a place where a girl could cut off her hair or excel at chess without every eyebrow in town going up. A place where you could mingle with the beats in the famous cafes of MacDougal Street (San Remo, Gaslight, Rienzi, Figaro, Cafe Passé, Cafe Lucia) while baroque concerti drifted out of speakers and mingled with the rococo curls of tobacco smoke. At last a place where sex was okay and money wasn't everything, where people like Marx, Freud, and Maxwell Bodenheim were precursors of *us*.

Us! World-shakers of the world!

Such were my musings as the train carried me East from Babylon. But now suddenly, abruptly, the train shuddered into a black tunnel changing its roar to a purr and the conductor announced, "Grand Central Station."

He said it as though the name meant nothing special; as Sheldon Aldrich said "I love you," by rote, on signal, betraying none of the shattering significance. I looked at that paunchy uniformed conductor repeating the mysterious New York name as if it were merely the last station on a routine run, oblivious of the blessed gift it was to be pulling into this station, and made my resolution. No matter how long I lived in this city I would never allow myself to grow blasé! No, I thought, as a porter wheeled my matched bags, with ZANE stamped in gold on each piece, through the site of the conductor's blasphemy: to me, even the most ordinary facts of life would always remain miraculous. Not only the existence of these crowds, these towering buildings, these neon lights, this energy (for now I was outside, waiting for a taxi), but even the most fundamental facts. For example, that under the blouse of every woman, including those hurrying past me to make the light, nestled the wonder of two nippled breasts; that the occasional beard passing on Forty-second Street, the mere sight of which triggered my desire, could be effortlessly grown by any post-pubescent Caucasian male; that under my own tailored suit with white blouse, white gloves, and spectator pumps Mama had advised for traveling beat the wild heart of a beatnik.

Settled in the spacious back seat of a Checker cab, I let the address of my hotel roll off my tongue with infinitely more appreciation and respect than the conductor had lavished on the name of his destination:

"Hotel Europa, please, on MacDougal Street."

The driver turned and looked at me for a second with what I took to be understanding. I smiled back proudly—not only for knowing enough to stay in the Village, but for having successfully negotiated the hotel and a week's rent without my parents' knowledge. Betraying nothing behind his New York eyes the driver started the meter with its brash New York prices, swerved abruptly into the deranged horn-happy traffic of Forty-second Street (another fabled name) and carried me headlong down to the hub of the Village.

Mama would probably have been shocked to see the room into

which, embarrassed, I followed my newcomer's ridiculous matching luggage, but I thought it a perfect place. Dingy as a garret, with tilted floor, sagging bed, cigarette burns on the table (ominous counterpart to the red hatchet mounted over the sign FIRE EXTINGUISHER in the shabby hall between room and community bath), the room had the unmatchable virtue of facing the one and only Washington Square Park. Music coursed through the hotel halls; a picture of a pair of frolicking butterflies torn from a magazine and Scotch-taped to the wall by a former tenant gave my room a touch of gaiety; across a tiny court two flowerpots and a pear sunned themselves on a window sill. Oh, how the cool Manhattan air stung my face as I parted the flowered drapes and threw open the window for the first time on that vibrant scene below. Quivering orange and yellow autumn leaves, unsynchronized guitars, motors racing, fast talk, ebullient laughter. Yellow taxis whizzed around the northwest corner of the park like circus clowns on unicycles. In case of fire I'd simply leap.

I didn't waste one minute unpacking. There was still half the precious Sunday left. I kicked off my telltale shoes and rifled my suitcase for the black slacks and turtleneck of bohemia. The boyish clothes in which I'd created smart effects in Babylon would have to wait till I'd studied the New York pros; a newcomer needed humility. I checked my new self in the rippled mirror—bangs to the brow, a three-millimeter gap between my two front teeth, red cheeks like a painted Dutch girl's splashed with Daddy's freckles—and then, tucking my notebook into the side pocket of my shoulder bag, dashed down the stairs, across the street, and straight up the nearest path of the park to the center where the famous fountain, long dry of water, overflowed with life and atmosphere. Ready to begin.

2 · A WOMAN

If anyone had asked me what I was looking for that balmy late-September afternoon in Washington Square where I floated with the stream of Sunday strollers, I wouldn't have known how to answer. Looking? But I had found it! Mingling in the huge swarm of New Yorkers sampling the music and life around the fountain—

where, among the hand-clappers, foot-tappers, folk-singers, steel-drummers, and innumerable guitarists, the spectators were indistinguishable from the performers—I thought I had only to open myself to the intimate vibes for my long-suppressed potential to emerge. Eighteen and alone, with an exaggerated sense of place, forgive me, I hadn't yet learned it took more than being on location to get a part in history.

Not that I felt entitled to a part. My having lighted in New York still seemed, despite my obsessive scheming to get here, more of a dream or a miracle than a fact, with all a fact's attendant train of consequences. The consequence of a miracle was simply another miracle, and here I was awaiting it.

Wandering along the paths of the park like any pilgrim in Jerusalem, I honored each holy landmark. The Arch, the Fountain, the green benches, the permanent chess tables where old men in tweed caps sat playing the game that had got me branded queer in Babylon.

Everywhere the miracle was manifest. Lovers kissed openly on benches, oblivious of gossip. Old men and women gathered the last rays of receding sun on aluminum reflectors they held under sagging chins. Dirty children climbed over statues and crawled in the grass without benefit of car pools—native kids who had actually been born here. The music, the bearded men, the chess players, the lovers, even the striking redheaded woman I noticed earnestly holding forth to a small audience of men on a nearby bench—all of them, alone and together, reflected a life so clearly superior to the one I'd fled, a life so inconceivable in Babylon, that merely being here among them seemed a preliminary fulfillment of Holmes's exhortation.

Naturally, I would have been grateful to find myself suddenly taken up by, say, a slim bearded poet with soulful eyes or some as-yet-undeveloped genius capable of discerning my own smoldering intelligence or perhaps a group of hot-blooded conspirators. But such fantasies hardly constituted "looking." For 1958, just being alone in New York City seemed quite achievement enough.

Of course, compared to the achievement of the Moscow Amazons, whose beeline to their capital took them straight into the swarming hive of revolution, my arrival in New York was like the purposeless flight of dandelion fluff. Those clear-sighted women would have judged this park scene irrelevant and promptly excised it from their memoirs. Though my purpose, no less than theirs, is to reveal the causes and contours of our rebellion, if I took so strict a view of the rebel life I'd have to eliminate entire decades from my story. At the time I knew nothing about Russians. American style, I'd come to New York to experience life, heeding Holmes's warning less with an eye to remaking society than to remaking myself. Am I to disown my own youth for being below the standards of a distant culture? No matter how often, looking back, I may have wanted to seize that foolish Zane by her shoulders and shake some sense into her ("What are you after?" I'd say; "What precisely do you want?"), or stand her in a corner to reconsider before she falls into bed with the first poet who smiles at her, or lock her up in a room with *Das Kapital*, or send for her aunt, or enroll her at Hunter College—anything to make her see beyond the decadent frivolities that had unfortunately infected even Greenwich Village in that unhealthy year, 1958—I still can't cover up the truth. I've heard the movement clamoring for "positive female images" and have recently studied Mao on propaganda; but what possible good can come of a false image, however positive? I have no thanks for those well-meaning writers who glorified sex just before I fell, who glorified marriage just before I agreed, who glorified self-fulfillment just before I indulged. Then how can I leave out half my story, the chancy half, even to glorify the revolution?

No! Better to put that muddle-headed Zane in the third person and pretend I barely know her, better to enter a special plea for leniency in the names of youth, ignorance, innocence, gender; better even to deny or denounce her than to wave the writer's wand over her weaknesses like those authors of "official" biographies and make her into someone she could never be. After all, 1958 was hardly a year in which a newcomer could easily find her way into the revolutionary underground in New York City, supposing such existed—certainly not Zane. In her shy mode (to which, to her dismay, she seemed increasingly prone since her arrival) she would have been considered unworthy, and in her rebellious mode she would have been dismissed as a show-off. Save your sneers for the real villains of that year—of whom there were more than enough.

Not that there weren't also a handful of exceptions who knew better, mind you. Though as we now know bohemia had fallen into the hands of misanthropes, individualists, opportunists, and misogynists when the War had ended a decade before, there were still clear-headed women in New York. There were some survivors from the twenties who'd been dubbed the New Women and still remembered *The Masses* and Edna St. Vincent Millay. There were the leftover women from the thirties, Louise's contemporaries, hopefully raising "red diaper babies." And there were even young women from the hinterlands whose heads would not be turned by published poets, women in revolt who knew what they were about.

In fact, the tall, striking redhead lecturing to a circle of respectful men, her foot planted firmly on the bench where her audience sat gazing up at her—the woman I had myself just stopped my stroll to watch—was (though I certainly could not have known it at the time) probably the number one exception in the Village.

I was a little too far off to catch what she was saying, but ardor and conviction lit her face. One hand gesticulated in support of some point that her other hand, now resting clenched and determined on her raised knee, had already presented. Unlike me in an argument, excited and intense, she seemed calmly assertive, scoring her points with an ease that looked like modesty. She could have come straight out of my *Debater's Manual*. ("Movement is language; motions speak. The voice tells something of the condition of the mind, but the look, the expressive action, mean quite as much.") Except for the shocking red halo of unkempt hair which no Babylon imagination could have anticipated, she struck me as a model of the person I wanted to be. True, she seemed older, much taller (five feet ten at least), probably wiser and more experienced than I, but as she leaned forward and removed her sunglasses to make a point, I recognized the gesture as one I had been at pains myself to master. ("Bring the body forward to express earnestness or enthusiasm. . . .")

Of course, an urbane New Yorker like her was clearly beyond those embarrassing but unavoidable compulsions I'd childishly pursued in Babylon in a vain attempt to differentiate myself from the rest; one who exuded such authority would never have had to study gesture in a book or resort for attention to exotic costumes or unbending stands. But I was new here and could change.

I moved in to eavesdrop. But at that moment the redhead's companions began exchanging handshakes and goodbyes. Then two of them headed toward the fountain while a third, a large shaggy man with the slouch and shuffle of someone who had grown prematurely tall, took the redhead's arm and started with her toward MacDougal Street.

Was I to lose her the very moment I had found her—as I had so often lost Birdland in the static Midwestern air? No! When your purpose in life is simply to experience everything, there is absolutely no reason not to do anything that pops into your head. I decided to follow both redhead and impulse wherever they happened to lead.

They led at a leisurely pace past the chess tables (where they paused), out of the park at the southwest corner, and straight down MacDougal Street.

Though it was still afternoon, the coffee houses and restaurants were crowded. Music spilled from the open doorways. At the corner of Bleecker Street, redhead and friend turned into a noisy cafe—the Figaro, a name from my New York notebook.

It was a crowded, dingy place I followed them into: two large rooms with yellowed French newspapers and posters decorating the walls, rickety tables and chairs, and a small garden in the back. The redhead waved to a group of people at a large rear table where a bearded man stood up and called to them. I tried to catch the names he mouthed, but the music overhead and the hum of voices muffled the sound; and before I could make out any name, the redhead's friend was squeezing two more chairs in at the table.

Not an empty table near them. I considered taking one across the room, but, embarrassed to sit alone like a tourist, I retreated to the street.

Safe among the nameless strollers, I retraced my steps slowly, looking, looking, taking everything in. Past windows of cafes where artists argued and lovers held hands across tables for two; past little shops devoted to single items, some unobtainable in all of Babylon (one for fretted instruments, another for clocks, a poodle shop, a ring shop, sandalmakers, spice stores, and at least one book or record store per block); past walls and lampposts hawking acting classes, poetry readings, socialist meetings, and dance ensembles, all vying for my patronage. I walked till the sun went down and the lights of the street ushered in an entirely different atmosphere. Early night people, clicks along the pavement, something brittle and impersonal on the street, something intimate behind the doors. When hunger overtook me, I ate a hot dog at a counter rather than risk another sit-down place alone. ("Wiener?" repeated the counterman with a smirk. But of course, they weren't called "wieners" in New York!) Then I walked back across the park toward home.

"Home." A furnished room in a fleabag hotel my mother would have sickened to see—the one place in the world I hoped to find myself. From my sagging bed beside the window on Washington Square I stared up at the peeling green ceiling and listened. Somewhere across a courtyard a jazz trio was rehearsing those Birdland tunes I'd bounced off the moon into my Babylon bedroom through my radio every night for a year. Now they had suddenly come to life, truer than the finest stereo. The fixture overhead was an aged disc with one red bulb, one yellow, and one empty socket. It looked like a winking god—the goddess of bohemia—perfect muse for the new wild dance in my head.

Out the window I could see the park in the middle of its act. It was at the latest ten o'clock, an hour when bohemians are just beginning their day. I thought I would rest for half an hour, bathe in the old-fashioned tub on four plump little legs, then consult my notebook and return to the street to look for the redhead and give another coffee house a try. But when I next opened my eyes, it was morning.

Above me the ceiling goddess was gazing fixedly down, an expectant, a magisterial look in her red eye. "Up!" she seemed to urge; she hadn't closed her eyes all night long!

I stepped from the bed to the ancient slanted floor, then raised the window. A new, enticing day. Across the tiny court the flowerpots of the day before seemed to have burst into bloom; the pear was gone, probably eaten. The green park shimmered under a radiant sun. Motors whirred with Monday-morning industry. It was altogether a different world from yesterday's, and I was a different person. At last, I was a resident New Yorker.

3 · AT KAPPY'S

Though I was panting and sweating from the climb up the stairs to the fifth floor of the tenement where Herb Kaplowitz lived, my hands were cold with anxiety. Behind the door I heard laughter and music. What would they think of me?

I had just completed a week in New York. If I had been a young Russian revolutionary arriving for the first time in Moscow—one of the martyrs destined to stand trial among the Five Hundred—by the end of one week I would surely have been deep in conspiracy. On the first day I would have contacted my contacts who would have put me immediately in touch with the underground and then I would have thrown myself into my mission, laying aside every other thought. If their memoirs are to be believed, those dedicated Russians of the 1860s never gave a thought to private life. There was a purpose then, a great ideal, a movement. And Emma Goldman the anarchist arriving in New York in 1889 to make revolution went straight to Sachs's Cafe where she immediately found among several dozen comrades a roommate, a lover, a mentor, and important subversive work.

But when I came to New York I knew nothing of the lives of revolutionaries, and my listed contacts—collected in the Midwest at a time when the rebel was merely a loner or a nut—were either commercial (bookstores on Eighth Street, cafes on MacDougal Street, Bigelow Drugs for breakfast, *Village Voice* for apartment listings) or emergency (a lawyer via Daddy, a few friends of friends contributed by Middletown's handful of self-styled beats). Notebook in hand, I wandered among the Village streets noting addresses only of shops; and when I forced myself to return to the Figaro for a coffee on Tuesday and again, despite my discomfort, on Wednesday, I wondered why. It was a silly position to be in, sitting there all alone with a tiny, long-empty cup (in which I had dropped a swirl of lemon peel), waiting for something or someone unknown—especially when nothing came of it but a growing conviction of the essential futility of waiting.

On Saturday I reluctantly admitted that it was not, after all, enough merely to be here. The elation of the previous weekend, which I had thought as much a feature of Village life as of my psyche, had withered before the vigorous new shoot of disappointment sprouting in its shadow. Even the park, which so recently had seemed an enchanted place, displayed another aspect. Sitting on the crowded rim of the fountain with the regulars Saturday afternoon, for the first time I noticed broken bottles strewn in the pit of the fountain. A drunk's despair? Aftermath of controversy? Then Sunday. At home Mama and Daddy, content with the reassuring lies I had found so easy to write from my safe distance, might have had the Philharmonic on the radio and a fire in the fireplace. But there'd be no game of chess in the afternoon and none of those fancy debates in which Daddy and I, warp and woof, once wove intricate patterns of argument. Who could Daddy contend with now that I was gone? Mama the peacemaker had never known the thrill we found strenuously embracing the other side of a question. Wrestling words to the floor, launching phrases on the air. Those Sunday duets which she merely applauded could hardly proceed without me. No, Daddy would be sitting there silent, with a paper or pipe, as here I sat, in the national center of all elevated controversy, alone.

I'd wanted to phone them then and be treasured audibly, unreasonably. But I hadn't trusted myself. What if they'd asked questions I'd have to answer with lies? What if I found myself announcing, against all my resolve, my imminent return? This tough loner, cracking at the first sound of her Mama's voice?

Phone booths had suddenly appeared on every corner around the park. In New York you had but to think a wish for the means to pursue it to materialize. Was this the city of opportunities or of temptations for those who would seize them? With my courage wavering, I decided to dial instead a number from my New York notebook.

The most promising name was "Kappy"—former army buddy of a school friend's brother, a "writer" she had said, and, according to her brother, "a character." An oddly named man with a Village address: perhaps the perfect antidote to loneliness.

But the minute he answered the phone I felt ashamed to be calling. It was bad enough to have called near dinner time; but then to have been pressed into accepting a dinner invitation on the slim grounds that "my wife's making spaghetti. There's always enough for one more. Besides, it's Sunday"—was unforgivable. Or would have been by Mama's standards.

"Are you sure?"

"Of course I'm sure. Now let me tell you how to get here. We're on Bedford Street. Do you know where Chumley's is?"

Chumley's was a literary cafe on my list. "No," I confessed.

"Never mind that. Turn right off Sixth Avenue onto Bedford. We're two doors in. Keep climbing. Apartment 5-G. We're pretty high up but don't give up. The ambitious always make it."

I followed his instructions exactly, until now, standing before a badly painted door marked 5-G, I wished I had given up. Too late. As soon as I heard the music come to a break I rang the bell.

A big man with a kindly face hidden behind fancy mustaches opened the door, spilling beer from a large mug. Puffs of flesh under his chin and jowls made him look soft despite the aggressive voice.

"Zane? Come on in." He ignored the spill and spread his jowls into a jovial smile. "I'm Kappy, your slightly inebriated host. Come on in and meet the rest of the folks."

He took my arm and led me down a short passage spilling over with books into a small cluttered room. Two walls were lined with books floor to ceiling, another had prints of modern art, and worn overstuffed furniture filled the center. My pulse throbbed as a circle of eyes and whiskers, human and feline, all focused in on me.

"We caught us a young'un this time," said Kappy announcing me. Then, proceeding around the room clockwise, he threw at me a jumble of names in a bouquet of occupations. Brad filmmaker, Wendy concubine, Paul bartender, Marshall writer, Leonore, baby Sue, Wolfe, cats, turtles, thinkers, beards, Villagers.

"Zane's from Indiana, friend of my old buddy. Up, Suzie." He lifted the child from a worn easy chair, poured himself into it, then replaced the child on his lap. I was surprised to find a beat type with a baby, it seemed out of place, though of course it could happen to anyone. It looked like any other kid.

"What are you drinking, honey, wine or beer?"

"Wine thank you." I thought beer collegiate.

"Kaye," he called, "show yer face to Zane. She's drinking wine."

A frazzled Kaye in black tights, dirndl, and pushed-up pullover sleeves appeared from another room bearing a jelly glass and a jug of red wine. She wore large round glasses that gave her a startled look. Her hair was pulled back into a ponytail, but little wisps of curls had escaped, leaving her disheveled, and I felt sorry for her.

"Hi," Kaye said hurriedly. She gave me the glass. "We'll be eating soon, so excuse me, will you? Make yourself comfy." And she disappeared back into the kitchen before I could even say hello.

Unfamiliar music was blaring from two speakers arranged on the plank bookshelves, but fortunately no one was listening. Instead, everyone was discussing a certain new movie, Swedish, some of them had just seen—excitedly talking on top of one another. They were discussing its symbolism and meaning as though it were a poem or a play, connecting it with the previous work of the director.

This was a revelation to me. Never before had I heard such enthusiasm and detail applied to the analysis of a mere movie. The furor over *The Miracle* had been a matter of free speech: politics, not art. I knew who the star was but not the director; I hadn't even known there were Swedish movies.

From this week's film they moved to foreign films in general and then to film as Art—a discussion worthy of all my hopes, embodying a new idea. I memorized the titles preparing to spend all my free time at the movies learning what I could before the next discussion. I prayed no one would ask my opinion or notice my silence. Of course, it wasn't my fault that there was only one "art" theater in Babylon or that since the crisis of *The Miracle* it showed exclusively British comedies; but I feared they would probably blame me anyway.

I needn't have worried: no one asked me a thing. Brad, Marshall, Kappy, Wolfe all battled one another for the chance to speak next, interrupting each other with their contradictions and contributions so urgently that the thread was difficult to follow. They worked together like musicians, both competition and counterpoint to one another, quite oblivious of the rest of us.

A bored Wendy plopped into a butterfly chair beside me and asked, "You're visiting from Indiana?" She was one of those tall skinny blond women with high cheekbones and no eyebrows I had always, with fear and envy, associated with New York. In Babylon, of course, there were no such women. Like me she wore a black turtleneck, but on her it created an entirely different effect.

"Not visiting, really. Staying, I hope."

"Staying? Oh—what do you do?"

This New York question was one I'd never been asked before. What I "did" had always been obvious. Though I didn't yet understand all the insidious implications of the question that I would have to face down soon enough, still, I was sufficiently defensive to try to excuse my flimsy answer. "Nothing yet, but I've only been here a week."

"Only a week!" She flicked her cigarette nervously against the ashtray and swung her long leg rhythmically.

"Yes. I still have to get settled and find a job."

"You look so young, I figured you were a student."

"I was. But I got my A.A., and now I thought I'd work and look around before going back to school."

"A.A.?"

"Associate of Arts."

I was sorry to be missing the conversation across the room. Wendy might have heard it all before, but I hadn't. There were so many new ideas, so little time to learn them; I didn't want to waste my precious life in small talk. But Wendy, smiling, was looking at me, and dutifully I asked, "And you? Do you take any courses?"

She sighed and exhaled at once, rolling her eyes—a profoundly sophisticated gesture, I thought. "Not now. I used to take acting classes with Fabio, but now I have a full-time job and don't have the time. That's how I met Brad," she volunteered. "He used to audition Fabio's classes for actors for his early films."

I looked across the room at Brad. He was white blond, practically albino, with hair so silky the pink scalp showed through; he had a little wisp of pale beard. They made a strikingly pale couple.

"Actually," she continued, "I was in his first feature film."

A movie star!

"Maybe we'll show it to you some time. We live just down the hall."

"How lucky!" I said.

She looked at me in a new way. "Oh? You're interested in the theater?"

"No. I meant how lucky to live here. I wish I could find a place like this."

She pouted, crushing out her cigarette in a full ashtray and immediately lit another as Marshall walked toward us. "You should talk to Marshall, then," she said, rolling her eyes at him. "He keeps up on apartments. Weren't you talking about a place earlier, Marshall?"

"Do you realize, Wendy, that you have smoked five cigarettes in the last five minutes?" he answered. "That's an average of one cigarette a minute. That's not too smart."

He had thick, black curly hair and a voice that claimed to know things.

"Oh, shut up, Marshall," she said. She blew a puff of smoke his way and stood up—as though getting out of a butterfly chair were merely a matter of will. "I'm going to help Kaye get dinner on," she said sourly and slipped away.

I knew I ought to offer to help too, but I wanted to talk to Marshall. He had been introduced as a writer, he had astonishing curls, and he was standing there with his hands in his pockets looking straight at me.

"So you're from Indiana," he said. "I'll bet you came to be an actress."

In Indiana where there were no actresses I would have taken the question for a compliment. There, actresses, like models, were thought to be chosen for their looks. I was puzzled, knowing it couldn't be my looks that provoked the inquiry. Some people said I had a pretty face, but there was too much of it. In those days I wavered between size 14 and 12, aiming for 10 while I learned to settle for 12. Compared to most people I was short. My cheeks were preposterously rosy; there was a useless gap between my two front teeth that made me look even younger than I was. No sophisticated shadows or hollows corrected the impression.

"I'm a debater, but not an actress. Why do people keep asking me that?"

He shrugged, then smiled. "Why else do pretty girls come to the Village? To be actresses, or students maybe. Why did you come? To debate?"

"I've just always wanted to live in New York. You can't imagine how impossible it is where I come from." I felt like a traitor as I said it, but I was here now.

He looked at me with amusement. "Really?"

I nodded. "In Indiana you have to be just like everyone else or they think you're crazy," I confided. "Really, I'd be willing to do almost anything to stay here. I'd even try to act, I guess, if I could get paid for it, since everyone seems to think I can."

His laugh revealed that I had blundered again, but instead of pressing me to defend myself, he passed on to ask, "You're looking for a job?"

"A job, an apartment, everything."

"You're in good company anyway. Everybody's looking for a job or an apartment. Or both. That's all anyone talks about here; jobs and apartments, haven't you noticed? What-do-you-do and where-do-you-live."

"It's a lot better than what they talk about in Indiana. It's useful, at least."

"What do they talk about there?"

"Cars and clothes. And communists in the government."

"Where are you from again?"

"Babylon. I'm sure you never heard of it. It's a suburb of Middletown."

I was ready to explain which Middletown, but I didn't have to. The name drew a blank. I was embarrassed. I'd thought since there were two books with Middletown in the title, everyone would have heard of it. After Aunt Louise had given me the books I'd somehow felt I was taking my place in history. But there was history and history. Now, having revealed my insignificance, I added hastily, "Wendy says you might know of an apartment."

"I might; it depends." He scrutinized me. "In my opinion, a good job is easier to find than a good apartment. Apartment, job, happiness, in that order. That's what people are after here. Except me, I mean. I have a great apartment, couldn't stand a job, and as for happiness—" He waved his hand and gave me a look that was clearly seductive.

"Where do you live?" I asked quickly, evading his look.

His face lit up; for once I had asked the right question.

"On Fourteenth Street near Eighth Avenue. Terrific place. Actually, I'm looking for someone to take it over for a while. I may be going away."

"What's it like?"

"It's in a big old-law tenement. There's no heat except the fireplace in the main room. But it's only thirty-eight fifty a month," he said with considerable pride.

Thirty-eight dollars and fifty cents was half of what I paid for one small room at the Hotel Europa. "When can I move in?" I asked eagerly.

But instead of answering directly, he said, "I may be going out West for a while." And though his evasiveness made me hunger for his apartment, remembering my manners, I let it drop.

"Now that I know where you live, I guess I should ask what you do. Kappy said you're a writer. What exactly do you write?" The very question gave me a thrill, even though it provoked another moment of that embarrassing scrutiny.

"Oh, words, sentences, stanzas, sometimes whole paragraphs."

"I mean," I retreated, regretting my foolish question, "do you write articles or stories or what?"

"Mostly 'what,' I'm afraid. This month I'm writing newsreel narration to get some bread, but that's on the side." He waited to catch me on another question, but, contrite, I said nothing. Relenting, he offered, "I've had some poems published and now I'm working on a long play and a novel."

"Watch out, Indiana," said Wolfe, who had walked over to pour himself some wine. "If Marshall is trying to snow you with his novel, don't believe a word of it. That's the oldest come-on in the book." Then turning to Marshall and speaking very fast, his Adam's apple bobbing up and down his skinny neck like the ball in a singalong, he continued, "It works every time. Do you remember Slim Garnett?"

"Sounds vaguely familiar."

"That old fart who was in Spain with the Lincoln Brigade. He published a novel back in 1949. Well, he was in the White Horse today pretending to be some big famous writer. Some of the guys were helping him with the put-on, and damned if the old bastard didn't walk out of there with four Benningtons hanging onto his coat." He shook his head incredulously. "My God," he said, "Slim Garnett!"

"Was it nice stuff?" asked Marshall.

"Lovely," said Wolfe. "Not one I'd kick out of bed."

"Just wait till they find out they haven't been sleeping with immortality," said Marshall.

"You think an old lush like that can still manage to get it up?" asked Kappy, who, with the others, had suddenly tuned in on Wolfe's story.

"It'll serve them right if he can't," put in Brad.

"What a waste," said Kappy, shaking his head. "What a goddam waste. Boy, I wouldn't mind helping him out, but shit, man, I'm married."

I was shocked to hear the pathos in Kappy's voice. Thank god Kaye was in the kitchen out of earshot. The only married people I knew personally were my parents and their friends, who would never have talked that way, even if they'd felt it. Of course, everyone knew that marriage was confinement; that was why I pitied all my poor classmates stuck in Babylon who had nothing else to look forward to in life. But to have a husband who complained about it in public, even in jest—that was a humiliation I would never be able to withstand. When and if I ever married, I intended to take exactly as much freedom as my husband, not a measure less!—and then let him complain about it in public!

"What's your novel about?" I asked, returning to Marshall and the prime subject. Beneath that dome of soft boyish curls was a headful of precious words, some of which he had bothered to address to me.

"Oh, about two hundred pages so far," he answered with a smile. He was probably making fun of me with his flippant answers, but he looked at me so intently when he delivered them, flattering me with his attention, that I gave him the benefit of the doubt.

"That sounds like an awful lot. Have you been writing it very long?"

He put his arm around me and said, "My god, girl, you ask too many questions, you know that? You'll have to learn not to ask so many questions. Don't you know writers are notoriously shy about discussing their work?"

I was silenced by his reprimand but gratified by his touch—though neither, I reminded myself, probably meant a thing.

"How come you bite your nails?" he asked, taking my hand. Talk about intimate questions!

I had a whole repertory of glib answers, always good for a shock, which I usually followed by two minutes of diligent biting. But the way I felt in that setting, I knew I could never bring it off.

"More wine?" called Kaye from the doorway, saving my face. "Fill up now, 'cause we're about to eat."

We all filled our glasses and stood. "To New York," I said,

raising my glass to Marshall, carefully turning my stubs of fingers toward myself.

"To Indiana," he said in return. And from the way he looked into my eyes, I knew he meant not the place, as I had meant, but me.

I felt my cheeks color with Midwestern blood, wiping out whatever treasured urban pallor I might have acquired in a week.

The kitchen, the food, the conversation were like no dinner party I'd ever attended. Pots set straight onto the enameled kitchen table, homemade spaghetti sauce thick as mud, enormous salad of unknown greens, long garlicked Italian loaves from which everyone tore a hunk, and wine. Besides gossip (stories to illustrate the superiority of poverty to riches, art to work, New York to elsewhere) the dinner talk was mainly about marijuana—how to grow, dry, cut, hide, roll, preserve, purchase, cook, and consume it. I hung on every word trying to memorize each vivid detail of the meal for a future in which I would have my own pad, feed my own friends.

For dessert Wolfe produced a leather pouch full of home-grown "tea." While he ceremoniously rolled the "sticks" and Kappy replaced the jazz with a Bach partita for unaccompanied violin, the rest of us settled down again in the living room until everything grew still.

"What about the mess in the kitchen?" Leonore asked reluctantly, lighting candles and turning off lights.

"What about it? Don't worry," said Kaye. Kappy, settling back into his chair, added, "Kaye's got everything under control. She's got it all down to a system."

He took a deep drag on the first stick and passed it on. My heart raced with excitement. The first dope in my life. As with my first kiss and my first temptation, I prayed my inexperience wouldn't show. Cautiously I only pretended to smoke when it came around, hoping no one could tell—like those canny ancients who poured their potions in the potted plants. But the sweet smell filled the air, and the next time it came around I took a real puff. After a while Wendy and Brad started kissing on the floor and Paul left for work. But Kappy sank deeper into his chair, Wolfe settled in a corner, Kaye took the baby out of the room, and

Marshall stretched out on the sofa, his feet elevated on an armrest, his head in my lap, practically purring like one of the three Kaplowitz cats. Everyone listened to the music, heads back, eyes half closed in the flickering candlelight.

Lucky, I thought, lucky. A week before I had been a mere child in Babylon burning my camp pictures and my diary, and now here I was smoking pot in a Greenwich Village apartment with real writers, listening to mellow music on hi-fi components with the head of a poet in my lap!

"The winning player is always lucky," Daddy had often said, quoting that chess champ of champions, Capablanca; and as often, I'd puzzled over what it meant. Did Daddy invoke the master out of modesty, attributing to sheer luck his own victories over me? Or, to the contrary, did he mean to caution me that the true winners make their own luck?

Whatever it meant, it was Daddy's phrase that popped into my head as I looked down at Marshall's in my lap. For here I was, only eighteen years old, one week out of Babylon—and my ambitions were all but fulfilled.

4 · MARSHALL'S PLACE

The subway ran directly under Marshall's building, roaring like a wild animal and making the walls tremble through the night. But each time I jumped up in response Marshall teased me or else he reached out to me in his sleep and touched my shoulder. Like Mama, when I'd padded down the hall to their room to present her with one of my rare nightmares: "There, there, darling," she'd say and let me spend the night in bed with them. Naturally I fell in love with him.

I fell in love in a night. Why not? He was silent and deep, a published poet, a dedicated lover, the first of either kind I'd known. I didn't even try to resist. If I was going to sleep with him (*de rigueur* for the rebel), why not fall in love with him? It seemed all pro, no con. Coming from the Midwest where every casual kiss was observed, counted, judged, and condemned, I wanted to live out my sexual fantasies in case the prohibitions were to take over again. I wasn't *looking* for it, you understand, but I did want a bit of the wild, free sex of books, as long as no one from home could see, with someone seasoned who wouldn't judge me, someone transient who couldn't hurt me, someone who might appreciate my trust and understand me.

"Well," you might say, "a smart girl ought to know a little more about a man before falling in bed, much less in love, with him. I'm sure you won't find your serious revolutionary women making such romantic blunders."

But I'm not so sure. Though it's true that most of them gave few words to love, maybe they banished love not from their lives but only from their memoirs. Even the militant Angela Davis, who came of age during the sexual revolution, only hints at love in her book. And though there were always a few—Emma Goldman, Elizabeth Gurley Flynn, Alexandra Kollontai (a member of Lenin's cabinet)—who bared their hearts and campaigned for Free Love, openly sleeping with anyone they liked, most of us learned about love the hard way. Even warnings are probably useless, for somehow, despite the severest warnings of parents and friends, hundreds, thousands of women have forgotten themselves at the last minute and succumbed to the lies, promises, flatteries, or mere attentions of lusting lovely men, landing themselves practically overnight in the most complicated predicaments from which some of them never recovered during their entire lives. And I'm not speaking only of your teenaged Midwesterners in 1958; I'm speaking of women of every age in every city in every year. The notorious sexual revolution itself has saved no one from the pain and confusion of love.

With a touch as gentle as a butterfly's Marshall opened my eyes with his fingertips. "Try it with your eyes open. Fucking is beautiful to watch. See us? . . . This is new to you, isn't it?"

Too embarrassed to answer, I let my silence be assent. Sex wasn't altogether new. There'd been mutual masturbation with Tony Horner, with whom I got carried away, and, once I'd determined it was time to shed my virginity, the real thing with clumsy though safe Sheldon Aldrich. But that had been more in the nature of an experiment than an experience, and a failed experiment at that, since I'd felt practically nothing. As for real sex ("fucking," as Marshall called it), Marshall was right. This was new. These naked bodies intertwined, this slow motion with eyes open, eye to eye, this giving up and in.

I can still see us that first night of first love. The double mattress on the floor, us on the mattress. New York, a private bed, a poet, an entire uninterrupted night. A luxury the price of which was supposed to be marriage! I see us in my mind—a pair of koalas—I the little one clinging to him with my legs, he feeding my mouth wet kisses like eucalyptus leaves. Beside us the idle fireplace gave off a mineral smell of cold ash and the walls smelled of age. Colorless lights from the world played on the ceiling in mysterious shadows as we went on and on, naked, making love.

Now, with nearly two decades of experience to enlighten me, I'm at a loss to explain the enchantment of that night. I was so intimidated, so terrified by Marshall Braine, that I ought to have been quite frigid. Instead, I promptly fell in love. Take it for a tribute to Marshall or the bottomless mystery of sex or the inestimable erotic promise of being noticed in '58 by a dark-haired poet or Beginner's Luck. I'll say this for Marshall, though: he knew just what he was doing. I was astonished to discover how long we were able to continue making love. My limited prior experience exemplified the other extreme, but even in the light of average performances, Marshall's seems remarkable: even nowadays in the new movies the act is normally completed in under a minute.

Twice we rested and smoked cigarettes while he, raising up on an elbow, honored me with intimate snippets from his private life. I was too shy, of course, to reciprocate: the loudmouth of Babylon had nothing to say that whole night long. Even the passionate I-love-yous that surged up through my kisses were uttered only in my head, not out loud. Such phrases, like white shoes, were dead giveaways. No I-love-yous, no demands, that much I knew; only passion and silence. But beyond that, I had no idea how to act—with a poet, a lover. Instead of speaking, I nodded and smiled a lot, until at last he asked me, "Say, how come you smile so much?" Then, mortified, I stopped smiling too.

Though I could have gone on making love forever, it was a relief when he eventually fell asleep. I had thinking to do. Safe from Marshall's scrutiny, I returned to the important—now crucial—question: how to be.

"Be natural," Mama always said in that encouraging voice. "Be your own sweet self."

Good enough. But what was really natural? All the warring

parts of you were natural, and still you had to choose which to acknowledge and which to hide, which to encourage and which to suppress. What was natural in one place might be totally artificial in another. Even impossible. Was it quite natural, for instance, to be lying naked in a poet's bed thinking and figuring, though I had just fallen in love?

To Daddy, how-to-be was a matter of sheer *will*. "Decide what you want and go after it." A teacher of mathematics, his world consisted of perfect points of no dimension, lines without the diverting distraction of thickness, simple, single answers. From the merest sprinkling of axioms and the rules of logic he was able to deduce answers to all the questions I could dream up, unhampered by the crusty interference of experience. Reason was his fixed star, and by example, mine. There was no place in his firmament for the irrational or the confused. If reason told you to do something, then whether it was unpleasant or difficult made no difference, you did it. Daddy lived in a harmonious orderly world. His mind was as clean as his fingernails, his life as neat as his dresser drawers. He rose each morning at exactly the same time, slicked down his rusty-colored hair by drying it in a stocking cap, peeled an orange for his breakfast, and went off to work on the 7:45 express. He returned at the stroke of six to correct papers until dinner time. Whereas I forgot the time, changed my mind, messed my room, dissembled. And though I had mastered my father's gift of the ready answer (which earned me a spot on the debating team) there were many things I did without any idea why. I bit my fingernails to the quick, I took power from the moon, I lied to my diary, I was filled with impossible ambitions. My days were sprinkled with inexplicable urges and irrational impulses that landed me in a thicket of inconsistency.

What I needed now, in place of Daddy's *will*, was dialectics. (Dialectics: that powerful tool, better than logic, for reconciling contradictions, understanding paradox, and seeing underneath a motive to its opposite, with which those shockers, Hegel and Marx, and Freud too, had challenged the old modes of thought.) But at eighteen, having studied no Marx or even Freud, I'd unfortunately never heard of the practice. If I'd had even a smattering of dialectics I might have accepted the paradoxical discovery, now beginning to dawn, that the spunky kid I'd been in Babylon—

"that nut Zane" who'd sided with the Lynds, flaunted her principles, and split for New York—had evidently panicked at the last minute and hidden herself in the Middletown station while I was boarding the train. Otherwise, how could I explain that overnight I had turned from that familiar, confident, rather loquacious, slightly eccentric, self-proclaimed loner, who delighted in challenging every convention even to the matter of hair length and dealt with rejection by embracing it, into this shy, practically tongue-tied deferential supplicant (Love me! Love me!), an exile craving nothing in the world so much as the reassuring feeling of belonging? And most distressing, most paradoxical of all, what had evidently brought on this unsettling metamorphosis was the very success of my Babylon schemes. It looked as though my cherished *will* might have its outward or inward effects, but not both.

Maybe the Nut had been smarter than I gave her credit for. Maybe she'd seen that only where one could take belonging for granted could one afford to ignore it. For though my classmates might laugh at me, snub me, even abuse me, they had to accept me: we had the same birthright. Whereas here, on my own, I found myself clinging to the local conventions of dress, speech, and even thought as scrupulously as a Go-Club girl. Appearance and reality had flip-flopped until I couldn't tell what was real. My very desires were turning inside out until they resembled their opposites! The nonconformist was a conformist of nonconformity! The show-off wanted to hide, the loner wanted to join in, the debater wanted to listen, the digger of tunnels wanted to soar. Now that my dream of freedom had become reality, my former reality, which I'd thought fit only to flee, was fast entering my dreams, until Babylon's grudging acceptance of me seemed cozy indeed.

Marshall's room had gradually grown cold. In his sleep he emitted a long, deep, male sigh, a strange unconscious snore that I knew had nothing to do with me. As far as he knew, his newest bedmate was merely a small, shy, smiling, freckled person, a rapt listener, uncomplicated, agreeable to a fault. It was disconcerting to be so thoroughly mis-taken, but I felt helpless to correct his impression; maybe it wasn't even so far off. Though the sleeping man beside me was a stranger, I huddled against him for warmth, and pillowed by these questions fell asleep.

The sun lit up a high, ornate tin ceiling colored like old bronze. What would Mama say if she saw me here? How could I ever explain my unclothed presence in a stranger's bed?

I looked around. The apartment looked different by day. Through a window facing the eastern sky over rows of city roofs sunlight poured in, illuminating a tiny arched fireplace beside the bed, arched cupboards, planked floors—remnants of ancient elegance amid disarray that I couldn't have imagined a day earlier. Fully clothed and armed with my notebook, I might have relished the setting; but now I only wanted to flee before Marshall could catch me trespassing.

Too late. Those poet-eyes, so intimately connected with the act of love, clicked open and held me. Then without so much as a *good morning,* Marshall drew me to him until we were making love again.

Better than trying to explain oneself, I thought. And though it was a new idea, now it struck me as perfectly natural for people to run their fingers silently through each other's hair and make love with their eyes open in the early morning.

Marshall got out of bed, stretching noisily, scratched back and stomach, then shuffled across the long room without bothering to cover himself.

"Right back. Got to put on the kettle."

Hoping he'd take for sophistication a silence that really reflected shock, I allowed myself shamelessly to watch him. He was like those paintings I'd always been too embarrassed to examine. Rippled shoulders and long arms, hip bones slung over narrow flanks: my first naked male. Hungrily I looked and looked.

He put a stack of records on the phonograph, flooding the morning with the Bird, then disappeared. When he returned with two mugs of instant coffee I watched the front of him. Christ, Saint Sebastian, a frisky pup, a boy. My morning: watching Marshall walk back and forth while I stayed safely in bed, covered with sheet.

"Well kid, what do you think about the pad?" he asked. "You want to take it over from me? Temporarily, of course."

I noticed that he didn't use my name. Mostly he called me "kid," and sometimes "Indiana." It was unlikely that he could have forgotten my name, it was so unusual, my most distinctive trait. But maybe. After all, I excused him, he was twenty-seven years old, a New Yorker, and a veteran of five years in the Village; he must have known many women.

"When are you going away?"

"I'm not sure. Maybe next month. I have some people to see on the Coast. What I need is someone to keep the place and pay the rent. Wolfe stays here sometimes, but he's not reliable."

I knew there was something fated about stumbling across the perfect pad so early on. But I didn't know whether it was a temptation to be resisted or a gift to be snapped up. Arguments beckoned for both sides; the problem was to interpret them.

"Let me fix the music and I'll tell you about the place," he said, turning businesslike. (Then was my being here with him only a question of real estate?) Technically the place was not Marshall's at all. It had simply passed from one artist to another, in the family, so to speak, without changing lease. Marshall had it from a poet who got it from a painter who took it over from another painter who'd lived there with a model who had previously lived with a jazz musician and a novelist. The novelist had kept it all through the war years and remained the legal tenant, though he spent only a couple of weeks a year in New York.

"And does he stay here when he's in the city?"

"Yes."

"But where?"

He shrugged. "There's room."

It was true, there was lots of room, the place was as big as it was seedy, going on and on in space and time, making anything seem possible. Perhaps that was why it scared me. I had willed myself to New York with no notion of how one lived. When I imagined life at all, it was with Mama's idea of poverty: a house like "a postage stamp." I could picture myself in a tiny basement apartment—a small room with kitchenette, small enough to carry a manageable rent but bigger than a hotel room—a place I could furnish with unique pieces I'd pick up one at a time for next to nothing, with character and charm to make up for all I lacked myself. Something like the efficiency with pullman kitchen and Murphy bed just above the Flats of Middletown where Aunt Louise lived without complaint—tiny but cozy, the radiator covers piled high with books, framed reproductions of great art on the yellowed wallpaper, replete with Louise's ideals and personality. Not a big cold rambling walkup. ("In New York Zane may have the chance to do the kinds of things, great things, we never had, Anna," Louise had said defending me. "You ought to be glad she's got the gumption to go. What is there for her here? Look at us. What's my life but losing battles? What's yours but a nice house? Now Zane has a chance to make something of herself." And Mama had said, "I know you're right. But a nice house is something, Louise, it is *some*thing.")

But then a quasi-legal cold-water flat like Marshall's was something, too. Once you got beyond the sinister landings of the ill-lit stairs and the inconvenience of the plumbing (bathtub in the kitchen, toilet in the hall), such places were full of possibilities. The tin ceilings and gingerbread moldings, the repeated arches had been there for generations. There was something about the place besides the unbelievable rent, frozen years before at $38.50, which more than made up for its drawbacks. I could see why former occupants remained connected to it. It was a place you could never sever from its stories. It had not only size and charm, but a history and genealogy. To live in it made you someone: a link in a chain. Its shabby disrepair had its own value: to free you of responsibility. Even not knowing who might be staying with you for weeks at a time might itself prove an advantage—given the right people.

"Most of the sculpture comes from three tenants back, and that glass bookcase in the hall? It must have the complete works of every writer who's ever lived here. They and the cats go with the place."

There were two lean crazy cats, one black and white, one tabby, who chased each other from room to room and seemed to bounce off the walls, or else slept curled up in drawers or boxes.

"I've never had a cat," I said.

"They're part of the deal. If you don't like cats the place may not be for you. Maybe it's too kitschy, anyway," he said surveying the room.

I didn't know what "kitschy" meant. "Oh no," I covered, "I didn't say I don't like cats. I only said I never had one."

He offered to help me move my stuff in whenever I wanted. "There's plenty of room. If you're willing to stay and take the rent while I'm away you can move in any time. Wolfe sleeps in the back and right now some neighbors stash their stuff here and use the place occasionally when they have more people than they can manage. All I need for myself is this bed and place for my books. We're pretty loose."

I didn't know if he meant to keep me as a roommate or a lover or simply install me as another transient. Was he being generous or selfish? Any way I might ask would sound either presumptuous or compromising. I let it drop. I didn't want to presume anything, for it was well known even to newcomers to the Village that artists must be free.

About four we went out together for sandwich fixings, which we bought at one of the several Fourteenth Street bodegas. "Let me help pay," I said, remembering that he had said he had no money. He generously allowed me to pay. We picked up two wooden crates from the street for firewood and returned to the studio.

"I want you to see that the fireplace really works," said Marshall, laying the fire while I made sandwiches. "Tonight you'll be a little warmer."

Tonight? Then he liked me. I had given him every opportunity to get rid of me that day, but my leaving was never suggested. On the contrary, he wanted me to stay. I laughed with gratitude.

"Tomorrow morning I really have to get back to job hunting," I said, eager to demonstrate my independence. While we were eating Marshall had begun removing my clothes. "This is all very nice but . . ." I waved my hand and asked, "is there a way you can wake me by eight?" I watched his face to see whether he was glad or sorry. Would he think better of me for acting independently or worse for joining the nine-to-five crowd? Was he glad to get rid of me or sorry to lose me?

"Sure," he said, "I've got a clock around here somewhere. I hope it works."

He lit a match to the crumpled paper and cardboard kindling and after locating a clock in a drawer pulled me down again to the mattress.

The heels of our unfinished sandwiches were forever abandoned, just out of reach.

My real qualms about taking his apartment I couldn't reveal. It was a find, a steal at $38.50, but I sensed that moving in, however loose the arrangement, would make me vulnerable. Would I be living with Marshall or not? Would he bring other women home? He had told me that others of the circle switched partners with ease. He, Brad, Wolfe, Kappy, and several others had a whole community of women they "shared" that bound them together. Wendy, who lived with Brad, was really in love with Wolfe, Marshall had confided. He himself used to sleep with Kaye with Kappy's blessing, once in Kappy's presence, he said. Had he been testing me? I thought it an admirable state to be beyond jealousy, but I knew I could never bring it off. And even if he didn't have other women, when he grew bored with me would he ask me to leave as he was now so casually asking me to stay?

And what about my parents? I thought, as he stroked me gently between my legs. How could I explain to them the telephone listing, the rent arrangements; how could I describe my roommates?

Suddenly Marshall sat up. "You're always thinking, aren't you?" he asked.

I was contrite.

Later, catching my eyes wandering during a kiss, he said again, "Can't you ever stop thinking?" I stopped my eyes obligingly, but the truth was, with my fate in his hands, I didn't dare stop thinking.

Of course he'd grow tired of me, I thought, but so what? New York was not Babylon, Indiana. Lovers might come and go, grow old and move away; but with rent control, a good pad was worth a certain amount of suffering.

When the alarm clock rang in the morning Marshall didn't stir. Just went on sleeping like a night person. I leaped from the mattress to turn it off feeling suddenly hopeful. Sun lit up a corner of the room. Perhaps it would be my lucky day. I'd go down to my own room on MacDougal Street, take a long bath, dress up, find a job. If I did take Marshall's place, a table of plants would do nicely in that sunny corner. Slipping on my clothes I decided yes, why not take it over? With a decent job I might really make it feel like home.

My jacket was on, my hand on the door, when Marshall opened his eyes.

"Give me a call in a couple of weeks, tell me what you decide, okay?" he said. "It's a good scene here, but I know it's not for everyone."

A couple of weeks? How deftly he established the desired distance. If he were really offering me a part in his scene, it sounded like the merest bit part.

"Sure," I said. "Sorry I woke you. Go back to sleep now. And" —Babylon taking over—"thanks for everything."

Out on the street, nothing looked familiar. The neighborhood, so recently enticing, seemed menacing. I'd be more comfortable, I thought, on Washington Square. Not that I was part of that scene either, for all my wandering along the pavements and eavesdropping from the benches. No, it would take more than proximity to find what I sought. Wherever the scene I'd come seeking was being performed, it was evidently not open to the public.

At least there was grass in the park, and music, and the poets who read their work in the coffee houses were not in a position to kick you out of bed.

I would find a job quickly, I decided, and look for my own place.

5 · NINA

Anxiously I studied the arcane significance of local customs and how to interpret certain events. I had to. For instance, the fact that Marshall and I bought a single copy of the Sunday *Times* at the Sheridan Square newsstand late on Saturday nights meant that, despite Marshall's continued aloofness, we were "a couple" three months after we'd met.

An ambiguous couple, though. Now, reading the *Times* in that slow, coffee-drenched Sunday afternoon ritual New Yorkers perform together after the heavy night of love, I wasn't sure how to interpret Marshall's cryptic praises.

"I'm really impressed, Zane," he said, looking up from the *Book Review* to watch me circle the want-ads. "You haven't even looked at the magazine section, and already you're picking out your next job."

As usual, the compliment was double-edged. People as immune to steady employment as Marshall's crowd could well have admired my facility for landing jobs. I'd had three in as many months, foolishly taking each change for advancement, while plowing too much of my meager paycheck back into the employment agencies. And still I filled out applications truthfully, innocently answering the fake come-on ads the agencies placed weekly in the *Times*. But at the same time, people who worked for a living were considered foolish south of Fourteenth Street. There, the purpose of life was to breeze through doing as little as possible. Discipline, ambition, even schooling were frowned upon with at least one half the face if they led to salaried positions.

Marshall explained: "If I could stand to work in an office for six months running I'd get myself on unemployment and take off for Europe. But I know I'd never manage it. I'd get canned a week before my time was up or I'd quit in disgust. I guess I'm just not the type. But you, Indiana—you're a *wunderkind*."

The only time he called me *wunderkind*, I noticed, was after a Saturday night. The time in between, when I worked in an office uptown and slept in my room at the Hotel Europa waiting to hear from Marshall, he failed to appreciate me. He had fine distinctions to draw—between being a parasite and being a drone, or between being reliable and being spontaneous. What he admired in me one day he might ridicule the next—if he thought of me at all between Saturdays.

It was just as well. I cared too much for his opinion to allow him to see how green I was—maybe the greenest eighteen-year-old who ever hit New York, learning everything the hard way. I was so green that weeks passed before I figured out that my hotel was a flophouse for addicts, transvestites, prostitutes, out-of-work musicians and actors, and those permanent transients who were temperamentally or financially unable to make the contacts, pay the deposits, sign the leases that would enable them to live better for less. I was so green that the first time I took a subway, I walked onto a stopped train thinking it a heated waiting room. (Weren't the people sitting silently reading newspapers as in a waiting room? Wasn't that a train track opposite?) When the train started to move I jumped up and ran to the door while everyone else just continued sitting there reading their newspapers. Sheepishly I sat back down, hoping no one had noticed my strange, startled behavior, and stared ahead concentrating on the numbers of the IND stops (14, 23, 34, 42) which, when I mastered them, would one day mark me too as a New Yorker.

Sometimes Marshall made fun of me. Once I'd asked why the steam billowed out of a grating at Sheridan Square. "That?" he answered, "oh, they're just letting off the pressure." I accepted the explanation until he began telling the story to his friends. But usually he simply ignored my questions, teaching me only such skills as might befit a poet's girl-in-training, as: how to "bite the sides" according to the *Kama Sutra* and how to "think in decent prose."

If I'd had to rely on Marshall for moral support I would have languished.

(I once let slip: "Do you love me?"

"Of course I do, baby."

"How come?"

"Christ, I don't know.")

But fortunately, I found compensations elsewhere. In the *Village Voice* I found plenty of authentic beat types—writers and commentators—who would certainly have perceived my virtues if only they'd known me. The *Voice* failed me for jobs and sublets because I was too green to realize you had to snap up the paper the minute it hit the stands, speed-read the ads, and be the first one on hand to fake credentials or bribe the super; but it did provide me with a treasured chess column called "Mating" by one Morgan Moore whose turn of mind was so like mine that I felt there might be hope for me in New York. It wasn't only the subject of chess, my own particular passion, that drew me to Moore's column. Like its title, the column was full of delicate ambiguities. The very conjunction of chess with sex—the purest of games with the most corrupt, a game of almost mathematical precision with the least predictable—made Moore's pieces intriguingly voluptuous —far more interesting, certainly, than any ordinary dry how-to column. I too had taken my chess as something more than a pastime. One column dealt suggestively with the use of the king's initiative; another discussed the titillating strategy of doubling; each was a perfect little essay, acid and quotable, presumably on some aspect of the gaming life, but occasionally about art or bohemia or politics or some other *Voice* subject having no discernible connection with chess. There was something about those columns, a turn of phrase or mind, that made me feel about Moore almost proprietary. In those polished essays I recognized some of my own most treasured thoughts, from insights I shared with no one to my father's favorite maxim: "The winning player is always lucky." Reading Moore began to give me the agreeable feeling that at last I'd found someone in the city who spoke to my unguarded self; and before long I found myself flipping right over the want-ads and real estate listings, the movie, lecture, and discussion announcements, where I had once hoped to find the ad that would bring me happiness, straight to the "Mating" column. I read it through quickly to get the gist, then once again slowly, savoring each image, each double meaning, as if those essays were letters to me. After the second reading I clipped them out. Watch this writer who says in print what you only dare to think, I told myself. And though the *Voice* had a devoted following of thousands of readers, I preserved the clippings as though Moore were my secret find.

For good or bad, Marshall didn't share my passion for chess and didn't read Moore, leaving me one arena to excel in. But as he held himself above my mundane interests and did nothing to discover my spiritual ones either ("Come on baby, forget about the want-ads. Stop thinking so much and come over here, will you?"), I had to find appreciation elsewhere.

It came on the second day of my very next job (temporary typist at the Clarion Research Publishing Corporation) in the person of the tiny and vivacious Nina Chase, who turned out to be the perfect tutor.

She made her appearance from overhead like the bohemian goddess in the ceiling at the Hotel Europa. There I was, desperately struggling to insert a ribbon into my recalcitrant typewriter, having ruined one ribbon after another and half a dozen copies of the "rush" letter I'd been assigned, when a voice from the ceiling said, "Can I help you with that?"

I looked up. There, peering over the frosted glass partition that separated our two small cubicles, was a pixie girl with bobbed hair, twinkling eyes, and a perfect cupid's bow mouth, incongruously chewing on a candy bar.

"Oh, please do," I begged. My fingers were covered with carbon and my voice, I was surprised to hear, quavered on the verge of tears. It was only my second day on the new job where I'd wanted to make a good impression; but all morning my typewriter had betrayed me.

She disappeared, then reappeared a moment later behind my chair.

"You're Zane, right? I'm Nina Chase." She flashed a crooked smile and held out her candy bar. She was like a toy-shop miniature, pert, crisp, with mischievous eyes. In a plaid pleated skirt and fresh white blouse and penny loafers, she looked like a schoolgirl. All she needed were pigtails or a bow in her hair to complete the virginal picture.

"Here, take a bite of this while I have a go at it," she said, and while I watched, she sat down in the typing chair and began attacking the ribbon with furious energy.

"Shit! This is useless," she said at last. "You've obviously got a defective typewriter." Then lowering her voice she asked, "Wouldn't you like a new one? I mean a really good one?"

"I thought of complaining to the supervisor," I confessed, "but I was afraid she'd think I couldn't type. This job is only temporary, so why would they give me a new one?"

Nina cocked her head and laughed a fast staccato laugh. "Don't be silly, every job is temporary. That has nothing to do with it. This job isn't too bad if you play it right. You won't have to do much. But you can't do anything at all on that malignant machine."

Malignant. I was charmed by the word. It was a perfect description, given the machine's multiplying betrayals in my two days at Clarion.

Nina looked around to check our privacy and said, "Look, I happen to know where there's an almost new executive Remington sitting unused. I think I can get it for you. Would you like it?"

I was overwhelmed. A new typewriter was precisely what I needed for happiness. "Yes. But what about you—don't you want it? Why me?"

"I figure anyone with a name like Zane deserves a break," she said, repeating the little laugh.

"You can't really tell much from that," I said, secretly commending her acumen. She was the first person I'd met who sensed some potential.

"I can. Besides, there are other clues. For instance: you bite your nails. Which means you're intense." (She understood!) "And there's the liar's gap."

"Liar's gap?"

"The space between your teeth. In our family we say it lets the lies flow out. I bet it gets you in a whole lot of trouble, doesn't it?"

It was an embarrassing question, but before I answered it she said, "Come on and help me," and set off through a maze of cubicles and corridors that led to a distant storeroom.

Not counting Marshall, a complicated case, Nina was the first person in New York to make a friendly, unsolicited overture. I was flattered and grateful. Nina's conspiratorial theatrics, though a bit frightening, were appealing, turning a dull typing job into a little adventure. Her unexpected generosity was touching.

"If you see anything you'd like while we're here," she said casually, dropping packets of labels and pencils and envelopes into her enormous shoulder bag, "just take it."

I wondered what her position was. She acted friendly like a hireling but fearless like a boss. "I don't need anything," I said, wondering if we wouldn't get into enough trouble just for taking the typewriter.

"Don't worry about getting caught," she said, reading my mind. "Look at it this way. The worst thing that could happen is we'd be fired, and then we could go on unemployment—the best job in the state. Anyway, no one knows about this stuff. Our department uses an entirely different supply room; this one belongs to the sales staff, I think. It will take them months, maybe years, to figure out what's missing and where it goes. Tomorrow I'll try to bring you some free books—remember, this *is* a publishing house. This company has a net worth of more than fifty million dollars, and you're getting the minimum wage. You really must take something."

I took a pack of envelopes and some rubber bands to placate her while Nina loaded the typewriter on a caster-bottomed typing table. And as we rolled it back through the corridors, peering ahead at each turning to make sure the coast was clear, I knew this would not be like my other jobs.

Nina's supply room turned out to be only the entranceway to

a whole underground life she had created for herself outside and inside the office. The next day, as promised, she brought me several books, among them an illustrated volume of Shakespeare's sonnets, a 1958 yearbook, Montaigne's *Essays,* and a small novel by Colette.

"I didn't know what you like, but these seemed safe. This company doesn't have the greatest list. The pickings vary every season."

"Did you . . . take these?"

"Does that worry you? Here—" she said, taking the books back and writing something in their flyleaves. "Now everyone will know they really belong to you."

I opened the books. *To Zane, for those old Paris days, Love, Colette. Second-best wishes from your friend Will.* I put the books in my bottom drawer and thanked her.

Down two flights of stairs through a pair of fire doors, Nina had rigged up as a private retreat a small, unused room, perhaps once a storage closet, off the executive dining room pantry. There, several times a day, she retired for her coffee breaks and lunch hour, and there she divulged to me some of her most useful New York secrets.

"The first thing you have to learn is how to get a job without paying an agency. That way, it won't matter if you get fired before you're eligible for unemployment." Anticipating my objection, she added, "They're parasites and swindlers, exploiting working people. We should take them for a change."

"But how?"

"A number of ways. The trick is to work with a partner. For example: two of us register with different agencies, using each other's names. After we get sent out with some assignments for interviews, we meet, switch information, and go for our own interviews. If we get hired, the agencies have no record of the people who take the jobs, only of the people who don't. No record, no fee. Easy."

I was surprised to learn that Nina had been working for Clarion only a few months, for she had uncovered details of the organization unknown to veterans of many years. She had been fired from her previous two jobs, she said, for trying to organize the typists; and though prospects of a union at Clarion were "not even worth speculating about," she was a whole intelligence operation on her own. She knew where all personnel records were kept, when each executive arrived, who was up for raises, how much, and who was sleeping with whom. She was semi-pals with most of the people in our unit, many of whom seemed to go out of their way to chat with her during the course of each day, the older workers lovingly patting her head or pinching her cheeks as if she were a favorite child, the younger ones exchanging secrets with her. I would have figured she was running some kind of illegitimate operation except that no one took her seriously enough. "Little Nina," everyone called her. If she was really pulling nothing she was wasting herself, for with that innocent schoolgirl exterior which gave her the power of obscurity, she seemed a natural conspirator. No Saturday night beatnik but an undercover original, for me she was a model, if unlikely, teacher.

Nina knew how to get the best dope in town, knew the phone numbers of several "safe" abortionists, how to crash private parties at Sardis, how to slip into plays without paying, where there were free wine-tastings, what movie theaters showed sneak previews, which clubs were rehearsing the best musicians, what stores were disposing of overstocks. She explained how she and her roommate Carole, an actress, were able to live like Titans on a single typist's salary or unemployment. And after I'd been working at Clarion a month, she confided to me her "best hustle."

We were in her clubroom one coffee break drinking coffee and nibbling macadamia nuts ("the most expensive nuts in the world; they grow only in Hawaii—have some"), which she had lifted from the executive dining room pantry.

"Now this is really secret," she said, "but I happen to know an alley in the theater district where guys will pay twenty-five bucks for a fast blow job. Twice a month is almost my half of our rent. Plus unemployment, that's all I need."

Equally shocked and impressed, I tried and failed to hide my astonishment. "Outdoors in an alley?" I asked foolishly, as though where she did it could matter. "Isn't that risky?"

She shrugged. "I don't have any trouble. The creeps are scared enough to want it over fast. They pay in advance, then zip-zip and it's over."

"But isn't it . . . *awful?*"

"Well, it's no lollipop, but it is a fast buck." She closed her eyes and slowly drew the steam rising from her coffee cup into her nostils. "My roommate Carole models for rent money, but I'm too small to model. Anyway, Carole had to hustle a long time to get up those contacts. You make it however you can."

The girl's nerve, compressed into a size 6 junior petite frame, was impressive. It put to shame my own defiance, which was currently restricted to such shared eccentricities as an occasional pipeful of Mixture 79 tobacco, black net underwear, and a studiedly foul vocabulary. Like many, I too had sometimes thought how sensible it would be to commit some fast sexual act for a good fee. Still, however "reasonable" it appeared, I had never come even close to doing it. And here was little Nina, looking younger and more innocent than I, going beyond the idea, beyond the question, beyond the desire to the act itself.

"Well, don't look so shocked," said Nina, greeting my amazed silence with an offended pout. "I only do it in emergencies."

But far from disapproving, as Nina thought, I was filled with admiration. Though I too considered sexual taboos passé, I could no more give them up than I could give up biting my fingernails. Nina's enviable indifference to opinion was quite beyond me.

"Look," said Nina, "if they're stupid enough to pay twenty-five dollars for a five-minute blow job, I'm willing to take the money. It's like sucking eggs. With easy money like that I can wash it out with good wine and still wind up ahead. It's more honest than a lot of sex. You get used to it."

Honest. Much was done in the name of honesty in New York that was considered unconscionable in Indiana.

It was time to get back to our desks.

"If you like the nuts take the rest of the jar with you," said Nina. "I don't like to leave a half-finished jar around even in here."

"Why?"

"Half a jar is suspicious. But a whole jar won't be missed—they've got a whole shelf full of them in the pantry. Capitalism!" she spat out.

It would have been impossible to refuse. "Thanks, Nina."

"Don't thank me," she said, breaking into her mischievous smile, "thank the company."

6 · THE TROTSKY TEST

"Do you really live with Marshall Braine?" asked Nina when she learned I'd moved. We were back in her clubroom where we could talk about anything, but the question made me uncomfortable.

"Well, yes, we live together. But it's not exactly what you think. . . ." I answered evasively.

She gave me a skeptical look. Did she suspect me of more passion than I admitted or of less? Of capitulation or of false modesty? The truth was, I'd moved my things into Marshall's place the week after New Year's out of sheer loneliness. He'd suggested it casually, I'd shrugged, and we'd done it: we'd been sleeping together regularly anyway. Though I pretended to have done it as much for the status ("A published *poet?*") and the rent ("Thirty-eight fifty a *month?*") as for love, actually after Christmas I just couldn't return to being alone. The move was as much a defeat as the triumph Nina took it for.

Nina cocked her head and asked, "Where have I just come across his name?"

"*New World Writing?* He had three poems in the last issue, and he's done a few readings at the Cafe Lucia and the Poetry Place," I answered proudly, placing myself smack in the middle of my dilemma. Now, as after each of Marshall's public readings, I had the witch's jealous urge to lock him up in a tall tower. If only we did live together as Nina thought! But though we now slept in the same bed, I knew I had no claims on him according to the mores of MacDougal Street.

Even the touching poems he handed out on emotional occasions ("Come on now, kid, don't be upset, I didn't mean it. Look—I've written you a poem. . . . Well, what do you think of it?") were less for me than for literature. Poems could easily be duplicated for rivals and successors; I even suspected the one he gave me for my nineteenth birthday had been left over from some predecessor. A poet belonged not to a woman but to the world. But if I'd voiced my suspicions, I'd be accused of acting *paranoid*, the catch-all word to explain the unacceptable used by that crowd only slightly less frequently than the derisive *bourgeois*, of which I was also guilty. "Now he's finishing a three-act play," I added, making the best of it.

"A play? No wonder you don't want anyone to know," said Nina coyly. "My roommate Carole's an actress; maybe you should introduce them. Invite us down some time."

I poured Nina some coffee hoping she'd drop the subject. Since she was so impressed by my living arrangements, I could hardly start explaining that it wasn't my place, despite my generous contribution to the rent. Through another of those dialectical reversals ("diabolical" I would have called it then) that had been turning all my motives upside down in New York until they looked like their very opposites, I felt more like a guest than a resident in our hip ménage.

There were lots of ways life had been simpler before I'd moved in with Marshall. Now, everyone who knew us had a private interpretation of our relationship. The way his buddies called to invite him out drinking, for instance—I could tell they assumed I was trying to hook him for good. "Is Marshall there, Zane? We really need him at the White Horse tonight—we've got something big on, and it would be awful if Marshall missed out on it." Before, they'd been respectful, but now they considered me the enemy.

I could barely hide my hostility. "He's not here. But I'm sure he wouldn't miss it." As though he ever stayed home for me. As though he had to be sneaked out of the house by prearrangement like some fettered husband straining at the leash like poor Kaye's Kappy. Husband? I'd sooner have married Sheldon Aldrich, who'd have treated me nicely, and got my sex on the side than one of the sexy artists of MacDougal Street. What great catches they all thought themselves, plotting to save each other from designing women so devious as to pay the rent. Well, they didn't have to worry about me; every Hoosier knew bohemians made the worst husbands. And even if one of them should drop out of bohemia to start up the tedious ladder of paying jobs, changing beard for necktie and denim for tweeds, settling sheepishly down to quiet evenings at home on Scandinavian furniture, disappointing his friends, he'd be just like any ordinary man—only a worse risk. Always wanting out and holding it against you. Marshall may have been one of the most attractive poets in the Village, but I hadn't come all the way to New York to be jilted.

My predicament would have been no more intelligible to Nina, who despised stability, than it was to Marshall's friends, who dreaded it. To her, bohemians were the only possible mates, passion the only acceptable basis for mating, though she personally doubted she would ever marry. Contacts, however, were another thing.

"Carole does a lot of things," she continued as we mounted the stairs toward our cubicles, "but she's really serious about the theater. She's seen the second half of every play in town—she slips in after intermission—and she can recite half the roles. She's really good. What she needs most at this point in her career are a few solid, legitimate contacts."

As usual, Nina's honesty was bracing. Marshall too cultivated contacts, but he'd never have acknowledged it. He scorned the very word "career." Like purpose (or money or love), it was something you were supposed to fall into but never go after.

"What would you say about a broad who claimed she didn't wanna fuck because she had to figure out the Purpose of Life first?" Albino Brad once asked the group.

"The *what?*" asked Kappy, slopping his beer in his astonishment.

"The Purpose of Life."

I'd felt myself blush, all but certain that Brad was referring to me. Not that we'd ever had such a conversation, but I'd often worked on uncovering the P of L when Marshall wanted to fuck.

"I'd say, what an asshole question! Fucking *is* the Purpose of Life, man. What other purpose could there possibly be?" said Wolfe.

It turned out they were probably discussing the absent Wendy, who was said to have the sexual problem of many thin blondes; but I knew the "asshole question" was the very one that had driven me from Indiana.

Now, it seemed, Nina's roommate (and maybe Nina herself) had also considered the asshole question, at least to the extent of thinking about careers. For myself, I would certainly have liked a "career," though I knew better than to say so; but to hear the beatniks talk, the only worthy career was Art, and even that was "bullshit," except as practiced by them. Otherwise, the Purpose of Life was to escape working. Success was redefined as failure and failure success.

I wondered how they all did it, those "artists," living on nothing. Some of them worked so hard at not working, trying to stay young, trying not to be swallowed up, that they were sure to be worn out by the time they reached thirty. True, you could always live on less money than you thought, especially in New York where there were free hustles for the smart, but no one could live on nothing. Eventually, even unemployment ran out. Nina, the ideal rebel, held down a typing job in addition to giving blow jobs on the side. Her roommate modeled from time to time and sometimes waitressed. Marshall wrote newsreel narrations. Kappy had a teaching job, and Paul tended bar. But Brad lived by selling pot to his friends and sometimes modeling as an albino Christ, hardly bringing enough to finance his films. And others, Wolfe for instance, spent their nights in bars, their afternoons in the coffee houses, their mornings asleep, and their weekends fucking, without any visible income at all.

I knew it was worse than mean of me to withhold Marshall from my friend, given our common plight of making a living. But what if Marshall preferred Nina or her roommate to me?

"Dammit, Zane! You've really been holding out on me, haven't you?" said Nina. I was afraid she'd read my thoughts this time for sure, but it turned out she wasn't thinking about Marshall at all; she was examining the fat book on my desk that I'd been plowing through on the subway for the last couple of days, and she had a delighted smile on her face.

"You've been reading Trotsky and never said a word. Now you really have to come home with me and meet my roommate. I know you'll just love each other. She's a Marxist too."

Too? Another embarrassment. I was indeed reading Trotsky, but I could hardly be called a Marxist. Two weeks earlier I'd known almost nothing about Trotsky. I was reading him now only in self-defense, because I had flunked what Marshall called the Trotsky Test.

"Okay now, kid," he had suddenly sprung on me, "who killed Trotsky?"

"Trotsky?"

"Yes, Trotsky."

Marshall was always springing tests on me or trying to teach me lessons. How to build a fire out of street trash in the tiny fireplace; where to find good firewood. How to blow my hard-earned money. How to massage his back. Which phrases to adopt, which poets to scoff at, which brands to despise. How to move my hips on his prick. To praise his writing. To laugh at Mama.

As always, I was a quick and ardent student, purifying my line, learning in minute detail the dos and don'ts of beatnik life. (*Do:* divest yourself of property. Get on welfare. Fuck. Learn a craft. Renounce your past. *Don't:* read anything with a circulation of over five thousand. Be a joiner. Stay sober. Tolerate the word beatnik.) Others, with achievements or credentials above suspicion, might take the rules into their hands and display a weakness for frilly clothes or indulge a taste for restaurant life, disdain dope, eschew sex, express jealousy, read tabloids or crime fiction. But I did nothing even slightly suspect, afraid that a small mistake would show me up as an imposter.

Louise had sometimes mentioned Trotsky, but I didn't know that he'd been killed. "You mean the writer?" I ventured. "The Russian writer?"

"That's the one," persisted Marshall, waiting.

"I forget. Wasn't he killed in a duel?"

"A duel!" He shook his head in disgust. "Trotsky is one of the greatest Russians who ever lived. You should learn about him while I'm gone."

"Gone? Are you leaving soon, Marshall?"

"Mmm. Maybe," he evaded.

The first Saturday after flunking the Trotsky Test, I slipped off to the encyclopedia section of the local library to research Trotsky and was embarrassed to discover he had been assassinated as a revolutionist. Was Marshall being sinister or just playing some sort of joke? I doubted he could really have wanted me to study Trotsky, for while Marshall and his friends were against McCarthy and the rich and in favor of freedom for communists in distant lands, for America they favored evolution over revolution except in matters of sex. Though they railed against the witch-hunts, they found all "mass movements" stupid, politics boring, ideology over, and theory naïve, and they were careful to sign nothing. Marshall was probably only making fun of me.

Nevertheless, I took out the only book by Trotsky the library had and wondered if it was merely coincidence that we landed that very night at the one rundown theater in Times Square that dared to show Russian movies. As we stood on the ticket line, Marshall pointed out the plainclothesmen snapping our pictures. I hadn't made much sense of the little Trotsky I'd read—it was all about events and battles waged long years before—but recklessly, with a fleeting pang for my family who'd had enough of investigations, I stuck out my tongue and flagged my ears straight into the cameras now that I, too, knew about Trotsky. See, Marshall, your daring Zane? He patted my proudly. And in my gratitude for his approval, I excused his occasional thoughtless cruelty as a consequence of the understandable arrogance of the vanguard or the pernicious influence of booze.

If Nina were suddenly to give me a test on Marx, I knew I'd flunk that too. Still, I couldn't go on evading her invitation forever. When I finished the Trotsky book a couple of weeks later (closing it with hardly more enlightenment than I'd had starting it), I reluctantly consented to go home with her and meet her roommate.

As soon as we walked into her apartment I realized why she'd been so eager to get me there. That Nina! I too would have been proud to show off such a place: in her usual fashion she had managed to turn up one of the last rent-controlled apartments in the most convenient part of midtown's east side, a section otherwise occupied exclusively by corporations and the rich, only two blocks from the office. While all other clericals rose at six or seven and rode from one to three subway trains to work, Nina got out of bed at eight thirty for a nine o'clock appearance at her desk.

"I hope Carole's home," said Nina, relocking three separate locks on the kitchen door, then leading me into a long railroad flat. I followed her through a rainbow of madly colored, sparsely furnished windowless rooms: orange kitchen, blue study (desk of door and filing cases), chartreuse bedroom, red second bedroom, mustard bathroom, and lavender-ceilinged yellow living room, where a beautiful woman, sunk into the pillows of a deep chair, sat slowly brushing her long black hair and studying a notebook open in her lap.

"Here she is, Carole," said Nina. "Here's Zane."

Carole stopped her brush midstroke and looked up at us to reveal huge eyes as lavender as the ceiling.

"Nina goddammit! What did you do with my other copy of the

script? I've got tryouts tomorrow! I've looked everywhere. How could you do this to me?"

"Take it easy, I have it. You told me it was an extra copy."

"But this one doesn't have any of the rewrites!"

"The whole thing is ridiculous, Carole. You know you won't get the part since you go around telling everybody first thing you're a communist. A communist! You're as bad as Zane, biting her nails in public whenever she has the urge, especially when the boss comes in."

I was sure it was some kind of joke. Who would admit to being a communist?--though what Nina said about my nails was actually true. In fact, conspicuous nail-biting was only one of the affectations I'd lately assumed in an effort to counter my growing image as a shy spineless person, particularly among Marshall's friends. Unfortunately, the affectations only seemed to compound their false impressions of me. As for biting my nails in public, my gesture had easily been outdone by Wolfe, who'd taken to sucking a pacifier in public as part of his regimen for kicking tobacco.

Among the other ridiculous attitudes I struck that year in a vain bid for my former distinction were:

Living for a week and a half on nothing but MPF (Multi-Purpose Food), a cheap, sawdustlike substance to be dissolved in soup, developed during the War for disasters and Displaced Persons (among whom I probably qualified).

Eliminating euphemisms: a fuck was a fuck; to shit, to shit; snot, snot; etc., etc.

Keeping my ashtrays overflowing with the butts of gold-colored Spanish cigarettes I smoked through a black Dunhill holder, my mark, when I wasn't smoking my pipe, and otherwise making a fetish of mess.

Maintaining a small shrine to Beelzebub, consisting of a small cast-iron statue of the Devil, standing on an agate base and thumbing his nose at the world, which I kept on a bookshelf surrounded by birthday candles.

Collecting all words and objects beginning with the letter Z.

These gestures did earn me a certain grudging respect from some of Marshall's crowd, but as it was fraudulently won (the real me was considerably more serious than they thought) I wound up feeling no less excluded.

Nina left the room in pursuit of the script, and immediately Carole smiled at me, obliterating all evidence of her recent outburst.

"Hello, Zane. I've heard all about you. Nina says you're a radical, right? And something of a character."

I didn't know what to say. Naturally I was flattered by Nina's opinion of me, but I sensed the danger at once. If she praised me unduly I'd disappoint; being overestimated could be as unnerving as being underestimated. Having had the comfort of actually relaxing when I was with Nina, I didn't want to sacrifice it to gain her roommate's good opinion, a strain compared to acceptance. Why was it so hard simply to be oneself?

I fitted a gold cigarette into my holder to calm my nerves and lit up. "I've read some Trotsky, but I don't know about the rest," I said, hedging my hedge and hoping she'd take it for modesty.

"Well, Nina says you go to Russian movies at the Hanley Theater and that you're game for anything. That's rare enough even in New Yorkers, but aren't you from the Midwest? I don't know any Midwestern radicals. Did she tell you I'm doing a study comparing Russian cinema to the theater of Bertolt Brecht? I stopped working on it when I got involved in this play, but I'll go right back to it when the play's over. I'd like to talk to you about it sometime." She leaned forward and said in a rush, "Not many people are interested in Marx these days. They'd rather get ahead than get to the bottom of things. They're too busy impressing each other."

She seemed so friendly and accepting with her complicitous smile that I couldn't bring myself to mention how little I knew myself. I had excuses for knowing nothing, of course. It was dangerous to love things Russian—Lenin, Trotsky, Eisenstein, the whole gang. In Middletown Marx had been banned, and if you had any books on related subjects you did well to hide them in the attic. The Rosenbergs had died, and plenty of people with dangerous ideas besides my uncle had found themselves out of a job. But in the Village, where one was supposed to pursue whatever was forbidden—sex, dope, justice, even socialism—such excuses were suspect. Even Marshall, who was hardly political, read a lot of Russians. I decided not to let on that my interest in Trotsky was only a month old or that I'd seen only two Eisenstein movies, total. An enthusiastic student, I planned to cram before I saw Carole again. No one was born with knowledge, after all; even Carole had learned what she knew from someone, sometime.

"And you," I said, easing off the subject, "Nina says you're an actress."

"I try, but it's hardly a living, I'm afraid." She twisted her splendid hair in one hand and held it up on her head. "But I shouldn't complain. So far, anyway, I've managed to escape the office racket. So far I've managed not to get up before noon since I left school."

"The man I live with," I said, using the ostentatious phrase, "is working on a play. Maybe I could—"

"What I really want to do, though," she said interrupting and looking at me severely, "is start a journal or have a radio show of my own. I love the idea of getting paid to tell people exactly what I think." She let her hair drop for emphasis. "But no one is begging me to take over the airwaves. Anyway, not yet."

The way her words boomed out, I figured she'd already studied elocution. She did sound like someone who knew just where she was going.

Nina came in with the missing script and three empty glasses. "Here's your script. Now what have you done with the wine?"

"Me? You're the one who had it last!"

I was afraid they were going to begin shouting at each other again. They were two strong characters—Mama's recipe for friction. But in another moment the glasses were filled, Nina sat down, and I soon found myself in on as engaging a conversation—vivacious as a dance, large as a symphony, engrossing as a game of chess—as any I'd had since my enchanted Sundays with Daddy, only broader in subject and richer in surprise: the conversation I'd come looking for. There we were, the three of us, leaning forward, waving our hands, furrowing our brows, pounding fist into fist in pursuit of understanding, expanding the discussion from politics to work to the class struggle to literature until it embraced the very Purpose of Life. It was so exhilarating I forgot all about my pose; and when eventually Carole touched on some burning issue I'd never thought about—why, I simply asked her what she meant. She didn't question or accuse me, snicker or sneer, but, leaning forward with those huge lavender eyes lit from within, without ado proceeded to explain.

7 · THE CAFE LUCIA

The two cavernous rooms of the Cafe Lucia, the coffee house favored by Marshall's crowd, were animated and buzzing. Cups clinked delicately against saucers, checkers clicked triumphantly across boards. Men argued, women agreed, girls laughed coyly; and I, coupling casual swagger with confident smile and leaning proudly on Marshall's writing arm, played to the tourists.

Who else could I fool? It was tourists or no one. Sheer residence had earned me the right to claim my difference from them. (Thronging to the Village on Saturday nights, they sat on the edge of rickety chairs, eyes fixed on the entrance, ready to poke each other in the ribs with the arrival of each new nut or notable, while I affected an air of unconcern.) But residence alone did nothing to establish me as one of that handful of dissidents I'd come to join, or differentiate me from every other long-haired artist's girl. I'd yet to distinguish myself.

Still, as I stood with Marshall at the entrance searching the crowd for his friends, I felt the old surge of hope that had drawn me East. There was something about this cafe. It wasn't all that different from the Figaro, the Vienna, the Peacock, the Rienzi, or the Black Pussycat, each of which I'd checked off in my notebook one by one. A little tackier, more makeshift-looking. But there was an excitement in the Lucia's air that appealed to my Hoosier side. Not only because it had been one of the first places not counting Paris where artists performed, or because it had been the setting for the six-page spread on the Beat Generation in *Look* (now taped in a corner of the window) that Marshall and Kappy liked to parody. ("Maybe if we give a real nice reading at the Lucia we can get some famous reporters' autographs.") To me, the Lucia, with its poetry readings and Bach, was the very cafe I had imagined during those long Babylon nights I had spent searching my radio for Manhattan sounds. Even Mama had heard of it.

"Quick! Let's grab that big table in the corner," said Marshall, who never seemed to question if he belonged. "We'll need the space tonight. I told everyone we're celebrating my final act." (Meaning: his play, which he'd finally finished that week, the last page of which I'd typed myself that afternoon, hoping it was as brilliant as he claimed.)

Not stopping to acknowledge a few scattered hellos, he steered me swiftly past the silent chess players and chattering couples to the biggest table in the place and gallantly pulled out my chair. Saturday night: the night of gallantry and couples, even here in bohemia. A night Marshall paid me compliments, Kappy told Kaye to hire a baby sitter, Wolfe found himself a woman, and even the White Horse regulars exchanged their boilermakers for sex.

I sat back and surveyed the scene, willing the warm Lucia glow to enter me. Other cafes of other days might have yielded up more easily what I wanted: some Berlin beerhall where ideas were incubated, a radical pub in Edwardian London's Soho, dim cellars in Vienna, cafes in Paris, a small back room in the Tsar's St. Petersburg where plots were hatched around a samovar and people led intense lives of commitment. But here, where I'd already put in my share of Saturday nights, I hadn't any idea of what exactly I'd have to do to qualify. Wolfe made it on love of jazz, Kappy had his famous scorn, and Marshall had his poetry. What was the common factor? Not accomplishment—of the entire gang only Marshall could be called accomplished in any ordinary sense; nor desire, for surely no habitué ever longed to belong more ardently than I. Neither was daring the key, doing the forbidden or unimagined, for people like Nina had dared more than any member of this inner circle, yet no one watched the entrance waiting for her to walk through. For some people not even being published helped: certain poets, "poetesses" Kappy called them, were ridiculed anew with each publication.

Maybe belonging was never more than a promise. The room was probably filled with girls who'd come to the Village from all over on trains and busses, found rooms and jobs, and rushed straight down to the famous places on MacDougal Street. There we all were in our black tights and ponytails trying to act gutsy, though underneath our clothes we were still sweet things with the smell of the Midwest just under our skins. Not yet knowing that innocence turned some men on, we tried to hide ours under black eye makeup, rose perfume, and seductive smiles, disguising our loneliness and origins by sleeping around. Some of the men, lonely too, covered theirs by growing beards and professing Art. Art, Art, Art, they said, creating community. (I believed every word!) They carried slim notebooks in their back hip pockets to scribble in as they sat in their favorite cafe night after night and played the out-of-towners' favorite game, mutual recognition. They acted as if to belong they had only to open their notebooks; but we had to open our legs: for us, art talk and scribbling were considered pretentious.

In theory, everyone was eligible. In theory, you had only to demonstrate your hatred of "mediocrity" (or, of "the multitude" with their "middle-class values")—preferably by some bold, original act, but something sartorial or sexual was generally considered acceptable—in order to establish your membership. In practice, however, unless you had already gained admission to the inner circle by some mysterious prior process, your efforts at nonconformity were more likely to earn you ridicule than recognition. No one was less tolerant of good intentions than Marshall's crowd. The rejections they heaped on their own (phony, faggotty, pretentious, artsy-fartsy) were crueler than those they hurled from a distance at their enemies. It was a hard crowd to penetrate. When the beats began taking over the Village after World War II, they had replaced the once soaring spirit of democratic debauch with something exclusive and harsh and mean. Even the standard reminiscences of the Lucia regulars, intended to produce hilarity, had an ugly twist to them. Wolfe's favorite story was about the time two separate customers brought pet monkeys who got loose and started mating on the espresso bar while the customers went wild. Marshall was fond of recalling the reading that ended in a riot when Kappy said to Sandor Ray, the Synthetic poet, "Sandor, I really liked your poem." According to Marshall, Sandor rose and said, "You . . . *liked* it? How dare you tell me you *liked* it!" And when Kappy, trying to make amends, repeated the offense, Ray began slugging.

("But why?" I asked Marshall every time I heard the story.

"I've told you, baby—you've got to watch what you say to writers.")

"What'll it be?" asked Marshall now, handing me a menu.

"Cappuccino," I answered quickly, returning the menu unopened, bidding for whatever meager credit might reward knowing what you wanted without needing to consult a menu.

And then I spotted her—the redhead I'd followed since my first day in New York—now sitting tall and tense two tables away, just as though she'd made her appearance expressly to answer my questions; for clearly, if anyone "qualified" here, she did. One in a million.

Eight million, rather. The first time I'd seen her I'd foolishly assumed there must be dozens like her in New York, moving briskly along my chosen path making the same striking impression on everyone she made on me. But if there were other women like her, I hadn't found them. Instead, I kept stumbling across this one, seeing her talking with her friends at the Figaro, walking through the park, browsing like me at the Eighth Street Bookshop, in line at the post office arguing with a surly clerk, or taking those long sure strides up Christopher Street, arms filled with packages, while I was walking the other way. Her frequent appearance probably meant only that we were neighbors, shopping in the same shops, walking the same routes; but as an enthusiast and a believer, I considered it nothing short of Destiny.

Which was precisely what I thought of now, seeing her only two tables away in the Cafe Lucia—and this the very beginning of the evening. I switched my chair to Marshall's other side to get a better view of her.

Though her face was partially concealed by one of her hands, there was no mistaking that red hair which announced her like the red flashing light atop a prowl car. Not only was she in my cafe, but she was playing my game: chess. Too close for coincidence. Seeing her head bent over the checkered board, a replica of mine, watching her bite a fingernail as I bit mine and push her hair off her face in a gesture like my own (only in her case, her fingers made it wilder still), I thought: but of course she plays chess. Naturally she bites her nails and smokes with a black Dunhill holder. It's no accident that we're both here in Lucia of all places, tonight. (As though it were the last place Villagers were likely to meet on a Saturday night!) Perhaps no stranger would notice the resemblance, but I knew that if my confidence hadn't been shattered on arrival in New York I might have been the one strategically moving the knight for all to see two tables away.

Imprudently I turned to Marshall. "Remember the redhead I told you about, Marshall? Don't let her catch you looking, but that's her!"

"Who?"

"There. Playing chess. Don't you remember? The redhead? I can't believe she's here. And playing *chess*."

He looked puzzled. "Her? What about her?" he asked vaguely. And realizing that she meant nothing at all to him, I felt her become all the more significant for me.

Instantly I regretted my revelation. Retreating, I said, "She looks awfully familiar, that's all. I thought maybe you knew her."

Before he could answer, someone I didn't know came over to talk to the great Marshall Braine and I turned back to the chess game.

She was playing against a man who was losing, you could tell. He shuffled his feet nervously and rested his chin alternately on one hand and then the other. And no wonder. The redhead moved her pieces so decisively. She was keyed up too: between moves she puffed at a cigarette, sipped her espresso, assaulted a fingernail, played with her hair, crossed and uncrossed her feet. But from the man's expression I was sure that nothing was going to save him. And remembering my own chess crises and defeats, I thought: Good. And then I thought for my redhead: Win.

"Who is she?" asked Marshall when his friend had left.

"I don't know. I thought you might." For indeed, Marshall seemed to know most of the beautiful women in the Village.

He shrugged. "I can't even see her face. But Wolfe should be here soon. He knows everyone. Ask him."

There were people—notable old-timers and ambitious risers—who prided themselves on knowing everyone. Wolfe was one of them. To me, the idea that one might know "everyone" in a city like New York was preposterous. In Babylon, yes—where everyone was the same and nothing ever changed. But the eventful world—even the compact bohemian zone below Fourteenth Street—seemed to me too vast, too strange and unpredictable, to be known. A born New Yorker, Wolfe made knowing his specialty. He could tell you secrets about each of the minor celebrities he'd never met, as he could give you synopses of every movie he hadn't seen and the thesis of every book he hadn't read. He collected gossip and scandals, which he could make sound far worse than they were. He identified plays by the theaters they were performed in ("The Majestic is one of my favorite theaters. It has those marvelous old chandeliers." Or: "The Rivoli is one of the few places left where you can get box seats for mezzanine prices") and restaurants by their decor. If anyone could recognize the redhead, it would be he.

"Two cappuccinos, sweet," said Marshall, examining the bosom of a tall green-eyed waitress in the requisite low-cut blouse. I felt a pang of bourgeois jealousy (my enemy) and considered waiting on tables here myself: an easy way to meet people. "Whipped cream on mine, okay?" he added.

Vivaldi started overhead, spreading Spring through the Lucia. At the next table, a couple (he slim and bearded, she booted and bangled) sat discussing literature. Their words, blending with the music, were obliterated by the periodic hiss of the *macchina*, turning out steamy espresso; and I, listening to everything at once, tried to fix forever in my mind this un-Midwestern atmosphere.

A moment later the gang walked in. Kappy and Kaye, Wolfe and a shy girl named Jill, pale Wendy and albino Brad, and several other couples in Mexican serapes or sheepskins whom I didn't know. They nodded and greeted me as they pulled up chairs and picked up menus, but naturally it was Marshall they turned to.

I assaulted Wolfe with my question.

"The redhead? Sure I know her," he answered with the pride of an expert. "She's one of those Village dykes who likes to skin men alive. In summer she runs a storefront chess studio over on Sullivan Street. In winter she plays in the cafes for money. Lures in the poor slobs and takes them for all she can."

"Why do you call her a dyke?" I asked. (She didn't look it.)

"I happen to know she is," said Wolfe, lifting his chin like a connoisseur. "Besides, just watch her play. She goes straight for the balls."

What was the difference between going for the balls and just plain trying to win? I figured Wolfe must have had some private reason to attack her so venomously, pulling out the ultimate insult. I wanted to defend her, using all my debater's tricks, but I never could argue with Marshall's friends. "Maybe she's just good," I offered limply.

"Good? If she were all that good she wouldn't have to go for the balls to win," countered Wolfe, making a grotesque grab for his genitals.

"Beware of chess-playing women," said Brad.

She was no dyke, I was sure of it, he couldn't offer any evidence; but I couldn't argue without evidence either. There was something mean in the attack I had no way to answer; I hardly even knew what evidence counted. New York was worse than Babylon! There at least I'd played chess despite them, but here I'd never risk it. Not once had I seen a woman playing at the tables in Washington Square—there had to be a reason.

"Can't you just see her radiating hostility?" put in Kappy. "Ambitious cunt."

Talk about hostility! No, what the redhead radiated was mastery. I recognized her state of mind by the way she held her cigarette and moved her hand in an arc through the air. Exactly so had I once moved my own cigarette hand, practicing that very pose before a mirror in Babylon while Mama tiptoed about the hall putting away laundry and Daddy graded papers. Chess was a joy. I'd have liked to see how Wolfe would fare in a game against her. I'd have played him myself—but then they might start calling *me* a dyke.

The waitress delivered two steaming cups of cappuccino, then drifted off.

"Hey!" called Kappy, snapping his fingers. "What about *our* orders?"

"Sorry," said the waitress, returning.

"You're new here, aren't you?" Kappy asked, demonstrating his own membership in the Lucia family. Flustered, the waitress readied her pencil while Kappy relayed orders, as though we were uptown in a hurry instead of on MacDougal Street where it was ordinarily a good hour before you got served on a weekend night.

I sipped my cappuccino, letting the frothy milk and spicy topping tease my tongue. At the next table the conversation had moved from literature to politics. "Who was Trotsky?" I thought I heard the slim man ask, looking deep into the eyes of his girl. Nervously she moved her bangle bracelets up and down her thin arm one by one. "Who?" she asked.

At the table beyond, the redhead was piling up captured pieces on her side, seeming taller and more imposing with each gain.

"See how she plays?" said Wolfe, watching the game. "She writes like a man, too."

"She writes?"

"Yes. She does the chess column for the *Voice*. Full of boring theories and pretentious words. The column is just an excuse for her to shoot off her mouth on subjects she knows nothing about."

"For the *Voice?*" I asked, hardly daring to believe what must be true. "You mean that's Morgan Moore?" I was suddenly immobilized by the revelation, unable to raise the cup to my lips or lower it to the saucer.

Wolfe, mobility unimpaired, nodded emphatically.

"So that's Moore," said Marshall, taking a belated interest. He craned his neck to get a good look. "Zane has a stack of her columns saved, as though she were a movie star or something."

I merely sputtered my astonishment.

"Why are you so surprised?" asked Wolfe.

"I always thought Morgan Moore was a man, that's all."

"You see!" he pounced triumphantly. "I told you she writes like a man."

"It's not that. I just never thought a woman would be writing a chess column. And *this* woman . . . well, I see her everywhere."

I was uncomfortably aware that everything I said in Morgan Moore's defense could be used against her by Wolfe. Giving points to your opponent was the debater's nightmare.

"Too bad you're leaving this week, Marshall. Morgan Moore probably devours girls like Zane. And now Zane knows just where to find her."

I turned abruptly to Marshall. "You're leaving this week? For where? What's he talking about?"

"I'm going to California. You knew that. Why do you think everyone's here tonight?"

I seemed to be the only one at the table who hadn't known he was leaving. But he'd threatened to go so often that I had long since stopped paying attention to his departure announcements. This was evidently a farewell party.

"With whom? For how long?"

Marshall shrugged in his maddening way. "A couple of the guys from Columbia are driving out and I'm going with them. Maybe six weeks, maybe six years. I don't know. We just decided to go."

It was humiliating to be told suddenly in public that the man you live with is about to leave for an indefinite stay in California.

As my stomach began its habitual frightened turn, I focused quickly on the chess game to hide my chagrin.

At that moment Moore leaned forward decisively, and my stomach paused while I watched. She picked up a pawn, advanced it one strategic space, and in a dignified yet uninhibited frontal assault (so perfectly synchronized with my own need for revenge) said: "Mate."

I took a last gulp of cappuccino to celebrate, and my stomach relaxed in vicarious triumph.

"You're really leaving, Marshall? You've said that before."

"But this time I'm going. The ride's sure and the play's finished."

I knew it wouldn't do to show distress. Marshall dumped people for being too serious. The trouble with the guys at Columbia, he once told me (probably more to instruct than amuse), was they took the wrong things seriously. Working like ants toward Ph.D.'s, studying the past, memorizing the causes of things, going all sad over politics. "I'll try not to miss you," was all I said.

Morgan Moore picked up the money at the side of the table, tucked it into her jeans, and stood up. Again, her height astonished me.

"See that?" said Wolfe, voice filled with contempt.

"She's got a fat ass," said Kappy. "That may be her trouble, you know?"

Her face when she turned toward us glowed with success.

"Where's our order? I'm sick of waiting," said Kappy.

"Let's get out of this place," said Brad. "Let's go somewhere you can get a drink."

Suddenly I didn't care if we stayed or left the Lucia. The last of Vivaldi's Seasons was ending. These people didn't care about me; why should I care so much about them?

"Do you know when you're coming back though?" I asked Marshall.

"I have no idea. I'm taking my play out there. Maybe I can get it put on. Maybe I'll find God."

"San Francisco isn't half as rough as this city," offered Wendy. "I was out there once—it's far more civilized. A better place for poets, they say. They appreciate you there. Someone like you should have an easy time."

Moore walked past us toward the door.

"If you like, Marshall, I'll watch out for Zane while you're gone," offered Wolfe.

"Thanks anyway," I said, "I'll look out for myself."

She paused at the door a moment, looking regally back across the room—Queen of the Cafe Lucia.

A dyke was she? No more dyke than I. She was a winner.

8 · A KISS

"C'mon baby," said Wolfe, putting a consoling finger under my chin. "Gimme a cup of coffee. There's nothing to be sad about."

According to the strict code of Cool by which we lived, only weakness moved anyone to extend a relationship beyond the initial passion of the moment. Once a passion peaked, you were supposed to let it go like a poem that had found its form. To "work on" a relationship as people take pride in doing nowadays was considered a barbarism that would destroy not only whatever feeling might be left but whatever good had gone before. The trouble with women, Marshall used to say, was they didn't know how to let go, they always tried to hang on after the natural end and drag everyone down to the ground. Just as they wanted to think instead of fuck and talk instead of sleep. The trouble with women . . .

"Look at it this way," said Wolfe stirring his coffee philosophically, "you're probably lucky Marshall split. He was getting restless. Now when he comes back he might be refreshed. It might pick up again."

He was clearly uncomfortable. Though he had been sleeping in the back room on an army cot, he had finally found a woman with a heated place and had come down to pick up his things. "Chin up," he said, chucking my chin again. He downed the rest of his coffee and left.

He was right, in theory. What had I to be sad about? There I was in the perfect pad, this time really on my own—wasn't that what I'd wanted? Each of Marshall's friends, including Wolfe, had made the obligatory pass at me in the first weeks after

Marshall's departure. But I knew they did it more for form than desire, as I turned them down more for form than disgust, for I'd never been anything to them but Marshall's pussy. After that I had my life to myself. Maybe it was lucky that Marshall had gone, forcing me back on my own. I hadn't come to New York to throw myself away on love.

But even when, with the pride of incorrigibles, I tried to count my blessings, I had to admit I was woefully lonely. Though I could read what I liked now that there was no one to comment on my taste, I found it increasingly hard to concentrate on a book. When I was finally free to tape Morgan Moore's columns up on the wall without risking a snide attack, it turned out she'd practically stopped writing them. Why was it that even at home with no one to observe me I was painfully conscious of eating alone? Could a place actually be too large for one person and two cats? To eat or not to eat, to make a fire or not, to get out of bed or . . . I was reluctant to burn up firewood just for me; and though I did have to get up in the mornings to go to work, at night in the cold I came to know the impending depression that's never more than a letter away from naïve Midwesterners alone in New York. I copied the cats—lying curled up in bed or springing suddenly up without reason, horrified to think that after all I might turn out to be one of those weak creatures who drifts along through life letting things happen to her out of sheer default. In Babylon at least people had the excuse that there was nothing else to do. But in New York? There was no excuse for needing someone.

When the new semester began in the marketplace of the spirit I forced myself to register for Russian Lit. at the New School and Life at the Art Students League. But it was embarrassing to sit in class aware that everyone in the room knew you were looking for "companionship." That they were all looking too only made the case against you tighter. It was a self-defeating prophecy, our shameful secret which transformed every pleasantry into a come-on and stripped our disjointed studies of their semblance of seriousness. Carole's Thursday night Marxist Study Group might have been more satisfying, for surely with the dangers they incurred no one could accuse those students of failing to be serious. But I was reluctant to join for fear they might ask me to sign something irrevocably compromising and get me blacklisted like Uncle Herman before I'd even begun a career.

Once, however, I did attend (anonymously) an open meeting of some Trotskyist group in a cold hall on Spring Street, thinking of Marshall's return, hoping to learn what it was all about. Unfortunately, the program entitled "Who Killed Trotsky?" was directed to those who already knew, for the speakers, shaking their fists in the air, invoked the names of men I'd never heard of and relived events that had occurred on distant continents decades before. As I slipped out, smiling sheepishly at the guards stationed at the doors, I was no less confused than when I'd entered. I consoled myself by ticking another credit off the list in my New York notebook.

To read about my escapades and accomplishments in the exaggerated letters I sent to Mama and Daddy or Aunt Louise—letters that bore the same relation to the facts as the secrets I'd once confided to my diary—you'd think I was out to capture the title of Miss Beatnik. And indeed, my life was hardly all negative. Wherever I went, I looked for a way to partake of the passion and action of my time, notebook in hand. I studied the New York streets, not uniform like Babylon's, but lined with history. Federal houses, attached houses, fifty-story apartment houses, tenement houses, carriage houses, coffee houses. To and from the office I mastered the art of subway rush hours: learned where to stand on the platform, how to wangle a seat, how to drill my way through the crowd to the door.

Weekends were seldom a problem, for I spent most of them with Nina. To her Saturday night escapades I sometimes added my own touch until my old Zanity showed signs of reviving. It was I, for instance, who suggested that we follow each subway line to its far-flung source, I who proposed that we dress up like boys and slip into McSorleys Old Ale House, the oldest bar in New York which claimed never to have been violated by a woman's presence. I was the one who devised the plan to write our names on the crown of the Statue of Liberty (a failure) and who insisted that we remain at the Five Spot until the last riff of the last set had been played at dawn (a success). As for lessons, it was a revelation to me to see Carole the actress brazen three of us past a ticket taker on one disdainful look. She flashed her lavender eyes and held her head so high approaching entrances that no one dared oppose her. With an expertly tied scarf and a masterly flick of her chin she could forestall or demolish every question. Sometimes I spent Saturday night at Nina's to be on hand for her occasional Sunday afternoon gatherings, where no subject was taboo; sometimes for no other reason than that we'd been out late boozing or dancing and I didn't want to go home alone. I was comfortable at Nina's—all the restraints and inhibitions I'd felt among Marshall's crowd disappeared the minute I walked through the door into that orange kitchen. With Marshall, not even the great relaxing weed itself had obliterated my excruciating self-consciousness. "I'm afraid pot doesn't do much for me except make me sleepy," I'd once confessed, too insecure to fake it. "I'm sorry. Maybe you have to be in the right mood." Apologizing for my failure to lose control, wondering as the stick went round how to pull the smoke into my lungs, when to blow it out, how to produce that accomplished hissing sound achieved so effortlessly by the others, how (lord!) to stifle my cough. And yet, the very first joint I tried at Nina's place took me out of my body into my mind where I discovered new, unexplored capacities. Whether it was the easy atmosphere and familiar surroundings at Nina's, or our mutual trust, or the quality of the weed itself (for Nina's sources were matchless), I never knew; but right there in that lavender and yellow living room my cerebral sight peeled back to reveal an unsuspected sensual core.

It started with music: a stack of a dozen of Carole's select LP's that dropped excruciatingly slowly onto a revolving disc to be tickled by a diamond needle on a long, thin arm that somehow simultaneously reached down through my ears to scratch the itch in my heart. Each endless note with its own evolution. But by the second joint (or was it the third? "Who cares?" said Carole. "No one's counting!") the music was merely background to the lush message of undulating color, colors never seen before, that materialized before my eye. My hungry, ravenous, neglected eye that had viewed these walls so often without seeing! A full decade before Day-Glo I saw the secret message of light in that familiar railroad flat with its lavender ceiling and richly colored rooms. As I sat stupefied at the far end of the living room, a candle flickering at my side, that series of rooms transformed itself into a set of gorgeous Chinese boxes, each of which opened into the unimagined newness of the next—for my private delight and illumination. Trying to fix my eye on the elusive mystical point where each hypnotically colored room impinged on the one behind it, and that on the next, deeper and deeper, at last I sought the single spot where all the colors merged, where all the rooms, stretching all the way back, could be seen at once on one plane, defying space, in one perfect place.

China.

"I've got to tell you what happened to me, Nina. I've got to tell you about the colors. . . . Is that what's supposed to happen?"

But Nina, half asleep and closeted with her own dreams, merely smiled contentedly at my satisfaction. "It was good, huh? I'm glad. I told you you could." And Carole didn't know what I was talking about. "Colors? Planes? Music, yes; but really, Zane, sex is the main thing."

That story, of course, I left out of my letters home. Not even Louise would approve of "drugs," though she applauded my attempt with Trotsky. Not that I ever actually lied in my letters; but the stories I told reflected the determined enthusiasm of an exile abroad. I wrote of my summer of fun; I told the truth of dreams. It was as if I thought ignoring my loneliness might make it go away or exaggerating my daring could induce it.

When the real test finally came, it made no difference what I had or hadn't put in writing. It took only one kiss to strip off my bohemian pretensions and reveal the marshmallow feet of this exile from Babylon.

I was dumfounded. Nina and I had been doing some Village bars—Carole was somewhere else that night—and were both slightly high. Nina had walked me up to Fourteenth Street from Sheridan Square. Then suddenly there she was inside the door of my building with her lips on mine—a gesture I could barely understand and found more than slightly ridiculous. (If only she'd been tall, I might have been able to handle it, but no, I was the taller one, which made me feel like a man.)

When I finally believed that she had actually kissed me, I started to giggle. "What are you doing, Nina?" I blurted out.

She backed away, saying nothing.

If only I'd said nothing too! But we'd always been open with each other. We'd always giggled when we'd felt like giggling.

Catching the disappointment in her face as she realized my

surprise, in a flash I saw everything—her expectations, my cruelty. How I must have seemed to encourage her with my dancing and awe, my pipe-smoking and complicity. And now it was too late to explain.

Quickly I tried to extricate myself by kissing her back, a peck on the cheek. But I had already blown it with that giggle and now whatever I did could only make it worse.

"I'm sorry, Nina, really, I—" (Worse and worse!)

"Sorry? For god's sake, don't be *sorry*."

"I am though."

"Don't worry about it."

"I'm not worried, but I want to explain. It's just that I—"

"Forget it, will you?"

Monday I felt sick and stayed in bed all day. On Tuesday at the office Nina and I avoided each other's eyes. Neither of us made so much as an allusion to our kiss. But all day long I remained acutely aware of her condition. She was one of those exotic women who made love to each other with fingers and tongues.

It was one thing to explore the lesbian night life of the seedy Mafia-run bars or go dancing and looking at the Cafe Bohemia for the joy of witnessing the whole panorama of life and sending the strange news home to Babylon; it was quite another thing to be one of those weird sisters, despised by everyone from Babylon to MacDougal Street. And how could I be sure I wasn't if Nina kissed me?

The following weekend—the first of many I spent alone—I opened the Sunday *Times* to read a sensational front-page story about a series of police raids of the previous night on Village and Harlem spots that netted 109 arrests and a million dollars' worth of pot and heroin. According to the paper New York City detectives, using names like Gorgeous George, Stone Face, The Sailor, and The Blotch, had posed as "beatniks" for months preparing for the roundup. One detective "even began to enjoy a vogue as a poet," reported the *Times*. Though his "major work" was considered "not printable," he had read "at the best-known of the Village's poetry reading coffee shops." One detective, continued the article, "in recalling the 'intellectual' discussions in which he had participated during his month in the Village, said that in general 'everyone was trying to outlie everyone else.' " He was smiling in the picture.

As I examined the photographs of the spies in our midst with their goatees and sideburns and berets, I became convinced that at least one of them was someone I'd met through Nina. There was no question that one of the raided spots was a place Nina had taken me to more than once.

I began to feel it was luck that had kept me from being with Nina that night; our friendship was actually dangerous. What if I had been arrested? What if they had called my parents? (I was still well under twenty-one.)

Persuading myself that I now had enough experience behind me to land a better paying job than temporary typist, I began checking the want-ads for Gals Friday. A new job turned up in a week.

When my typing pool took me out for the customary farewell lunch the following Friday, and with her usual style Nina presented the goodbye gift (a large, gilded wooden Z, suitable for hanging), I scarcely remembered why I'd quit. But I was not a person to hang back hesitating while the future beckoned; and well before five o'clock closing, I'd emptied my desk and moved on.

9 · INDIANA DANCE

"Zane? Is that you?"

I jumped half a foot, practically overturning a bin of lemons, so unusual was it to hear my name in New York City. Though I'd been here over a year now, since Marshall had gone and I'd stopped seeing Nina, only a handful of people knew me by name.

Besides, it was a Babylon voice: the last thing I'd expected to hear at the corner of Eighth Street and Sixth Avenue in front of the all-night grocer across the street from the Women's House of Detention in the middle of a snowy Saturday night.

There was another reason I jumped. Guilt, which was turning me into a jerking marionette.

I'd come out to treat myself to a mango—a fruit I had only recently discovered whose fragrant meat made me think of tropical rainforests. I liked to eat it with a spoon as I stood at my window late at night when I couldn't sleep, holding the ripe, slippery fruit on my tongue, watching the unending stream of cars and people and the fluorescent lights of Fourteenth Street, thinking: If you hadn't come to New York you'd never know about mangos. Now if you can only hang on there's nothing you can't taste in this city.

Not that there was anything wrong with mango hunting. New York was a microcosm of the world; it was said that a total of eighty-nine languages were spoken within the city limits; and as I'd had no luck finding their speakers, it seemed to me that getting to know the exotic treasures that filled the street markets was a tolerable substitute. But midnight mango hunts were suspect. Did I want the mango for itself or had I manufactured the need to justify the solution? Like Mama, endlessly shopping for the perfect hat, was I buying supplies one at a time in order to have an excuse to wander alone in the city? I was unable to do anything without a rationale, certainly not walk the streets at night like a drifter or hooker or other needy person. But I couldn't stay home either, using up my life to no visible purpose; and without Marshall or Nina I had almost no reason to go out. The fact was, even the lushest avocado lost its savor when eaten alone.

If only I were one of those people able to sit in a cafe with a book or hang out in the bars I wouldn't need excuses; but I was too proud to be seen wanting. Instead, all summer long I'd haunted the streets and bookstores and bodegas searching for untried wonders until now my quests were habit, a routine of living alone.

Again, the Babylon voice assaulted me. "Zane?"

I turned around. Broad Babylon grin. Jim Eagle.

"It *is* you, Zane. How extraordinary. What are you doing here? And what in sweet Christ's name are you going to do with *that?*"

We had never been even remotely friends. Though we'd known each other since kindergarten, Jim Eagle was not my kind. In high school he'd played tuba in the band and then had gone on to one of the Big Ten colleges. But burdened by months of loneliness, I felt a surge of tender fellowship toward him.

"Jim! What are *you* doing here?"

"I've been living in New York for a while now. I work for an ad agency. But I'm going home soon. What about you? What are you doing here?"

"The same—working, living."

We stared at each other incredulously. I couldn't imagine him anywhere except marching red-faced down a field with a tuba at his lips. It was hard to think of anyone from Babylon High in New York City.

"How do you like it?" he asked, breaking the silence.

"New York? Oh, I love it." I could hear the enthusiasm that always accompanied my only answer bubbling up through my words. I'd passed the critical one-year mark and was publicly committed.

Jim laughed. "No, I meant the fruit. What is it, a pomegranate?"

"This? No. It's a mango. Haven't you ever tried one? That's the great thing about this city. There's almost nothing you can't do or find right around the corner."

He took the mango from my hand and slowly rotated it: a delicately shaded elliptical red and green ball. Then he handed it back and said, with a weighty shrug, "So what?"

The question shocked me. To experience the new, to gain knowledge of the world, of every unknown part; to feel, to see, to taste, to know everything possible, had seemed to me the unchallengeable goal. In the months of loneliness I'd just come through, I had measured my progress by just such evidence as unusual species and exotic fruits. For my notebook I made extensive inventories of all the sensations just beyond my reach. Brains, tripes, sweetbreads, testicles, tongues, pigsfeet, sheepsheads, and oxtails; mangos, guavas, starfruit, pomegranates, collards, dandelion, kale, and artichokes, all undreamed of in Babylon; even the vast variety of canine species that filled the parks, the pulis, poodles, pomeranians, whippets, wolfhounds, as well as every imaginable human type. Then I ticked them off as I tasted them and rushed the news to Babylon. "So what?" The indifference of the world to the wonders of the city seemed to me a matter of ignorance or maybe timidity or that irrational smugness I'd found revealed in *Middletown*. But after living in New York Jim Eagle could hardly claim ignorance; his judgment, like mine, was after the fact, based on experience. I was annoyed at his too easy "So what?" carrying the suggestion that a mango was merely a fruit, that there was nothing miraculous to the untried, that, in short, the belief that had enabled me to hold myself together in this cold, indifferent city for the balance of a year was flawed. And though I had to concede that he was probably sincere, I took his question as an attack.

"So what?" I repeated, growing instantly defensive. "But that only proves you've never tasted one. Here—you must let me pick one out for you. As a present."

"Thanks anyway, but don't bother. In a couple more weeks I'm leaving New York. After Christmas I'm moving back home."

My heart began its crazy Indiana dance. "Home," meaning Babylon, was not a word I allowed myself. A coward's refuge. I had packed my Babylon clothes in my graduation luggage and hidden them away, I had worked on changing my Midwestern A's and R's, I had cultivated urbanity, trading my tear-stained diary for my New York notebook. The secret wishes I sometimes entertained at night (I confess it!) to escape the lonely struggle to survive in New York were self-betrayals, thoughts requiring vigilant opposition. Though I hadn't a suspicion of the heroic future awaiting me in the Third Street Circle, I still had the naïve faith I'd brought East with me, which I nourished daily on tripes and mangos. No, whatever loneliness I suffered I took for my initiation rite—arduous but temporary. Donning again the tailored suit and going "home" was out of the question.

Still, it was with a hint of dread that I brought myself to ask, "To Babylon?"

"Yes. I have a good job offer in Middletown—in an office with a real window."

"Aha!" I snapped, debater-fashion, rapidly massing my defenses. "What good is the grandest window that looks out only on Middletown?" I tried to bring out my question calmly, with the lightest touch of irony, retaining my control, like Morgan Moore. But even before it was out I knew my cause was hopeless. Never had I been able to hide my passions, only to obliterate them. I heard the condescension in my words, the contemptuous overkill in my voice that marked me as a turncoat, a hothead, a fanatic.

"Well, at least I'll know some people there. I'll know what's going on."

"Oh, you sure will," I jeered. "In fact there's nothing there you won't know all about in under two weeks. I'm afraid the only surprises in store for you in Middletown are the tragedies."

I was ashamed of my overreaction, my parochial response, which, by plainly revealing Babylon's continued pull on me despite my year away, only shamed me the more. For what quarrel could

I still possibly have with Babylon now that I had moved except that very pull? The people there had made their compromises with life like people everywhere; and if they weren't the compromises I chose to make, it was nevertheless no longer my place to judge them. To be standing free at midnight in Greenwich Village condemning mightily a poor little city hardly anyone here had ever heard of (and those who had, invariably confused with another of the same name), a city that merited no more than a five-line entry in the WPA Federal Writer's Project *Guide to Indiana,* which I had once inexplicably troubled to look up in the reading room of the vast New York Public Library, an entry restricted to latitude, longitude, population, and major and minor industries, hardly distinguishable from a dozen other Indiana towns beginning with the letter B, an entry which provoked in me only a mild surprise that it had been included in the guidebook at all—to be guilty of such an unfair attack was tantamount to confessing my own shaky resolution. Loneliness and weakness—how I despised them! New York had its own liabilities: however strenuously I denied them to Jim Eagle, I couldn't fairly deny them to myself.

"I don't know," he was saying. "What do I get here? I work in a little cubicle like a coffin. I spend half my salary for meals in greasy spoons and a lousy overpriced room-and-a-half, with a curtain to hide the so-called kitchenette—a hot plate and a sink full of roaches." He picked up a handful of brown slush and with a little dip of the knee I recognized instantly as a Babylon baseball-snowball gesture, formed a ball. "Even the snow—you call this snow? Look at it," he said with disgust.

Now it was my turn to shrug and say, "So what?"

It was silly, of course, to argue about the relative virtues of city and town when it was obviously a matter of taste. But something impelled me. I too worked in a glass cubicle for the minimum wage, I pointed out; but I was not so naïve (I spat out the word) as to expect happiness there. Happiness? I laughed. Some things (as Aunt Louise always said) were more important than happiness. But even as I was parading before him as a counterexample, I knew it was a pointless tactic for the argument. What good was a counterexample when our difference was a matter not of logic but of will? Still I went on, pressing Jim Eagle to acknowledge that I, at least, belonged here, that it was possible for someone, if not him, to be quite beyond Babylon, that cockroaches and confined quarters and, yes, even loneliness, were a fair price to pay for the rare chance to see each new Bergman film as it came out, to taste mangos on a whim, to play chess in cafes (it was beside the point that I personally had never done so), to hear new ideas and passionate debates, and to live where the action was!

He tossed his soft snowball from one hand to the other and guffawed. "Action? A lot of good it does to be where the action is if you don't give a shit for Bergman films. Sure you can get anything here *if* you can pay for it, or *if* you can enjoy it alone." His snowball had disappeared; he picked up another handful of slush and made another. "But who wants to eat alone every night? I've been here nearly two years and I still don't know anybody except a few other Midwesterners in the same fix."

A bad sport, a loser, I thought, stubbornly refusing, despite my own not dissimilar experience, to acknowledge his point. The truth was, even in the Village it was not "new ideas" that filled the air but folk music and "art." Instead of passionate debates I'd witnessed only occasional happenings or impersonal parties. The highest goals on MacDougal Street, it seemed, were to get laid or be an artist, and after that to be included at a poetry reading or open a sandal shop or maybe a bookstore. With ideology purportedly "finished," everyone seemed embarrassed to discuss ideas: no one wanted to and if ever you did there was always someone from Columbia Graduate School, a modest sneer on his lips, ready to prove that you knew nothing. The truth was, I'd been in this city of eight million, the largest city in the hemisphere, trying to find my place for over a year myself and knew only a sprinkling of unconnected people. The people at my office whose real lives were lived elsewhere; a neighbor who felt sorry for me since Marshall had gone; a handful of classmates from the New School and the Art Students League. I'd even made impudent overtures to strangers in an effort to go native. I'd cooked a disastrous dinner for Wolfe and his new woman, who mistook it for a play for Wolfe; I'd secretly spied on Morgan Moore; and I'd introduced myself to an electrologist named Zane Zagreb, a Yugoslavian refugee whose shingle hung outside a Thirteenth Street apartment house, but who was too sensible (or insufficiently lonely) to try to build a friendship on so flimsy a connection as our common name.

"How long did you say you've been here?" asked Jim.

"A year. A little over."

"And you live alone?"

I could hear the pity in his voice. "Now I do, yes. But I have a great place. On Fourteenth Street."

He shook his head sadly. "Listen, I'll lay you even money that within a year you'll either be married or back in Babylon. Look at me: I used to feel just the way you do."

It was insulting to have my life and defeat predicted. I'd been considering inviting Jim to the Cafe Lucia for an espresso, but I didn't want to hear the anti–New York line he'd subject me to.

"I'm going your way. I'll walk you home," offered Jim. "I have nothing else to do."

While I paid for the mangos, Jim made another snowball out of the brown slush. Across the street women locked high up in the House of Detention shouted down to their relatives waiting at the curb. It was two days after the last snowfall—an ugly time in the city. Everything conspired to back Jim up that night; even the grocer who dropped my mangos in a paper bag slapped change into my palm grumbling something insulting about handling the fruit.

As we started uptown I reached into the bag for a mango and offered it to Jim. "Here. I got you one anyway. Try it before it's too late. Maybe you'll change your mind."

"And here's for you, Zane," he said, offering me a handful of the cold brown mush. "Your great city. Maybe you'll change yours."

10 · THE FACTS OF LIFE

The letter came just in time. "Get ready," said Marshall. "I'm coming home and I'm bringing a friend." Otherwise, Jim Eagle might have had his laugh.

Of course, Marshall Braine would never do anything predictable. Having announced his return, he immediately set off in the opposite direction, taking a three-month detour through Mexico and Guatemala, dispatching me enticing postcards from each, before finally heading north. He stayed away just long enough to miss the winter gloom (that *bête noire* of lonely New Yorkers that had taken Jim Eagle and almost got me) and managed to arrive in time to see the city's miraculous greening.

I'd had such a close call that I forgot all my lessons. Each postcard made me itch for his return. With a few suggestive phrases, that adept poet was able to lull my disbelief into complete suspension until all I remembered of him were the black curls, the nights, the slow kisses, that boyish manner that packed the wallop of a man. Suddenly, against all my interests, I found myself longing again for the old sparkle of the Cafe Lucia where we would sit with the friend he was bringing back—maybe one of the rising poets from the City Lights Bookstore or a suntanned Californian conferring health on us all—to talk about poetry and the nature of reality, while people who hadn't seen us in a long time would stop at our table to welcome us back.

What I didn't expect was the woman named Blanche whom he installed without a word of apology or explanation in the room formerly occupied by Wolfe.

As it was Marshall's place (though I paid the rent), I had no right to object. Even if it had been my place I could hardly have raised a fuss. We believed in share; I had no claims on Marshall at all. Even between the committed, jealousy was considered a bourgeois indulgence, and we were anything but committed. Besides, Blanche was over thirty with a child on the Coast, so what was there to be jealous of? Marshall was a connoisseur of youth ("I'd almost forgotten how special an eighteen-year-old body is," he'd once said to me, giving mine the distinction it had always lacked but at the same time prefiguring my downfall), boasting he could tell a woman's true age from the firmness of her thighs.

Blanche's thighs, to judge by the rest of her, would be large, fleshy and dimpled with age. But Blanche was a long-time member of Marshall's crowd from his treasured "Tenth Street days," a writer in her own right, though self-published, and a one-time girlfriend of the famous Kerouac. Though she intimidated me, the truth was I liked her. She reminded me a little of my Aunt Louise. Not that she was earnest or political like Louise, but she was firm-willed and generous of feeling and she took an interest in me. She teased me about my now-abiding shyness, scolded me for biting my nails, set out food for me whenever she cooked exotic dishes from places like Indonesia or the Andes (the spices for which alone filled one of her bags), and was careful to include me in conversations. Once when I admired a necklace of hers, she insisted I keep it. "You like it? It's yours!" she said, lifting it off her heavy breast and slipping it over my head.

"Oh Blanche, thank you, but I couldn't keep it."

"Couldn't? There's no such thing as couldn't!"

She was one of those pure, independent spirits of an earlier time like Isadora Duncan, who expressed herself with dyed feathers and diaphanous scarves and dared the forbidden. She wore rings on every lacquer-tipped finger, layers of beads and amulets, makeup of her own invention, and unique, flowing, gossamer garments. She had been everywhere, done everything. After a raid on a notorious nude loft party of a few years back, she had made a name for herself by offering to strip before the judge as Exhibit B. ("Why B?" "B is for Blanche.") Afterward, she had lived in Europe for several years, returning with a baby named Aurora, whom she carried around in an oriental sling and nursed in public. Such maternal displays eventually got her thrown out of the San Remo, where she'd nursed Aurora at the bar—an insult which propelled her to the "more natural" California, where she plunged straight into Buddhism.

But now that she was back in New York, she was full of reminiscences of the Tenth Street days, a wonderful time "before the silly word 'beatnik' had ever been invented," and her London days, and her running with the bulls in Pamplona. As she lit her lemon incense or rubbed me with almond oil, she wove nostalgic tapestries in which the names of the famous glittered like sequins, outsparkling all of Marshall's stars.

I studied her. (Not that I hoped to be like her—no more than one studied Voltaire or Trotsky to be like them.) But no amount of study ever suggested to me that a woman of her age and experience, however delicate of sensibility or feature, could still be sexually desirable to the youth-hungry men of MacDougal Street. So it was a shock to me when, at the start of the long Memorial Day weekend, I came home from work midafternoon on Friday to find one of Blanche's oriental records blaring from the phonograph, the room filled with the sweet marijuana smell, and Marshall and Blanche in my favorite sexual position on the very mattress on which I had first fallen in love.

"Oh, excuse me!" I heard my Babylon self apologize for the intrusion. Only the night before I'd been the one; my diaphragm was still inside me. I hastily left the room.

In the kitchen I made a soothing cup of tea, Mama's antidote to all upsets. In full earshot of the lascivious activities behind the wall, I sat at the table and sipped tea, trying to determine what to do.

It was not their having sex that upset me so much as my own blindness, which had allowed them so easily to deceive me. It was their hiding it from me under my nose, assuming I would be easily fooled. Suddenly a dozen clues I had ignored, thinking Blanche too old, popped into my head and snickered.

A few minutes later Blanche, hastily clothed, came into the kitchen and sat down next to me. "May I talk to you?" she said, putting her hand over mine.

I wanted to snap mine away, but I didn't want to seem ungracious. "Sure," I said, trying to appear unruffled.

"It's not what you think. Marshall and I are just old friends. It has nothing to do with his feeling for you."

"I know that," I tossed off. I didn't like her treating me like a child. "You can't seriously think I'd be jealous over Marshall, can you?"

She scratched her eyebrow with a long greenish-tipped pinkie and said nothing.

"What bothers me," I continued, "is something else."

"What?"

"Your . . . your sneaking around behind my back!"

She threw back her head and gave a long whinnying laugh. "Sneaking around? Believe me, darling, I don't ever sneak around."

"Then why do you sleep together only in the daytime?"

She leaned back and closed her eyes. "Actually, I've always preferred to sleep alone. But there is something more, it's true. I didn't want to taunt you with it; you were sure to misunderstand. You hardly seemed receptive to . . ." she let the sentence hang. "I like you, Zane. Frankly, when I met you you seemed so far over your head in this crowd that I was afraid you might flip right out if you had to handle something like this. But no one was trying to put something over on you. *Au contraire.* We were all trying to help you. How old are you for god's sake—eighteen?"

"Nineteen," I said, offended. But though I hated being told I was out of my element, I liked Blanche even now. In telling me all this she was still trying to protect me. She made me want to try even harder to please them.

"Come on, now," said Blanche warmly. "I've got some fine pot from the Andes. Why don't you join us and then you'll see how little you need to worry."

How little! If I hadn't been stuck with my Babylon deceptions I would have recognized the instant I met Blanche how *much* I needed to worry. Her silky brown hair that hung loose like her limbs was beginning to gray, but it was hardly unattractive. It matched her clear-seeing gray eyes. Though fine lines decorated her temples at the corners of her eyes, she had good bones and full lips, a face of character and feeling. Her husky voice was sultry. Now that I knew, I could hardly believe I'd been so naïve as to have considered her too old. The question was not how Marshall could find Blanche attractive but why she would bother with him. At that moment he seemed to me the last person on earth anyone would want to make love with. Blanche was wasting herself.

"Actually, I only came home to wash up. I'm on my way to meet someone. Maybe another time, though," I said, adding a "thank you," in case the invitation meant they did accept me as one of them after all. Then I put my cup in the sink.

Blanche shrugged. "Okay, suit yourself. We'll see you later." She smiled encouragingly. "Have fun."

"Hi. Don't I know you? I'm Guy," said the man leaning over my table. He had a nice face—honest and ruddy, balding a little on top.

"Do you?" I said. "Maybe from the New School? Or the Art Students League?"

"Sure. That must be it." He sat down and signaled for a waitress.

It was so easy; why had I taken so long to do it? Even tonight, after I'd vowed to give it a try, I'd wandered aimlessly around downtown for quite a while trying to work up the nerve to start, wondering which cafe to begin in. Finally I settled on the Cafe Lucia because, though Marshall had a prior claim to it, it was the most familiar to me too, and now I was on my own. I'd only had to sit down and order a cappuccino before the man had come over and introduced himself.

"You're a student then?"

Now the conversation was familiar. Like the dancing school ritual in Babylon, with standard introductions and responses. Easier than I'd expected. The New York way.

"No. Actually that's just a sideline," I said, inserting a gold-colored cigarette into my holder. I leaned forward for a light. "I've got a job in publishing, but my real line is debating."

I was pleased to find I knew exactly what to say to sound like a regular, and Guy was happy to cooperate. I think he may even have been impressed. Impressed by my description of our pad (as good an opener as it had been when Marshall had used it on me), impressed by the stories I'd picked up from Blanche, impressed by my friends: he had heard of Marshall Braine.

Soon we left the Lucia for Guy's own favorite, the Cedar Bar, a painter's place where he was known. We sat at the bar drinking boilermakers with the crowd, then moved to a table to get to "know" each other before going back to his basement apartment on Barrow Street for the night.

The sex wasn't bad; between the drinks and the setting it was rather good. But I didn't want to free myself of Marshall only to be dependent on someone else. A long weekend was beginning; I couldn't spend it all with Guy. To be free meant not to get involved with anyone. People had been saying precisely that since I'd come to New York, but somehow I hadn't really heard it until a few hours before, when it came in a flash in the kitchen. Of course: sex had to be as loose for women as for men. That was the big accomplishment in the Village, those were the simple facts of life.

The time had come to prove myself. On Saturday I thanked Guy for the hospitality and told him to give me a call in a couple of weeks. Then I put my clothes back on and returned to the Cafe Lucia.

Usually after an evening at a party or in a coffee house I went on home, where I now slept on the cot in the back room. But sometimes I closed the night at someone else's place. Neon lights flashing at the window, dirty blankets, red wine, dust on the floor.

"Baby, let's not talk now, okay? Now like this. Hold me. Turn around."

Drink helped, pot helped a lot to wipe out consciousness.

"Sorry. Is this good? Is this?"

Old cheap prints Scotch-taped to the walls, stacks of little magazines and manifestos when you opened your eyes. A typewriter, a phonograph, no picture of mother.

"Now. Yes, *now*."

Not till morning, waking under a stubbled man (instead of ironed sheets smelling of happy sleep and breakfast mother sounds) —a man wrapped up in himself—would I feel misunderstood. Early trucks stampeding up Ninth Avenue beyond dingy curtains. Someone slightly snoring. Somewhere out of town clean rain would be falling.

Sordid mornings in someone's bed, dreaming of revenge. Countering embarrassment or boredom, I offered new amours or my own breakfast service.

"Just wait here. I'll be back"—with a big smile and a Midwestern kiss on the nose. Then I'd pull on my shirt and pad down a narrow hall lined with orange-crate bookcases into the kitchen. Covered bathtub for a counter, empty fridge, and in the sink dirty dishes and artless roaches busily pursuing male politics. Somewhere instant coffee.

But who can putter gratis for one who doesn't love you? No—scratch the breakfast scene; back to troubled sleep. Better to laugh than be laughed at, kick than be kicked.

After the pipes clanged or hissed me awake at dawn (for often as not it was a weekday, and secretaries were due at their desks at nine sharp, no excuses) I opened my eyes to three other choices. Slip out while he sleeps, wait and make him adore me, or exact payment. I had no nerve for the first. The second was problematic and at best a stalling action, for even after they "adored" you, they were still dirty boys with lazy limbs and pimply backs rising on ego or lolling in lost causes, incipient alcoholics. Even after they "adored" you they didn't want you calling them at night or during their working hours. The women they adored didn't make unanticipated demands or try to have the last word. Which left number three: payment. That summer I was satisfied if I could get a key to his place. With his key in my pocket I could walk out holding my head up, smiling cheerfully, heels clicking like a winner. "So long. I'll be back soon." And maybe it would be soon and maybe it wouldn't, but I'd have another piece on my key ring.

But sometimes when I struggled out of someone's bed in the morning, tripping on the overflowing ashtray that had been placed carelessly on the floor the night before, I fancied more than another key for my expanding collection. Perhaps permanent commitment, or a crack at a really fine job.

After my vacation that summer, I couldn't go back to my old job. For two paid weeks I'd gone on a reading jag, starting at Go with the *Odyssey* and getting high each night on Blanche's Bartok. When my vacation ended, I was so enthralled I blew my unemployment and just went on reading and improving my mind till my money ran out.

But people who skip college and try to make it up on their own often have a harder time than they expect. Without a stipulated purpose, they feel they have to keep long reading lists and be able to quote from all their sources and utilize everything they know. A strain. When they realize how much they have left to learn they may grow restless. They find it hard to concentrate, as though they were dying of boredom.

After Virgil, I found myself a new, promising job. It was a good move. Not that I expected typing in a law firm to be more stimulating than typing in publishing or insurance; but what could be more liberating than new faces and money in the purse—$5.00 more a week than I'd ever earned before?

I wasn't there two weeks before I began a sweet affair with a clerk named Gordon ("Sonny") Sunday. Not one of those ambitious Villagers who launch their seductions with chapter and verse of Freud or Reich, he was a hard-working boy from Queens with huge moonlike eyes and muscular arms that caught my attention as I was waiting behind him to use the duplicating machine.

His fiancée was returning to New York come fall, but he had nothing to do for the rest of the summer. "I go to Central Park with a sandwich on days like this. Want to come?"

"Sure. What time do you get out for lunch?"

After that, we spent lunch hours making love behind a certain tall boulder—none of your sordid basement studios smelling of stale butts and flat beer and the arrogant disorder of voluntary poverty. We took off our shoes (mine thong sandals, his clean Oxfords without a spot of paint) and kissed. We ate potato salad and Jell-O, and shared a pint of enriched milk each day. We never mentioned politics, modernism, unfinished dissertations, splitting for the Coast, orgones, or orgasms. We lay on Sonny's jacket on the dry grass covering Manhattan schist, and when we did talk it was clean talk about our bosses and offices, about what we hoped we'd be doing in ten years, about cloud formations overhead and rock formations underneath.

Of course, we never intended that our idyll would last beyond the summer. Not only because Sonny was engaged and once the weather turned we'd have no place to go. But also because, however refreshing it was to relax in the park with a sweet boy like Sonny, I still hoped somehow to add my little tributary to the great city gush. As long as I privately stuck to my regimen for self-improvement (which Sonny knew nothing about), making regular entries in my New York notebook, I thought it could do no harm to speak as summer lovers may still speak, for all I know, in Omaha, Kalamazoo, Cincinnati, Middletown, St. Louis, Des Moines, Buffalo, and all the places we forsook on busses and trains in the fifties looking for better than love. And not like the fast-talking name-dropping philosophers of MacDougal Street.

PART III

Behind the Window

The days got longer. About as long as they get. The changes began. . . . When we looked out the window again we were someplace else.

—DIANE DI PRIMA,
Memoirs of a Beatnik

1 · RICKY

It was not that so very much time had passed, but such astonishing changes were packed into those volatile years that they seemed to be happening doubletime. All my life I'd had exactly one birthday a year, coming at regular, predictable intervals. But now, no sooner had Sammy's passed than Ricky was ready to celebrate, and then Tina with her "Me, too!" and little Julie's first and mine again—all whizzing by so quickly I could barely keep track. How do you get from one life to another without so much as a lesson?—that was the mystery. Again, if I'd studied my dialectics I would have known that every period is a period of transition, that each state contains the seeds of its opposite, that no matter what you forgo or gain today, surprises are coming tomorrow, nothing ever stays the same. But immersed in the elusive present, I didn't study anything.

The sad thing was, it had been precisely in order to insure that I might stay forever within the magic circle of those centuries-old trees in Washington Square that I had made my compromises. But I married and birthed three babies before it hit me that the stage is one thing, the play quite another.

We lived on the top floor of a crumbling old brownstone near Washington Square, only two blocks from the seedy Hotel Europa I'd fled to years before. Our place had its drawbacks—four long, rickety flights to drag the shopping cart up and down, faulty plumbing, and the usual cockroaches in the kitchen; but it had a working fireplace, which made it attractive to my husband, and for me there were tall shuttered windows overlooking a garden on the roof of the next building, beyond which lay the living park itself.

I'd meant to turn my back on that park only long enough to

have my babies—but when I returned to the window I barely recognized it. People who only yesterday would have hesitated to sign their names to a personal check were handing out leaflets and daisies; everyone was making love on the grass (now freely trampled on) undisturbed by police whose patrol cars had been banished from the park. The clothes were unrecognizable; our ponytails had fanned into flowing hair; and all the music was new. One old saxophonist still haunted the fountain in the mornings, weaving sad arpeggios of Parker themes, and a few folk singers lingered on, but all around them a new breed beat on bongos to accompany the strange new rock sounds that blared from radios on every bench. A year had once seemed such a long time; but now it was gone before I had learned to date my letters correctly. MacDougal Street was dying: shops were closing while new ones were opening up across town. Now, instead of a handful of ardent eighteen-year-olds daring their luck away from home, hundreds came to the city every summer, thousands, tens of thousands. And not only eighteen—an age which itself had once seemed so vulnerable—but sixteen, fifteen, even fourteen. Mere children—and I a mother now.

Half a decade earlier I'd tried to be one of the handful traveling underground, giving secret signs because we were such a tiny band. But now the band had swelled and multiplied like winter rivulets swollen in spring, spreading from the fountain of Washington Square to parks all over the city: vest pocket parks, Tompkins Square Park, even Central Park itself, and I couldn't keep up. Now every weekend the beards and jeans by which I had once recognized our kind flooded the city. Thesis had merged with antithesis until vanguard and mass had changed places; and no sooner did I manage to take up permanent, proprietary residence in the Village than I became a stranger there. Though I still sometimes felt that lilt of camaraderie smelling our secret potions as I wheeled the stroller past a group huddled in a doorway, my cryptic smile was not returned—no, not even by the girls in the park to whom I lent quarters and cigarettes en route to the playground every day. The marks that had once revealed us to one another no longer signified. Though I traveled along the same streets going for groceries, to the playground, taking Sammy to nursery school, and occasionally let the children play in the garden behind the

Cafe Lucia while I sipped espresso pretending nothing had changed, almost nothing had remained the same. And from the respectful air of every shopkeeper and baby sitter I could tell that I too was a new person. Once Daddy had admonished me not to make a spectacle of myself; but now the spectacle was all out there, lavish and visionary, while I had become a spectator. A mother now, sitting on a playground bench with my back to the scene; an onlooker upstairs gazing out the window.

I'd married with the best intentions, resigning myself to a second-best life but only briefly acknowledging that I was going over to the other camp. Though historians might one day pinpoint that season as the beginning of a new era, when Ricky Thompson and I flew to Babylon for an Indian Summer wedding in the late fall of '60, we pretended not to think of change, historical or otherwise. I was secretly aware that by the bohemian creed I had espoused, marriage signified capitulation, but with the confusion of those who marry at twenty and the impertinence of youth, I clasped Ricky's hand in the garden before Daddy's friend Judge Branigan (only feet from my tunnel to China), determined to let marriage alter nothing.

"To Zane and Ricky—a long and happy life," toasted Mama, at last beginning to believe we had both said yes.

How relieved she'd been the day she'd met Ricky, staying carefully in the background, afraid to scare him away. After two years of fretful nights imagining the worst for me, she and Daddy could finally relax. In her eyes, dewy with hope, I could read her relief that somehow, despite the youthful rebellion and the failed years in New York, her daughter had managed to come through undamaged by the beatniks, dope fiends, religious and sex maniacs, homos, communists, anarchists, and other criminal elements I'd fallen among. Perhaps I was too young, as Daddy said, but better young than never. I could almost hear them congratulate each other that their reckless, impetuous daughter with her bitten nails, stringy hair, and what Daddy had long ago identified as "an air of being on the verge of doing something unacceptable," whom they had nevertheless so imprudently indulged and adored, had managed to land this promising husband.

It was the wedding they'd always imagined. "In the garden,"

said Daddy, "if the weather holds. There's room for everyone. All the people who watched you grow up; and the faculty, what the hell; and you can invite all your friends."

(My friends?)

"To think," said Mama philosophically, "that we started out here with a barely cleared woods and a mortgage, and now"—she waved a limp arm to the universe—"Zane's grown up and we own the house and the garden is finally starting to look the way I want it—"

"Too bad the roses will be finished by the wedding, but won't the zinnias be out then, Anna? And the mums? Autumn has its points," said practical Aunt Louise.

"If you want roses, though," insisted Mama, "we'll buy roses, and we'll have a cake from Mrs. Kelly-Cooper, three-tiered, and champagne, yes!— Oh, Zane, I'm so happy!"

It wasn't hypocrisy that made us opt for a bourgeois wedding. If anything, the opposite. If you're going to do it at all you might as well make your parents happy. To have one of those anti-weddings that became fashionable a few years later, or to pop down to City Hall on your lunch hour pretending the whole insane formality was the work of the State which had nothing whatever to do with you, was a sham I held myself above. To marry was to capitulate—I'd always known it despite the Babylon creed that the Purpose of Life is to grow up, marry, reproduce, and in due course die, all as richly and happily as possible. Back when Dee-Dee Larson in a memorable debate had said she'd never marry for less than passion, against the prettier Barbie Pratt who said she'd never marry for so little, I'd known that the real question was not how to choose a husband but whether to marry at all; for it was already a matter of record that passion failed after marriage took hold. The Lynds suggested it and Kappy summed it up in his refrain, "Kaye, you're crowding me."

Of course, like every modern bride I secretly hoped that by some miracle my marriage would prove to be the exception, permitting us to escape the deadly taint of compromise and routine that made marriage anathema to the philosophers of MacDougal Street. I'd even taken steps to minimize our concessions. I had Ricky's sworn promise that we would never move out of the Village or hire a cleaning lady or give dinner parties for the boss or empty ashtrays compulsively or watch television or subscribe to *Time* magazine or have the papers delivered. But these details did not alter the fact or act of marriage; and as a former fanatic, a one-time disciple of Joan of Arc, however confused I'd become in my two-year sojourn in bohemia, I still couldn't deny that to marry was to go over to the enemy. If I was so weak or needy or demoralized as to succumb to the temptations of marriage—to its false promise of lifelong security—I'd do it openly with a wedding cake, thank you, not sneakily like a hypocrite. Not for me the excuses of the sly brides and bridegrooms who married out of the same weakness as everyone while pretending to be doing it solely for the landlord, the tax break, the Draft Board, the Blue Cross coverage, their parents, or the wedding present money. No—better to admit defeat, then clear the board and start a new game.

This is not, mind you, to deny that there have been model revolutionaries who married for legitimate outside reasons. Rosa Luxemburg and Emma Goldman each married a volunteer for the purpose of citizenship, afterward reimbursing the husband for expenses or thanking him for his trouble before going her own way. Of course, many never married at all; but even those who did it for the usual reasons didn't waste words trying to justify the deed in their memoirs. Elizabeth Gurley Flynn attributed her brief marriage to extreme youth and a "romanticized view of life." La Pasionaria explained: "My mother used to say, 'She who hits the bull's-eye in her choice of a husband cannot err in anything.' To hit the bull's-eye was as difficult as finding a pea that weighed a pound. I did not find such a pea. May the happy wives forgive me; but each of us judges the market by the good values we find there"—putting an end to the subject. They had more important things to write about, they were busy with revolution.

But for me, arriving in New York at a time when the Great Causes were obscure and the known ones were proudly exclusive, the question of marriage could not be glossed over. More than an act, it was a statement, a definition: You were *someone who did it* or *someone who didn't*. And if it was not hypocrisy that placed me in Babylon on that late September Sunday in a yellow silk sheath (no white: no virgin) drinking champagne toasts with Mama, Daddy, and Ricky's widowed mother in gray lace, come from Philadelphia for the day, it wasn't all smiling acceptance either. It was more like disarmament: the war had finally been resolved in favor of a lasting peace.

"I can't believe it, Zane, I just can't believe it," Dee-Dee Larson was repeating, shaking her head above a plate of hors d'oeuvres she had conveniently rested on her eight-month pregnancy. Ricky's accent (part Harvard, part Philadelphia) and his mustache, whether affectations or achievements, were so far outside Babylon experience as to be intimidating. With no visible flaws beyond his Eastern origins and a divorce (not mentioning the slight overbite obscured by the mustache), Ricky inspired incredulity. To me, swayed by love, but probably also to most of the people at the wedding, like the cousins whispering across the yard, he looked liked an enviable catch, a walking tribute to his family's gene pool with those deep, brown, intelligent eyes beneath eyebrows that met decisively in the center, the cleft chin, the long straight backbone, and a gentle voice that implied a temperament said to be rare in a Harvard grad. His degree from the Law School of that top-quality institution (which, minus his alimony payments, equaled a guaranteed ability to provide for a family) disposed of most doubts entertained by the older guests. Like my parents, who nudged each other over each of Ricky's melting looks, they seemed relieved that I had pulled up from my suicidal plunge. When Dee-Dee congratulated Ricky and wished me luck according to wedding convention, I knew she really meant the congratulations for me.

"She's all yours now," said Daddy jovially, elbowing my groom. "She can be quite a handful, be warned. I hope you have more luck handling her than we've had."

"Zeke!" cried Mama. "Is that a thing to say about your own daughter?"

Not that Mama thought otherwise. I'd heard her defend me to my teachers more than once with the explanation, "But Zane has always been different from the other girls." ("Incorrigible," the principal had pronounced; "fanatical," averred the counselor. To which Daddy had nicely countered, "Exceptional is what you mean.") But Mama, my faithful defender, saw no reason to let Ricky in on it before the marriage had been consummated. Having gradually resigned themselves to an indefinite stint of parental worry over the shocking life I led, Ricky's unexpected appearance to take their troublesome daughter off their hands was a welcome windfall.

What would Mama have said if she'd known that Ricky had had the same crush on bohemia I'd had or that it had been my beatnik veneer that had attracted him to me in the first place? There we were, standing in the crater of a contradiction blithely drinking wedding toasts: I forfeiting bohemia by marrying Ricky while he thought he was joining it by marrying me.

I admit I understood nothing. If only I'd seen through the shallow philosophy of MacDougal Street—but I was still too green to see through anything. I was a failed bohemian, not an enlightened one; a beatnik manqué, reconciled to moving on. What does a child of twenty know of marriage, much less of that itch to switch that turns lawyers' eyes to typists, doctors' eyes to nurses, when they hit thirty? Ricky had been a victim of two suburban lives, his parents' and his first wife's, so naturally I believed him when he said he wanted to change. Hadn't I, too, preferred bohemia to the suburbs? It was my Zanity he most admired, inviting his friends to debate me or play me at chess as though he himself were the contender. "Watch yourself with her, I'm warning you," he'd say proudly.

Straight, sheltered Ricky—a man of the world but so easy to impress! He'd lived such a square life—neckties for work, suburbs for home—he was a pushover for a beatnik. The other women in our office tried to please him with pretty dresses and yesses; but I wore my old black tights, read Sartre on the subway, cursed like a man, flaunted my key ring, and lived by myself in a shabby walkup—all the ingredients for salvation to a hopeful like Ricky.

It was nice being the hip one for once, the teacher instead of the student, my payoff for two sullen years of apprenticeship. Though I knew what flimsy tricks I used on Ricky—Marshall's tricks, Blanche's tricks, all the old tricks the hip had used on the square for generations—it was a relief to be appreciated. Ricky glowed with gratitude when I gave him his first joint, took him to his first reading at the Poetry Place, stayed up all night making passionate love. And when I inveighed against Harvard and money and marriage, he began begging me to marry him, absolutely oblivious of the anxiety hidden in my words or the contradiction contained in his.

"Ah, Zane," he'd said the night before we finally decided, filling my room with the lovely musk of sex, "you're so different from other women. How did I ever find you?" And in that elevating post-coital serenity, I wanted to say yes.

What a position to be in! I knew if we married I'd no longer be "different." Still, I did want him to save me from my failure and confusion.

I'd considered the question from every side. I'd analyzed, embraced, regretted, hesitated, measured, and reconsidered, arguing myself to a draw. I'd used all my debater's tricks against his lawyer's ones, secretly hoping he'd win, too green to realize that for every complicated question with a multitude of reasons beckoning from every side, the side you finally come out on may depend on the merest accident. "A good debater can always successfully defend either side of a question," said my *Debater's Manual*, and I, a specialist in having it both ways, could throw my skill to either side. Which side? I hadn't yet learned that not reason but desire must win in the end; in the critical moment of decision impulse takes over. Something once overheard pops into your head, you read a line of poetry in a magazine, you imagine your life in twenty years, you see your fourth grade teacher's face, you're suddenly overcome by unbearable fatigue.

He was a lovely man—mustache flecked with gold and red in the black bush, a dimpled chin, a man who committed himself to foreplay as though it were a matter of justice. He could dissolve my shyness with admiration, restoring my charm. And suddenly through my mind flashed a passage from the *Debater's Manual*, the section on Gesture, that tipped the balance. "Do not be grotesque," the passage read. "Do not use a strong gesture of the hand while the knees are weak." In that passage I seized upon what seemed to me an unshakable motive to marry, a motive to be proud of, one that held dignity and outweighed the shabbier ones like safety and happiness so suspect to Aunt Louise. I would marry in order not to be grotesque!

When Ricky announced that he had found us the perfect apartment—"It's rent-controlled, it's got shutters and a fireplace, and it's just off Washington Square"—I decided to put my faith in that standard New York solution to every personal problem. All the while I'd used the strong-hand gesture of the rebel I'd been weak-kneed with my nagging need for love. But not all the efforts

I'd launched with the strong-hand had made me an acceptable bohemian. Even if I'd been able to manage on less money, sleep with more men, live with more dirt, smoke more dope, than all the rest, still my knees would tremble. Where had the strong-hand gesture got me? Who had any of us thought we were impressing with our ratty jeans and false phrases if not people like Ricky? Let the others drown themselves in typing pools in the name of Art or squander their futures for some half-articulated doctrine, shaking their fists in the air; I would stop. In the end, what was the difference between living off the minimum wage, unemployment insurance, a cushy grant from the Association for the Advancement of Art, or a loving husband who would be drawing the same salary anyway, married or not? A man who loved you was worth the world.

Aunt Louise, that incongruous blend of insight and eccentricity, came marching across the yard in the same space shoes and tweed suit she wore for birthdays, picketing, and other public occasions. She had bowed to Babylon convention only to the extent of having donned a ruffled shirt for the wedding. While all the other women, in their stiletto heels, sank into the lawn like croquet wickets, Louise stood firm; for her shoes as much as for her principles, she was patronized as Babylon's eccentric. The more they patronized her the firmer she stood ("You know what Karl Marx said? He said, 'Follow your own course and let people talk!' Actually, he was quoting Dante, but Karl Marx said it too.")—and the more I adored her.

Over the freshly coiffured heads of the other relatives waiting to kiss the bride and meet the groom, our eyes met. Louise's hair, side-parted and straight, was cut like mine. A small thing, but like the music we'd shared and the books we'd traded, it connected us. What did she think? Everyone else showed satisfaction, even glee, to see this strayed daughter of Babylon rejoin the flock through marriage. But Aunt Louise had different standards.

Not that she was opposed to marriage on principle, like the beats in New York. She's been married herself—an action she'd never have undertaken if she'd disapproved. But her marriage, to a sickly communist Jewish musician who'd spoken shamefully little English till the day he died, was original. Whereas mine might have disappointed her as hopelessly ordinary.

Louise had managed to stay pure and independent despite

marriage, proving marriage was not the determining factor—or at least that exceptions were possible. If mine were to be an exception I needed Louise's blessing. I couldn't hope to be pure like her; it was too late for that. Ricky's strongest qualities were all sterling bourgeois virtues. He was hard-working, devoted, punctilious, pragmatic—necessary in a husband if compromising to a beatnik. But he did seem open-minded about how to live. It might still be possible to qualify as exceptions—to find together what I'd been unable to find alone—*if* Louise gave us the go-ahead. She moved closer, smiling, with her champagne glass aloft. Disappointed or pleased? I had to know which, for if anyone could spot an exception, it would be she.

At last she was kissing my cheek and squeezing my hand. Then she stood back, grinned, cleared her throat, raised her glass and said: "To the union, as I always say. Long live this union—of my beloved Zane and her Ricky!"

"Hear, hear," cried Daddy beside her, a little drunk. "Long live the union! They're probably too damn young, but I'll drink to it anyway."

In what was probably my first act of marital duplicity (or was it "adjustment"?), I took Louise aside and asked, "Well? What do you think?"

"You've made everyone very happy," she said warmly.

"Including you?"

"Oh, Zane, darling, I'm for *you*. Don't you know that?"

"But what do you think of him?" I pursued. It was not that I wanted to win her over; I wanted to know what would happen to me. She'd always seemed to be one of the few people with answers.

"How can I say? I don't know him. But if you picked him out he must be fine."

And I saw that already Ricky and I were reflecting off each other.

The rest was as expected, it's all there in the photos. Cutting the wedding cake, throwing the bouquet, the going-away suit (white gloves for Mama), stepping onto the train in Middletown Station for our overnight honeymoon in a sleeper. From the smiles on our faces and the determination in our stance you can see we were as committed as any pair of newlyweds. Past wondering if our marriage was a mistake, we sheltered our heads from the rice like outcasts in solidarity. Whatever doubts may have survived the ceremony made no impression on the photographic plates.

2 · THE SECRET

I hope you got a good glimpse of Ricky at the wedding, because I don't plan to let you see much of him later on. This is my story, not his; I've spent long enough being "Ricky's wife." (Not that I blame him—he was the lawyer, the Harvard man, everyone knew it, and I was the nutty kid with the space between my teeth. Nor am I being vindictive, condemning him to the same isolation in which I found myself raising the children while he was lawyering. That wasn't his fault either, it was just the way things were done then.) For the purposes of this history any husband will do, why focus on Ricky? Since the revelations of the past decade I've heard essentially the same story in a thousand variations. Why muddy the picture with the distracting lines of Ricky's face or his particular mustache and overbite, his character? He deserves his privacy. This is no case history that I'm submitting to the reader for a verdict in which each side deserves a fair hearing. (Even if it were, the other side, if I may say so, has never gone begging for advocates!) I am trying to show "the experience of the individual in relation to historic events"—the negative moment, the unique conjunction of circumstances that made us after whole generations of isolation suddenly rise up together and say no! Such an uprising can't have been because of this husband or that husband, this marriage or that marriage, this grievance or that complaint! The particular husband is beside the point. In fact, I've probably been one of the lucky ones—but that's no reason to accept things as they are.

I'll say this for Ricky: he was a decent husband, he did all that husbands were expected to do in those days—breakfasts on weekends, the midnight bottle, paying the bills including his first wife's alimony for several years. And even later, when we were hurtling through life so fast we were barely able to stop to speak to each other in passing, he did no worse than the run of husbands, waiting (as far as I know) the usual seven years to have his first affair, apologizing for being out of town so often and for always working late at the office. We were both products of our times. . . . But there I am, bending over backward to present his side when that is precisely what I said I wouldn't do.

I can cite plenty of precedents for keeping Ricky out of my history. Those who chart for posterity the stories of their public engagement in the passion and action of their time seldom dwell on their family lives. Few of the women revolutionaries who left memoirs behind ever married at all, and the others either cut their marriages short or knew better than to invite the world to judge them as wives by writing about them. Instead, they hid their tears like men. On the other hand, most public men who write their memoirs hardly ever feel the impulse to detail the domestic side; a reference on the dedication page, some brief acknowledgment of the wedding and the birth of each child will usually do. Of course, there are notable exceptions. Malcolm X, after a profound tribute to his mother, spends a whole chapter explaining how, though women are "only tricky, deceitful, untrustworthy flesh," he came to marry "one of the few—four—women whom I have ever trusted." At the other extreme, John Stuart Mill (a feminist) so unequivocally insisted on his wife's importance to his intellectual development ("friendship [with her] has been the honour and chief blessing of my existence, as well as the source of a great part of all that I have attempted to do, or hope to effect hereafter, for human improvement. . . . What I owe, even intellectually, to her is in its detail almost infinite") that his biographers have since been bogged down trying to prove that his feelings led him to "exaggerate" and that her influence on him was "peripheral." And even Trotsky, who in his diaries makes frequent reference to his children and all-suffering second wife, is vague to the point of confusion about his family in his *Life*. But the example of Henry Adams, that giant among memoirists, though extreme, is closer to characteristic. Never once in his thousand pages does he so much as mention his poor wife, though she profoundly distressed him with her suicide.

No, it would only obscure the issue to show you the handsome, devoted Ricky before his work took him away and his hair thinned, or let you join us on our nightly walks through the Village that first year we were married, strolling leisurely hand in hand along the streets on which I had become an authority during my lonely beatnik trial and now eagerly shared with my husband. It wouldn't help to let you stop with us while Ricky popped in and out of the neighborhood shops to buy me some little present, some surprise, something I admired in the window or remembered having tasted once, some souvenir of our delight. It would be foolish to let you hear the intense conversations we held late into the nights, interrupting only to make love—passionate attempts to describe the precise states of our feelings, or intricate analyses of our pasts (in which each of us exaggerated what the other longed to hear, I coming off more Zany, he coming off less straight than God would probably have judged us), or long speculative flights about how we would live and what we would do in our never-to-end intimate future; equally foolish to let you see us on Sunday mornings waking late, lying about, with a Bach cantata on the hi-fi to start the day and orange juice Ricky would get up to squeeze in my Good Will squeezer and pot after pot of fresh black coffee and the special kind of omelette with herbs and cheese Ricky had learned how to make from his first wife but I had rechristened "Ricky's eggs" and sometimes croissants from Sutter's and then in good time getting the Sunday *Times*, joining the crowds in the park around the fountain, and later maybe taking in a local play we'd just read a notice of or catching a few sets at the Village Vanguard depending on who was playing or just putting on our favorite chamber music or choral work (for it would still be Sunday) and letting the night slip down on us. Nothing is more misleading than happiness! If you saw the fine moments during the week when we showered together in the morning, gulped our coffee, and rode the subway to work, days when we had nothing in the world to do before and after work but resolve our disagreements and make each other happy—in short, if you were to witness the newlywed bliss we fostered that idyllic year before the babies came, when even an argument held the consoling promise of our making up (for I was as much a fanatic in love as in anything, we *would* be the exceptions, if you do a thing you might as well go all the way, I say!), it could lead you to ask, *But why do you want to change things?* Readers of romances forget (if they ever knew) that some things, as Aunt Louise says, are more important than happiness, and that the changes are coming anyway, whether you like it or not.

As I learned long ago in the *Debater's Manual*, "Only the inexperienced think they should contest every statement made by the opposition. The disposal of irrelevant matter limits the question to the main issues and centers interest on the proposition. Unrelated evidence is worth little. The fact that a certain thing happened cannot constitute proof."

Okay—I concede: Ricky was a decent husband. Now, try to understand our revolt.

Like any guilty daughter I had been proud to take Ricky home to Babylon. But when I walked into Bigelow Drugs less than a month after the wedding and heard a familiar voice at the counter ask: "Hey, Zane, is it true you got married?" I was instantly ashamed.

Naturally, it was too late to deny it. The marriage had been consummated and then some. But that was precisely what I wanted to do when I turned around to face my accuser.

Wolfe sat sipping coffee at the counter with that leisurely air of abandon sometimes assumed by the hip to antagonize the straight and a superior look on his face.

"Who's the lucky guy?" he asked, Adam's apple bouncing.

"You don't know him," I said, torn between protecting my husband and defending myself. "His name's Ricky Thompson. He's a lawyer. Civil liberties."

It wasn't exactly a lie. Ricky had handled several civil liberties cases in the course of his work for Legal Aid in Philadelphia. But now that he was in a large general law firm, he could hardly claim that specialty. But pitting my loyalty against integrity, I defended him the only way I knew.

"Yeah?" said Wolfe, raising one skeptical eyebrow. "Well, congratulations."

The smile that spread across his face made it clear to me that no matter how thoroughly I could justify Ricky with credentials, nothing could keep Wolfe from his conclusions: I'd married a lawyer—older, straight, and potentially rich; I was a sellout.

I'd never really expected to escape the charge; I hardly needed Wolfe to point out that the bourgeois virtues I'd been at pains to wipe out in myself were the very qualities I treasured in Ricky. One could hardly do without them in a mate! I had known, examined every side, and married anyway, with as wide a spread of reasons as any twenty-year-old bride assembles. Nevertheless, from the beginning certain embarrassing facts began to emerge that made it impossible for me to ignore Wolfe's slippery smile, no matter how many worthy justifications I hurled at it.

The very day we moved into our apartment, for example, to my dismay Ricky squeezed twelve suits (twelve!) into our bedroom closet, dramatizing our differences with alarming clarity.

Naturally, I said nothing. According to my scruples every person's clothes were strictly his own business, a matter of self-expression (and cash). Like my idol Joan of Arc I had waged several youthful battles over matters of dress when I'd lived in Babylon and would not be so hypocritical as to object to Ricky's. But there the suits hung, exactly opposite our bed (squeezing my own motley wardrobe to the edge of the closet), arrayed along the rack like twelve disciples, ready to taunt me with my compromise whenever we made love, reminding me of the fragility of one's image. I could not even figure out whether saying nothing made me a martyr or a collaborator.

Then there was the apartment itself. Two and a half rooms in a converted townhouse, stylish and shabby enough to suit us both, it was a model of compromise. We furnished it half from the street (my style) and half from the better shops (his). I saw Ricky's disgust at some of the bedraggled finds I carried home like a retriever: a shadeless metal floor lamp, chipped coffee mugs, and particularly the ugly old upright piano two men from Good Will deposited in our living room to sit like a schoolmaster dominating the room. But in good faith he said nothing. Likewise, when Ricky moved in a thick Persian rug and then began adorning the walls (walls I would have left Spartan bare) with old prints of New York and other objets d'art, I said nothing either. The floors and walls were as much his as mine, and the money he spent on them was his alone: how could I object? I couldn't start out the marriage taking a negative stand over matters I'd always insisted were trivial. Each point of difference between us was a small matter, in itself unworthy of a fight. I would not be so small-minded as to elevate them to the status of principles. Yet it was clear that with lush rugs on the floor and framed pictures on every wall, even the brick walls of a Greenwich Village apartment, I could hardly hope to retain my self-respect. Ricky's new heavy presence in my life (and on so intimate a basis as marriage!) was becoming a constant reminder of my own impurity.

For a while I managed to take Wolfe's snide accusation and stand it on its head in a virtuoso resolution. Sellout? How could I possibly be a sellout if the so-called benefits of my "advantageous" marriage felt exactly like liabilities, making me embarrassed to walk into a cafe with my own husband? On the contrary, if I had turned down the man I loved solely for material reasons, *then* I would have been guilty of the same order of vice as selling out!

Poor Ricky had no idea of the storm that raged within me. All he saw were my incomprehensible moods, which he attributed to my bohemian temperament.

But why, I wondered, had I married a man so innocent or foolish that he couldn't see through me? And how could I live in a place I would have been ashamed to invite my old friends home to visit?

3 · CHANGES

When Ricky called me at home to announce that President Kennedy had been assassinated, the baby was gagging on a zwieback and I had to hang up fast. "Sorry, Ricky, I can't talk now," I said; and for a long time that was my pattern, especially when the children were little. Rebellion spread beyond the wildest hopes of the fifties, rebels found their cause, the Left came out of hiding and multiplied, the most important events of our time exploded around me, but I was unable to participate.

Not that I'd grown complacent in my new life. If anything, the riveting drama of *should* against *is* I'd come East to play in was more exciting than I'd ever hoped, with new scenes unfolding daily outside my window just beyond my reach. But I had married by choice, submitting to some basic human weakness or need that increased each day of my dependency, making a sham of my old ideals.

Gradually I had to concede that Daddy had been right. Already I was sorry I hadn't finished college. It was one thing to be a daring drop-out in a cold-water flat using your precious time to live instead of learn; but once you were married you were just another person with no marketable talents who hadn't finished college, and the time you'd "saved" was more like squandered. I might as well never have led the Babylon debating team or come to New York to change the world for all that they mattered now.

Things kept turning out differently than one expected. ("It is vain by prudence to seek to evade the stern assaults of destiny," wrote the radical Transcendentalist Margaret Fuller.) Aunt Louise had finally launched her journey around the world through the St. Lawrence Seaway thinking at last to enlarge her life, only to pick up a mysterious intestinal parasite in India that contracted it instead, leaving her an invalid. Two male-to-female transsexuals were reported in the *Times* to have died tragically of breast cancer. And I, too busy to be sorry, began to hide my bohemian aspirations like some guilty passion.

The time I saw Blanche swathed in chiffon waiting to cross Eighth Street, I pivoted the stroller and walked quickly the other way. If it was too late to flee when I saw someone from the past I averted my eyes, pretending not to have noticed. It was probably unnecessary—mothers looked different from other Village residents and by then most of the old crew who had stuck it out would not have recognized me even if they'd remembered me; but I didn't want to risk confronting my old desires. The months melted into seasons, the seasons into years, history unfolded, while I rose at six and collapsed at eleven, whirling madly through each day, from the time Sammy was born, and then smiling Tina, until Julie, her hair done in skinny pigtails, tears rolling down her puffy cheeks, braved her first day of school.

It wasn't the children alone that drove my old longings underground. Even before they were born I'd stopped seeing anyone from the old days, partly from circumstance, partly from shame. With Wolfe's smile before me I avoided taking Ricky to the cafes where I'd once listened to the young poets and old-timers fight over politics and love, in the same spirit with which I'd once burned my childhood diary. Anyway, Ricky preferred the big sidewalk cafes now springing up on the avenues where he could drink an aperitif after work and watch the colorful flow of pedestrians as though it were Paris. Unaware of the difference, he assumed anything below Fourteenth Street was "bohemian."

"Well, isn't it? Really?"

"What?"

"Bohemian."

I shrugged off the question. For our new life Ricky's understanding was true enough: all over New York people had begun easing themselves into the scene via good Mexican dope and little European cars, or latching onto research jobs and government grants, at once altruistic and self-serving, then moving into the Village. If they called themselves hip, who was I to dispute it? Having walked out of bohemia voluntarily, I was hardly pure enough to spoil our fun with my old sour all-or-nothing outlook. "I suppose so, love; cappuccino is cappuccino," I conceded in the interests of harmony—now deliberately fudging the very distinctions I had once struggled to maintain.

But old longings are hard to suppress, and for every generous gesture the loving wife composed, the rebel inside had a nasty rejoinder. The old debate over how to live that I'd thought to have settled by that decisive act of marriage had merely taken time out for the wedding, resuming as soon as we moved into our new apartment. Back and forth I raced from one side to the other, listening in on all the old arguments from a new perspective, half partisan, half umpire, as ashamed to be watching this display as any peep-show patron, but equally unable to resist.

Only once in those early years of marriage do I recall both sides of me acting together on my old ambitions; only once did the little rebel come out of her marital cave to stand up and defend herself in Ricky's name.

Ricky had finally taken me to meet his one-time Harvard mentor Leo Stern, now a fast-rising power in publishing whom Ricky held in the highest esteem. Though they saw each other infrequently and had only a few years of age between them, Leo was the closest thing to a father in Ricky's life, and naturally Ricky wanted Leo's approval for his newest bride.

We all met at the Harvard Club after work. I wore my "dressy" beatnik garb—a blue printed cotton shirtwaist dress with my longest hoop earrings and black tights, a compromise between the jeans I would have liked to wear to that exclusive club and the appropriate costume for Ricky to present me in.

Women were never permitted in the main dining room, so we

had to eat in the small, auxiliary dining room up the stairs from the diminutive side entrance (the "Ladies' Entrance") to the club. But even there I felt the thrill of doing the forbidden, like crashing parties with Nina in the old days, and had the urge to perform some slightly sensational act: smoke a big cigar over coffee, say, or strip down to my underwear.

The dinner was uneventful. Leo, freshly showered after a stint on the squash court and dressed impeccably in dandy Harvard grays, ignored me. Only over coffee, when Ricky dropped some boast about my chess game into the conversation, did Leo show any interest in my side of the table.

"You?" he asked, turning to me.

Though I knew it was trouble, I heard myself answer with a touch of defiance, "Of course. Why not? What's the big surprise?"

"Nothing, nothing," he said, backing off. "Actually, I know a lady writer who's quite a champion at chess."

"Morgan Moore," I said.

"Yes."

Despite his "nothings," he continued to eye me with curiosity. For once I was grateful for Ricky's enthusiastic wife-promotion; and though I probably knew where it had to lead, I felt so inflamed by the setting and the company that I did nothing to try to deflect the inevitable challenge from Leo that followed: "Okay. Let's play."

Not until that instant did my voice falter, making way for the shyness I had hoped to have exorcised once and for all on my wedding day. It took over my throat, my tongue, my fingers and limbs, infecting my knees as Leo asked our waiter to set up a chess board for us in the lounge (the small one, where women were sometimes permitted entry).

"You can have white," he said magnanimously, moving for a psychological advantage.

"No. Let's play by the rules," I countered, as though we were playing for the largest stakes.

Actually, I didn't even hope to win. I wanted only to make a decent enough showing to justify Ricky's faith in me. He'd never seen me play, had only my own word to go on. Now I was Moore at the Cafe Lucia, Zane in Babylon, hoping to defend the honor of my past and make Leo Stern take notice.

When Leo made a fatal error in the twenty-seventh move, enabling me to move in quickly with my black bishop ("Checkmate!" I cried, a bit too eagerly, surprising us all), for the first time in my memory both wife and beatnik were so perfectly united, bringing equal glory on Ricky and myself, that it would have been impossible to distinguish them.

"Bravo," said Leo limply. (I don't know who was more astonished—Leo, Ricky or I.) "*Checkmate*, you may be interested to know," Leo quickly added in his distress, "is one of the two words in English that derives from the Persian. The other is *gazelle*."

Later he argued that he'd had too much to drink (probable) and had lost less to my skill than his own carelessness (true). Nevertheless, I had played fairly and well, and to Ricky's joy, Leo immediately began to treat me like someone worthy of his esteem: someone who, in one thing at least, was his equal.

Unfortunately, that game was the last time for years to come that I was able to identify myself with Moore. Once the babies came and I left my job and we moved to a slightly larger apartment in the same building, the rebel crawled back into her cave. The last thing I'd ever do was go off to type in an office while some poor Else took care of my children! After that, the raging debate over how to live was an irrelevant mental diversion, an occasional entertainment to listen to late at night, for there were neither means nor time to pretend I could be anything but what I was: a harried, married mother-of-three who spent her days planning meals in advance, hounding roaches out of the kitchen, chasing back and forth to the playground, investigating nursery schools, phoning endlessly for a baby sitter.

Not even a working mother, either, despite the free-lance copyediting job Leo Stern threw my way that I pursued in all the hours the children napped. Since Ricky earned enough money, my part didn't count. Anyway, it paid hardly more than I paid the sitter when I worked longer than the baby napped. But I needed the job to insure a continuous record of employment (just in case) and to deflect the charge of parasite, to which I was especially sensitive, having married a good provider. At least I was able to write something besides the dreaded "housewife" under "occupation" on my passport, which I kept current—also just in case.

In case what? It was hard to imagine. In case Ricky died in a plane crash, in case the children were stricken, in case the sophisticated act I put on for visiting Hoosiers should some day happen to come true and the person I'd once hoped to become could climb back into the body of the one I was.

Even Morgan Moore, who had remained a tenuous thread connecting me to my past, had mysteriously disappeared from the neighborhood after the arrival of my firstborn. It was awful: one week she was there, an inspiration, and the next, gone.

Her last *Voice* column, an ambitious piece on the mythic consolations of losing, had appeared about the time I was looking into natural childbirth. She didn't announce it as her last, but afterward there were simply no more of them. As her columns had always been erratic, I drew no conclusions. Toward the end of my pregnancy, after I'd left my job and once again briefly enjoyed the old luxury of exploring the Village in the daytime, I took to walking past the chess studio on Sullivan Street where she had set up shop, hoping to catch sight of her through the window. Everything was as expected—chess sets of "original design" on display in the window, neat checkered tables set up with wooden chess sets in rows, a few people playing—but I never saw Moore. And then it struck me that I'd stopped seeing her on the street as well.

I had a curious thought. Suppose the changes in my own life that had dropped me out of bohemia into the oubliette of love had some counterpart in Moore's life? Perhaps she too had thrown up her hands at the impossible struggle and dropped out of the scene—had run off with some devastating Grand Master, tall and silent, who alone was able to defeat her.

But I drew no firm conclusions until, just after Sammy was born, I wheeled the baby in his new, navy blue carriage across the Village stage, proud as an understudy with one chance to perform (not yet aware that a child was with you for the rest of your life), toward Moore's studio on Sullivan Street only to find it, to my horror, gone.

Gone! The building remained, but the door was padlocked, no chess sets were on display in the window, chairs were stacked on tables, and a FOR RENT sign leaned forlornly against the windowpane.

I stared unbelieving at the window. It was like the time I'd returned to elementary school after two weeks in quarantine for chicken pox to find all the seats reassigned and my best friend taken by someone else. Now I realized how foolish I'd been not to have walked into that studio when there'd still been time, sat down opposite Moore at one of the tables, paid my dollar and had a go at it. But I'd always put it off, hoping that in another week (or month or year) our talents would suddenly be equal and I'd be able to do it without requiring any special courage.

And now it was too late. She had vanished. Another drop-out, or maybe a casualty of the rising Village rents the *Voice* had been noting lately with alarm. Some of the cafes had already closed, with dull chain restaurants and shoestring boutiques opening in their places. Even the old MacDougal Street clientele, said the *Voice*, had begun drifting eastward to the Lower East Side, newly named the East Village, where there were still bargain rents in tenements. I should have seen it coming, ought to have trusted my earlier instinct that Moore would disappear. It happened all the time in New York. People, shops, streets, neighborhoods, whole populations could disappear from under your nose. One day they'd be there for you to count on and the next time you looked around they'd be gone. The park was changing, and even the Eighth Street Bookshop, that unshakable Village landmark that had headed my list of sights, had closed its doors one day and opened up across the street the next, never again to feel the same.

We too—there we were, footloose beatniks thumbing our noses at the world, then young marrieds inhabiting the park on weekends in matching sweaters, wandering in and out of little Village shops, then abruptly, before we knew it, we were something else entirely.

A unit; a schedule; a family.

Don't worry, I have no intention of telling you the now-familiar sad housewife tale the Women's Liberation Movement bravely ripped the cover off. Just as I plan to be discreet about Ricky, I won't complain about my kids to you, either, you can count on it. Despite the potent mother's rage unleashed in the latest wave of feminism, don't look to me to mine that vein. Frankly, with my children half grown, the anxiety of those years, like the pain of childbirth which we conveniently forget, is getting a bit dim.

Except as motherhood swept me into or barred me from the passions and actions of my time, I'll try to leave that chapter out. Not only because I'm sure by now you've heard all about the all-consuming clutch of tiny fists plucking at the mother's flesh, heart, patience, liver, until she's a walking reflex, a living response to those shuddering sobs and needs that absorb all her sympathy and passion, turning romance and even reason into distant luxuries. (And remember—I had not one baby but three: well beyond the point where quantity turns, as Marx says, into quality.) Rather, such is the swing of the pendulum that what cries for exposure today is the opposite of what was needed yesterday. The new taboo, the truth that needs recalling now, is the sheer enchantment of a baby's yawn, the delicious milky smell you breathe when you kiss the soft spot on a baby's head; the flutter of live eyelids that accompanies the last sigh before sleep descends; the blissful sound of those delighted giggles you can evince at will by noisily blowing love into the creases in a velvet neck; the terrible beauty of trusting eyes depending on you (on *you!*); the intricate arrangement of fingers learning how to hold a thread. And that's only the beginning. Such undreamed of sensual joys are mere moments beside the gradual steady awakening that comes of exploring the world anew through uncorrupted eyes; getting a second, third, fourth chance to live; discovering this time round what you'd forgotten or never known, belonging so completely to another that you become twice-born, thrice-born, twice and thrice your size: responsible, caring, connected—you become someone you never imagined could live inside you.

Of course, it's risky to say these things today, for there are many—particularly the young readers of rebels' lives—who will hear in them only a new version of the old call to the womb. Better for me to take no stand at all, give no advice. Inform yourselves elsewhere. I'm afraid there's a passionate case to be made on either side, having children or doing without, and both sides are for humanity. Have your babies or tie your tubes—whatever you decide, you'll find out soon enough that you've lost something precious. "The negative is to an equal extent positive," says Hegel; the truth, as usual, is dialectical.

Disclaimers duly made, now back to the story. Chapter Four: The Raffle.

4 · THE RAFFLE

As I pocketed the stub of chance number 1940 and dropped the other half in the crepe-paper covered box set up on Eighth Street by CORE, I had the sudden feeling I would win. Not only because 1940 was the year of my birth—by any system a lucky omen—but because I so needed to win. Three months had passed since I'd lost my precious free-lance copy-editing job—three months that had included Tina's birth and my birthday—and how many jobs were there a mother could do at home in the few erratic hours a week her children were occupied or napping? A sewing machine was capital equipment, never mind the symbolism; winning one in a raffle was a sign of luck; who was I to pass up any opportunity?

Not that operating a sewing machine had ever been one of my ambitions. Even the secret longing I'd lately begun to harbor of teaching a course at the New School (in something, anything—debating, child-rearing, fantasy, chess—whatever specialty I might manage to work up) was, however grandiose, a considerable comedown from my former desire to signify. Still, knowing how people pored over the New School catalogue spring and fall, year after year, searching for salvation, there was some connection between my grand and my reduced ambitions; whereas sewing for a living could hardly open up a life. But it was better than nothing. One of the park mothers crocheted a line of berets for swank boutiques like Capezio's, and another was quilting on spec. The pair of them sat in the playground doing their work with a certain pride the rest of us lacked. I'd once heard another mother ask the crocheter: "Isn't that just like the hats they sell at Capezio's?" And she had stayed her hook for a moment while she answered with exquisite dignity, "I *make* the hats for Capezio's." After that, she commanded a certain respect among us all. But work could bring more than pride: it enlarged one's future. Emma Goldman, the famous anarchist, had come to New York with no other resource than her sewing machine and she'd gone far. If I won the raffle, like her I would seize my opportunity.

Besides, at that moment I desperately needed the money. Birthdays and Christmas I wanted cash. I wanted an independent sum that I could dispose of myself with neither guilt nor gratitude, a sum (or a skill) to fall back on if Ricky died or left us, or to give to my favorite cause if he didn't. Money absolutely my own. For though we always pretended to be exceptional, the truth was, now that we were a family we were increasingly like any other couple: with one toddler and one newborn I was only a divorce away from welfare.

Already I'd seen it begin to happen all around me. Dreamy Mrs. Gregory downstairs from us was reluctantly moving her family back to her native Iowa where her mother would be able to watch the children while she went to work, because her husband had decided to leave them. (She sounded almost hopeful saying goodbye. I'd never liked her husband, either.) According to the playground gossip, Jan, the jolly park mother who'd preceded each of my pregnancies with one of her own, was in a hospital for suicidals while her husband and his actress friend visited the children on weekends at his mother's. Though only a handful of sandbox parents lived apart, it seemed that half the ones with school-aged kids were splitting up. In front of the big swings that was the big topic, as big as nursery schools, for some fathers wouldn't pay tuition once the fights began. Linda Bennett, Connie Kandel—clearly, it could happen to anyone, it was only a matter of luck and time; yet everyone expected (at least hoped) to be the exception. No, it was impossible any longer to ignore the fact that money was survival and in our family Ricky—capricious, romantic Ricky—had all of it.

It was said that if you scraped and saved and moved to the suburbs, you'd presumably have equity in a house to sell when he left you. On the other hand, if you stayed in the city you'd have a better chance at a job. Some people went for the house, but for myself, I placed my bets on the job.

My only previous job had fizzled out after a small disagreement I'd had with a translator of Kierkegaard over the capitalization of God (god). Not that I cared if it were upper case or lower, but I thought the spelling ought to be consistent. The translator, however, wanted it upper case in some instances and lower case in others. I'd tried to accommodate myself to his pleasure (what did I care? I had no truck with his God), but I was unable to fathom his system, and though I'd successfully completed three other projects for that company, halfway through the new project I'd been replaced. That job had been a windfall, a piece of patronage from Leo Stern who had overlooked my lack of higher education and given me a contact. But having failed one editor, I could hardly ask Leo to recommend me to another.

Ricky probably made more money than we needed, but I never knew for sure. He never told me what he earned, and when I tried to find out he evaded my questions. "How much do you want? I'll have it tomorrow," he'd answer instead. If I persisted, he'd reward me with injured pouts and doubletalk, but no answers.

I had reason to want to know. He himself was a capricious spender; and the pile of unpaid bills I occasionally stumbled upon (including the obstetrician and sometimes even the rent) sent me into flights of anxiety. Was it carelessness or poverty that kept the bills piling up? Ricky wouldn't tell. If I'd been the earner I would have done things differently, but as it was, I had no recourse but to worry. As long as Ricky gave me enough cash to cover expenses, he felt I had no right to ask about finances. "Don't I take care of the family?" he'd say—"Don't I give you whatever you ask for? Then what's it to you which bills I choose to pay first and how I choose to pay them? You make me feel like an animal on a leash, asking those questions, trying to control me. Do I try to tell you how to run the household?"

The more freely Ricky spent, the more I felt the need to conserve, always afraid that at a crucial moment we would simply run out of funds. Years before I had learned to live on next to nothing, paring my desires down to necessities in order to be free; now I did it to forestall panic.

It didn't work. Ricky was able to cancel all my efforts. While I studied the specials at the A & P, Ricky bought equipment; what I managed to save over several weeks, Ricky spent on one business lunch. When the rent rose, when Ricky bought, I pared and pared until there was nothing more I could cut, leaving me pressing right up against my anxiety.

Not that he wasn't generous. He was maddeningly so, willing to go into debt to fulfill a whim of mine. But as it was his money, not mine (a fact he established with his very generosity), I felt free to spend it only on incontestable necessities. I couldn't even make use of our joint checking account because Ricky always kept it on the verge of overdraw.

Only a week before the raffle we'd had a big blow-up over

money. I had returned from the playground the Saturday before my birthday to face one of Ricky's double-edged surprises.

"Now get ready, Zane. I've got a big surprise for you. I think you're going to love it," he'd said with ominous enthusiasm, leading me into the living room.

There, against the far wall, stood a new Steinway spinet, gleaming in its oiled fruitwood case, its ivories beckoning. The very piano I'd been foolish enough to admire in a window on Fifty seventh Street.

"Happy birthday," he said, kissing me.

I was speechless: appalled at the sheer extravagance (the piano must have cost hundreds, maybe thousands, of dollars, whereas I didn't have enough money in my name to buy an airplane ticket home to Babylon), incensed that he had used my birthday as a pretext for one more debt. Like the cases of wine he'd bought "on sale" and the car he'd sprung on us, the piano too would have been bought on credit, to be paid off over the years, costing me nights of sleep as well as years of interest.

"How could you?" I said, tense with resentment.

"But you said this was the perfect piano," he replied, feigning innocence. As though he didn't know my true preferences; as though admiration were mere prelude to possession.

"But how could you buy something like this without discussing it with me first?" It came out in a hiss, for I wouldn't allow myself to scream before the children—which always gave Ricky, who lacked such scruples, an advantage in any argument. Once I might have won an argument on points but now all Ricky had to do was threaten to raise his voice in front of the children and I would usually give in immediately.

"Come on, Zane—how could I have discussed it with you? It's your birthday present."

"*My* present! Like the car, I suppose, which was also 'for me'?"

"It *was* for you. It was for all of us. And the piano—well, you're the one who plays."

"Plays? I just fool around sometimes. The same as the car—have I ever actually driven it? I prefer to take the subway."

"The kids can take lessons some day."

But it did seem mean to complain about his generosity. I threw my arms around his neck and wailed, "Oh Ricky, if you really wanted to give me a present I'd love, something for *me*, you'd give me cash. You'd return this 'present' and make a deposit for me in a bank account. Interest free. How can you talk about piano lessons when we haven't got one penny saved for an emergency? We haven't even put anything aside for nursery school."

The piano was gone the next week, but I never did see the cash. Naturally, Ricky acted like the sole injured party. Immediately he returned to his financial silence that kept me in a constant state of uncertainty, never knowing if we were rolling in surplus or in debt. Only once a year, at income tax time, could I get answers to my financial questions by threatening to withhold my signature from the joint return. Even that technique yielded little more than a false and momentary sense of power, for Ricky, a lawyer, used every obfuscating trick to conceal the truth from me. Debts and credits danced in some mysterious, precarious balance that kept me ever fearful, while with brilliant doubletalk Ricky told me only enough to insure that I would sign.

No wonder, then, when the phone call finally came asking that I come up to the CORE office right away to pick up my sewing machine ("I won?" "You're 1940, aren't you?") I took it for the kiss of luck that would change our lives.

"We won! We won!" I screamed, twirling a stunned little Sammy in my arms till he begged me to stop. It was only moments before supper time. Nevertheless, I bundled the children into their snowsuits and mittens and put them in the stroller, covered the pots and turned off the flames, and marched straight over to the CORE office.

The machine was a brand I'd never heard of, a Japanese imitation of a Singer, with a walnut cabinet that had a drawer for threads and pins and a cubby for patterns. Hardly an item to catch my eye in a store window, but now a vehicle of fate that inspired reverence. Already I could see my creations (as yet undesigned) in all the nicest windows in the Village, with a discreet sign in the door saying: WE CARRY DESIGNS BY ZANE. Already I could see the letters of thanks from the head of CORE and the head of SANE for my generous donations to the cause out of my first year's earnings. Sammy sensed the significance, for right there in the CORE office, in front of the volunteers, he jumped and squealed.

Sewing machine, stroller, children, and I all taxied home, my first expense against future earnings. All through dinner I studied the manual. In a matter of mere days I was sewing children's jumpers (who but I would notice the mistakes?)—a fanatical seamstress.

I learned to sniff out sewing scraps from local sources as I'd learned to scavenge firewood from the street when I lived in Marshall's studio. Outside a pair of clothing manufacturers in the South Village, on the Thursday trash piles, on Fourteenth Street at the mill-end shops, at the festivals and rummage sales of the neighborhood. In a month I had actually put together a small group of lined satchels, each one unique, which I scurried to place on consignment in several of the local boutiques. No bohemian ever joined the petty bourgeoisie more willingly. Then came ponchos (so easy to make, I learned to do two an hour—that is, two per naptime if I didn't have to rip), and after I found a discarded roll of laminated silver cloth on the counter of one of the mill-end shops, I sewed a set of weird aprons, children's and misses', I hoped would catch on.

Business was slow. My financial return was dismal—even in my best week my hourly return was a fraction of what I'd earned at my old copy-editing job. But I didn't care. My needle pointed straight toward the future as into each item I sewed a hand-lettered label: *Designed by Zane.*

5 · WASHINGTON

When the campaign for the big Washington Civil Rights March of '63 was launched—posters everywhere, volunteers taking signatures and passing out leaflets at Village Square—Aunt Louise's benediction kept popping into my head.

"It is required of a man that he should share the passion and action of his time at peril of being judged not to have lived."

I watched the young activists with fascination. Were they an old element or a new? They sat behind card tables at the street corners with the look of defiance I once had worn. But they collected signatures without a qualm, faces lit with righteousness: a living reproof to those who, only yesterday it seemed, would not dare to sign anything. Only yesterday a rebel was one who scoffed at "joiners"; and now here were these rebels sticking their necks out, scoffing at caution instead. Pushing the stroller past them on my way home from the A & P, I signed everything they asked. I admired them. I wanted them to know I supported them. Secretly I envied them.

Of course, my going to Washington was out of the question. For me to dash out of town with a picket sign leaving my babies behind would be the height of self-indulgence; Tina was not yet weaned! I might justify fighting the fallout that poisoned their milk, but I could hardly justify leaving my post for the joy of momentarily linking my life with suffering humanity in the service of a Great Cause—if I hadn't known that already, Ricky would have made it clear. But as the momentum for the march continued to build, it captured my imagination as if it were the Prince's Ball.

If Rosa Luxemburg, that revolutionary martyr, could confess to "feeling that life is not within me, not wherever I happen to be, but somewhere else, far away," then understand how I, despite having chased life vainly to New York, despite the terror and joy of raising my precious babies, could feel I might capture life at last in Washington, D.C.

I knew what life looked like. I saw it all out my window every night as I nursed Tina. While Ricky slept I watched the revelers winding down in the park, heard the winos fight, saw the drag queens comb each other's hair and lovers tear themselves from each other before sun-up brought the paddy wagon. In the morning I could tell intriguing stories to Ricky as he dressed for work or amuse the mothers in the playground, letting my eyes grow large and my voice high as I described the details of all I saw and heard, or weave stylish stories in my weekly letters home to Mama and Daddy or Aunt Louise. But no matter how many dramas I witnessed or how fancifully I embellished them in the retelling, I knew a spinner of tales was not a participant.

Nor was a connoisseur. By the time my ponchos flopped, I was an expert on the Village. Not only on the coffee houses and dives of my beatnik days, or the architectural treasures I'd collected with Ricky before the babies came, but even on the fabled Village wares. I bought my coffee beans at the Italian Store, bread at Zito's, fresh noodles on Houston Street, cheese at Murray's, pâté from Nicola's, vegetables from the pushcarts on Bleecker, fruits at

Balducci's, and pralines from the tiny, triangular Miss Douglas's Bakeshop, the pride of West Fourth Street. But knowing the neighborhood and being known, even being greeted by name by the renowned Miss Douglas herself, could do nothing to change patronage to participation. Miss Douglas baked; I merely ate.

And suddenly, indulgence or no, I knew I had to go to Washington.

I knew Ricky, who scoffed at causes, would disapprove. ("You really have to join a mob to prove you believe in integration?") And Tina had barely learned to sleep through the night. Yet, words without deeds, beliefs without acts to batten them down in reality, were mere bravado, like the empty notebooks of the cafe boys. I had already maternally sat out the sit-ins and the freedom rides—soon the whole civil rights movement would pass me by, and instead of a worthy life I'd have only a secret one.

If it had been possible, I would have slipped off quietly to Washington without ever telling Ricky. As I'd signed petitions and even once stopped en route to the pediatrician to carry a picket sign in front of the GM Building without telling him. ("You're so naïve, Zane," he'd once accused me. "You'd sign something without even knowing who was sponsoring it just to feel good.") As, also without his knowledge, I'd sometimes slipped off to MacDougal Street in the late afternoons before Tina was born (with Sammy asleep in the carriage) to read through the names of the poets who would be reading at the Poetry Place, or twice sat nervously in the Cafe Lucia for fifteen minutes with a cup of espresso, or let my eyes catch the eyes of other seekers sitting on their front stoops on fine days with unopened books in their laps, and peeked inside the windows of the brownstones hoping to see the pictures on the walls and fathom the amazing lives of the occupants. For each of these breaches of my isolation I felt as guilty as a wife with a lover and hid them from Ricky.

Not that he would necessarily have opposed me. He was free enough with his blessing, based as it was on ignorance. After all, what could be the harm in a coffee or a walk?

But nothing is innocent in marriage (that battle between loyalty and integrity), and if Ricky had known my true motives, if he had guessed at the wild hopes I was unable to dispel, he would surely have retaliated. If he'd understood me for a single moment he would have known that my most innocuous gesture might, carried to its end, have overthrown him, his pleasure, our love, our marriage, the very world he inhabited . . . I didn't want his blessing lightly given.

But going to Washington without him was out of the question; if I'd suggested it he surely would have suspected that I had a lover. Instead, one day I just showed him the full-page ad for the march in the *Voice* and blurted out:

"I think we should go to this demonstration."

"Why?"

"Come on, Ricky. You know why."

"But to Washington? Isn't there one in New York we could go to instead?" It wasn't the cause he opposed, only the nuisance.

"Not like this one. This one will make a difference."

"What about the kids? We can't take them; the crowds'll be impossible."

People who stayed in their home towns could leave their children with grandparents. Those who ran off to New York to make history and stopped to have babies had to find other means. "You could stay with them and I could go down by myself," I offered. But Ricky's suspicious scowl made me quickly add, "Or else, if you'll come with me, maybe we can hire a sitter to spend the night."

He knew something was up. I had never before even considered leaving my babies overnight with a sitter.

"Where will you find someone who'll stay all night?"

"I'll check the agencies."

The next day I reported what it would cost. "Thirty-six dollars just for a sitter?" he said, his eyes popping. Not that it could have seemed so much to him, but it was an unprecedented extravagance for me. I saw him trying to decipher my motive. Could I, who made a fetish of frugality, trying to save myself from the corruption of Ricky's income, I, who'd last earned two dollars for each laborious hour I worked, be willing to blow thirty-six dollars on a baby sitter for one night, plus forty more for bus fare and expenses, just in order to join the mobs in D.C.? "That's a lot for a sitter, isn't it?" he asked.

Embarrassed or not, I persisted. "I suppose so, but I have to go. I really don't care what it costs."

Other people bought clothes and tickets to the opera, other people took taxis and hired cleaning ladies with their husbands' money. But not I. Even if I'd been married to Rockefeller I'd have ordered from Sears and taken the subway. What I wanted were other things. This.

"What about Tina?" asked Ricky, suddenly remembering.

"It's more than two weeks off. I'll wean her." I stumbled as I said it.

Ricky stopped short and gawked at me. Sammy on his daddy's shoulders grabbed onto his hair. "You'll wean her for *this?* You really want to go that bad?"

Oblivious of our concern, Tina lay asleep in the carriage; and in that awkward moment I had no place to hide my true desires. Tina, whom I'd planned to nurse, like Sammy, for a year, would be only six months old in August. But my conscience pulled me both ways. And besides, it was now more than a matter of conscience.

"Yes," I said simply.

We'd probably have done more for the cause if we'd stayed home and donated the sitter money to CORE. But I didn't want to cheer from the sidelines for the rest of my youth or give up half of all I'd longed for just because I'd gotten married. I wanted to be in the thick of things, sweating and signifying. The world went reeling on—Strontium 90 poisoned the food, Cubans made a revolution, martyrs died in Mississippi, everywhere there were wars, calamities, assassinations—while I pushed the stroller back and forth to the playground, accomplishing nothing of importance. ("Nothing? No, don't say that, Anna," I once heard Aunt Louise counsel Mama. "At least you've raised a family, Anna, at least you can point to Zane and say: I've produced her, I've done that." And from my listening post at the top of the stairs I took a moment's pride in having given Mama an accomplishment. "But I?" Louise had continued, "I've never made anything but a little trouble. One three-week strike that came to nothing in the end because they said, you know, we were communists; and maybe Herman, bless him, lost his job because of me. Well, before I die I'm going to do something. God knows what, but something. Something significant!")

I knew going on this march with thousands of others was only modestly "significant." Some people went to jail or even death for their beliefs, not just to Washington. But it was a start.

I liked to believe that a couple of years earlier, before the children were born, I'd have been on the first bus heading south. If I hadn't so abruptly retired the hip persona I'd once been at such pains to cultivate (abrupt was the only way: abrupt as "I do"), I would have been a freedom rider or an organizer, not just a body on a march. Now, though, even an occasional demonstration was hard to manage, and every one of them was disloyal to Ricky. Because no matter how often I renounced the aspirations that had lifted me out of Indiana and landed me in New York, I always knew, and somewhere Ricky knew too, that one really critical experience, one chance to signify, could start the eruption of all my old desires. It was not another man he had to fear—I'd never met one who was irresistible. It was my own lusting spirit.

"Okay, call the agency," said Ricky, lifting Sammy to the ground and smiling benevolently on his wife and son; "I'll check the busses through the office." And though I would rather have gone with CORE or a Village group than other lawyers and their wives, I threw my arms around his neck in gratitude.

On the bus (NAACP) we stuffed ourselves with bagfuls of peanut butter and jelly sandwiches. "Integration sandwiches," we called them ever after, because we'd all been told to pack food that didn't need refrigeration, and what other kind was there? We sang campfire songs from our youth, old union songs (I'd learned them all from Aunt Louise, but Ricky didn't know the words), and "We Shall Overcome." Arm in arm we marched through the dusty summer streets of Washington to the Lincoln Memorial where we lounged on the grass and listened to Martin Luther King tell his dream, and would have listened twice as hard if we'd guessed what was coming. We congratulated each other on our huge presence, bowed our heads for the delegation from Alabama who'd come on foot, rose to our feet when the President came. On the way home we smiled out the bus windows at other smiling people on other busses massing on the highway, filled with the incomparably cozy feeling of brotherhood. We lined up for hours at Howard Johnson's johns, letting one dime spring the toilet booths for all comers in urinary solidarity.

"Now aren't you glad?" I said, squeezing Ricky's arm. I could see that he was. I hardly ever thought of the children, it felt so good to be out there, marching on the right side, making trouble again, declaring myself, joining history and all the good people I no longer saw now that I was married.

I was quite sure they had all come to Washington, though I hadn't seen them. How could you hope to find anyone there with two hundred thousand of us? But I felt their presence. All the bohemians and fanatics I'd left Babylon to find, all the Progressives and Trotskyists, poets and pacifists, all the like-minded people marching in solidarity, two hundred thousand strong. Nina and Carole, Wolfe, Kappy, Kaye, Blanche, the whole Lucia crowd, even Marshall if he were in the East, and Morgan Moore. They'd all have got there somehow—borrowed money for the bus fare or hitched rides or rented a car or ridden the rails if necessary. I hadn't seen them in years, but I knew they wouldn't have missed it. We'd never had such marches in my day—only local demonstrations to ban the bomb or unban folk singing, or get the busses out of the park, plus a few petitions to save one doomed building or another. Nothing like *this*.

I knew that Nina, at least, had been working for civil rights from the very beginning. I hadn't seen her since I'd married, and then one Sunday back in '61 I saw her again when Sammy was only a few months old. Ricky and I had been sitting in Domino's, a recently opened sidewalk cafe rated tops by the magazines and a tourist favorite, when I heard Nina's voice. I was surprised. Though I was always vaguely on the lookout for people from my past, they never seemed to turn up, and Domino's was too expensive for them anyway. (Naturally, I would still have preferred one of the humbler cafes on MacDougal Street, or even the Riviera, but Domino's was one of the few places where you could keep a baby carriage beside your table without rousing the ire of the management. The White Horse had a sign in the window that said straight out: NO DOGS, NO PETS, NO STROLLERS, NO CARRIAGES, McSorleys didn't admit any women at all; and if you had a stroller you were asked to leave the Lucia unless it was practically empty.)

There was no mistaking that voice. I looked around to see her, now stridently, now entreatingly, urging the customers: "Sign our petition. Won't you please join us at Woolworth's Monday? We're going to close down the lunch counters until every counter in the South is integrated."

I suddenly felt embarrassingly exposed. There was Nina, stalking the tables, pressing her pleas into every conscience like a blind beggar tapping through the subway, while Carole passed out leaflets, and I sat sipping coffee in a family tableau. I was dying to talk to her, but it was impossible without at the same time revealing all the changes that had taken place in me. I didn't want to see her disappointment. Years had gone by since I'd known those two; years in which I'd slipped from one life to another practically as easily as learning a new tune. Yet here were Nina and Carole, pure as poppies, seemingly uncorrupted by time.

"Nina?"

"Zane!" She stopped short and looked at us.

My hand moved to Ricky's. "You knew I got married, but I don't think you ever met my husband. This is Ricky Thompson. Ricky, Nina Chase. And that's Sammy, our son, in there asleep."

I felt awkwardly like a tourist myself, introducing the whole family. ("See that building there? You could probably fit the entire population of South Ridge, South Dakota, in that building," I'd heard someone say that very day.) I started talking fast and smiley to cover up my discomfort. "It's great to see you, Nina. If you knew how often I've thought about you. What are you up to now?" I said—making the very small talk we had once, together, risen above.

"Same old things," she said winking pixily as she had always done, as though the whole world hadn't changed at all. And imagining myself again on her side of the table it struck me that even the sexual complication would have disappeared now that I was safely married.

"Where are you living now?" I asked.

"We've got part of an old house over on East Tenth Street, opposite Tompkins Square. Terrific place I fell into—"

"Fell into? You always managed the best apartments," I laughed.

"I'll bet I know where you're living now. You're near the ocean—right?"

I was hurt by her assumption that I'd moved to the suburbs.

"Wrong. I'm just a couple of blocks from here actually, off Washington Square."

At first I was proud to say it, glad at least to have insisted on staying in the city and the Village. But then I thought of our place and what we paid in rent, and what Nina probably paid, and I was ashamed.

"Really? But I never bump into you. I figured you'd moved out of the city."

"No, you're the one who disappeared, Nina."

She pressed a leaflet into my hand. "Listen. Maybe you can come sit-in with us tomorrow. We need people desperately. We want to occupy every seat at the lunch counter before the lunch crowd comes in, and if they arrest us we want to fill up the seats with more people." The old twinkle was in her eye, along with something dramatically serious.

"I don't see how I can. I'm nursing my baby."

Nina looked mystified for a moment, as though she didn't quite understand the words. "All the time?" she asked.

"No, but I can't leave him for more than a couple of hours. I certainly can't get myself arrested."

"I guess not," she said. Then she added, "But you can at least sign our petition. It's a support statement."

Ricky leaned over. "Who's sponsoring it?" he asked.

"SMLA."

"Who are they?"

"Zane remembers. It's Carole's old group."

Ricky kicked me under the table, meaning: don't sign. And though I was mortified to be stalling, Ricky was a lawyer and felt strongly about such things.

"Look, it's long, and I can't sign anything without reading it carefully, Nina. The baby's going to wake up any second. But call me, and we'll talk about it. We're in the phone book: Richard Thompson on—" and I gave her my address.

At that moment, Carole, her lush hair bobbed but looking no less arresting for that, looking, indeed, like a fashionable Joan of Arc, passed our table in distress, pursued by a waiter. "Come on, Nina, quick," she said, "let's get out of here"—and they were gone before I could see Nina's look of disgust or formulate a greeting for Carole.

"Who were they?" asked Ricky.

It was painful to realize how little my present overlapped with my past, how little my husband knew the secret me.

"They?" I smiled. "That was Nina Chase and her friend Carole Buxbaum. They were my best friends for a while when I was new in New York."

"Strange, you never talked about them."

"No? That's funny," I lied, knowing perfectly well why I hadn't mentioned them. Not that my normality was in danger of being challenged any more, now that I was a mother and safely married; but why needlessly reveal my cowardice?

As I watched them make their way up the avenue, heads high, chanting their message and handing out leaflets to every pedestrian they passed as though the changes coming were all by their design, I knew Nina wouldn't bother to call me.

That was the first and last time I'd seen her since I'd married. Most of the others I hadn't seen at all. Brad had turned up at Ricky's office one day half a year after we'd married to ask for money. At first he said I had suggested that Ricky would be interested in investing in a film company. Then he changed his story, claiming to be a close friend of mine—too close to want to bother me—and would Ricky lend him fifty dollars for three weeks? Ricky telephoned me at my office to ask what to do. "There's this funny albino-headed character saying he's a buddy of yours, but honestly, Zane, he looks like some kind of weird-o. Do you want me to give him the money or what?"

"Oh, Ricky," I cried, knowing what contempt Brad would feel for him either way. "Oh, Ricky, honey, I'm sorry. I guess you better give it to him. . . ."

All the way home from Washington on the bus I felt jubilant, uplifted. (That's what history remembers too: "They were like a vast army of quiet Americans at a church outing. . . .") We sang the songs all over again as busful after busful of black and white rolled triumphantly toward New York.

What was a sellout anyway? I wondered, having begun in a tiny way to redeem myself. A sellout was one who sat comfortably back and did nothing, or merely sent a check. Not I, surely; not us.

Then I got home and had to pay the sitter and all the hideous questions came rushing back.

Her name was Felicity. She was black. She had a couple of kids of her own way uptown, but she had come downtown to take care of mine while my husband and I marched in Washington.

The children were both asleep when Felicity made her report. I smiled, pretending to listen, but all I could feel was my shame. Shame at having gone to Washington, at our full drawers and cupboards (which she had certainly seen), of my carelessly kept kitchen, of the giant button on my sweater that pictured black and white hands clasped over the ridiculous legend: "WHOOPEE! EQUAL RIGHTS IN '63!" I'd bought the button for a dollar from a vendor, had not designed it or thought about it. Nevertheless, I was implicated.

Equal rights? White Else who had lived in our attic in Babylon had cried her eyes out with probably less reason than might black Felicity, now calmly closing her sweater and waiting for her money.

"Is it okay if I give you a check?"

"Rather have the cash if you don't mind."

In my absence she had straightened up the kitchen, even cleaning the bottoms of my pots—more than I'd ever done!—and suddenly I couldn't wait until she was gone.

"Quick, Ricky," I whispered frantically in the next room, "give me some money!"

Then returning with a smile to Felicity, painfully I counted it out. "I think that's right," I said.

Most of all, I was ashamed to have had practically everything I ever wanted and still not be satisfied.

"Let me give you my phone number," said Felicity. "Then if you want me again you can call me direct and the agency won't take any of my money."

Slowly she wrote out her number, each digit a stab in my flesh, and handed it to me. I tucked it into my address book, though I already knew that despite her need I was too cowardly to invite her into my life again to witness my privilege. The contradictions were insupportable. No, if I had to go out, I'd hire local sitters from the neighborhood as I'd always done: people who could not judge me so mercilessly.

6 · THREE DOCUMENTS

How quickly the changes escalated in those years when the children, like the sixties they inhabited, began to grow up. My duty letters to Babylon were filled with one kind of electrifying news—the leaps by which the children began to master the seemingly miraculous feats of the human species—while the papers reported equally spectacular events on another plane. Assassinations, ghetto riots, bombings, war, terrorism, student uprisings—changes that tumbled upon each other so quickly that I could scarcely follow them.

Too quickly you were required to adapt. Just as you rejoiced to have adjusted to one phase (Tina lights up with recognition, holding out her pudgy hands when you walk into the room), another was upon you (her lip trembles as you move toward the door) demanding of you a different, sometimes opposite, response. One year separation anxiety required your constant presence and reassurance, and the next thing you knew you had to leave your baby screaming for you in the cold entranceway to nursery school ("I'm sure he'll stop just as soon as he realizes you can't hear him, Mrs. Thompson")—a traitor, a villain.

What went on outside the nursery was equally demanding, if you could stop to see. But for me, mired in maternity, the world was remote. Sometimes in the mornings Ricky put down his coffee, patted the *Times*, open before him, and said, "Listen to this, Zane." And while I diapered the baby or took a temperature or brushed Sammy's hair for school, he reported the latest outrage in the awful war of *them* against *us*.

Malcolm X gunned down, marchers clubbed in Selma, U.S. bombs falling on Vietnam, police shooting rioters in Watts, students beaten for protesting—

"No, Ricky, no!" I cried. "What can we do?"

He looked patronizing and sad. "Do?" he said as I might have guessed. "There's not much to do. You don't know what's really going on. They only let you know what they want you to know."

I didn't believe it. Others, a few, seemed to know what to do—from small gestures to great sacrifices. They were spreading the truth at the teach-ins, fighting back in the ghettos, blocking troop trains, burning draft cards, organizing sit-ins, marching, signing, saying no! no! no! in a thousand ways, even dying. But all their gestures struck Ricky as problematic—salves for the ego.

Not that he was on the other side. He had even gone South for two weeks of his vacation during Mississippi Summer after Leo Stern recruited him. "Just for two weeks," said Leo, combing New York for volunteer lawyers. "They really need men like you. They get a lot of volunteers, but they're almost all white women."

"I don't know. Zane might not like it," Ricky had said skeptically.

"Zane? But isn't *she* the big liberal?" asked Leo with that insinuating smile of his.

They were both looking at me. What could I say? Frankly, I was frightened to let Ricky go South with all those college girls on the loose, and he with his mustache and dimpled chin the perfect catch. And, yes, it did seem unfair that Ricky, who was really indifferent to causes, should be needed instead of me with my passion. But more than anything I wanted him to join the good fight and share my passion; to hold him back would be unthinkable, a sacrifice of principle to ego. He was the lawyer with the vacation, after all, and I had the babies to keep—how could I possibly be resentful?

"Don't be ridiculous. I *want* you to go!" I said, coating my resentment in pride.

But he had returned from the South if anything more cynical than when he'd gone; worse, he considered himself an authority, describing half the volunteers as in it for the fun and the real source of change in the South the federal government. To him, consequences of individual acts were unpredictable, all self-sacrifice at bottom self-serving. A prudent man. How much our positions had changed since we'd married! Once I'd been the hardnosed one, exposing the truth about "romance," and Ricky the naïf. But now our stands were reversed. Now I was the softie and Ricky the one who found me naïve.

I couldn't help it. To me it was intolerable to stand around helplessly doing nothing while every sort of horror was committed; soothing to take a stand whether ultimately useless or not. I recognized the sentiment as soft; knew the uplift of carrying a picket sign was a luxury that must not interfere with my real obligations; knew it was folly to want to participate when there were plenty of others to man the barricades but not one other in the world to keep the life going in my three babies. If Ricky were right that such gestures made no difference, or, worse, that the consequences of your actions might be other than you'd planned, then they were indeed "self-indulgent." ("Go ahead and indulge yourself, soothe your conscience if you like, but for god's sake, Zane, spare me your righteousness!" he said.) But while Ricky scoffed, my response was to try still harder to purify my motives.

Once I had seen a picture of purity in the *Times*, shocking, unforgettable. Following the example of the Buddhist monks who'd burned themselves to death in Vietnam, a saintly Quaker named Norman Morrison had anointed himself with kerosene on the steps of the Pentagon (while eager photographers got it down on film) and lit a match, shaming us all.

Pictures of the war dead, of the ghetto dead, of the children, the hungry and maimed, squeezed your heart unbearably for the horror and the waste. But Norman Morrison had deliberately touched the match to his body, had chosen to give his life. It was the purity of saints, perfectly uniting motive and act; whatever the consequences (or lack of them), his act had mattered, his death was not a waste. ("I have no regrets about my fate," said Sophia Perovskaia, facing probable death for her act of regicide. "I have lived according to my convictions; I could not have acted otherwise; and so I await the future with a clear conscience.")

If you weren't prepared to die like Norman Morrison or Joan of Arc, how could you decide what to do? How could you choose where to draw the line? How could you sign a petition proclaiming your mind without following through with your life?

Trying to entertain Tina and the new baby Julie while waiting outside the nursery school for Sammy to be able to do without me for one single morning, I knew how futile it was for a mother of three preschoolers to speculate on motive and act. Only someone prepared to give up her life could be considered (as I once had been) truly "incorrigible." (Vera Figner was so determined to prove her willingness to die that she had to be "reprimanded for seeking personal satisfaction" and sent to Odessa by the Party.) One who did less, as Ricky was only too quick to say, was a hypocrite.

And yet, despite my hesitation and isolation, those maternal years were crucial times in advancing my radical will. While the young Students for a Democratic Society were moving off campuses into "the community" and thus, as one spokesman phrased it, "giving birth to themselves," I, who had so far given birth only to others, was quietly preparing for the time of my own entry into the birth canal of the coming revolution.

In the middle desk drawer, where I kept nursery school applications and teachers' reports, I have recently uncovered three prophetic documents from 1965—the year Johnson began systematically bombing Vietnam; the year the Figaro closed down for several weeks to repair the ravages that followed a shameful racial incident; and the year Sammy Thompson, barely toilet-trained, entered St. Christopher's Village Nursery School—documents which reveal the early gropings and irrepressible stirrings of the once and future fanatic.

One is a letter I sent to the Board of Directors of Sammy's school—my first public statement in the seven years since I'd left school myself—in which I express "concern and dismay" over the Board's expulsion of one of Sammy's classmates, impish, black, impossibly wild Benjamin Clark. Though the letter betrays my continued dependence on the *Debater's Manual* and bears traces of autodidactic pedantry, it eloquently and, I think, bravely argues an unpopular position, presaging the soon-to-emerge agitator who will not be silenced. "There may be several legitimate reasons for you to suspend a pupil, even in November, without abusing your authority. These I shall take up in a moment, one by one." (*Debater's Manual:* "The safest course is to admit all that can safely be admitted.") "But first I must seriously ask the Board this question: Is it possible that a 4½-year-old child can ever, under any circumstances (let alone after only three months of nursery school) be reasonably considered 'incorrigible'?" My first enterprise as a PTA activist (carbon copies to each parent in the school), perhaps my first independent political act undertaken on my own initiative out of sheer conviction, the letter still fills me with pride. Though most of the parents in the school initially shouted good riddance to poor Ben, making Ricky dismiss my cause as "lost" ("All causes are lost causes," he sometimes said, taking the longest view), still I dared to stir up an entire parent body over one indefensible injustice.

The second document I salvaged from those days is a schedule, neatly penned on yellow lined paper, projecting the impossible goals I set myself that year, hour by hour, task by task, into a visionary scheme: to squeeze between the shopping, cooking, feeding, cleaning, washing, juggling required to keep alive three children under five, a full half hour alone with each of them every day for anything in the world they chose to do.

Reading it now, I have no doubt that if the Red Squad had

ever had a glimpse of my schedule they would certainly have known they were dealing with a fanatic of extraordinary proportions. I can barely believe it myself. So far above the standard ideals of the day did I set my maternal sights that only the whackiest child-care expert would have acknowledged me. Having failed in my first life, I was zealous in my second. My decreed day included the usual 6:30 awakening, meals, airings, naps, and prescribed escortings to nursery school, to the doctor, to the playground and library. Like other conscientious mothers I struggled to provide the necessities: adequate protein, calcium, B-complex, sleep, sensory stimulation, discipline, distraction, quiet moments, and two stories per child at bedtime. But beyond such standard minimum requirements, beyond the expected and even beyond the optional, were the unrealizable demonstrations and devotions I required of myself. No child's question could go unanswered, no kindness unappreciated, no achievement unrewarded, no failure of patience in myself unpunished. There they are in my dogged scrawl: the minutes and hours of my dedicated days, all arranged to dispatch with maximum efficiency the endlessly proliferating crucial chores in such a way as to leave me time to bestow on my helpless offspring all possible tools for understanding, all possible proofs of love. But as always, my ambitions far outstripped the practical realities, and I probably never once managed to live up to the standards I set myself in that Utopian schedule.

My third and most treasured item from that year is an article torn out of *Time* magazine announcing the sudden apotheosis of "our newest prophet": my own long secret hero, Morgan Moore.

I remember the exact moment she reappeared in my life after an absence of almost four years. I had been pregnant with Sammy when I lost sight of her, and there I was in the pediatrician's office with Sammy and two more babies besides when I suddenly and unexpectedly came face to face with Moore's picture. Julie was asleep; Tina was stacking blocks at my feet; Sammy was pushing the yellow miniature bulldozer he never went without that year; and I, flipping lackadaisically through the pages of an old issue of *Time* while I waited out the Mother's Wait, recognized her face.

Sandwiched among the photos of hippies, marines, and fat politicians, a woman warrior's eyes flashed pugnaciously back at the camera, a hand cut the air; the caption confirmed it: Morgan Moore.

Four eventful years had come and gone without her. Kennedy's assassination, Freedom Summer, protests in Berkeley, and now suddenly Moore was back again, writing again (or still), peering out of *Time* (of all unlikely places!), looking as serious and triumphant as I remembered, and being hailed, not as a new Grand Master, a dyke, or even a wit, but as the spokesman of a New Generation, author of a Very Important Book.

I gulped down the flashy words. A candidate for the coveted Grandville Prize, already "a classic on publication" said *Time, Motive and Act* had established Moore's place securely and permanently in the intellectual firmament. No mere collection of essays, her first full-length work was a dialectical treatise on the nature of power which bore "the mark of an exciting, original mind"; and though Moore was hardly the "newcomer to the literary scene" that *Time* alleged, having written for the *Voice* for years, it was still a jolt to see someone whom I had independently discovered and championed now suddenly risen to stardom and hailed as "one of the most brilliant minds of the New Generation."

That was the one disturbing note in the article—the acknowledgment that indeed there was now a new generation loose in the land. Unlike ours (called sometimes the Silent and sometimes the Beat) whose lights had already flashed and faded, the new generation had not yet been named. But I could tell by my awkwardness wheeling the children through the very streets my generation had claimed as exclusive turf that a new one had, as *Time* confirmed, succeeded ours. It was a generation of joiners (where we had been suspicious of every group)—noisier, more numerous, less defensive, more rebellious, than ours. A generation that could not distinguish me from every other mother-of-three.

I studied the picture, hoping for illuminations. Moore was somewhat older than I; but like someone pushing onto the last car of the subway train just before the doors close, she had managed to squeeze into the new generation in time while I stayed behind in the station with the stroller.

The nurse stood up at her desk, holding a list. Stealthily, I tore the page from the magazine inch by inch, losing a few letters of a few words from the inside margin but keeping the precious photo (the first picture in my collection) intact and slipped it into the diaper bag at the exact moment the professional voice announced, "Mrs. Thompson, doctor will see you now."

In we went. I could barely jolly the children through their ordeal or listen to the doctor's warnings, I so needed to get to a bookstore and buy that book. And all the way downtown on the Fifth Avenue bus, stopping for passengers every two blocks in rush hour traffic, then through the cranky aftermath of inoculations, and dinner and baths and bedtime, I waited to open the sealed Brentano's package that contained my prize.

Ricky didn't come home till late that night. Sometimes when he had to work late I couldn't read at all. But tonight, with Moore's book in hand, for once I wasn't disappointed when Ricky called.

From the back of the jacket Morgan Moore looked straight into my eyes. Unlike the action photo in *Time*, this picture was posed and premeditated. Even in black-and-white, the wild hair all but shimmered red; and the eyes, calm and serious, demanded to be considered.

"When you finish this important work," the man in *Time* had said, "you will find yourself troubled by its gloomy, disturbing vision. Do not be fooled by the effortless style, the feminine wit: Despite appearances, this stunning young redhead is a weighty talent, one that will have to be reckoned with. Miss Moore's vision is as tough as a man's; it is ultimately too radical and transforming to allow any response but the deadly serious."

It was indeed a brilliant book as the critic said; and now, reading it, I felt subversive stirrings of my own buried aspirations. Not to shine—I had too many children to shine—but to make trouble, to say no again, to stick my foot in the aisle as Moore had done and send complacency sprawling, to face injustice head on no matter who might sneer and, linking my own rebellious will with Moore's, somehow to affect the world.

The pages of the book went by, building point by brilliant point toward Moore's compelling climax. "You see?" I wanted to shout to the world and all the misogynists of MacDougal Street who had so meanly attacked her. While they'd guzzled beer and posed and talked, pausing now and then to scribble in their notebooks, she had thought, worked, written.

Not for me the gloom the man in *Time* had felt. On the contrary, as my eye descended the last page toward the concluding words I already understood so well (for I was still Moore's perfect reader), I felt my dormant spirit rise until, closing the book at last (to see her once more looking up at me, this time with the firm gaze of authority), my smile spread into a triumphant grin. Once again in the presence of Moore I rejoiced in the unexpected achievements that turned out after all to be possible for a strong single-minded woman.

Now, with dialectical hindsight, it is easy to see those three documents as embodying thesis, antithesis, synthesis of my confused desires in 1965. See how perfectly the clipping and schedule exemplify the two conflicting tendencies that held me in precarious balance before I fused them in the feminist synthesis, as the letter to the School Board reveals my first pathetic attempt to unite Rebel and Mother in a single act. And in the strained years that followed —from the moment Morgan Moore's name appeared among the stars on the statement protesting the first bombings in Vietnam until I found the Third Street Circle in '68—the warring parts of me vied for control as I attended every demonstration I could swing without neglecting the children.

Devoted disciple of Moore, I circulated petitions in my building, baked cakes for the Peace Center, stuffed envelopes, leafleted on my way to and from nursery school, got gassed at the Pentagon and jailed in the Tombs. But nothing I did was enough. Assailed by the futility of each effort, guilty that people were dying and poor while I was discontent and comfortable, I was always the intruder, the housewife, the hanger-on, who either had to bring her brat or dash off to relieve the sitter or cancel at the last minute because of a sudden crisis at home.

At demonstrations I was the loner with the stroller at the fringe of the crowd, always ready for a fast exit. Remember me?

At the Pentagon, where I went with Women's Strike for Peace in '66 in response to Morgan Moore's appeal, we were denied the audience we'd been promised with the Defense Secretary. We saw the brass peeking at us from behind their curtained windows, while soldiers guarding the entrances snickered and grinned; but no one received our delegation. And when, enraged, we stormed the entrance, beating against the Pentagon doors with our shoes, the soldiers went up to the roof to watch us, amused. (When Mailer and Spock led thousands, including me, against the Pentagon many months later, it seemed to everyone such a fine idea; but back when we did it it fell flat, winning us only a tiny story in the *Times* and a snicker from a reporter on the evening news.)

Still, I tried. At the Peace Church around the corner (where Moore's name now lit the masthead) I volunteered to help type the newsletter and get out the mailings while the children played in the basement nursery room. But if I happened to be there on the day of the Policy Meetings, Father Percy politely asked me to leave before calling the meeting to order.

Even the bimonthly Intellectual Forums, the most serious political debates in town, held in Leuticia Bracci's famous loft, eventually turned me out—though I paid my annual dues early and twice helped with the mailings. ("I don't know what keeps me doing it," Leuticia had complained, "handling a million details, making all the arrangements myself. It's far too much for one person, but if I didn't do it what would happen to the Forums?" "Perhaps I can help you," I offered. "Good," she said. "The next mailing has to be out by Tuesday or we simply won't have a Forum. But don't show up before three tomorrow, I won't be there. And for god's sake, don't bring any children with you!")

For two years Leuticia accepted my twenty-five-dollar membership dues, sending me a pair of tickets for each of five Forums held in her loft. There, surrounded by Leuticia's huge, ugly canvases, I watched Morgan Moore take her occasional place on the makeshift platform, a lone woman among the intellectual celebrities, to debate the burning questions of the day. I was too shy ever to risk a comment in the hour reserved for "discussion" following each debate, though my brain reeled with questions. Despite my debating skills I had not finished college. Still, there was never a more enthusiastic patron than I. On those long-awaited nights I invariably arrived at the Forums before the doors opened, happy to stand among the rattling pipes in the cold stairwell for a chance at a front-row seat. Others complained about the lack of air and the smoke and the narrow wooden folding chairs; but for me all discomfort faded before my joy as the speakers picked their way over the mad tangle of wires up to the platform. Smiling

Leuticia fixed their mikes around their necks and lovingly poured their water; I fixed Moore in my eye (a graceful poppy among those drooping vines) and sank myself into her performance.

When the discussions were over and a preening Leuticia, trailing the mike, took the stage to thank each of the speakers personally (popping their names against her tongue like caviar) and invite everyone to stay for "our special intellectual punch" and cookies, I stayed till the last possible moment, milling inconspicuously among the intellectuals, listening to their talk. Never once did I leave that stuffy loft, not even when Ricky begged me, until I was absolutely certain Moore had gone. And afterwards, in the days following, I continued to debate in my mind the seductive pros and inconclusive cons. But somewhere toward the end of the second year, Leuticia decided to reserve the front rows for celebrities and the wives of panelists, whose names she lovingly taped on the backs of the chairs; and by the third season, when the debates at Intellectual Forums were making a national splash, having grown in proportion to the spread of the war, my annual check was returned with the following letter:

> *Due to the increased popularity of the Forums and the limited seating in the loft, we are no longer able to offer seats to every member. Henceforth attendance is by invitation only. Those members who, by profession and position, are potentially able to make the greatest contribution to the Forums will be allotted seats.*
>
> *Those of you who wish to continue as inactive members of Intellectual Forums ($15.00 per year, tax deductible) will be considered first should seats become available or should we locate larger quarters.*
>
> *Leuticia Bracci,*
> *Director, Intellectual Forums*

Compared to other mothers at the school who less restively performed their tasks or more docilely accepted their state, I must have seemed quite the activist: a wearer of buttons, bearer of picket signs, vocal yearner after basic change. But as for really participating in the passions and actions of my time, a busy mother could hardly swing it.

Now that I've made a study of the subject I know that only a tiny handful in history ever managed, except for certain suffragists who took the problem head on; that rare indeed was the dedicated activist like Mother Bloor with a brood to raise. Mother Jones began her political career only after her four children died of yellow fever. Elizabeth Gurley Flynn, though she dedicated her memoir to her "dearly beloved only son," ditched her husband and turned her one baby over to her own mother to keep till the difficult years were over. Margaret Fuller, torn between her maternal and revolutionary ardors, recognized that "children involve one too deeply in this corrupt social contract and truth is easier to those who have them not." La Pasionaria, grieving over "how difficult it is for a mother to devote herself to a revolutionary struggle," let the Party send her children off to school in Moscow. And the tortured Olga Liubatovich, who was banished to Siberia after the Trial of the Fifty, proclaimed forthrightly: "It is a sin for Revolutionaries to start a family. But in your youth you somehow forget that Revolutionaries' lives are measured not in years but in days and hours."

No, however daring I may have looked to the PTA, I could never have fooled those who made history. From a performer ready to storm the stage where history was being played, I had become a stage mother, coaching my children in the wings. If I had retired to the suburbs at that moment, Father Percy, Leuticia Bracci, the Secretary of Defense, or the ghost of Justice Holmes, like the FBI and the Red Squad, would never have noticed. As far as any of them knew, I was just another housewife.

7 · A NEW SITTER

I thought it would be a delivery when I opened the door. No one else ever called. But instead I found myself facing a small, dark, sexy, bearded man, one of the new people. Full, black, untrimmed beard, shaggy hair down below his shoulders, uncertain stance, a harmonica protruding from his jacket pocket, and pressed against narrow jean-sheathed hips, Morgan Moore's book. My throat tightened in the sudden presence of this Other, this Beard from my past and future, standing in my doorway.

"Mrs. Thompson? I'm Bonnie's friend. She said you were interviewing for a baby sitter."

He spoke very softly and avoided my eyes. Staring from behind round, wire-rimmed specs (while I stood holding the door, peering at him stupidly) his black eyes told nothing. But I surmised. Bonnie's friend, he would be a radical, maybe a revolutionary, at least one of those who declared himself. I stood there immobilized. He couldn't have known that he was applying not only for baby sitter but for a role in my life.

The fact was, in recent years I had become intimately involved in the lives of my sitters. Mainly because from the time Sammy was born they were the only people I saw with any regularity outside the family; but there were reasons other than proximity. My sitters' built-in promise of temporary relief from the burden of total motherness awakened in me an immense gratitude. These would-be actresses and dancers, these activists and students, attempting despite prodigious confusion to persist in a life I'd abandoned, were my rescuers. If they too were lonely, they easily became like family, leaning, confiding. How could they not when they came smack into the intimate part of your life, nuzzled around, rummaged through your closets, glanced at your mail, answered your phone, read your books, listened to your music, evaluated your life? They stirred me with their needs and appreciated the way I scrupulously left them lavish snacks and paid them an extra hour's wage for each fraction over. I was so glad to be made their confidante that I let them smoke my cigarettes, dirty my dishes, entertain their friends at my expense, rely on me for every kind of information and support.

Naturally their tribute also had its negative side, driving home to me how soon I'd be hitting their enemy age of thirty, of which they in their naïveté remained oblivious. Mostly recent arrivals, they could ignore the proliferating evidence that time was rushing on. But I confronted new alarms every day. Seasons, birthdays, the children's outgrown clothes, the paint beginning to peel again on the window sills, the grease spots on the red chair, recipes tattered from use, papers piling up, Ricky's closed files, forgotten music; everywhere, warnings that I had somehow turned from a wayward kid like them into an eccentric woman, someone principled but matronly, a creature, I was shocked to find, remarkably like my Aunt Louise! The metamorphosis was already out of my hands; my aunt's matronly persona entered me without invitation. Sometimes it came over me in a public place—at the library or the supermarket when I balked at some bureaucracy or stood on principle only to be dismissed as a crank, a troublemaker in white sneakers. Once the feeling came over me in the park when a frisbee player leaped in front of me shouting, "Heads up, lady!" taking me, despite my jeans, gambol, smile, for a *lady*. But it happened most frequently now with my baby sitters, the very ones who honored me with their confidence, for they addressed me in precisely the same appreciative tone I recognized as the one I had always used on my Aunt Louise. It was a tone that turned me into a special case, making me sexless, avuncular, obsolete—and why? For no better reason than that I had preceded them to New York by a number of years and decided to have a family.

"Listen, Mrs. Thompson," said my caller at last, as I continued to stare at him, "maybe this is a bad time?"

Mrs. Thompson—the two words in the entire language that could most efficiently bring down on me the dread matronly persona.

And then, looking suddenly puzzled, my visitor cocked his head, shuffled his feet, hesitated for one precious moment, and asked, clearly embarrassed, "Uh, you are the mother, aren't you?"

A shiver of gratitude passed through me, a shiver of lust, such as Aunt Louise, I was sure, could never have felt—followed on the instant by profound embarrassment. How unseemly was lust in a mother! Even in my single days when lust had been acceptable I'd always tried to control it; directed toward a sitter, someone younger and free, it was pitiful. Yet there it was: the first lust I'd dared acknowledge since I'd married and renounced it, lust brought on by the irresistible blend of black beard, book, and that precious moment of doubt before he asked if I were "the mother."

"No, it's a fine time. Come on in."

I said it quickly, praying nothing would show. Unnerved by my own feelings, I began the breathless, enthusiastic chatter with which I'd learned to disguise the unacceptable among them. "I hope you don't mind. I was about to feed the children. But if you'd care to wait—?" Fighting back the resident matron by smiling too widely, talking too fast. But no matter what tricks I employed to preserve a semblance of worldliness—my valid passport, Village residence, peace buttons, boutique attempts, occasional free-lance jobs—I was precisely, as the new sitter so bluntly put it, "the mother."

"Sure," he said with the calm of the childless, "take your time. I'm in no hurry."

I led him down the hall past the bickering children in the kitchen, into the living room. Painfully aware of Ricky's art on the walls, Sammy's wooden trains all over the floor, my disarray, baby clutter, I took him without pause straight toward the sanctified window with the view over the rooftops into Washington Square—my one visible achievement besides the children for my years in New York. Near the window on the wall were peace posters, Che's message of love, my gilded Z, clippings that mattered, a picture of Moore, and in a secret place, like the chains of a saint, the photo of Morrison aflame.

Back when we'd first moved in, just before Sammy was born, Ricky and I had had time to drink our morning coffee here, watching the early morning dog walkers and the changing styles. Then, I had covered this window table with a pretty cloth and arranged it with two chairs—our private cafe. But soon the children came and we no longer had time to sit and enjoy the view. Responsibly we'd had protective bars installed on every window, including this one, to forestall disaster. Ricky began to stay later and later at his office; my days merged in a blur of chores highlighted only by crises; time alone together became as rare a luxury as passion. Still, somehow, long after good sense dictated a move to the suburbs, I managed to remain in this place, dragging strollers and shopping carts up and down, holding on. Despite the bars, I built a little shrine to my hopes around this window. I piled the table with reminders: a bowl of buttons, an overflowing ashtray, a tiny vial of black Tahitian sand. No matter how baby-littered or Ricky-chic the rest of our place, no matter what music Ricky played on the stereo or who might be crying in the nursery, in this spot I kept alive my old hopes that some day, if it wasn't too late, I might still do something that mattered.

Now, as this newest sitter eased himself into Ricky's chair, his fur-trimmed face fitting so well into the window picture, I was again beset by my ruling contradiction. Though I might fool the neighbors and the PTA into thinking me one of the new people, no range of posters or buttons or desires could change the fact that I was really a late fifties Villager, early sixties at best, still hooked on Bach, self-improvement, and civil liberties, whose development had been diverted some years back; whereas this shaggy young man in my living room, like most of the others who answered my annual ad in the *Voice* for Baby sitter to care for 3 preschoolers 2 pms a wk, occasional eves, Wash. Sq., call after 7, was one of a new enigmatic breed who had taken over the park and the Village with obvious designs on the world. Though he had the look of the bearded boys of MacDougal Street which never failed to arouse me, we really belonged to different, unbridgeable generations; he was a new type.

Outside the window comrades cavorted like puppies suddenly released from their leashes. Perfect Sunday, '67: Vietnam Summer and Summer of Love: even the reactionary press was predicting a turnout for today's march in the tens of thousands. Through the window you could practically see the vibrations on the air as the pageant of stark militants, gossamer hippies, assorted park people, and police spilled over the paths onto the grass. Demonstrators were assembling around the fountain and performers doing their acts. All there—framed in my window. Not even the Parks Department prohibitions could interfere any more. The grass and the very trees had been liberated along with imagination and spirit. Only a week before a riot had barely been averted when an innocent hippie who had climbed a tree in pursuit of his pet squirrel had been prodded down with hoses and poles by a bitter Fire Department gone berserk. Martyring that hippie, sending him plunging through the air into a net below in which they had tied him up and carried him off while the crowds looked on, had been the last desperate act of defeated officials before yielding the park to "the people." Now, as dogs bounded and frisbees flew, as flower children distributed daisies and demonstrators distributed leaflets, as the rich music of bongos and guitars set the undertone of sex and excitement, even a spectator could feel the summer rising to some unprecedented climax.

"Take off your jacket," I invited, looking beyond him to the park. I pretended it was my park too, my community. But membership from behind a window or a stroller didn't really count. This bearded newcomer could probably walk through the park more comfortably than I, who'd lived here for nearly a decade.

Below the window several plainclothesmen, wearing berets, goatees, and turtlenecks, lounged against the railing that had once been dubbed the Meat Rack for the cruising gays who formerly gathered there. Perhaps the very police who, in clean-up squads, had hounded the gays out of the park west to Christopher Street, now munched sandwiches and sipped soda like civilians, evidently snatching a final bite before infiltrating the demonstration.

"You can watch the festivities while I go finish up with the children. Use the binoculars if you like. Do you want some coffee or maybe tea? I have rosehips I picked last summer—they make a wonderful tea," I offered, going into my hospitality act.

"Sure. I'll try some," he said, "thanks." And taking the binoculars I held out to him, he turned to the window.

"Hey," he said and whistled low. "This is some view." He adjusted the lenses and lapsed into a silence that excluded me.

"See those men leaning against the fence?" I said, insinuating myself into his view with conversation. "They're police. This is where they meet. They wear little red buttons and drive up in their patrol cars, and sometimes they have a snack right there in plain view. One of these days," I said, "I'm going to take their pictures and post mug shots of them in the Peace Center. With Wanted captions reciting their long records. Larceny. Illegal entry. Perjury. Assault."

He turned to me and raised one eyebrow, giving me the interested look I craved, the look that clearly recognized me as not your ordinary mama. I might have been encouraged by the look if I hadn't known from experience that the more exceptional my sitters found me, the more surely I would wind up feeling like my matronly aunt. It was no use: whether I evinced in them the deference due an employer or the interest I desired, my situation insured that I would remain elevated and avuncular.

"By the way," I said, as though years of experience could be reversed by a moment's desire. "My name's Zane." (Dodging the matronly Thompson.) "What's yours?"

"Victor Levinson."

"Victor Levinson! Oh! Bonnie's talked about you. Aren't you a singer?"

He nodded modestly.

Bonnie had talked about him at length. He wrote songs for the revolution. Now, having him here in my living room, knowing more about him than he knew about me, knowing that because of his moment's doubt something sexual had stirred in me, I felt increasingly awkward, agitated. "I won't be long," I said and hurried off to the kitchen.

The children had been playing with water. My fault. I wiped up the mess, then guided them back to their food and sat down before the high chair to feed Julie.

Spooning food into my baby's mouth, I knew that no love affair ever provided a solution, that no man would waltz you into the passions and actions of your time. That much I'd learned in my beatnik days when, sleeping around to distinguish ourselves from the straight uptown types we were otherwise fated to become, we wound up feeling all the more excluded. This was one of the reasons I'd always disdained adultery. It was for the muddled, the weak-willed, the desperate, or the drifters. At best it was a diversion that not only solved nothing but created dangerous risks for a mother-of-three without independent means. As I held out plump yellow kernels of corn to Julie, urging, "One more spoonful?" I reviewed all the good reasons I'd had for renouncing MacDougal Street.

Julie shook her head adamantly, tightly closing eyes, lips, mind: total yes, total no. And as I kept an eye on how much chocolate Tina poured into her milk and how dangerously Sammy teetered on one leg of his chair, I saw how inappropriate in a mother was lust, how it could only make me more ridiculous. Though I was now as lonely as any wife with three small kids and a driven husband, dignity demanded acceptance. I'd already wandered too deep into my woods, each step the consequence of a consequence, to find my way out and begin again. Only once, when Ricky had betrayed certain classic signs (acting moody, listening to Schubert like someone in love) threatening to render this marriage, which I had entered for its permanence, quite as ephemeral as any, did I even think of adultery. Imagined and rejected. For though I'd once been adept at seduction, I'd been out of practice for years.

Julie dribbled corn on the floor, smeared her bib in her plate, and was done. When Sammy and Tina had finished too; when I'd put Julie in her crib and bribed the others to be good with soap bubbles (a rare treat which, if I set it up right, might keep them both occupied for up to half an hour); I somehow forgot everything I knew. For not only did I wash my face and brush my hair, but, carrying two steaming cups of rosehip tea to the living room, I summoned all the charm and confidence I could muster to guide me through the interview.

Victor Levinson was an on-and-off student at the New School: on when he had saved enough money, off when he was broke; a regular at the Free University; a musician; a dreamer. Though he'd have liked to join the guerrillas in Peru, he scraped by on occasional gigs in the bars and coffee houses and on odd jobs like mine. Six years my junior, he was marked clearly by that shaggy hair as part of the new generation, as I was marked by my children as part of the old.

No, he had never done baby sitting before. He was applying for this job because his friend Bonnie, who was leaving New York for the summer, had told him it would be perfect for him.

"Oh, really? What did she say?" I asked. I looked out the window and tried to sound offhand, though my pulse quickened.

"She said she likes the kids and"—he hesitated, embarrassed like me—"that you're a fine person to work for."

A second-hand remark but a first-rate opening, one I could treasure and use. A fine person to work for. Would Victor think so too? I had no doubt I would hire him, inexperience or no. You couldn't let one of the new people who was well disposed toward you, who carried Morgan Moore's book, who played the harmonica and wore a full black beard, walk out of your life for lack of experience.

In Victor I saw both the person I had been and the one I wanted to be. I wanted to draw him out, let him know me. There were gaps in my life (like every woman's) that needed to be filled and a story in him to pursue. He was hinting about his childhood, about a secret, about a trip to Cuba. And what of the silences in which he clothed himself, the gentle manner? Did they hide contradictions and implications? Nearly a decade had passed since I'd come to New York, the beats had vanished into history in a puff of lore till they were as quaint and dated as flappers. I had tried to adapt to the changes, but they were too swift. "Anyway," I offered, "the hours are flexible. And there's usually a good show on outside."

Now the fence was deserted; the demonstrators were obeying a bullhorn as up through the open window drifted this year's slogans, enveloping us in an aura of community. I watched Victor sip his tea like someone who lives on cheese sandwiches and Coke and seldom stops to sit before a window, and I tried to make the most of his appreciation.

"Mama?"

My name. I turned guiltily to see Sammy standing at the entrance to the living room staring up at Victor. Down the hall came Tina, trailing her brother. The game was up now. Whatever effect I had managed to create, the mother would take over—and so much for Victor's appreciation.

Sammy stared at the beard. "Did you close up the bubble water jar?" I asked in my mother-voice.

Sammy nodded without moving his eyes. Though beards were now all over the neighborhood, they seldom came into our living room.

I lifted Tina to my lap before she could begin to fuss, took Sammy's hand, and made the introductions.

Victor improvised a greeting by running his harmonica playfully along his lips. Timid Tina, unsure of its meaning, threatened to cry, and Sammy (who, though older, could also have gone either way) wandered across the room to his trains—good, I noted with relief, for half an hour at least.

"They really do like music," I said, apologizing for them. But it was useless to try to distinguish myself from them in order to escape the embarrassment of motherhood before the childless.

Victor pocketed the harmonica with an unconcern that easily divided the whole world into matters worth discussing and all others, shrugged, and said: "No sweat."

The rest of the interview was matter-of-fact: rates, schedules, favorite children's books, emergency procedures—anything to cover up my now intrusive awareness, oppressive as steam heat in winter, that I was a woman facing him, a man.

Tina had begun climbing onto my lap and down again, up and down, pulling at my hair and my shirt, pointing up the absurdity of my position. "Please stop, Tina!" I said, stifling my irritation. And in one last futile effort to seem other than "the mother" I indicated the red volume that lay neglected on the table, Moore's book. "If you like Morgan Moore, I'm probably one of the few people in the world with her complete works," I offered.

"You've read this?" he asked—taken once more by surprise.

"Oh yes. I've read every word of Moore's. I've followed her from the beginning, when she was doing chess columns for the *Voice*. That's a picture of her over there."

He looked at my strangely decorated wall and back at me until it was there again: that puzzled baby-sitter look, the look of perplexity I got sooner or later from every one of them. From this reader of Moore no less than the others who'd worked for me over the years—ambitious unemployed actress from Pittsburgh, undergrad from Long Island, revolutionary from the Bronx, hippies from Newark and Durham and Brooklyn, folk singer from the East Village. A look that choked and reduced me; a look that simply could not reconcile this mother-hostess-homemaker (babies crawling over her feet, simple sentences, detailed schedules and lists of neighbors, doctors, and the indispensable twenty-four-hour Poison Control Center to call in case of emergency) with my taste and Zanity. Perhaps Victor could accept my posters and even my window, knowing there'd been an older Left before the new, a bohemia before the counterculture. But a housewife's devotion to a guru of his sect—this he could not understand.

The more I revealed the more incredulous he grew, like every sitter before him. And though their incredulity was always tinged with admiration, it was not the admiration of peer for peer. Rather, it was the admiration of the unattached young for that rarity among adults, the older, sensitive, married woman. I knew it well—it was the same admiration I'd once so callously showered on my aunt. "Mrs. Thompson, if you have a little time I'd really like to talk to you," sitter after sitter had said in those cruelly familiar tones. And even in my own measured responses—concerned exclamations with knitted brow, supportive promises to help, gentle reassurances, pats on the hand—I was shocked to recognize the very gestures, even the voice, my aunt had used with me.

Too soon! It was as if Louise's aging, generous, but sexless soul had been lurking inside me all along, just waiting for a chance to take over. She was fifty at least and wasting away, while I was not yet thirty! But children made up for many years.

"Victor has to go now, Tina, so let him have his shoes," I said, hoping to end the interview without sacrificing all dignity. Whatever had made him wonder, if only for an instant, if I were "the mother" was now irrevocably buried under the palpable, inescapable presence of my large-eyed, velvet-skinned, infinitely precious children without whom my life was as inconceivable as was theirs without me.

"Sammy, say goodbye to Victor. He's going to sit for you some time."

"Bye," said Sammy without looking up from the elaborate construction of tracks he'd managed to build directly across the passage to the hall.

We stepped over them. "He's very easy to take care of," I confided. "Once he gets interested in something, your only problem is getting him to leave it."

"I don't think I'll have any trouble, Mrs. Thompson. They seem like nice enough kids."

I helped him on with his jacket, conscious of new unsummoned feelings when my fingers touched his shoulder.

Tina opened the door and pushed him out.

"I'll telephone you," I called after.

But because life was dashing by so quickly and I was not, really not, the person my sitters took me for, when Victor was halfway down the first flight of stairs I rushed to the banister and forced myself to yell after him: "Oh, Victor? You don't have to call me Mrs. Thompson. You can call me Zane."

8 · THE JUNK

I don't know how I heard about the junk in the East River (a junk! from China!), but with the first rumors my childhood longings bubbled up again.

Naturally, in a waterfront town like New York City, most people were blasé about strange vessels, having seen quite a variety. Not like landlocked Babylon, where everyone had to await the completion of the St. Lawrence Seaway to know the strut of a drunken sailor. New Yorkers had seen replicas of the *Niña*, the *Pinta*, and the *Santa Maria;* the pleasure launches of the Eastern rich; the wrecks of a variety of tankers; the *Andrea Doria;* that Norwegian fishing boat to which a desperate Russian defector had leaped in vain; and the yacht of some Persian shah who had marched his entire entourage of veiled concubines and turbaned eunuchs across Forty-second Street. Most of those nautical visitors had attracted only seamen and inveterate boat-buffs to the piers.

But when the Chinese junk appeared sporting those three red sails, not even jaded New Yorkers (who took the Staten Island Ferry solely to avoid the heat, who left seaside Battery Park empty on all but the sunniest Sundays, and would as soon take their children to the model sailboat pond of Central Park as attend the live exhibits on the swarming Manhattan rivers)—not even they could take-or-leave the mysterious wooden vessel that began making its way up the East River from the harbor toward Harlem. There it was, a dark silhouette obliterating Welfare Island, blocking out with its red sails (yes, red!) the Fifty-ninth Street Bridge; and as it advanced northward toward City Island, the word spread through the city.

It was definitely the thing to know. "Have you heard about the junk in the river?" "The junk?" "A slow boat from China." Like the legendary hurricane of '60 that drove straws through two concrete buildings on Fifty-seventh Street, like the snowstorm of '61, the blackout of '65, and the transit strike of '66, that Chinese ship in our midst brought out the best in us. "Are you taking the kids to see the junk?" park mothers asked, and People's Radio gave it half an hour live.

As usual, I was among the last to go. Reluctant to accept that I was one of them, I avoided doing exactly what other parents did. I felt no need to give my children ball games, circuses, TV, war toys, candy, or anything nationally advertised. Their Halloween costumes were handmade, their invitations painstakingly handlettered. A boat in a river seemed perfectly dispensable. But after the *Times* ran a large photo of that now historic silhouette in the Sunday paper (drawing hundreds of kids and their daddies from midtown to the river that afternoon) I remembered something precious from long before, something leaped inside me, and I decided to bus across town to the river "for the children's sake."

There it was, splendid and dark against the sky. Around it lesser vessels buzzed and chugged, trying to get a close look or a touch as devotees follow the stars, while the stately junk, its red sails spread on bamboo ribs like Chinese fans, bowed graciously up and down the waves.

A sudden gust of wind off the river filled the tapered sails that rose up three mahogany masts. "Look!" said Sammy. And I thought how lucky for me that Ricky was away or he might have done the honors like half the other dads in town—and then I might not have remembered my Chinese dream.

Across the flat prow a sea serpent leaped while on the bow a large painted eye looked out at us and the river. As I stared back into that eye, it seemed that once again I was looking down into the deep pit of my aspirations, so long before forgotten.

"See the dragon," said Tina, sighting the serpent. I wanted to explain, but the children were too young to understand what a rare thing was a Chinese junk in New York waters. What lies west of Ninth Avenue to a native of Gotham? Too bad—my city-bred children could never undertake such a project as my dig, for where was there earth for them to dig in?

All the same, that night at bedtime instead of reading them their usual fare, I tried to tell them about my tunnel through the earth, and Marco Polo who took back word to Italy of great sailing vessels with room for fifty merchants in separate cabins and three tall sails spread on bamboo battens like the very ones we saw, and the terrifying dogs with eyes as big as saucers who guarded vast treasures unknown to us.

9 · THE COOL LADY

Victor did stop calling me Mrs. Thompson—at least that was something; but he never would call me Zane. Each time he came to sit, there was that strained moment of greeting when sex and some unspoken longing hung in the air, but no one broke the formality. I called him Victor and he, insuring my decorum, called me nothing at all.

Even when we began to talk about intimate matters (the fourth time he sat, about par for my sitters), he used no name for me. "I wanted to ask your advice about something," he said one Saturday night while I was figuring out what I owed him and Ricky was parking the car. "I know it's no good tonight, but do you suppose I could stop by some afternoon next week?"

I looked at him sharply. This was the very line I'd given him in one of several recurring fantasies.

Ricky was due to be away Thursday and Friday. I suggested Victor come "toward the end of the week."

The week dragged by. What could he want? I considered every possibility, no longer pretending to fight my preoccupation, no longer maintaining it was inspired by Ricky's interest in Schubert. Maybe he simply wanted to enlist me in a cause or discuss a personal problem. What if it were something about the children? Maybe he needed an employer's recommendation or wanted to borrow some money. Over the years my sitters had spoken to me about each of those things, and I had always been obliging. I found them shrinks and lawyers, got them passports and abortions; I wrote letters for their teachers and went bail for their boyfriends; I lent them our place for meetings, readings, couplings, even weddings. (Our most splendid party was the wedding of one of my favorite sitters, performed right there in our living room. The groom's friends did the music on guitars, Father Percy of the Peace Church made the sermon, the bride wore white, and since it was a warm night in June we threw open the windows and drank toasts to every passerby—a gesture preserved in a *Voice* column the following week by an astute reporter with an eye for local color.) Or maybe he wanted what I wanted.

Victor came at 5:30 on Thursday—my kitchen hour. Naturally I offered him dinner. Like any undernourished student, he was happy for the chance at a home-cooked meal, as I, too long the nanny at dinner time, coveted a meal accompanied by adult conversation.

(Dinner with Ricky hardly counted. Whenever he was home in time for dinner I wanted us to eat as a family, which limited conversation. And when he came home after the children were in bed, even if we hadn't both been too exhausted to scintillate, we would have sat together in silence. Our preoccupations no longer overlapped, our differences had long since slipped into taboos in the interests of peace—such is the trade-off of marriage. As for our occasional smiling dinners with other couples, conversation was chit-chat or shop talk, predictable and polite: I preferred the conversation of our children.)

I fed the children in the kitchen. Victor helped. With shameless promises I got them to go to bed a little early. Then Victor and I piled our plates with food and carried them to the window table.

In that setting, backed by a parkful of freaks, I battled the matron down and helped the lover to emerge. To inspire trust, I confided tantalizing moments of my past, however vulnerable it left me; to gain Victor's confidence I listened to him as intently as my aunt had listened to me, trying to figure out what he really wanted. And gradually the red lips inside the black beard told me where he had grown up, how he'd managed to get to Cuba, what he hoped to accomplish when the revolution came; I got him to sing me his songs and look me straight in the eye until we seemed ready to dish up our pasts to each other like new lovers.

He ate avidly, accepting seconds and thirds. Unlike the children he even praised the salad dressing and at dessert lapped up the last drop of pudding (tapioca: Sammy's favorite). It was such a pleasure to be talking to someone unjaded about the future, uncynical about the movement, someone appreciative and fresh, that I barely remembered to eat. I wondered sometimes what it was he had come to discuss, but I wouldn't risk spoiling a perfect meal by asking.

After coffee, over a snifter of Ricky's cognac, Victor pulled a neatly rolled joint out of his shirt pocket, fingered it tentatively, and asked, "Like to smoke?"

A gift of trust. I hadn't smoked pot ("grass," he called it—all the words had changed since I'd had my babies) in half a decade. I hadn't stopped by design; it was just that my sources had disappeared. Ricky was a beer and brandy person; the children had come—

"I'd love it," I said, already forgetting that no man could fix your life.

We left the dishes near the window and moved back inside the room. Easy chairs and dimmer light. Victor licked the end of the joint, lit up, took a long, deep drag, and handed it to me across the table between us.

We smoked a long time, it seemed, looking past each other

from opposite chairs. When my bitten stubs of fingers made it impossible for me to take the joint from him again, he leaned toward me across the table and held it between his nails to my lips. My lips grazed his hand, but he didn't pull away.

"Wasn't there something you wanted to tell me?" I asked in my mellowed state.

Dope was a truly wonderful thing. With what appreciation I watched him lean his fine head against the back of the chair; with what pleasure I saw his red lips gyrate slowly inside his black beard as, from a seemingly great distance, he began to speak.

Intervals as long as songs passed between his words and my comprehension; it took a great effort to hear him. I was too moved to think. Something about a woman? Something about love? He spoke so slowly that I couldn't remember the beginning of his sentences by the time they reached their end. But I tried to be encouraging anyway. "Go on," I heard myself say repeatedly; "yes, yes." His lips were all but disembodied, issuing a staccato of "like" and "you know." The form of the words escaping from his mouth was so alluring that I could barely reach the meaning.

But meaning slipped through all the same; for abruptly I was aware of a nagging pain at the back of my eyes that wasn't the marijuana. And as it spread to my limbs and into my throat, I heard the reassuring voice of my Aunt Louise comforting me, as she always had whenever I'd gone to her for help. Only now it was Victor she was comforting—every time I opened my mouth.

How had she got here? I wondered. I couldn't figure it out. I only thought: what a pity.

"I don't know what to do," Victor was saying as I strained to understand him. "Like, she said she'd live with me after the summer, but then I got this letter."

The pain had turned to sadness that made me want to cry.

He leaned forward, speaking with urgency. "Tell me, please, what do you think I should do?"

The words were coming out so slowly now I couldn't follow them. Bleeding together like cheap dye they obscured all pattern until they hardly made any sense. "One reason I'm asking you," he continued, "I hope you don't mind, is that Bonnie admires you. To her you're one cool lady."

Cool lady. Was that a compliment? Given all the other things she might have called me, I supposed it was. All the same, the revelation stung me, declaring me smart—perhaps even wise—but sexless.

"I don't mind. Why should I mind?" I said—and remembered how, even as they eagerly solicited my help, the girls I hired always lowered their eyes chastely (as though my having borne children insured that I could know nothing of the torments of love or sex); and the boys (for though they might be nearing my age, they were footloose and still boys) watched their language when they spoke to me. Whether I was a mentor to college girls, confidante to lovers, Samaritan to runaways, or benefactor to hippies, I could not stem my growing resemblance to my Aunt Louise. A wonderful woman—the very one I had taken for my own mentor (and perhaps similarly reduced to fossil, taking so freely and giving nothing back); but sexless, selfless, matronly.

Victor was waiting for an answer, quizzical eyes filled with trust, lips pursed expectantly inside his woolly beard. And suddenly I was flooded with shame for having hired a bearded flatterer ("you are the mother, aren't you?") with no experience in the vain hope that by stirring my passion he might save me from the unbearable prospect of becoming my aunt. I had gambled once on a savior and lost—because no matter how loving your mate or how decent your marriage, no one could save you. In some ways a good husband made it worse—making all your discontents betrayals. And betrayed, even the best of husbands could leave you flat with three small children, no job, and no prospects—and then where was your salvation?

My mistake, I decided, had been to think that an act of will, even so extreme an act as renouncing rebellion by having Ricky's children, could extinguish my desires. I had thought that if you started out your marriage with anything less than absolute commitment, you'd be setting yourself up for an ugly divorce that would probably overtake you when you'd be least equipped to handle it; if you were to marry at all you had to go all the way. Part of me had foreseen everything, had even wavered. But sensing that too often hedging simply ends in a botched job, changing a swan dive into a belly slam, I had finally renounced my Zanity and plunged. And now I had to admit that after everything, I was still perfectly vulnerable! I had accepted the limitations of married life in exchange for its satisfactions, and still a black beard on a free spirit could move me; still a disenchanted husband could frighten me; still an unjust world could accuse me.

I looked at that face now filled with pain over a young woman I'd employed, a face that recalled my subversive desires but reflected all the differences between us, and as he poured out his anguish, I realized what folly it would be to ask him to sit again.

Half an hour later I tactfully indicated I was growing tired. At the door Victor clutched my hands, looked deep into my eyes, and thanked me. I smiled my matronly smile.

I washed the dishes from our perfect meal and then, still slightly stoned, sat for a long time at the window watching the endless procession of changes in the park, the restless movement of the night.

10 · THE REAL MOORE

For quite a while Morgan Moore had been living with me rather comfortably in one of the larger rooms of my mind where we frequently discussed politics and culture in the mornings and more personal matters at night. Since her public star had risen, I had followed it zealously, in print and out. When she sponsored a rally, I attended; when she praised a book, I read it; when she defended a position, I embraced it. (Later I learned that all over the country there were dozens of others like me quoting from her treatises, tacking her picture on their walls, taking solemn oaths in her name. But at that time I still considered her my own private discovery.) Since, however, our peculiar relationship had for years been uninhibited by reality, I was thrown into confusion when I saw the real Moore emerge from a small yellow brick building two blocks from my own, carrying a bundle of laundry under one arm and a fat briefcase under the other.

She was the last person in the world I expected to see at that moment. It was early morning—halfway through that precious daily hour after I'd dropped Tina at nursery school and could at last give myself entirely to Julie. An hour I steadfastly reserved for the two of us, not only in pursuit of my Utopian dream of making every child of mine as strong as a firstborn, but for the lovely feel of it.

We had stopped at the edge of the park to watch a black

squirrel scamper up and down a tree (how it thrilled me to see Julie's green eyes grow huge and her tiny hands clench and unclench with excitement as we watched another of the amazing antics of this surprising world); and after the treasured squirrel had disappeared, leaving the child bereft, I had lifted her out of her stroller and offered to console her with hide-and-seek, her favorite game. Her unabashed delight each time I found her in her hiding place, the irrepressible giggle, quite obliterated the embarrassment I felt as a grown woman indulging in such a game.

Then suddenly, while I was waiting for Julie to hide a second time, my back to the park, my gaze across the street, there was Morgan Moore emerging from the yellow building with her laundry, embodying all my suspended hopes.

I was jolted by the sheer reality of her—no mental image, no speaker on a platform or disembodied word in a book as she'd become through the years, but a woman again—still unexpectedly tall, rosy-fleshed, dressed in ordinary Village clothes like mine (black pants, a peacoat, garments that had been tried on and purchased in a store), now walking unswervingly toward us.

A briefcase could mean anything; the laundry could only mean that she lived there!

Instead of searching for Julie, I abruptly ended our game and frantically ordered her into the stroller.

"No, Mama," she cried. "Find me!"

I had no time to reason. Instead, I grabbed my baby and strapped her into the stroller as the great tears began to roll.

Moore walked toward us. Julie, resorting to her most effective bid for control, demanded between sobs to be taken to the toilet.

I stood paralyzed, unable in that instant to choose between proceeding with the imperfect life I had accepted and . . . shooting the moon.

Julie clutched the handle of the stroller in her fists and shook it. With all the power she could push through her miniature lungs she screamed, full of my betrayal. But her screams only summoned up in me forbidden thoughts, murderous thoughts—like the first time you give your body without desire, the first time you slap your child, the first time you deceive your spouse. I wanted to overthrow my confining life.

"Mama, Mama, Mama," cried Julie.

"Stop, Julie!" I hissed through my teeth.

Moore had turned toward Sheridan Square and was receding from us now, walking purposefully away, her red hair spread out on her shoulders. In a moment she would turn the corner.

What did I want? If I followed her now, after I had chosen my course and made my compromises, after dropping my pose and having my babies, now when I had given myself to Julie, it would be not out of caprice or curiosity as it might have been in the past but from some absolutely irresistible need.

"Ma-ma-ma-ma," chanted Julie.

I spun the stroller around. Wishing to kill my baby. With one hand I squeezed her shoulder and with the other I pushed the stroller down the block, racing after Moore.

Moore proceeded to the Sheridan Square Launderette, where she disappeared down four short steps.

I waited at the curb, bending over Julie with wild threats to keep her quiet, trying to make myself invisible until Moore reappeared. A moment later she emerged without the bundle and proceeded toward the subway.

When her back was to us I started after her. At the corner she stopped at the newsstand for a paper, then descended the stairs into the station where I couldn't pursue her. I watched till the last strand of red hair had disappeared.

There was nothing I could do for Julie now. I had taken away her game and hurt her for no apparent reason, and now it was too late for the potty. I had wrecked her morning with betrayals as I would probably wreck her life—giving in to my impossible fantasies.

"I'm sorry. I'm so sorry, baby," I tried to tell her, sick with contrition. Against my principles I bought her a candy bar at Sheridan Square. But it was useless to pretend that today's guilt and resolutions could overcome tomorrow's desires.

Moore now lived two blocks from me, I was sure of it; a disturbing fact if you believed in destiny, or even just luck. From then on, each morning I awoke thinking of her opening her eyes down the street and beginning her day, and of my own still unfinished possibilities.

I have an image of myself from those nursery school days—lurking in doorways, waiting on street corners for Moore to appear. Like every Village screwball, I was powered by a private fire that produced a wild light in the eye. I could be distinguished from the others chiefly by the stroller I always walked behind; otherwise I was as driven as the desperate old man who begged from children on the library steps, or the poem peddler wrapped in furs, or the shopping-bag woman delivering her endlessly sad, incomprehensible sermon.

Call it crazy; Ricky certainly would have if he knew. But now when I stretched in the morning I felt I was reaching for something.

11 · DEE-DEE

I was working at the sewing machine again when the phone rang.

Having failed with satchels, aprons, and ponchos, this time I was trying my luck with tunics, as long as Ricky, caught up in an important case, was working late. The children, supper completed and bedtime approaching, played contentedly at my feet with sewing scraps.

Sewing was something of a soporific to me. Once the designs were worked out and I had only to sew the seams, I could let my mind drift along in fantasy, warmed by the hum of the machine's motor. So when I heard the voice of my old high school friend Dee-Dee Larson, in town with her husband on business wondering if we could all have dinner together, I was momentarily perplexed.

I hadn't seen Dee-Dee since my wedding. The various lives I'd led overlapped so seldom it was always a shock to find them juxtaposed. Sometimes Mama wrote me news of my childhood friends —who had married whom, who was working where—and I imagined them unchanged except that now they lived in new houses a little farther out and concealed their foul language and sexual transgressions from their children instead of, as formerly, from their parents. Now, hearing Dee-Dee's broad Babylon A's in fast-talking New York City, A's that had once been my own but had come to sound positively foreign, I felt myself torn by the contradictions.

"I'm dying to see you, Zane. I've thought of you so many times. I always wondered what happened to you."

A good question. What would she think of me if she knew? My life was rather different from what I'd intended.

My first impulse was to hide. But realizing what it meant to be a Hoosier visiting New York, I knew I could probably get Dee-Dee to believe of me what I chose.

"I'd love to have dinner with you, Dee-Dee. I'm afraid my husband won't be able to make it, but if I can find a sitter on such short notice I'll come myself. Maybe I'll take you and your husband around the Village. Would you like that?"

"Oh," she squealed, "I'd love that, Zane. We'll go wherever you say—but it's on us."

I looked at my watch, then around the room. A lot to do, but—

"Okay," I said, "why don't you pick me up here?" I gave her my address. "If I can't get a sitter we'll send out for some Chinese food."

"A sitter? I just can't picture you with kids, Zane. You of all people!"

It was always painful to face my Babylon image since things had turned out so differently. If Dee-Dee had seen me the next moment—hair disheveled, nerves on edge, piling children's tunics on a sewing machine, frantically straightening up the mess—she would never have connected me with my racy past. Surely anyone who saw me feeding the children in the kitchen would doubt that such an obviously devoted mother ("Perhaps a trifle too devoted?" my own mama once suggested. "Nonsense," replied Daddy. "You know Zane never could do anything with moderation"—and both agreed that devotion was better than neglect) had ever made herself ridiculous as a youth taking unbending stands on basic questions; had been the youngest customer of Babylon's Movie Palace ever to walk out of a Saturday matinee on principle; or had spent her senior year in high school dressed as a boy—not because of any deviant tendencies, but because if you wanted to take a public stand back then, clothes were the way and boys' clothes meant business! Now, like so many, I was a hard-working mother trying to make ends meet.

After contacting a sitter, I showered in a rush and picked up most of the toys, careful to leave whatever underground papers and left-wing leaflets I could find in a conspicuous place on the coffee table. If only my image didn't matter. But if it weren't for my image, which alone I was able to manipulate, I would have had nothing in the world to distinguish me.

"My god, Zane! Look at you!" said Dee-Dee when they showed

up at the door in their travel suits. With a potent mixture of fear and envy they looked at my long hair and Village clothes, outlandish for Babylon; they spoke to my pale precocious children; they observed Ricky's pictures on the walls, Veronica my hippest baby sitter, and the view from my window; and with relief I could see that I hadn't let them down. I was still an adventure to know; they could go home and describe me to their credit.

(There were hippies everywhere by now, even a colony in Middletown, but the Village was still, would always be, Sin City.)

"What kind of food would you like?" I asked. "Italian? French? American? Chinese?"

After the first shocking instant Dee-Dee looked the same as always—same smile, stance, even the same old hair-do. Her husband, Douglas, though only four years older than us ("Didn't you know Doug? He graduated from High a year before we entered," said Dee-Dee), looked to me like a plump, middle-aged Midwestern businessman.

"I love them all, but Doug likes Italian," said Dee-Dee.

"Perfect. The Village is really an old Italian neighborhood; there are lots of good places." Slipping on my wildest poncho, the one with the peace dove for a clasp ("You like it, really? I made it myself. Yes, I used to sell them to some of the local boutiques") and adjusting my Mexican bag on my shoulder, I led my eager visitors out the door.

"I'm surprised to hear the Village is Italian. I thought it was the place artists live," said Doug, looking apprehensively across the street to the noisy park.

"And rebels," added Dee-Dee.

They were going to be the perfect visitors. I decided on one of the older Italian restaurants, a place a few blocks away where old men played bocci in the back and wine bottles decorated the walls. But to get there I led them on a long, indirect route through the throbbing park and the most enticing shopping streets.

My Village. Playing it up for the Hoosiers was like flirting: a tourniquet for loneliness, temporary first-aid for the bleeding ego.

It was a fine evening—a restless frenetic Friday. It seemed everyone was out. En route to the restaurant we passed half the poseurs of the neighborhood. The blind clarinetist competed for dimes with an upstart woodwind trio on Eighth Street, the proud Cavalier in plumed hat and velvet breeches paraded up Sixth Avenue stroking his waxed mustache; a dog walker with eight on leashes stood like a maypole under the arch where a shopping-bag woman laughed at the strutting dandies and the proselytizing prophets circling the fountain. "Who's that?" asked Dee-Dee, her eyes popping; "who's that?"—like a toddler first learning the names of things.

As Wolfe had once named everyone for me, I proudly named them all for the Hoosiers: "That's Tiger Rag, that's Moondog the poet, that's the Sartorian"—and explained about the shopping-bag women lurking in doorways laughing or crying, and the porn peddler, and the woman writing an endless novel in that second-floor window, and all the rest. As though the ability to name them somehow conferred their magic on me.

Doug was intimidated. "Do you walk alone at night? You're not worried about your children?" But Dee-Dee was impressed. "I always said, Zane, if anyone got out of Babylon it'd be you. I bet you fit right in here, don't you?"

For the moment I was happy not to disappoint her. The pose was easy enough to pull off. All it took was the right clothes and the right line in order to seem to fit right in; no visitor could tell the difference. By the time we reached the restaurant I'd accepted six leaflets, signed two petitions, and given change to half a dozen panhandlers (after all, those were the sixties).

Still, I knew I was a fraud. It was the same every day. I was inundated with leaflets on my way to and from the playground. I took them, considered their messages, attended those rallies that didn't interfere with nap time, signed every petition, cared; but the ebullient life around me only intensified my isolation. The children woke at six, the police rounded up the bench sleepers in the park as I watched from the window with my coffee, Ricky went off to work, the Captain who lived next door did his morning exercises, I made my daily resolutions, the blind clarinetist tapped his way toward Eighth Street stopping to look both ways before stepping off the curb, while I readied the laundry for the machines in the basement, took Sammy to school, made the shopping list, and ran my sewing machine—but I was hardly more involved in the ferment around me than any Babylon housewife. An acute observer of all that went on, I sensed all the more acutely what

I missed and knew that everything would have proceeded exactly the same if I had noticed nothing at all.

We took a table in the back, near the bocci court, and examined the dittoed menu. Dee-Dee and Doug exchanged a look that meant the ambiance contained exactly the right mix of seedy and scintillating they had hoped for. I ordered wine, then answered knowledgeably each of the eager questions put by my visitors as though I were privy to all inside information. Crime rates, art trends, new theaters, old restaurants, the odd shops, the next revolution. I played it both ways, straight and dramatic, smoking a gold cigarette before the hors d'oeuvres and letting the hair fall into my eyes, but talking knowingly to the waiter. Having watched the best perform I knew just how to do it. Though I wouldn't have tried to impress a local friend, who could object to a little showmanship for a home-town visitor?

Dee-Dee and her husband seemed to love it. Perhaps, I thought, duplicity was at the heart of all social relations, not only the sexual ones.

Dee-Dee reached into the basket for a piece of whole wheat Italian bread. She buttered it slowly, then took a crunching bite. "This is the best bread I've ever tasted," she said, closing her eyes to seal the hyperbole. "God, it must be exciting to live right here in the center of everything," she breathed.

I smiled and agreed. It was like hearing a lover call you beautiful despite the truth. (She was so easy to impress; I envied her her enthusiasm.)

"Yes, once you live here you never want to live anywhere else in the world," I said, only wishing I could be the person they thought me. It wasn't an absence of principles that made me play to them so blatantly. It was just that I had once been one person, then had become another, without exactly willing the change and I could never have explained. My scruples had gone the way of my hopes—gradually, without a fight—the way one probably watches one's children grow up and move away. I had married and let my purity lapse, like an insurance policy too costly to continue, and now, instead of hopes and scruples, I had hopes and pretense.

We finished our antipasto and dug into the main course. In counterpoint Dee-Dee and Doug named the eight plays they'd seen since they'd arrived. There was something about New York—even visitors had to see their accomplishments piling up, had to match their expectations.

"Do you see much theater?" asked Dee-Dee, twirling pasta around her fork with better will than skill. As though the form of your life mattered more than the content. I'd been prey to the same idea myself—thinking that all you had to do was be in the right place at the right time, and everything else would work out. As though what you did in the right place didn't matter. What could I tell her? Actually, I had been to no more than two or three Broadway plays in seven years. But I didn't want to insult her gratuitously by repudiating her taste. "I only see the plays around here," I said. "Experimental theater, street theater, Off-Broadway, Off-Off-Broadway."

"Off-Off-Broadway?" she asked, her eyes lighting up.

"Political stuff. Poetry readings," I said, hoping to discourage her from wanting to attend. Going to a restaurant with them was one thing, but a play would be something else. Some time before I'd foolishly taken my parents to see the Fugs, a "revolutionary" rock group whose specialty, it turned out, was four-letter lyrics accompanied by obscene gestures. "Mister, you aren't gonna like this," someone in the audience had warned my gray-haired dad as we were going to our seats. If only I'd heeded the warning. The first number was "Fuck" set to music, with the lead singer simulating intercourse with the mike. Even strangers had been able to see that my well-intentioned parents in their hats and suits could only be mortified by the Fugs, though they were too polite (or insecure) to say so; but I didn't know it until intermission. "Quite interesting," was all Mama would venture, and Daddy, less bold or more restrained, changed the subject. No wonder they urged us to visit them in Babylon but tried to avoid New York.

"If I lived here I'm sure I'd spend all my money on Broadway. Why don't you go, Zane?"

I shrugged and confessed: "Actually, I never go north of Fourteenth Street if I can help it."

"Fourteenth Street," offered Doug, "is the northern boundary of Greenwich Village."

"Well, to tell you the truth, we're the same way at home," confided Dee-Dee, leaning forward across the table. "Remember when we were kids, we used to go downtown shopping by ourselves every Saturday, and then if we had dates we'd go to Brownsville Saturday nights to hear jazz at the Black and Tan and sometimes we had those rummage sales down there, and it was all perfectly safe? Well, now we don't dare go downtown, not even for shopping. I could tell you so many stories."

I had a sickening knowledge of what was coming. "Oh, come on now," I said vaguely, hoping the cloud that was gathering over our table would just blow away.

"No, really. It's terrible. The blacks have taken over the whole downtown, haven't they, Doug? You wouldn't recognize it, Zane."

"That's right," said Doug. "Our city is totally changed. Even the suburbs aren't too safe. Though of course in a place like New York it must be much worse," he added in tones of sympathy. "I noticed you brought us to this restaurant in a very roundabout way. I kept wondering what you were trying to avoid. I understand, though. With kids, you must be pretty scared in a neighborhood like this."

"Scared? Of what?" I asked with dogged naïveté. As though refusing to recognize his meaning could hold off the storm.

"Of everything. You know—the violence, the blacks, the communists, all the screwballs in this crazy city."

I knew what he meant. Compared to the calm and order of Babylon, I lived in the midst of chaos. I never knew what might happen when I turned my back; I hardly knew anyone who lived in my building, while Dee-Dee probably knew every soul on her entire block and precisely what they were up to at a given minute. Such knowledge, such assurances were comforting: they made you know where you belonged. Jim Eagle had succumbed to them. And even to me in my loneliness they had once looked so consoling that I'd had to take drastic self-disciplinary measures to keep them from tempting me back. Always fighting the knowledge that if you only believed what *they* believed and did what *they* expected you to do, you could be recognized, accepted, even loved in Babylon. Your place was always there, no matter who you were, if you wanted it.

But I couldn't believe what *they* believed; I couldn't promise to do what was expected; and so my place had been to leave. I'd left Babylon once; twice; I was doomed to leave it again every time I contemplated home, no matter what my precise geography.

Now Doug was going on about crime and the Viet Cong. I watched his mouth move across a small screen in my mind but the sound was off. I had the eerie feeling all this had happened before, everything was repeating for the hundredth time. In another moment I'd be shouting, calling them racists, losing control, and there was no stopping it because it had already happened.

I didn't want to fight. It would be senseless. When I was growing up no one in Babylon had ever argued about politics. (I remembered Dee-Dee saying once: "I know it's wrong to be prejudiced, but I can't help it. That's how I feel." Dee-Dee or someone else.) But the fight was coming all the same. Because I couldn't bear to be swallowed up by the assumption that naturally I agreed with them. It was to escape that assumption that I'd had to flee Babylon in the first place. I couldn't suddenly submit to it here in the heart of Greenwich Village.

"Don't you think the blacks have more to be afraid of from whites than the other way around?" I heard myself ask.

"Zane, you know me," said Dee-Dee. "I'm not prejudiced so I would never generalize against Negroes. But you've got to admit that when you can't even walk around your own city, things have gotten out of hand." She smiled a conciliatory smile, trying to smooth things over. "I wouldn't go as far as Doug, but with the drugs, the crime, now the looting, and even the war, everyone is frightened to death." She placed her hand over her husband's.

I was suddenly overcome by lethargy. I felt far too tired to listen to the conversation. The outcome, the very words, theirs and mine, I knew by heart, like lines from a familiar play; a new improvised phrase here or there would make no difference. The light emitted a million years ago (or a million million) by some distant galaxy got to earth in its own good time while people went on about their business; it was too late to stop it now. I yawned an endless yawn and stopped eating.

"Look, Zane," said Dee-Dee comfortingly, "I'm not saying it's all of them or anything; they didn't used to be this way so it's not in the genes. Don't you remember how nice they were at the rummage sales? And I don't think everyone who wears a peace button is a communist. But the same way we can't give in to the reds, we can't let the blacks take over, either."

It seemed sad that Dee-Dee Larson and Doug whatever-his name on a trip to New York were sitting across the table from me saying the very things we had said as children selling white junk to poor black people at a rummage sale in Brownsville. As though nothing had happened since then; as though we were all still back in high school, with the girls giggling together and the boys playing their brutal practical jokes and me dressing like a kook and Daddy, distressed, asking, "But why, Zane, why?"

Did nothing ever change? Were the upheavals of the sixties for nothing? All at once I began to see connections. The agonizing attacks of conscience I'd been suffering for years, my qualms over my motives, my terrible self-doubt, flew off like a flock of startled terns. The debating champ rose from her bed to deliver a savage rebuttal as all the anger of my childhood—that need to say no, to hold myself apart, finally to escape from that place, to think, to breathe—exploded in a great burst of polemic.

"Oh, please," wailed dimpled Dee-Dee when I had stopped. "I'm sorry I ever said anything. Let's not get into a big argument." Doug called for the check.

While the waiter added up the bill I could see Dee-Dee thinking: still the rebel, still the kook. We sat in a tense silence, cooling down. Gradually my hands dropped the gesture for *defiance* in the *Debater's Manual* they had automatically assumed. "The argument, not the opponent, must be destroyed," I recalled of the rules. By the time Doug had paid I was already ashamed to have displayed my big-city righteousness when I was anything but pure myself.

"Would you like to go some place for espresso?" I asked politely, hoping they'd refuse.

"No, we're leaving early tomorrow. We'll just take you home and grab a cab back to the hotel," said Doug.

"I can go home by myself," I offered; but that took us back into the center of our argument and of course they wouldn't hear of it.

This time we walked directly back to the Square. As we passed the all-night drugstore, the seedy bars, the newsstand with its splash of porn and poetry, Dee-Dee took my arm, friendly despite all. "Remember the year you fixed all the records in the office so we could have triple lunch, Zane? We had to go all over town because we couldn't risk staying around school and getting caught. Remember how you used to take on any boy at chess? I always put my bets on you, though. Some of us were talking about you just the other day—I think that's what made me call your mother for your number. Judy said she used to be afraid to eat lunch with you in high school because she never knew what you'd be cooking up for the afternoon. Cutting school or trying to pick up soldiers. She thought you were kinda crazy."

"Soldiers? My god, I'd forgotten all about that. That must have been during the Korean War. We could always find soldiers hanging around the Movie Palace or the roller rink, but even when we wore lipstick, they always knew we were way too young."

"I think I was afraid of you too, sometimes. You were always so unpredictable."

"Remember? you always used to say to me, 'I'll go with you Zane, but you have to do the talking.' "

Dee-Dee laughed. "But I did admire you, Zane. I always stuck up for you. I always said you probably had a reason for those things you did, even if we couldn't get it. I never said anything against you."

I had always tried to have reasons. Acting without purpose or reason, drifting along and letting things happen, still seemed to me the one inexcusable act, a willful waste of your one and only life—even though nowadays I had to follow necessity more than reason, and what reasons I had seemed to me less and less convincing, balanced as they were by their opposites.

We said goodbye on the street, hugging as though my outburst in the restaurant had never occurred, Dee-Dee still playing scandalized straight-guy to my Zany rebel. As they crossed the street to hail a taxi, I thought how subjective a thing was freedom; how relative was nonconformity.

I climbed the familiar stairs toward my sleeping children, trying to see through Dee-Dee's eyes, past the stroller chained to the banister and the tricycles piled in the hall, until by the top floor I was breathing the thinnest domestic air. But at least, I rejoiced, it was this air! At least I was still here where it was possible to resist the seductive pull of comfort and my past and find a truer place for myself, if only I tried hard enough. Ignoring that I was still, in fact, alone among the many, wanting amid the glut, with relief I threw open my window on the park, rested my hands against the bars and breathed in the great changes that were about to happen. Though I had not yet found the way to participate, still I had managed, despite all the odds, to get this far, instead of dying misunderstood in Babylon.

By the stoned chanters below I swore that the very next morning I would try again. Julie was still in diapers and Tina was in school only half a day; but I would find a way to render my services. I would donate my new tunics to the Peace Center, I would make dissident posters for the PTA, I would send money to the Panthers, I would volunteer at the clinic, I would sign up (god help me) for courses at the Free University, I would read the *Times* cover to cover to know what's what, I would make bread, donate blood, study Marx, take up yoga, impeach Johnson, read Marcuse, sew for peace, join the Resistance, attend the conference, sneak into the Forums, listen to People's Radio, and somehow, before Tina had to be picked up, before Sammy got home from school, while Julie was still napping or after they were all asleep (if Ricky would only stay home with them of an evening), I would insinuate myself into the passions and actions of my time that so far had eluded or excluded me and make of myself someone I might respect! Someone quite certain of what she believed, who could argue calmly using facts, who wasn't ashamed of her position, who wasn't afraid to appear ridiculous, who could take it if they called her pushy, who knew how to follow orders, who wouldn't be touchy about making coffee, who would do the talking, who could get her husband to agree, who could discover exactly what needed to be done and, whether anyone liked it or not, would do it!

12 · WHITEHALL STREET

The list of sponsors appeared in the usual tiny print at the bottom of the announcement, but my eye zoomed straight into the crests of that pair of M's as familiar to me as waves to the beaten shore.

> *Stop the Draft. Help us smash the War Machine. Join us at 39 Whitehall Street on December 6 to close down the Induction Center. This time, only jail will stop us.*

One more chance, I thought as I read over the leaflet, to become worthy. One more chance to vindicate my life before 1967 ended. For the past year, my demonstrating, like the terrible war itself, had escalated as I went from one rally to the next, hoping to produce two miracles: ceasefire and ease of mind. Sometimes I circled behind the stroller with a picket sign trying to invoke the spirit by obeying the marshals and cheering the impassioned leaders in the cold drizzle that seemed to fall on the Left that year. More often, I hovered at the edge of the crowd merely mouthing the slogans for the few minutes remaining before I had to rush back to the Village to pick up one of the children. Either way, I knew that nothing could save me from my increasingly tainted motives which, despite me, invalidated every act. The blue peace button with white dove I forced myself to wear every day in a prominent place on my outer garments was my badge of hypocrisy, as much a promotion of self as of peace. Self, with its dirty sneer, lurked behind every action and inaction ready to mock me with its exasperating "you can't fool me!"

In April Ricky and I had taken the children to the last safe peace march in New York. At that huge, self-congratulatory affair old friends rendezvoused and famous rock stars sang. We'd bumped into the Leo Sterns around Sixty-fourth Street and had marched together, Leo and I flirting and sparring as always in our endless return match. Everyone was tickled to have seen and been seen—it was the social event of the season. When we saw the demonstration on the news that night, I remarked that it had been no sacrifice for us, we'd all enjoyed ourselves, even the children. "Sacrifice?" said Ricky. "You demonstrate for the good of your soul or to save the soldiers?"

In October I'd tried harder. Leaving supplies and instructions at home, I'd kissed my babies goodbye and bussed down to Washington where, with one hundred thousand others, I had assaulted the Pentagon and faced the tear gas. Oh, how I'd longed to cross the soldiers' imaginary line and go limp, following the leaders to jail and glory in a triumph of passion over prudence. But I knew I couldn't saddle Ricky with the children, placing politics above family; knew too that not even jail would be enough to silence my sneering self.

The demands of ego were insatiable. Knowing how sacrifice caressed the conscience, sacrifice itself was corrupt. Instead of crossing the soldiers' line into glory, I'd martyred my hopes for one sacrifice on the demands of another, dutifully mounting the bus that would return me home in time to get the children up in the morning. With only strangers on board and no one to challenge or acknowledge my act of self-denial (on the contrary, the whole bus was whooping it up in a celebration of our heroic performance, mindless of the implications of our being in transit instead of in jail), I'd argued myself to a draw across the entire two-hundred-mile stretch of highway home. Absolutely unable to decide which side of me was the hero and which the coward.

When I'd walked into the apartment about midnight to hear the baby sitter say: "Hi, Mrs. Thompson. Mr. Thompson went to the movies. I hear it was a great demonstration. They arrested Norman Mailer and Dr. Spock and Abbie Hoffman—" I was swamped with regrets.

Now, two months later, I had another chance.

"Only jail will stop us," promised the leaflet in my hand. This time I would not waste myself in agonizing debates. I would ignore the nuances of motive and act. I would act on impulse, on passion.

The announcement was unambiguous. "Join us" meant only one thing to me: Morgan Moore would be there. I would be too.

It was 5:30 a.m. and still night when I emerged from the tube of the Seventh Avenue subway into the narrow streets of lower Manhattan, ready for anything. The air, which in a few hours would pulse with the clicks of office life and the tensions of industry, was now strangely quiet; the occasional mournful wail of a ship or foghorn in the harbor, the smell of seaspray, only heightened the sense of unreality that always accompanied me on my walks through the movement.

(In landlocked Babylon the ocean itself had seemed a dream. Barbie Pratt, who visited New York City in the summer of '55, was the only person I knew who had ever actually seen it. Over and over I'd made her describe it to me. "Huge waves as tall as a big man; water with the taste of salt." Coney Island and the Statue of Liberty I could imagine, but not a body of water that tasted of salt.)

Small clusters of early arrivals stood around speculating about what might happen, sipping coffee dispensed by those clever New York vendors who were always the first to arrive at every important demonstration. Today's action marked a new phase of struggle in New York City: mass civil disobedience. All available troops had been called out. On horses and in trucks they had begun to arrive, filling the surrounding streets, setting up their barricades against the thousands of protesters expected to circle the Induction Center within the hour. No one knew how many would show up or how many, beyond the leaders and the small core of unwavering, committed militants, would actually sit down and be arrested, though that was the question on everyone's mind, from the mayor's to mine.

I hoped today I would be worthy; I hoped I'd go through with it. Not that I now embraced the cause with more ardor (or less) than in the past. Reading the body counts, seeing the pictures of the dead, the villages set aflame, the children and parents ripped apart, filled me with precisely the same horror as the first time. But I was sick of being a bystander. Yes, I knew that despite my best efforts the war went on through protest after protest just as Ricky said; knew that my main work was still to get the kids to school, note the specials on the groceries, prepare the meals, check the vaccinations, keep the animals and plants alive. (The war had not let up for millennia. My own mother's labor pains began as Europe was collapsing before Hitler, but nothing could keep her from pushing me into the world. No more than could her own mother, who'd given birth to her on the eve of Armistice. Even the great La Pasionaria agonized over her priorities: "Did I have the right," she asked, "to sacrifice my children, depriving them of a secure and warm home, of a mother's care and affection?" The Party finally took her children off her hands while she fought in Madrid. But I, partyless, balanced duty against duty.)

This morning, however, after leaving a three-day supply of food in the refrigerator and alerting the baby sitters, I'd banished duty from my mind and prepared capriciously for jail. And by the time dawn broke, and the little clusters of people had swelled to an enormous crowd, I was all but committed.

Thousands of us packed the narrow streets till it was difficult to move. Even the marshals, waving their megaphones in herding gestures, seemed to have been crowded to a standstill. For an instant I thought I caught a glimpse of the march leaders just beyond a row of police barricades (Moore?), but before I could see clearly, I found myself being pushed along rapidly in the other direction, caught in the human stream.

One minute, it seemed, everyone was standing around waiting, exchanging obligatory observations about the war, with the police a safe distance off, and the next minute everyone was being swept along in a surge of movement toward the site of the action, while mounted police galloped alongside. Now suddenly, as far as one could see, there were people rushing forward. (And only a little farther uptown other people were on their way to their offices as usual, some oblivious of our war; and at home the children would be just waking up and rubbing their eyes.)

As soon as the surge forward was over I felt a hand on my shoulder. I looked around. Victor Levinson.

"Victor!" I cried, so happy to know anyone at all in their movement that I conveniently forgot our last awkward meetings.

"I thought that was you," he said, equally surprised. He kindly spared me the pain of being called "Mrs. Thompson" and made no allusion to our past connection, which had ended an embarrassing number of months earlier.

"Where's Bonnie?" I asked.

"I don't know. I came by myself."

"You did? So did I!"—as though that too were some amazing coincidence. Funny how at a demonstration anyone you recognize always seems like an old comrade.

When the next wave of bodies pushed us ahead again, I struggled to stay near Victor.

"Are you planning to sit down and get arrested?" I asked, joining the general spirit when we stopped again.

"I'm not sure yet. Are you?"

"Oh, sure." I said it as though I'd always been a hard-core militant. "I've arranged—" But before I could finish, I found myself being pushed ahead, while Victor slipped away from me.

"Here," he shouted after we stopped, "take my hand so we don't get separated again." He reached across the people between us and firmly clutched my hand, wiping out the ambiguities of our relationship in that single gesture. We were comrades now, by mutual agreement, sharing a goal and an enemy.

Again the crowd surged forward, then stopped abruptly. It was impossible to see beyond the demonstrators, impossible to know if we had reached our destination or a line of police. Not that it made much difference, for the crowd was so dense we couldn't have left if we'd wanted to. We were stuck like soldiers in a war, unable to turn back.

All at once from a distance I heard a terrible chorus of screams; then another spasm went through the mob, a shock wave, and I lost Victor's hand.

"What's happening?" I shouted back to him, feeling the cold thrill of fear. But when the wave had passed, half the people around me were sitting on the ground and Victor was no longer in hearing range.

I sat too. Wondering if we were anywhere near the Induction Center, anywhere near Moore. I suddenly thought of Ricky receiving my phone call (in case of arrest, you have a right to make one phone call, we'd been advised) and turned queasy; and though I could think of no overlooked detail at home, still I filled with guilt for being here where I was but one more passionate body instead of home where I was indispensable.

Rumors flashed like sparklers all around me. The police had charged on horseback into the crowd, someone said; demonstrators were fighting back; the leaders had been arrested.

Another mass scream. Whatever onlookers remained were suddenly separated from the rest of us as the police moved in.

Fear and triumph coursed through me. At last I had really done it! Whatever my motives, they no longer mattered; for all of us, heroes and adventurers alike, saints and sinners, were going to be arrested. There was no turning back.

Flanked by a half dozen lackeys, the police captain approached, a look of grim determination on his plump face. Behind him a string of paddy wagons crept toward us, their gratings leering in green triumph. From my window for years I had watched the same vans eating bench sleepers and bums in the early morning roundups in the park. I'd always felt sorry for the victims, huddled under ragged overcoats; but for me arrest would be a victory.

The captain consulted his walkie-talkie, then turned to us. "In the name of the law, will you stand and leave?" he asked us one at a time, incanting the magic words of the law. Around me, dutiful protesters took down his badge number in little notebooks or snapped the captain's photograph; applause accompanied each arrest.

"No."

"Arrest him, officer. In the name of the law . . ."

Then all at once it was my photograph being snapped, my name being taken by a huddle of reporters and press photographers. The arresting officer took my elbow to dispatch me behind the others into the paddy wagon while the supporting crowd applauded. I shook my elbow free and climbed unassisted into the windowless truck.

It was startlingly black inside, with the only light coming from behind me. Before I could sit down on one of the two long benches that spanned the airless space, the doors slammed shut, closing out the last ray of light, and the vehicle jerked away.

I fell onto the bench, squeezing between two bodies. Next to me I felt a familiar presence.

"Victor?" I ventered on a hunch. "Is that you?"

"Zane? It's me."

There it was between us: my true name.

At a corner, the truck lurched, sending me flying against him. I felt his thigh pressed against mine, jean to jean, and was grateful for the protection of the darkness. There was no penalty for thoughts that could not be seen in the dark.

Nevertheless, I covered up with my old fast-speak.

"Do you know where they're taking us? What happens next?"

"Beats me," he answered.

At the next swerve, Victor steadied me with his arm, and when I righted myself again his large hand closed over mine.

And because it was dark and we were old friends and my children were nowhere near and no one knew what was going to happen to us, I lay my head on his shoulder and he slipped his arm around my back. Like the sleigh rides of my Babylon youth, like the Tunnels of Love, the total darkness of the truck provided the intimate atmosphere in which even the shy could play out our scene in the incredibly erotic drama of the movement. Human bodies pressed together, thousands of strangers sharing an idea, all the emotionally charged atoms pressing toward some singular release, the intimacy of danger, the danger of arrest, the adventure of love, heroism—all came together for us in that Black Maria. With the next lurch of the truck the vast distance between our lives dissolved in our pressing mutual need. His mysterious beard touched my skin; we kissed.

It seemed only a moment afterward that the doors were opened. The guards stepped out and we were ready for the next unknown.

"Men to the right, women to the left," directed an officer as we piled out of the van one at a time and lined up against a concrete wall.

Over already? But before he disappeared behind the next paddy wagon into the Tombs (Manhattan's quaintly named, most venerable prison), I saw Victor Levinson smile at me, hold up two fingers in the victory sign, and press his harmonica to his lips.

Short, I noticed as he walked away making his music, but very sexy.

"Here you go," said the guard fumbling with his heavy key ring. He gave the slightest shove to my shoulder to prove who was prisoner and who was guard. It was sheer elation I felt as I crossed beyond the iron door into the cell.

The cell was already so crowded with women that I was surprised they'd try to fit one more body in; yet our guard had left three of us here, the last three of our group to find a home. Maybe it meant our action had been successful and we had filled the jails as hoped.

Instantly we were surrounded by questions.

"What's the news?"

"Have they started making indictments yet?"

"Last we heard they'd arrested more than two hundred. What's it up to now?"

"Is the Induction Center closed down? Tell us."

But as soon as the prisoners discovered that we knew even less than they, they moved away disappointed.

I made my way to the back of the cell where I found a leaning spot against the wall from which to survey my new family. There were twenty of us at least, all herded into a room no larger than an extra bedroom. All politicos, to judge by our clothes. One toilet, open to the room, a few benches against the concrete wall—nothing else. People leaned against the walls or squatted where they could on the concrete floor in various postures of discomfort. Bored, drained, waiting for action or news, but with an air of mutual admiration and respect I'd never felt before.

There was no place to sit. Too bad—it seemed as though I had been standing for hours at the ends of lines in identical green corridors: waiting to be booked and questioned, waiting to surrender my purse and watch, waiting to be photographed, fingerprinted, searched for hidden weapons. ("Remove your underpants and squat, front and back," ordered a red-faced matron who had somehow gotten it into her mind that I had smuggled contraband into prison in my privates.)

In a corner seated on benches I spotted three older women—prestigious wives of old movement leaders—who seemed to be holding court for the young women near them, all deep in conversation. I recognized them from Leuticia Bracci's Intellectual Forums, where they'd regularly filled the front seats emblazoned with their distinguished names: Mrs. B., wife of the poet; Mrs. W., whose husband had already been indicted for conspiracy in connection with the destruction of draft files in Omaha; and Mrs. van T., doubly famous as the daughter of the retired minister of Boston's pacifist Episcopal church and wife of Harvard's most distinguished radical historian.

How lucky, I thought, to have wound up in the celebrity block; and though I felt a momentary pang of shame for my impure motives, I started across the cell toward their corner.

Why not? Wasn't that why sponsors lent their names to these actions in the first place?—to attract and inspire a following among the uncommitted? Wasn't that "leadership"?

But halfway across the crowded cell I stopped, suddenly aware of the implication of their presence. Quickly I scanned the walls, the clusters of prisoners in the corners, until I spotted Moore.

There she lay, stretched out on the floor, talking with a small group. She rested her head on one hand, her red hair spilling over her arm, the rest of her long body sheathed in black. I knew it would have seemed perfectly natural for me to join the little group and introduce myself. (What could I be accused of? It was not my doing that we were locked together in a cell.) But once again, as with each opportunity to meet her that had come my way over the years, at the crucial moment I stepped back, reluctant to approach her.

Instead, I took my place against the wall and listened to the group on the floor debate the relative merits of pleading guilty or not guilty. Guilty, we'd been told, would probably bring suspended sentences to first offenders; not guilty would involve a trial but would preserve your first-offender status for another protest if you were acquitted. It was a question of urgent interest, but I kept my distance, content to listen unobserved.

An hour or more must have passed like that—the others earnestly talking with Moore on the floor while I watched from the wall—before two prison guards came to our cell and read out the leaders' names. Mrs. B., Mrs. W., Mrs. van T., Morgan Moore.

For an instant as she sat up I thought Moore paused to look at me. But the next moment she stood up, stamped the legs of her black pants down over her boots, ran her fingers through her hair, suppressed a stretch, and walked without pausing past me toward the gate.

"That means they've started the arraignments," whispered the woman beside me.

The guard unlocked the bars and took the leaders away.

13 · ADULTERY

I waited for Victor at the back of the platform in the Sheridan Square station of the IRT, imagining all the things that could go wrong. I'd fall in love; I would be caught. I didn't care: This was what I wanted.

Each time a train exploded into the station I filled with such alternating currents of hope and dread that I thought my pulse would burst through my constricting veins. I had committed small betrayals against Ricky—drinking coffee in the Lucia alone, thinking resentful, even hateful thoughts, hoping for a savior—but never (except for that single stolen kiss the week before) the real thing. Now, if Victor only showed up as planned, I was going to plunge headlong into adultery. By prearrangement and complicity: he had arranged for the place in Brooklyn, and I'd arranged to get rid of Julie. My tongue still burned from the lie I'd just told when I'd dropped her off at her friend's. But a preparatory lie, even the first of many, was nothing to what I planned. If Victor showed up in time, we could get to Brooklyn and spend four hours making illicit love (four more hours than I'd spent in all the seven years since I'd married)—and who could tell what would happen after that?

It seemed as though innumerable trains had come and gone

without yielding up my lover. (Lover: how much of the structure of my life did that word imply?) I stood there huddled inside my warmest coat counting trains and losing count, remembering instead every word, every erotic pause in our phone conversations.

I'd been expecting his first call: that kiss in the paddy wagon had not been the sort one could simply walk away from. From the moment I picked up the phone and heard his first "Zane?" (feeling the shiver of intimacy run through me at the sound of my name on his lips), through the detailed recap of our day in jail that served as our common bond, until finally, hesitatingly, he gulped and proposed: "I have some clippings about the demonstration from a few movement papers. One of them has a picture of us in it. If you'd like to see them, maybe we can get together."

"I'd love that," I said too quickly.

"When?"

Now, I thought; tomorrow, today. Whatever the impediments, I'd dispose of them. But instead, I said lightly: "Oh, it doesn't matter. Whenever you say. My days are pretty much the same, except Tuesdays when I have to take Sammy and some of his friends down to the music school."

Victor was a slow speaker, like many of his generation. A chooser of words. Before he had chosen, I added, "Maybe I can arrange for Julie to visit a friend one morning; then we won't have to worry about interruptions." It was a brazen thing to say, but we had so little time and I was afraid he might slip away again.

"That's cool."

"What would you like to do if I can arrange it?"

There was a long pause in which you could almost hear our hearts beating.

"Play a little music, maybe make some, uh, love."

My heart turned over. Then in a sudden panic I said, "But you can't come *here!*"

"I'll find us a place. I have a friend in Brooklyn—I think he'd let me use his pad."

"Brooklyn?" I said gaily, my excitement mounting toward hysteria. "Sounds nice. I've never made love in Brooklyn."

Instantly I regretted the remark. It sounded too flippant, like a statement from my key-collecting days, implying an ease with sex, with casual sex, I both lacked and abhorred. I'd never intended it to come out that way. After seven years of isolation, my delicate bond with this beautiful bearded man was exceedingly precious to me, too precious to dissipate in a sordid encounter or a casual affair. Victor was a serious boy, even earnest, whom I had never known to engage in banter. That was one of the things about him that I loved. The way the solemn intimacy in his voice provoked my heart—intimating it might expand to fill the empty cavity in the pit of my life—it seemed calamitous to constrict it with misconceptions before it even began to swell.

Of course, we really knew nothing about each other. I took him for one of the new people—perhaps a slightly more serious, somewhat more intellectual, specimen of your ordinary New Left counterculture radical—but someone, like the beats of my youth, for whom sex was a pleasure like a good Cuban cigar: something to sniff and savor after dinner, to light and appreciate and then quickly let die. And I knew from certain subtle indicators (for example, his surprise at my insisting we meet down in the subway instead of out in the open for the world to see) that if he no longer mistook me for a person like my Aunt Louise, for which I was already half in love with him, he probably had me pegged as one of those bored, sophisticated, even dangerous married women who was always on the lookout for a new adventure.

Suddenly there he was, ambling toward me in his beard and jeans and sheepskin, looking so beautiful and poetic I was afraid he would vanish if I dropped my gaze.

"Hi," he said barely moving his lips; and except for his glasses, which were definitely this year's, and the harmonica peeking out of his pocket, he could have been Marshall or Wolfe or any of a hundred other heartbreak boys who had passed through this Village station in the years since it was built. Like the part of New York they inhabited, all right to visit but disaster to love.

I smiled, reluctant to speak and give myself away. He took my arm and did not let go of it the entire time we stood in the station; or as we sat on the next train holding hands like kids, reading the station signs, making little revolutionary remarks; or as we trudged through bright Brooklyn snow keeping perfect thigh-to-thigh lockstep past rows of family houses and blue-gray tenements; or as we took the stoop, the stairs, found the key, wrestled open the door, read the note on the pillow (*Vic: There's some stuff you should try in the parsley jar on the window sill, papers on the bureau. Sorry there's no food. When you leave put the key back where you found it. Have fun. Talk to you next week. Fred*), and fell into each other's arms.

Not for seven years had I been touched by the outside world, seven years in which it was said there'd been a veritable sexual revolution. For seven years I'd been dormant inside a fat cocoon, coldly, darkly alone. Such a rigid shell could hardly be dissolved by sudden sex. If the living creature inside were to be reached alive, the thread would have to be delicately unwound, revolution by revolution.

From Marshall I had learned to kiss with my eyes open; but I didn't dare let Victor see the longing in mine. Inside his arms I closed my eyes fast, preserving my shell.

But the kiss was like a cool drink to a parched mouth. Perhaps silent men saved the motion of their lips for this. When our clothes lay in a heap on the floor our kisses spread like spilled water on a polished mirror seeping to the edges until we were bathed in it. Wriggling up the bed toward the pillows I felt sunlight from the window behind the bed hit my skin. When I opened my eyes I was blinded by sun.

I shot up and hastily pulled up the sheet.

Though I had once zestlessly flitted from bed to bed, now, seven years later, I suffered agonies of shyness at the prospect of exposing this used, married body, from which three new humans had emerged, to the scrutiny of the young, matricidal counterculture.

"How about trying your friend's grass?" I said. Dope had helped in the past; now I needed all the help I could get.

"Now?" said Victor, incredulous. Clearly it did not strike him as the best moment to begin a new activity. He didn't understand how I needed it.

I nodded.

"Sure," he said, shrugged, and popped out of bed to collect the fixings.

While he walked to the window, I drank in his round buttocks, his firm thighs, that erect organ, as though I'd never seen a man or might not see another. (How different from one another they were. It was always so surprising to see. He would misunderstand this look too, if he saw it, but there was nothing to be done.)

He rolled a joint, and as we smoked my anxiety began to subside. (Some things in the world you could still count on.)

"You won't tell Bonnie about any of this, will you?" I remember giggling as the dope began to do its work.

"Not if you don't want me to."

"*If?* I don't want you to tell anyone, not anyone. It's one thing for you, but if this ever got back to my husband!—"

"Really?" asked Victor, his curiosity suddenly aroused. "What would your husband do?"

I closed my eyes and shook my head, holding the smoke down in my lungs while I contemplated the disaster that would follow discovery. Obviously, Victor had no comprehension of married people's lives. (Why should he?) I'd never be able to explain. (Why try?) It was foolish to dwell on such thoughts when we had only a couple of hours in which to undo (or do) so much.

The conversation ended with the joint. Victor sang me one of his sad beautiful songs that moved me like love. Tenderly I lay the back of my hand against his black woolly beard while he sang, feeling his music with my hands.

First our fingers joined. He took hold of the fragile thread and began very slowly to open the cocoon. It might take a long time, but he seemed to be in no hurry. Was it his knowledge or my need or the seven years or the new dope? I didn't know or care. I opened my eyes to see. His black beard was spread across my breast like an oriental fan, his lips brushed my arm: a moving sight. I watched the muscles under his skin, the veins in his arm, I watched the blood move through him, his thick neck, his strangeness; I watched and watched, able at last to see what Marshall hadn't been able to show me. And when he moved his body onto mine and came into me, I kept my eyes open, watching the thread unwind turn by turn, trusting Victor not to break it, not to stop until it was completely done.

My last thought before the final turn that exposed to the sunlight my happy, throbbing self: My eyes are open.

14 · TRASH CANS

Just as the trees of Washington Square were preparing to green again, Lyndon B. Johnson, who had been the President since Tina was born and Kennedy died, conceded defeat to the movement (us!) by declaring his intention of retiring forever to his Texas ranch.

Hundreds of Villagers burst into the park that late March night in a spontaneous victory celebration. I happened to be there when the first ones appeared, for I was looking out the window for Victor, who was already a little late.

"We did it, we did it!" the celebrants shrieked, lifting each other into the air.

Well, I'd always wanted to be on hand where history was made. If I'd had a sitter and no other plans, I would have dashed down the stairs and joined their snake dance through the streets just to partake of that rare communion, though never for a moment could I pretend that Johnson's defeat was in any part because of me. Having failed to burn myself before the Pentagon, my actions seemed arbitrary. Between motive and act lay as dense a tangle of accidents as ever. All I knew for sure was that the winter had come and gone, the children were each another year older, my *Designs by Zane* on which, unaccountably, I had once placed so much hope had grown shopworn and dated in their East Village boutiques, and even my affair with Victor, which had created such great upheavals in my heart when I had first fallen a few months before, had accommodated to my routine. Guilt and passion canceled each other out, leaving my life essentially unchanged: we made love at least once a week, we spoke to each other secretly every day; but my true desires lingered unquenched. Though I had undertaken jail and passion in the vain hope that they might commit me to some destiny, at the end of that eventful winter I was no closer to saving myself than I'd been in the fall. Objectively, in fact, I was two steps closer to disaster: the State now possessed a perfect set of my fingerprints; Thursdays I risked calamitous exposure. Otherwise, all was as before.

He had said he'd give the signal at 9:30, a safe hour after the children would have fallen asleep. We used the following system: one light in the living room meant it was safe on my end (Ricky was usually out of town on Thursday but we couldn't take a risk); a riff on the harmonica followed by two matches lit at the curb meant Victor was ready. As soon as I saw the double flash, I was to count to twenty and buzz open the downstairs door so

Victor wouldn't have to ring the bell. Then we would have until nearly dawn to dope up and make love.

But instead of Victor's matches, suddenly I saw a trash can in the northwest quadrant of the park burst into flame. A moment later, from another spot the same message shot into the March sky, then another, as the revelers ignited their uncontainable enthusiasm.

Dangerous: the war was hardly over. One tempted fate by celebrating a victory in advance. But one thing this generation didn't fear was the backlash of fate. They did not think far enough ahead to imagine retribution, fancying the future to be the day after tomorrow. Lacking the prudence inspired by fear or family, for them it was not enough to feel or anticipate their victory; for them it was necessary to act on it. To do something, anything, to proclaim their power, so long as it was a palpable action. *Put your body on the line,* they importuned each other and asked incessantly, *where's the action?* never bothering to consider (as I was cursed to do) how complicated and mysterious were the connections between cause and effect, between purpose and outcome. *Never trust anyone over thirty,* they advised, never noticing how their own days were numbered.

I had lived through one cycle already; I had seen my world turn on its side, stand on its head, and then roll over again. Common sense told me it would happen again. And again. But the people in the park igniting their passions from trash can to trash can knew only one kind of change: from the way it was before them to the way it was now. They thought they had changed the world forever.

Just so, when Victor brought his super-grass and piled stacks of records on the hi-fi, he did not think of afterward—when he would slip out the door and the children would wake up and Ricky would come home. When with exquisite timing he removed my clothes item by item (as though he could so easily remove my qualms and hesitations) and launched the ancient mysteries, he was not plagued like me by guilty fears or distracting questions. Not even the best dope in Manhattan could bar the perverse intellectual (or practical Midwesterner) who climbed into my bed with us to whisper in my ear: Why is he here? Why gamble your chances? Or, as we fell deeper and deeper into habit:

What can come of this affair? What will you do with your life?

Of course, "affair" was not a word Victor would ever have used, preferring instead the unwieldy, less informative "relationship" favored by the young, single, or psychological. But the connection that had coupled us for the past half-year was, despite the misleading music and dope, precisely what the married had always called an "affair." And affairs were, almost by definition, superfluous to the progress of a life, however affecting. They always came to an end—and then what? Then even the feelings vanished; they might just as well not have existed. Like the fires now burning in the trash cans in the park, they would flare up and go out, rich as a moment's expression, leaving nothing usable behind.

As I scanned the park for Victor, I thought of a line delivered a decade before by one of Marshall's Columbia friends, a line everyone but me had found funny at the time but I had only recently come to understand: *September's gone, and what have you done about it?* Back in those days, when I was able to account for each September of my life in a different concrete way, a new September meant nothing to me. A veteran of nothing yet, I wanted the months to zip by like headlights, proving I was going somewhere fast. Each month was an occasion not for regrets but for rejoicing that I was on my way. Not till many years later, when a Labor Day signaled time to get the children ready to begin school again and I counted time by their summers as I had once eagerly done by my own, when the months slipped into seasons and the seasons into years without my having done anything to affect the world, did I find myself thinking (not with amusement, but bitterly): *September's gone, Zane, and what exactly have you done about it?*

A set of chords and a run on the harmonica let me know my lover was outside my window. Two matches flared and I began my count. But already I knew that love couldn't save me—no more than had my peace button or my sewing machine, in each of which I had also placed my faith. The President had withdrawn, Victor had momentarily rescued me from becoming a creature like my aunt; but both were false and temporary salvations. In fifteen minutes, I thought as I buzzed open the door, we would be smoking the magic weed that would take us to that place where Victor's arms and beard could make me imagine solutions; a place where the uncommitted lived and I was welcome to visit. But as soon as the drug wore off and I awakened to the roar of early morning garbage-grinding trucks, I would know the truth again. September would come and go again, the killing would go on, Ricky might or might not abandon us, Victor would move to a commune, the children would grow up, and there was nothing, nothing, I could do about it.

PART IV

The Third Street Circle

We take the woman's side in everything. We ask not if something is "reformist," "radical," "revolutionary," or "moral." We ask: is it good for women or bad for women?

—*Principles*
of New York Radical Women

1 · FIRST MEETING

And now the changes begin again. How lucky I am to have been born at this time, to be living in this place. Something that has not been seen or heard in generations, not remembered in half a century, something potent and transforming, is about to come thundering down Fifth Avenue, sending tremors through all the cities. A new idea (or as near to one as can be found in this late century), a heresy that delights me the instant I think about it, one I know in my blood to be true.

Memorandum: Director, FBI
From: SAC, New York
Subject: WOMEN'S LIBERATION MOVEMENT (WLM)

Informant [deleted] who has furnished reliable information in the past, advised that the WLM, so far as the informant is aware, is not an organization as such but rather a cause and philosophy. She stated she knows of no formal headquarters or officers on a local or national basis. She has no information concerning the finances within the WLM.

Informant stated that the philosophy of the WLM is for complete equality in all facets of life for all women. The basic difference between the liberal and the radical groups is that the radicals state that male chauvinism is a direct result of the "establishment" and existing institutions and that these must be torn down before women will have their equality. Informant stated that in the New York area the Women's International Terrorist Conspiracy from Hell (WITCHES) is a radical group active for Women's Liberation. Another group is an offshoot of the WITCHES, the "Red Stockings," considered to have split off from the WITCHES because of a more radical approach to the problem. Still another radical group believed to have formed in the New York area is the "Third Street Circle."

It was a bleak Thursday in the second week of the New Year when I found myself outside the raunchy tenement on East Third Street, debating whether or not to go in.

I was late—a victim of my now habitual vacillation. The block was forbidding, with motorcyclists making menacing rumblings down the street and icy patches on the broken sidewalk. Across the stairs to the building lay the sodden remnants of Christmas '67. Tinsel, wrapping paper, empty wine bottles spilled out of the garbage cans leaning against the stoop.

A women's meeting? Another revolution? Once again, I considered going to a phone booth, calling up Victor, and arranging to see him instead, since I already had a sitter.

I had agreed to go to the meeting in the first place, canceling my regular Thursday date with Victor, only to oblige my insistent friend Kitty Kramer, who didn't want to attend a meeting alone. But that afternoon her youngest had come down with the flu, and she called to cancel. Remembering my long antipathy to clusters of females, from PTA to Women's Strike for Peace, when I got her call I decided not to go either. But Kitty wouldn't hear of it. "Oh, Zane, go. Wait till you hear them. They're just like us."

Like us? It seemed improbable. Until I had found Kitty in the playground scribbling in a notebook, underlining, turning back, striking out, with a bitten stub of a pencil choked between nervous manicured fingers, I wouldn't have believed there were any "like us." A pair of exceptions, talk-starved as others were sex-starved. Even after we acknowledged each other I was skeptical, for we were the unlikeliest combination. I, plain, aloof, and be-jeaned, beside that tiny, talkative, made-up, high-heeled Kitty who shamelessly called herself a writer. I hardly knew what to say or how to behave, having spent the good part of a decade in solitary. But once Kitty and I started talking, nothing could stop us. Even the hateful playground became tolerable. All other playground conversations were small, suspicious, and particular, and I avoided them. But the moment ours got under way they ascended like smoke rings to the gloriously universal. I had always found it impossible to think in the playground, with heads splitting and guts spilling whenever you turned around. But somehow Kitty knew how to follow a theory down a slide or back and forth with the swings. Our relationship was peculiar. We asked nothing of each other in the usual way of friendship: no listening to troubles, helping out in a pinch, exchanging presents or hugs or friends or meals. All we demanded was: a willingness to talk, to read, and, above all, to speculate.

Kitty had awakened me at 2:30 a.m. to tell me about this meeting.

"Quick, Zane," came her voice through the phone. "Turn on People's Radio. Some women are talking and they sound like us. Only instead of just two of them, there seems to be a whole group. And instead of just talking, they want to *do* something."

Do something? I was for that. Something surely needed to be done. But in the middle of the night? Sometimes Kitty got carried away.

"What time is it?" I asked, trying to wake up.

Kitty and I had talked for hours earlier that night. Once we'd discovered that both of our husbands went out on Wednesday nights (mine on Thursdays too, usually), we'd started to hold our conversations on the phone after the children went to sleep. It was much better than the playground where there were constant interruptions. This way, we could even preassign ourselves a topic or a text as though we were in college. Of course, like Marxists in Middletown we kept our topics secret. Even our husbands would have laughed at the pair of us pursuing metaphysics without a college degree between us. But it was silly to pretend to each other we weren't serious when there was no one around to intimidate us.

"I think it's about two thirty. Does it matter? Ricky isn't there, is he?"

Kitty was a night person who sometimes forgot I was on days. I got up every morning with the children at 6:45, but she left breakfast out for her children before she went to sleep and let them watch TV in the morning while she slept. "The only time I can write is when they're all asleep," she explained. Though she seemed to me anything but a writer—she was too short, her voice was too high, and she wore entirely too much makeup—like Marshall, she was writing a play.

"Listen, they're about to announce a meeting. I've got to find a pencil, quick!—" Then she hung up abruptly.

Dutifully I tried to tune in People's Radio, but after a few minutes of night rock I gave up and went back to sleep.

And now here I was, in a part of town I knew only by day, feeling as out of place as I had in my own neighborhood a decade earlier.

I stepped over the garbage on the stairs, pushed open the door, walked into a dark foyer that smelled strongly of old urine, and pressed the button for 6-C (F. D. NEWMAN). When the buzzer rang, I pushed open the door and began my anxious climb up the rickety stairs.

"Come in, come in," said the tall blond woman with calm blue eyes who opened the door for me. She was strikingly slim, with long graceful limbs; on the street I would have turned to look at her. On her lips played a reassuring smile.

"My name's Faith. And you're . . . ?"

"Zane. My friend Kitty called up for us, but it turns out she couldn't make it after all."

"Oh yes," said Faith, as though she knew all about me. Her blond hair fell over one eye as she nodded. "She called a while ago. I'm sorry her kid is sick, but I'm glad you could make it. Come in."

She seemed genuinely pleased to have me as she led me into a small kitchen, neat but shabby, lined with old glass-faced wooden cabinets and ancient fixtures. From the next room I heard the excited voices of many women talking at once.

"I'll take your things. Just go on in," said Faith, pointing me ahead and disappearing down a small hall.

Resolutely I made my entrance.

A charged, crowded, whitewashed room. A room tense with subdued excitement, animated with purpose. You could feel it the instant you stepped through the door. You didn't have to hear a single line from the conversations scattered through the room to know that not one word would be frivolous, not one motive wavering. You could see it in all their faces, sense it in the undertones. The room was a den of conspirators, and every person in it —female.

It was shocking to see only women. (At the PTA or in the women's prison, yes; but in this atmosphere? In such an atmosphere as this, one usually found a bearded center with a smell of pipe tobacco.) There must have been a dozen or more clustered into small, informal groups—all young, all earnest; not like the women I knew. One group huddled together on straight-backed kitchen chairs, talking avidly. Another, evidently examining a newspaper, nibbled snacks from a table laden with potato chips and pretzels, nothing fancy. Other women sat cross-legged on the big, pillow-covered bed in the corner, collating and stapling mimeographed pages. Still others sat on the floor in a semicircle around a low coffee table, deep in discussion.

They all looked more like students or secretaries than my idea of revolutionaries. Marshall's friends had always had a joke about Marxist girls in secret cells with fuzzy hair, spectacles, and faint mustaches on their upper lips, joining the Party to get a man. These women defied the image. They were scrubbed and pretty, like students at the Art Students League, but there was a special look on their faces, a light in their eyes I'd seldom seen on students. Not even the activists in my cell at the Tombs had had it.

I stood in the doorway taking in the room. Seatless wicker chairs made usable with pillows; a couple of small, threadbare rugs on the painted floor; plain wooden tables, floor cushions, Japanese paper lamps were the furnishings—the usual trappings of voluntary poverty. But there were touches—a mass of green plants before the window, odd fabrics on the homemade pillows (instead of the burlap of the fifties), hand-thrown pots neatly interspersed with the books on the shelves—that made it different from the careless disarray of cold-water flats, the austerity of artists' lofts, or the endless clutter of family quarters. This was neat, poor, cared-for. On the walls were several posters. One showed the dove of peace; one was of a sharp, old-fashioned woman with bright, intelligent eyes; one depicted the blue sky with the single word, REVOLUTION; and in the place of honor over the bricked-up white-washed fireplace was the largest poster of all, showing Chinese peasants marching under the legend: *Speak Bitterness to Understand Bitterness.*

Faith returned to the doorway. "Come on," she said, putting her hand gently on my shoulder and accompanying me into the room.

I noticed that most of the women wore jeans, shirts, sneakers—a simple enough uniform, but one I happened not to be wearing. Here and there I saw a miniskirt, but even the skirted had an air of belonging I lacked. I was suddenly glad that Kitty, with her high heels and makeup, was not beside me to announce more blatantly how little we fit in.

I sat down on the floor at the edge of a little group, and, searching for some nonchalant pose that would help me appear inconspicuous, I began examining the books and pamphlets on the coffee table. *The Second Sex* by Simone de Beauvoir, Sartre's lifelong companion; Engels's *The Origins of the Family, Private Property and the State;* a mimeographed paper with the intriguing title "Dialectics of Housework" and another called "The Politics of Sex"; pamphlets on birth control, on welfare, on women in China, on psychology; a collection of essays by Rosa Luxemburg (whose picture on the jacket matched the woman on the wall poster), another by Mao Tse-tung, a fat book on China called *Fanshen,* and *The Feminine Mystique.* An intimidating assortment; I wished I'd read them all.

Directly across from me a fiery woman who seemed no more than twenty was speaking excitedly to the little group. Listening to her was irresistible, however impolite. Though she seemed a mere girl, slight and pale, she had such piercing eyes and such intensity in her face that she reminded me of the picture of Saint Joan I'd cut from a child's book and taped to my wall in Babylon. A saint, I thought as I watched her, or someone who's going to make history. Her light brown hair was clipped as short as a boy's and her clothes were unadorned, giving her a look of severe simplicity; mainly I was drawn to something in her eyes. Clear, deep eyes beneath a smooth, high brow, eyes that glistened as she spoke (deliberately, severely, emphasizing each separate word): eyes that looked inward for knowledge, outward for power; the unmistakable look of a visionary.

Not wanting to seem to be staring, I turned back to the books on the table and continued to listen.

"Ask them to help us?" she said with a high-pitched laugh. "Are you crazy? We'll demand it. If they want our support they'll have to prove themselves first. Their word won't do any more. They haven't seen anything yet."

"We could give them a list of demands," said someone else, "starting with their Steering Committee. Let them hold half the places open for us."

Saint Joan laughed again. "Yes," she said, "and the major speech at the rally."

"Right, Marya," said another. "And some concrete evidence that they really intend to do something. No more promises."

"Maybe we can let them run the mimeo for our leaflets." (Laughter.)

"Or serve us coffee." (Laughter.)

"Let them take care of the kids when we demonstrate."

"Let them make our buttons."

"Distribute our literature."

"Pack our lunches."

"Darn our sox."

And in another moment they were all laughing, fierce, bitter laughter, their eyes flashing with righteous anger.

A short woman in patched jeans and a blue cotton workshirt approached the little group, leaned over, and conferred with the saintly Marya for a moment; then she walked across the room to the fireplace, stood beneath the Speak Bitterness poster, and rapped for attention on the mantel.

"I think everyone who's coming tonight is probably here," she said, running her fingers through her short black ringlets and adjusting her glasses, "so we better get started. We have a lot to cover. Some of us have been working every evening this week already, and we'd sort of like to end early." She looked over at Marya and smiled. "I drew the lot to open this meeting, but I've never done it before and I'm a little nervous. I know, I'm not supposed to apologize." She adjusted her glasses again, thrust her hands into her pockets, leaned against the fireplace for support, and, speaking very fast, began again.

"Okay. My name's Golda Feldman. I'm a founding member of the Third Street Circle, a small group of women interested in Women's Liberation. Some of us have been meeting for the last three months or so trying to analyze the situation of women as an oppressed class."

Women a class? An oppressed class, like the poor? Me, a member of an oppressed class? I could already hear Ricky breaking up over that one. It was beguiling to hear Golda use the familiar jargon of the Left on such a shockingly new subject.

"Right now," Golda continued with an air of importance that was probably only a cover for her nervousness, "we're trying to develop a concrete analysis of the situation, so we're holding these discussions. There's so much to understand. But pretty soon we're hoping to start doing some actions."

"What kind of actions?" asked someone.

Golda looked knowingly at several of the other women in the room and said: "We haven't decided yet. There are a lot of really important issues to organize around"—she held up one hand and with the other pushed down one finger at a time, ticking them off systematically until she had made two fists—"abortion, sex, prostitution, job discrimination, child care, maternity layoffs, education, marriage, divorce, rape—I could go on and on. But we really have to develop an analysis first and figure out our priorities before we decide what to do."

It was an impressive list of issues, all obviously related now that they'd been named, though I'd never have thought of connecting them on my own. The truth was, I'd never thought women treated unfairly given their difference; I'd only thought me treated unfairly to have been born one.

"The main action we're doing now is organizing," she continued. "We're writing pamphlets, appearing in the media, holding these meetings. We're trying to make people aware of how all these issues are used to keep women down, how women for centuries have been kept apart and in servitude to the Man. We need to build a mass revolutionary movement, not just remain a vanguard."

There was something didactic, even patronizing, about Golda's speech. They were probably all fanatics, I conjectured, interpreting the universe in one ray of light, ignoring the spectrum. But still, the audacity of the core idea positively tickled me. A women's revolution!

When Golda sat down a few minutes later, Marya herself continued from across the room. "Since early December we've been trying to draw up a Manifesto that everyone can agree on. We've had a terrific response to our talks on People's Radio. We've been getting piles of letters asking for our literature and speakers. And though the Third Street Circle has only about twenty active members right now, we know this movement is going to be tremendous. We can hardly keep up with our mail now, so we're holding off on outside actions for a while and concentrating on these meetings to raise women's consciousness."

I suddenly remembered meetings in Babylon—smiling girls sitting in a circle, talking about money and boys.

"Now Faith is going to tell you a little bit about what these meetings are for," said Marya sweetly.

Faith was sitting on the floor against a wall, clasping her legs at the knees. She didn't get up, but smiled the relaxed smile that had already put me at my ease, and began to speak.

"What we're trying to do here is find out about women's lives by examining our own experience." She was soft-spoken and calm, the opposite of Golda but no less serious. She made everything sound reasonable. "We started as a study group about half a year ago, an offshoot of a larger group of radical women who were trying to get at some general understanding of the condition of women. We started out reading some basic texts like Marx and Engels and Freud to see what they had to say about women."

Maybe that was what Kitty had meant, then, saying they were like us. They read books and discussed them. Unusual enough for women, true, but enough to make us seem alike?

"But we found out very soon that those male theorists had nothing much to say about our lives, and what they did say about women was probably not reliable."

There was a murmur in the room, a murmur of assent. "It was pure bullshit!" yelled someone from across the room.

"We knew we'd have to try something else if we wanted to

understand," continued Faith. "In China, during the revolution, the peasants were able to change their lives by examining their own personal, everyday experience of oppression. They got a lot of strength from talking about it and comparing stories—they call it Speaking Bitterness. We decided to try the same technique. After all, it makes sense. Before we can begin to *change* the system, we have to understand how it works, how it keeps us down. Sexism goes so deep that at first it's hard to see; you think it's just reality. Well, instead of trying to learn from a lot of books by men who aren't even aware of the problem, we have to learn from each other. Examine our own experience and develop our own theories. If we can find out the truth about women's lives we'll have something solid to build our revolution on, the way the Chinese peasants built theirs."

Marya's voice popped in again. "Read *Fanshen* if you want to see what the Chinese did," she said. "And Mao. There's a lot to be learned from China."

I felt intimidated. China? Mao? Another version of the Trotsky Test?

Faith went on. "What we're doing here is really pretty simple. We refuse to accept anything as true that we can't confirm by our own feelings and experience. And we try to view everything in terms of women's interest: How does it affect women? Is it good for women or bad for women? It's a powerful method, you'll see. Even just among a few of us, we've already begun to learn so much from each other that it's changing our lives."

I couldn't begin to imagine their lives. Who were they? What did they do? Had they all read Marx and Mao? These women, who at first glance might appear rather ordinary, spanning the ethnic, racial, and physical types, now seemed nothing like the usual run of females. Unlike the women one saw on the street, in the subway, at the supermarket, they had a distinct and fascinating presence that made me feel like an imposter in imminent danger of being exposed.

Faith lit a cigarette and continued. "Usually we take one topic and examine a specific aspect of our lives, though of course, everything is connected. For the last few weeks we've been talking about what goes on in our jobs, our feelings about money and work. And before that we talked about sex."

"Sex?" repeated a young woman across the room, her round eyes opened wide. She sounded scandalized. She wore a short skirt and had her dark hair pulled severely back like a dancer's. Another newcomer, I figured.

"Sex is central," said Faith, standing up. "And if you're shocked that we discuss it, that's because we're not supposed to. Don't you think that's odd? We have hardly any reliable knowledge about sex, since almost everything that's been written about it has been written by men; but women don't talk about it to each other. Almost all anyone knows for sure is what we each know about ourselves. Well, now we're going to pool our knowledge."

She was right. Not even with Kitty, my one close friend, had I ever exchanged a word about sex, though half my life seemed to have revolved around it. We talked about books and ideas and the children, but nothing really personal. She knew nothing of Victor.

Now Marya, all defiance, was speaking excitedly. "Since sex is forbidden, it's one of the subjects we're going to deal with first!" Her nostrils flared. "Who are they to shut us up? The more intimate and personal the experience, the more important it is to examine. We're fed up with hearing that our problems aren't political, that they're 'just personal.' The personal *is* political," she said, her voice rising, as around the room people nodded in agreement.

The personal is political: a stunning new thought. All my life my big conflict had been the personal *or* the political. Whether to keep my mouth politely shut or take a stand. Whether to act on feeling or principle. Whether to accept the sweet security of family or live rebellious and alone. To nurse my baby or demonstrate. Sign a statement or please Ricky. Attend to dinner or go to jail. Sometimes I decided one way, sometimes the other, but always dissatisfied and guilty, seeing every political act subverted by the rude intrusion of ego. The personal and the political seemed incompatible until suddenly, in Marya's defiant vision, I glimpsed their reconciliation.

"There are reasons for every one of our so-called personal problems. Political reasons. Reasons of power. Why is it that women are stuck with all the housework and shitwork? We belong at home, right? But is that fair? And why do we take the rap for all the bad sex? We're frigid, right? And all the unwanted babies? We're careless, right? For being treated badly by men? We're bitches, right? And for all our other 'personal' problems? Do you think it's because women are stupid and irrational and weak-minded? No. It's because we're *oppressed!* We're oppressed by men. It's because men run this world for their own benefit. Men have power over women. Power. That's political!"

She paused. No one breathed. Then she said: "Now we're going to stop blaming ourselves. We're going to listen to our feelings and put the blame where it belongs and start taking some power for ourselves."

Yes! I thought. Yes.

Marya sat down. After a moment Faith continued. "We have three rules, that's all. We have to tell the truth about our feelings; we don't deny anyone else's experience; and we try not to pass judgment on each other. We just want to accept the evidence of our feelings and try to uncover the truth."

She looked around at us all. "That's it. At the end of the testimony we try to summarize what we've learned, maybe draw a few tentative conclusions.

"Let's start by going around the room and introducing ourselves; then we can decide on a topic. For now, just tell a little about yourself: your living arrangements, the kind of work you do, what brought you to this meeting, and why you're interested in Women's Liberation. Okay? Who wants to go first?"

Faith looked from one of us to the next. I pretended to be examining a pamphlet so she couldn't possibly catch my eye. My living arrangements? The work I did? These women probably all had glamorous jobs with futures, whereas I was nothing but a housewife, a mother, a Midwestern drudge. I had no idea of what I would say when my turn came up. The dangerous prospect of revealing "the truth" to a roomful of strangers made me skittish—though I had to admit I was extremely curious to hear their stories. The truth about my sex life and my work life—the two subjects that had been mentioned—filled me with shame. Sneaking a lover into my apartment while the children slept; Ricky's betrayals; feeling frantic about money while pretending it didn't matter; knowing I'd never finished college or held a decent job—these were things I took pains to hide from everyone, and all the more these high-powered strangers who would certainly blame me for my failure if not my discontent.

"Okay, then; if no one else wants to, I guess I'll begin," offered Faith.

And suddenly there I was, turning the key, entering my new life.

Once the heat is applied, once the invisible ink darkens and the message appears, it's hard to remember the blank page of the moment before. Like secrets penned in invisible ink, like faces disguised among the lines of those hidden pictures of childhood, in that woman-filled room the confusing jumble of disconnected lives I'd led began to take form. Slowly, as I heard my story repeated in as many variations as there were women in the room, the pattern began to emerge. Gradually my own life's aims and shames arranged themselves until at last all the hidden faces in the picture were manifest.

Yes—in quite a different way than Kitty thought, they were "like us." They led women's lives. They, we, and more. All were revealed: Else weeping in the attic, worried Mama, the baby sitters, me; and the refusers too: Nina, and Blanche, and Aunt Louise. Of course! The wonder was how I could have lived in that picture so long without ever perceiving those hidden faces.

I'm sorry I can't slip you into that first meeting, let you know each woman in the Third Street Circle, give you Faith's story, Golda's, Marya's, Olive's, and Kitty's too—instead of only mine. This synthesis is the climax of my story, and I'd like to offer it complete. I'd like you too to see those faces, know how various and ordinary we were. I want you to see where we came from: our childhoods, the bitterness, our families, the sex, the demeaning jobs, all our once-shameful secrets. Then you too might feel the shiver of new consciousness that went through us each time someone, speaking the forbidden, released a precious or shattering truth. Then you too might learn how that moment changed us forever: *Before:* uncertain, alone, adrift. *After:* one clenched fist; one perfect unbroken circle.

But of course, I can't. I'm sworn to secrecy. It's a private meeting and I can't talk (even though the FBI managed to get a full account!). I can tell you my story; but of this group with its visionary cause that turned me at last from an *I* to a *we*, I am free to reveal hardly more than is a matter of record: our public statements, projects, conferences, demonstrations—events like those that fill the pages of all the volumes of revolutionary memoirs. The hard-earned insights, the transformation of consciousness we achieved together by holding nothing back and offering each other our most intimate secrets—these must remain hidden, like forbidden books in the attic.

No wonder rebels' "Lives" so often read like position papers: There's so much they may not tell. The famous passion La Pasionaria lit her speeches with is strangely absent from her memoir. Sensitive Alexandra Kollontai, who often declared "the complete liberation and sexual emancipation of women" to be the "highest aim" of her life, blue-penciled the personal from her autobiography under last-minute Party pressure. Angela Davis, that loyal communist, veiled her most intimate feelings in judicious calm through a long, temperate autobiography. And even uncensorable Red Emma Goldman was temporarily silenced by censors at an International Anarchist Conference when she attempted to speak of Free Love. Those who defy the censors and say their say have it worse: Chiang Ching, Mao's widow, was castigated as a traitor for making taped revelations about her personal life. Ting Ling, modern China's most famous woman writer, was purged from the Party in '58 for writing passionately of the unhappy plight of women. Richard Wright left the Party in order to write freely. And for refusing to recant Joan of Arc died at the stake.

No Party stops my pen. But never shall I forget those strained meetings in which we looked for the informer among us, or the large stormy speak-outs where we voted to eject all reporters, or that hushed moment when a frightened sister gravely told us that something she'd said in the strict confidence of our Circle had been repeated "outside."

If I thought it would help our cause I might tell you all. But you can't build a movement on betrayal. Having myself confessed to perfect strangers my most carefully guarded secrets, I know silence is better than treachery. This is no fiction, where the author may write what pleases her; this is true.

(In fiction I wouldn't dare introduce six new faces three-quarters of the way through my tale, as in life. I'd keep my story small, start Chapter One with Our Circle—disguised, of course; then follow each character all the way through. I'd merge Nina and Faith into one person, maybe Carole and Marya into another, I'd bring Dee-Dee back as Kitty—it would be neat above all. But you could dismiss my story as untrue, and then what would be the point of it?)

No—better gaps than lies! I'll stick to history, even if it sprawls. Better to name the names, as the Lynds did for Middletown; let Victor and Marshall disappear, as lovers do; drop Nina; repeat nothing told me in confidence. But let the lessons be clear, and let every word be true.

At last it was my turn to speak. I meant to be cautious—honest but minimal. "Frankly, I came to this meeting," I began, addressing myself to the stipulated question, "because my friend told me it sounded interesting; and since we're both alone with our kids all day, we're always on the lookout for interesting conversation."

At the mention of kids, Faith nodded encouragingly and Marya sent Golda a triumphant look. Still, with or without their encouragement, I never intended to reveal to a roomful of strangers the damning facts or divided feelings that gorged me.

But after I'd listened to the other women's stories, all different yet underneath the same; after I'd viewed my own life through the prism of this new illuminating idea and seen its simple repetitive pattern uncovered for the first time; after I realized that all my attempts at freedom had ended in failure because I'd lacked this knowledge; I heard myself say to the assembled room: "But now that I'm here I think I must have come to save myself."

How they listened to me then! Who among them could have guessed I was the same timid soul whose carefully formulated questions to the monthly Intellectual Forums had died unasked on frightened lips? Once I found my tongue there was nothing I couldn't say. My guilts and confusions melted in the light of this stark new understanding. Indeed, the very aspects of my life I had found hardest to accept glowed as precious nuggets of experience for the Third Street Circle. To hear their eager questions, you might wonder if they'd ever before met a genuine living housewife-mother. My failures, my compromises, even my three children, those starlings on the runway who had kept me grounded, were suddenly assisting my ascent; and all that had seemed so humiliatingly unexceptional in my life was welcomed and accepted by these women. They were interested not merely, like Father Percy of the Peace Center, in the services I might volunteer or, like the PTA, in my vote or my dues; they were interested in my life, in me.

All listened rapt as I spoke; no one questioned my authority. And as I pronounced without a thought of discretion secrets that had never before passed my lips, as I began dimly to see connections I had never seen before, I knew I would not again be able to step back into darkness.

Now I had a key to explain my life. Perhaps it would even enable me to change it.

> Informant, who has furnished reliable information in the past, advised that a WLM meeting was held on [deleted] at [deleted] New York City. Each woman at this meeting stated why she had come to the meeting and how she felt oppressed, sexually or otherwise. Few of these women, according to the informant, have had political backgrounds. They are mostly against marriage, children, and other states of oppression caused by men. The informant stated that a mailing list was passed around at this meeting and she will try to obtain a copy of it.

2 · MISS AMERICA

"Go back to Russia!" shouted the fat man with the narrowed eyes and sneering lips. From a mutter, his sneer had picked up momentum until it had grown to a menacing threat. A short woman with dyed black hair and dark lipstick stood beside him smiling as he gathered around him a little mob of hecklers.

It was our fifth straight hour of marching in a slow oval before Atlantic City's Convention Hall, just down the boardwalk from a half-naked woman stretched out across a mammoth billboard advertising suntan oil. Inside the hall, the annual Miss America pageant was in progress: a perfect place for the first "mass" demonstration to launch our infant movement. Between the symbolism and the media coverage, it was a natural.

Or so it had seemed until we came up against the crowd. Now, it appeared, we had more explaining to do than we'd anticipated. Our signs, simple and straightforward, were evidently not clear enough. Of the boardwalk strollers who stopped to watch us, some were curious, some puzzled, but more than we'd expected were suspicious, hostile, and even, like the fat man, enraged.

I paused for a moment directly before him and, holding up to him a poster Tina and I had painted that said, simply, FREEDOM FOR WOMEN, looked him in the eye. The fat man slowly licked his lips as though my poster were an obscene picture and began shouting abuse, while the black-haired woman beside him (his wife?) and the other hecklers laughed their encouragement to him.

It was hard for me to understand that they hated us. Why? It was such a simple, such a sound idea—freedom for women. Equality, freedom: what could be more innocent? If I hadn't known better I would have thought the difficulty lay in dreaming up an argument against it that wouldn't fill one with shame. "Why did we need to have this movement at all?" Faith had asked. "To me, women's freedom is just common sense." And Marya had answered cynically, "Sure. To *you*."

And yet, they evidently had no trouble at all opposing us. The Left called our movement a "diversion"; the Right saw it as subversion. Trivial or critical—objections that canceled each other out. Even the apolitical hated us, just on general principles. The fat man, for instance—from the look on his face I thought he would try to wipe us out, given the chance.

Their hatred was a mystery. All we wanted was justice. "Oh, is that all?" I'd half expected them to say. "Of course, darling, everyone should have justice. Here, let me help you with your poster."

Instead, they threw around countercharges. They accused us of being bitter, envious, ugly, discontented. As though we hadn't ourselves proclaimed our discontent. As though anyone were supposed to rest content knowing how you were wronged. And when we went right ahead and pressed for our rights, they accused us of behaving "unnaturally."

Unnaturally? How could it be unnatural if that was the way we behaved? What was natural?

Or they said we didn't know what we wanted—when we clearly named and spelled out for them precisely what it was we wanted. ("The best way to reduce your adversary's argument to absurdity," said my *Debater's Manual,* "is to supply such an abundance of evidence and sound reasons against his argument that the audience can draw but one conclusion—that the argument is untenable.")

"Look, don't be foolish," Marya had warned. "Women's liberation is revolutionary dynamite. If we ever got equality—forget freedom for now—the entire system would collapse. People aren't stupid. They know. They can see the implications."

And indeed, that was always the problem: the implications. Galileo's insistence that the world went round the sun was innocent enough; it was the implications that caused all the trouble. One thing led to another and before you knew it the whole structure of the universe was being closely questioned.

Frankly, I could understand why some of the men felt threatened. If they went along with us they might have to give up certain things they cared about. They liked their dinners on the table when they came home, they liked their shirts folded neatly and their sox picked up, they liked their children tended to, their beds made with their women in them, ready. And they liked knowing that no matter what they did there'd never be a woman to boss them around.

But the young men, the men on the Left, movement men—what a disappointment they were. They claimed to want to turn the world upside down; they could go on endlessly about oppression and injustice. But when it came to us, they were unwilling even to think about it. You? they said, laying their hands on our knees or stroking their beards or our hair; what do *you* have to complain about? They too liked their privileges, it seemed. They liked their coffee made, their mailings done, their speeches typed, and particularly their freedom to love fast and run. Shades of beatnik charm. It was all too depressingly familiar.

Ricky had received the news of my sudden commitment with indifference, then suspicion, and finally apprehension. Even when he tried to hide it I could see he was jittery. No wonder: Suddenly I had my own plans; I was accepted where he wasn't; I was out of his control.

What about the children? he soon learned to say, as I started going to meetings every night. (He'd spent few enough evenings at home, but that was another story.)

Well, what about them? I said.

I had some other new ideas, too. For one thing, money. Why should he keep all our money? His ability to earn so much more money than I could earn was a privilege which ought not to be compounded by keeping me begging. I worked as hard as he worked, maybe harder, he couldn't deny it. Out of the joint checking account I began to draw money for the first time. Money to pay the extra baby sitters, money to finance some of the activities of the Third Street Circle (*Their financial needs are small*, reported an informer to the FBI, *and the individuals within the separate groups are able to supply the necessary funds*), money to put away for my old age, dammit, or sooner. Why shouldn't I?

"But didn't I always say I'd give you whatever money you wanted if you just asked me?" said Ricky, hurt.

"Yes. And you also made sure I would never ask!"

For another thing, I defied his will and even his orders, going one Sunday to a speak-out in the church across the park to give public testimony on my two abortions.

"I don't care if you attend, Zane," he said. "That's not it. I'd just rather you didn't discuss the abortions, that's all."

So reasonable. Was it true after all that every girl marries her father?

"Why not?" I asked.

"I just don't want you to discuss our private affairs in public."

That line. "It's not private, Ricky. It's political. They're trying to give that doctor ten years, remember?" As though our bodies belonged to *them!*

He tried to jolly me. "Come on, Zane—do you want to be Dred Scott?"

I ignored his little joke. The jokes that had once endeared him to me now tended to make me furious. "How will we get the laws changed if we don't start talking about it? You can't really object."

"No? You're such a nut, Zane. What makes you think there won't be police there? They've advertised the thing all over the place. They could arrest you."

"Let them arrest us! We're the victims, not the criminals! If they got all of us, they'd have to arrest hundreds of thousands of us, maybe even their own wives. Let them arrest us, I don't care!"

"Well, I do care. I'm a lawyer, remember? Abortion is illegal. How will it look if it gets in the papers? They prosecute people for having abortions, don't you realize that?"

At last, the true reason! It reflected on him. "I'm sorry, but I have to go," I said. "They haven't got so many people willing to testify—only five or six—and I'm the only married one with children. I said I'd do it. I have to."

"And I'm telling you, Zane" (eyes narrowing, voice at a whisper, the threatening signs of a long marriage), "I don't want you to go. I don't want you making a fool of yourself. It's my privacy too. I'm ordering you, Zane: don't go."

I did feel sorry for him, "ordering" me, but I was also furious. No, he couldn't control my new ideas, maybe couldn't even understand them. I was no longer subject to the old bargain, the old intimidation. I might feel shaky or ashamed about my secret lover, but giving testimony in public, defying the law, acting on principle was different: It could make you invulnerable. I refused to respond to Ricky's sarcasm. If anything, his attempts at intimidation only strengthened me. (Says Vera Zasulich of the first moments after she shot the hated Governor of St. Petersburg, General Trepov: "Every minute my joy increased . . . because I found myself in an extraordinary state of the most complete invulnerability, such as I had never before experienced. Nothing at all could confuse me, annoy me, or tire me. Whatever was being thought up by those men, at that time conversing animatedly in another corner of the room, I would regard them calmly, from a distance they could not cross.")

I suspect that for a while Ricky assumed I must have a lover. ("Oh, Zane, Zane—what's happening to us?") What but another man, a rival, could have captured my passions and transformed me so? My mother-in-law didn't help when she asked him archly, "Meetings, Ricky? Every night? I don't know—Zane never liked to leave the children before. Are you sure they're meetings she goes to?" He began waiting up till I came home and sometimes I suspected he was even having me followed. There was a certain man with a black beard and sometimes a painter's cap I saw standing in view of my window leaning on the park fence at all hours, day after day. Whenever I checked the window, he was there. The spy, I called him, wondering if I were turning paranoid.

But if he were Ricky's hireling (I never had proof), he wouldn't have seen much. The truth was, Victor lost his pull on me after I joined the Third Street Circle. The mood of the group was critical of men, and I had little time left for him. From the start, Thursdays were out, and soon my other nights went too. One night a study group; another night a business meeting just to answer the mail now daily pouring into our post office box; another night to develop theory and work on position papers; meetings to plan new strategies and actions; speaking engagements to spread the word (and prove we could do it); and after a while even weekend meetings to help other women get organized into new groups of their own. There was so much to be done, there was no time for men. Lenin's comrade Alexandra Kollontai had summed it up: "I have read novels and I know how love takes possession of one's faculties to the exclusion of everything else," she wrote. "But I have no time." Nor had I.

Dirty commie jew queer lesbian ugly cunt whore bitch!

There was something terrifying in the fat man's look. His freckled arms hanging from shirtsleeves ended in clenched fists. Even the black-haired woman beside him wore an uneasy expression. But at least the hecklers were taking us seriously, which was less demeaning than the Left's contemptuous dismissal. "What's the position of women in the movement?" someone had asked at an important Left conference, and the answer had come back, "The position of women in the movement is prone!" Prone was where I'd placed the speaker then—prone on my private list of offenders and traitors who would one day be sorry. Just wait, I'd say, adding them name by name; just you wait. Already my list contained selected relatives and leftists, half the famous beats, the President of Yale, the husband of my neighbor on the third floor, and Emanuel Popper, the principal of Sammy's school; and more were coming. A place was reserved for every man who continued to dismiss us after we'd troubled to explain, particularly those who ought to know better.

It was too soon to expect many people to understand us, much less support us. That morning sixty of us had mounted chartered busses at Union Square with our posters and leaflets—all the activisits we could assemble in New York. At that moment there probably weren't more than another two or three hundred women in the entire country who could claim to understand our struggle. An outspoken group in Boston, another in Washington, a group in Chicago, a few people in Florida, and strong beginnings in California. But we were all zealots (one could hardly have withstood the reprisals and jeers without zealous commitment); and a small core of zealots today could start Mao's prairie fire tomorrow. Soon we would be spreading; then let the enemy beware! Within the hour, inside Convention Hall a delegation of our women would be shouting and unfurling a giant red banner that read, WOMEN'S LIBERATION. With Ricky's money (rather, mine!) we had bought a block of tickets in the center of the front row of the balcony. The cameras would turn from the stage to us and all over the country, in every living room where people sat watching the pageant as they did each year, it would be known that women had stood up for their freedom; women were standing up. ("The people have stood up," proclaimed Mao victorious in '49.)

We had invited the press, alerting all media that we would speak only to female reporters. An outrageous tactic, and correct: Some papers had to pull reporters off their women's page to cover the story since they were the only women on staff. ("That ought to teach some people something," said Golda gleefully, and hardheaded Marya had added, "That ought to earn us some loyal media allies.") For guerrilla theater, we ceremoniously crowned a live sheep "Miss America" (as we sang "There she goes . . ." to the TV cameras, while Olive played the harmonica and Faith and Kitty danced), tossed bagfuls of high-heeled shoes, *Playboy* magazines, girdles, bras, eyelashes, and other accoutrements of oppression into a Freedom Trash Can; and otherwise put the world on notice that after half a century in eclipse, women were back. Back and fighting! Women were henceforth to be reckoned with!

"Let's move it along a little faster," said Golda waving her megaphone. "There's a group over there turning mean. Keep marching. Remember our decision: no personal confrontations."

The dangers surrounded us: hecklers, police, and even our own fanatics. A woman none of us knew had lettered a sign: THE ONLY GOOD MAN IS A DEAD MAN. Luckily, Marya had seen it in time and had managed to persuade her not to carry it. We wanted to reach women, support sisters, make people understand—not simply attack men, though some people couldn't seem to see the difference. Planning this action, deciding nuances of policy, we had agreed to abide by group decisions, but we couldn't control the newcomers. One lone, starry-eyed woman on the boardwalk had said, "I've been waiting so long for this," and Kitty, handing her a sign, had invited her to join us. But there were others who watched and said nothing as the occasional hecklers, turning meaner and louder every minute, trotted out the old arguments and names we'd heard all our lives: "Back to the kitchen where you belong!" (the fat man was shouting as I came round again). "You're jealous of Miss America!" "Bitch!" "Hag!" "Not one decent-looking broad in the bunch of you!" "Uglies!" "Dyke!"

Now their names could no longer scare us. These "hags" were beautiful. A "bitch" was a fighter. And where was the bite in "dyke" now? A dyke was a woman who lived without men, a dyke was a woman-loving woman.

"Bitch!" yelled the fat man once more as I neared him. He lewdly licked an ice cream cone, gyrating his tongue in attempted insult. Beside him the black-haired woman frowned and placed a hand on his arm. With a quick upward jerk he threw her hand off him. I turned to face him, raised my chin, and held out my sign: FREEDOM FOR WOMEN.

It was a new strength that surged through me now. At every demonstration until today's I'd felt myself part charlatan, shamelessly joining someone else's struggle in order to be counted among the saved. I'd been tortured like any unbelieving believer, wretched as St. Augustine, begging God to reveal Himself, even as he led a worldly life. Not even the enraged whites in the early sixties shouting "nigger-lover," or the soldiers with bayonets staring us down in Washington, or the indifferent Villagers hurrying off in the cold to buy their Sunday morning croissants at Sutter's French Bakery while I stood in freezing Village Square during the weekend Peace Vigil that went on unbroken for years, had made me feel justified as this fat man, hurling his insults, made me feel now.

"Don't you think maybe it's too late for us to join this movement?" Kitty had asked me after I ran down for her that first enthralling meeting of the Third Street Circle. "A meeting every week, I don't know. . . . What about the kids?" And I'd known instantly what she meant. Weekly commitments were reckless for mothers. Someone always got sick or recalcitrant or the sitter didn't show or your husband felt neglected. Still, I'd known Kitty was wrong. It was not too late: we were just beginning. Our lives supplied the data, our minds the theory; if we couldn't get a sitter we could take the children with us. This was our struggle. Never again would I hover on the edges, a suspect white in the black movement, a lawyer's wife in a worker's cause, a campus radical off-campus, irresolute, dispensable. This was my fight and I was essential. Never mind the confusing debates over which horror preceded which or which people were more oppressed. All oppression was interconnected. Sexism was as outrageous as racism, poverty, imperialism, and every other vile injustice—perhaps more so for being unacknowledged. If we—if I personally—did not fight for the interests of women, who would? Gone at last was that endless inquisition into my own motives that had turned even my highest purpose sour. Now I knew precisely what I was struggling for. Not glory (for which women had always sold themselves to love), not love (a spinoff of glory for a clever man), but justice.

The shouting had stopped, replaced by an eerie silence. Something told me to watch out.

Then I saw: the fat man was sending a missile arching toward my head.

Had the light in my eye provoked him? Or the sign I'd so lovingly painted? It was I he was attacking, not a symbol, not a messenger. I myself, with my gap-toothed smile, I—now for the first time in my life one with my beliefs.

Quickly I averted my face (turned, not ducked: I was standing up now) so that the ice cream cone, missing my cheek, landed in my hair. I threw it to the ground, then turned back to face my assailant. There I stood, with ice cream melting in my hair but my chin high, a martyr in glory, a martyr fulfilled. I barely noticed the people shouting all around me.

Then an amazing thing happened. The black-haired woman, leaning over the barricades the police had erected hours earlier "to protect us," handed me a wad of Kleenex. "Here," she said, "wipe yourself up with this."

The fat man turned toward her with a look of stunned disbelief.

The woman said nothing to him, but to me she repeated her gesture with another handful of tissues, her eyes blazing like ours.

Golda, exhilarated, thanked her profusely before shouting into the megaphone, "Come on. Let's keep this line moving." Kitty leaned across the barrier to shake her hand. I beamed my thanks silently, and in a moment we were marching again.

One casualty; one sister (maybe many sisters?) stronger. Not yet time for the action inside the hall, but already victorious.

Subject: MEETINGS AND ACTIVITIES OF WLM

The following report appeared in the October 1968 issue of Rise-Up:

"On September 7, in its first major action, WLM staged an all-day demonstration on the Boardwalk in front of Convention Hall where the Miss America Pageant was taking place. . . . Picket signs proclaimed solidarity with the Pageant contestants while condemning the Pageant itself as racist, militaristic, commercial, and 'degrading to women.' Sporadic violence erupted. At night an 'inside squad' of 20 women disrupted the live telecast of the Pageant, yodeling the eerie Berber Yell (from the Battle of Algiers), shouting 'Freedom for Women,' and hanging a huge banner reading Women's Liberation from the balcony rail. Two women were arrested for spraying Toni Hair Conditioner (a sponsor of the Pageant) near the Mayor's box."

As the police handcuffed Marya and Golda, Golda told us later, they charged them with "emitting a noxious odor." Golda had jeered, "Yeah? Tell it to Toni!" But Marya had smiled and said, "Thou sayest it."

3 · LEO STERN

"Stop it now!" snapped Leo Stern to his son Clifford who was dipping a chopstick into his tea while the rest of us finished our hot-sour soup. Leo threw his wife, Rhoda, an ugly look, then returned to fulminating over the faulty logic in several reviews in that morning's *New York Times Book Review* in which two of his prize authors had been trounced.

I tuned out. The authors were male, the reviewers were male, the subjects of their treatises were male, that whole world of books and publishing and ideas and politics was male; and Leo Stern too, who had recently been appointed executive editor in one of the more prestigious publishing houses, was himself smugly, complacently, arrogantly male.

Clifford was dipping again. "Can't you do something?" said Leo to Rhoda. This time his disapproving look took in our entire table —one of the large round ones in the center of the currently popular Mandarin Palace on upper Broadway: Ricky and me, Leo and Rhoda Stern, and among us a present total of five children.

"Really, Leo," said Rhoda, "you can't expect them to sit still if they're starving and they don't have anything in front of them to eat. Can't *you* do something? Get our waiter?"

"That's right, Leo," I seconded with a little smile in support. "Why do you put it all on Rhoda? You're the father; what are *you* going to do?"

He threw me a quizzical look; it was probably the first time in our long history that I had ever plumped for Rhoda against him. Well, many things had changed.

I fished a mushroom out of my soup with my chopsticks and held it out to Julie. Ordinarily I avoided taking the children to dinner where adults were present. I hated the strain of dividing myself between my charges and my friends, even if the children were officially welcome. "Oh, we don't mind if you bring your kids," some people offered, misunderstanding my objection. Of course they didn't mind: It wasn't their meals that would be ruined; I was too conscientious a parent to permit that! If one of the kids started to whine or spit up, the adults could just raise their voices a little higher or lean a little closer to whoever was talking (as Ricky was now edging his chair toward Leo) while I withdrew from the conversation. Rescuing utensils and settling quarrels were definitely bad for the digestion and even worse for the image—especially the image of one who had once flamboyantly rejected the trivial trappings of family life in the name of perfect freedom. There were some, of course, who sacrificed their children to their images—like the spaced-out parents we'd seen sharing their joints with their toddlers at that afternoon's Love-In in Central Park. But I had early resigned myself simply to forgetting about image, restaurants, dinner guests, cafes, and coherent conversation unless the children were home with a sitter or until they had all reached a certain age.

Today, however, I had made an exception. It was a long time since we'd seen the Sterns, and being uptown at dinner time we'd decided to call them. I wanted to apologize to Rhoda for my long flirtation with her husband.

At that moment the waiter arrived with a huge platter and began piling tureens of delicacies on our table. Shiny rice noodles, shredded spiced beef, plump dumplings, tiny shrimp, a whole fish with staring eyes in ginger sauce, chicken with walnuts, delicately sautéed vegetables that kept their color, mounds of steaming rice. As the waiter raised the covers from the serving dishes with a flourish before leaving us to indulge ourselves, I was suddenly struck by the alien ambiance of the restaurant. Despite the usual handful of students and sprinkling of Chinese, the place bulged with soft, overindulgent New Yorkers. The last thought in the minds of the comfortable people proudly wielding chopsticks or lining up for tables behind the red velvet rope at the front of the restaurant was of revolution. Fashionable restaurants, private people—though I'd once come close to joining them, since I'd joined the movement I could hardly even remember how to behave.

Distinguished, dandified Leo Stern was unaware of the vast changes that had taken place in the world and in me since our last meeting. He pursed his lips and raised his eyebrows as though he were still and always the undisputed star of our table. Since I'd seen him last, he'd sprouted a trim little salt and pepper beard (unlike Ricky who refused to pander to fashion even to the extent of growing sideburns), had traded his academic tweeds for denims and his horn-rimmed specs for wire-rimmed ones; but he was as slippery and aggressive as the late fifties savant he'd been when I'd met him.

"I've been told," he said, "that the chef at this restaurant was literally kidnapped from Peking by a ring of Hong Kong adventurers who supply the best restaurants in the world. They held an auction for this man with bids reaching to six figures. As though he were a hot manuscript going to the reprint houses or a baseball property. You're the connoisseur among us Zane—let us know how it measures up."

I was no connoisseur, but Leo had a selective memory. Once I had cooked an exotic meal for him when Ricky and I were first married, and he had typed me. He was not a man to examine his judgments frequently. I was sure that once he noticed the small feminist button blazing on my shirt like a red flare (clenched red fist inside a female symbol), signifying to initiates that I had withdrawn my allegiance from every man, including this molder of opinion, he'd be less generous with his flattery. In fact, once the button registered, I had no doubt I'd be in for it—not only because feminism threatened to interfere with free-trade in adultery, but as an ism on its own. Leo hated the giddy sixties and was well known for his venom.

We passed the platters around the table, Rhoda and I helping the children, Leo and Ricky helping themselves. Eagerly Leo opened a dumpling with his fork—the only adult at the table who had not mastered chopsticks. As long as the food had still to be tasted, he wouldn't notice my button, but afterward it would be only a matter of moments until politics was on every plate.

Sometimes my button embarrassed people as it sat on my breast announcing my passion like an indiscretion. A button was a breach of taste, a belch calling attention to some fact or process people would rather not acknowledge. When its symbolism was known, my button was sometimes greeted with curiosity or even sympathy by women; but to men, it was an affront, the palm across the cheek to be met with counterattack.

Men far less arrogant than Leo found the challenge irresistible. Frequently they could defend their confronted egos by dismissing my button with a laugh, placing themselves above such absurdities as my obsession. "Women? What next!" Daddy had said when I'd begun systematically defending Mama. Sometimes they found it necessary to issue me a short reprimand for not devoting my energies to a worthier, less Byzantine cause. "Women?" it might run. "But what about the working class?" (Victor); "What about the war?" (Father Percy); "What about the blacks?" (the husband of my neighbor on three)—neglecting to notice in their concern that half the working class, half the Vietnamese, half the black people in the world were women who, even after every revolution conceived or achieved, still wound up the bottom half. But sometimes they were sufficiently threatened by the accusation implicit in my button to undertake a full-scale ideological attack. Today, I was certain, was such a time and Leo Stern, whose style was combat, such a man. Okay. I was ready.

"What's this?" asked Tina.

"A nut. A walnut. The kind we crack. You love them."

She poked it around her plate. "In my chicken? I don't want it."

"You loved it last time."

"I didn't."

"Try it anyway, Tina," intruded Ricky, "or leave it there, but don't play with it."

Time was, nothing would have filled me with more dread than combat with Leo Stern. Maybe I'd become more political than he, but he'd gone to Harvard, he'd read everything, he knew the authorities, and he humiliated his opponents. People were included in his "us" or they weren't, and there were consequences. People did (like Ricky) or didn't (like me) play squash at the Harvard Club with its separate Ladies' Entrance; people were impressed or they weren't by the names he dropped. I confess, I had been—at least by his first-name basis with Morgan Moore and by his letters that were occasionally printed in the *New York Review of Books*. He had the passion of debaters, the wit of literati, and since I had miraculously defeated him at chess eight years earlier, he had honored me with a grudging, if gratifying, respect, the only man in New York besides Ricky ever to do so. As the years had passed, he never forgot the game (I never forgot it either) and with amazing ingenuity always managed to work some reference to it into every conversation, even those that appeared most resistant. Like spouses who publicly boost their mates knowing how they reflect upon each other, Leo affirmed my talents because they had once for a moment outshone his. Perhaps he did it as a self-inflicted penance for having lost to me, perhaps in a vain attempt to exorcise the memory, but whatever the reason, he paid me the unique compliment of taking me on in debate and turning his charms on me. His attention to me gave me just that edge of confidence I needed to do my best, and I always welcomed that continued acknowledgment of my moment of triumph.

Today, however, my feelings were mixed. Not only because of Rhoda, but because the considerable charm Leo had always held for me had shriveled up like a dead balloon when I'd joined the movement. How, I wondered, could I ever have been so vain as to fall for his conceit? Now that I had replaced my bumbling confusion with analysis, my old insecurity with belief, I found his good opinion of me self-serving and patronizing, his conversation shallow, his insights trite, his demeanor elitist, his ideas as predictable as I had once (oh, how?) found them interesting. Compared to the absorbing talk I now pursued daily among women, Leo's talk was dull and frivolous. Even his style, which I'd once found so compelling, had grown irritating to me now that he was unmasked. The paltry scraps of flattery he had thrown to me from his immodest table and for which I had so shamelessly groveled now filled me with shame. Who was he but another misogynist, cruel to his wife, unfeeling with his children, a bully to the world?

"Zane," said Ricky, calling me back from my giddy stew, "can you pass the shrimp? Everything's piling up near you."

Hatred was surely distracting. It was counterproductive to engage in individual struggle with the enemy, yet something in me still wanted to fight Leo. Though my duty was to concentrate on rallying Rhoda, who could, if enlisted, do an inside job on Leo, armed with my vision I wanted to battle him to the ground, then turn like a matador trailing cape in the dust and walk victoriously away.

"I suppose you saw the review of those books in the *Times* this morning by your friend Morgan Moore?" Leo said when he had arranged little mounds of each kind of food in a circle on his plate.

His reference to Moore was a good offensive opening for the game we'd always played, for though he despised Moore almost as much as I revered her, he was her friend while I was merely her fan.

I had several good moves available to me: a defense of her review, a defense of her person (longer range strategy), or a counterattack.

Actually, Moore's review had disappointed me, for she had not yet embraced our cause. I was convinced it was only a matter of time until she joined us. Indeed, that morning's piece, like every new article over the past year, had brought her one small step closer to us, though her progress wasn't fast enough for some of the impatient women in our Circle who were already preparing to denounce her. Faith had dismissed her as acting more like the opportunistic bourgeois women who claimed to have "made it on their own" than the radical I knew her for; militant Golda said with contempt that Moore's equivocation held us back, accusing her bitterly of being more concerned to defend her position among the male intellectuals who had elevated her than to assert her solidarity with us. But I, her perfect reader, recognized her seeming aloofness as a matter of scruples. Hadn't she already denounced chess as a vainglorious distraction from politics? She was coming along. My own espousal of our cause was connected with her, whose lone example had sustained me during my long years in captivity.

But while I could defend her to my sisters, it would be perilous to defend her to Leo. I would have to use premises he'd never accept or arguments I no longer believed. We were worlds apart.

That very morning I had gone through the whole *New York Times* with red pencil poised, counting the paltry token female entries, circling the insults, underlining the names of the enemy. Ricky had watched me alarmed, but Leo would have laughed to see it. I red-penciled his entire world; the only books I read now—those by and about women—he would probably not even have heard of.

"Yes," I said, "I saw the review," and dropped the subject.

Across the table Marcia and Clifford Stern, four and six respectively, were getting up and down from their chairs, oblivious of the busy waiters carrying heavy trays of steaming food among the tables. Evidently the Sterns had a different set of restaurant rules from ours. Rhoda, with an attitude that alternated between frantic and resigned, was making only cursory efforts to seat them. And I realized that I was really more concerned to keep my own children from being hopelessly corrupted by the Sterns's example than to defend my politics from Leo's inevitable attack. His challenge, his opinion, which had once kept our meetings tense with excitement, was now of no consequence; nothing was at stake but my energies. Could this be "liberation"?

"She should have stuck to chess," said Leo in one last attempt to engage me in battle and at the same time prepare the way for his inescapable allusion to our match.

"Listen, Leo," said Ricky, "if I were you I wouldn't bait Zane. She's likely to snap your head off."

Ricky spoke from experience. His racy jokes, his "honey" and "sweets" to waitresses and telephone operators, his lack of vigilance with the language and lack of patience with the children continually provoked my wrath.

"Really?" asked Leo, his curiosity piqued.

"You'll see," said Ricky.

I jumped on Ricky. "Thanks, I can speak for myself. You don't have to interpret me."

"Well," said Leo, "this is beginning to sound interesting."

"Forget it," I said and engaged my chopsticks.

"Tea?" asked Rhoda the peacemaker, filling cups. And seeing he could not get a proper response from me, Leo turned his attention back to Ricky.

I was too jumpy lately, true. Little jokes, words, sexist comments let slip in all innocence, I could not let pass. I was like a coiled spring, set to snap at the first ruffled hair. I laughed only at our jokes, never at theirs. Even this dinner, which now pained me, would have been the highlight of my week a year before, providing me with a week's worth of images to ponder and conversation to contemplate while sitting in the playground. I would have been grateful for a chance to engage the worldly Leo, for the experience, capital E. The weekend excursions—to Chinatown, to the pushcart markets on Delancey Street, to the pulsing San Gennaro's Festa, to the serene Cloisters, a swim at Coney Island, a stroll through the Diamond District, to see the lions in the Bronx Zoo, or whatever treat Ricky would offer us on his day off—had seemed our only remaining adventures in New York. Now, however, I had more important things to do than mark time or collect experience. Now every minute counted. Conversations were interesting or dull as they illuminated or evaded the Question. The very talk I'd come East to hear now left me bored or irritated, while the back-porch chatter of Babylon girls I'd so eagerly fled had begun to excite my curiosity. (If only I'd saved my diary!) I knew that other people continued to live their lives day by day with only the vaguest of plans and hopes, as I'd long done myself. The restaurant was crowded with such people waiting for tables, examining menus, savoring flavors, impressing each other, hungering after what was called "fulfillment" or the sheer accumulation of sensation. But I could barely remember what it had been like. Now, even the simplest of my old pleasures—a book, a movie, a stroll through the Village, an hour in a coffee house (unless it were a relevant book, a woman's movie, a leafleting stroll, a discussion hour)—held no appeal, and the grand, once moving experiences—music, literature—were mystifying. What satisfactions could they yield? A momentary delight, an afternoon's entertainment, an evening's diversion.

A diversion! The very accusation our leftist detractors so unfairly hurled at feminism, I threw up against daily life itself!

"Do you ever cook Chinese?" Rhoda was asking, and took a bite of shredded beef. "The idea of it. The idea of everything cut up in advance, of chicken with nuts, my god, of shiny noodles like these. Who would ever think of it? I have a friend who's taking a course in Chinese cooking. I've never tried it. Did you know Marco Polo discovered noodles in China and took them back to Italy to become spaghetti?"

She chewed thoughtfully. A source of esoteric information like her husband, but hers was culinary. "Isn't this spiced beef marvelous?" she said.

I wondered if this were the moment to begin my pitch. Around cooking. Any point of common experience would do, anything could serve the organizer: cooking, child care, the supermarket, the twenty-hour mother's day, not to mention in Rhoda's case the constant derogation of her opinions and desires to those of the great Leo Stern.

"Miraculous, I'd say. That's why I'd never attempt to cook Chinese food myself. First, I know I could never do it well, but besides that, I don't think I want to know. I have this feeling about China, about the orient."

At that moment Leo shot an arm out to grab Clifford who was balancing on one foot. "Now will you sit down and behave?" he said between clenched teeth, squeezing the boy's shoulder and sending another searing look across to Rhoda.

I decided to use a direct approach. "Anyway, nowadays I go to so many meetings that I hardly have time to cook anything that takes much preparation."

"What kind of meetings?"

"Women's Liberation."

I waited to see her response. She looked blank for a moment, then asked, "What?"

"The Women's Liberation Movement—have you heard of it?"

"I don't think so. What is it?"

I lowered my voice, leaned across Tina to get closer to Rhoda's ear and began to explain. One recruit—especially a wife and mother—would justify my having taken a day off and come uptown. Helping Rhoda would be penance for my once shameless pursuit of her husband.

Tina pushed me away.

"It's really hard to talk about it here," I said, "but if you're interested I'd love to take you to one of our meetings."

She looked puzzled. It was true, I had never before, in all the years I'd known her, invited her to do anything with me. But, as I was now learning daily, it's never too late.

"Do you think Leo would enjoy it?"

"Not with Leo. Just you. Men aren't invited to these meetings."

"No? Why not?" She looked positively bewildered.

"We have to be able to talk honestly." I lowered my voice still further. "You know how hard that is when men are around. Besides, they might not like what we're doing."

"What exactly *are* you doing?"

How could I answer such a question here?

"I mean, what do you talk about?" she said.

"Everything. Right now the group I'm in is working on making abortions legal. But that's just one issue. There are so many. I'll send you some literature."

Her eyes reacted to the word abortion. There was hardly a woman I knew who didn't respond to the abortion question, hardly anyone who hadn't had one or needed one at some time in her life. Even the most ardently single women in the Third Street Circle, women who vowed they would never marry, had been pregnant at some time in their lives, and not for ignorance of birth control. There was more to it than simple will, something beyond reason.

"Your . . . group?" she said.

"Yes. The Third Street Circle."

"Is it a therapy group? An encounter group?"

I laughed. "No, nothing like. In those groups, I understand, you try to change yourselves, you try to express yourself and adapt to the world. We're doing the opposite. We want to change the world."

She looked blank.

"Men have been getting away with murder," I whispered, "don't you think? They're the ones who ought to change."

She looked over at Leo talking to Ricky. "When do you meet?" she asked.

"Sundays we have meetings for new people. There's one tonight if you'd like to come. Do you think you can?"

But instead of answering, she asked, "Is that what the little button is for?"

"Yes. The struggle symbol inside a female symbol. Women's Liberation."

Despite her evasion, she was clearly curious, maybe curious enough to come to a meeting. Better not push it, though, I decided, better to give her space and time to build up courage. Leo was probably a tougher husband to buck than many—in some ways harder even than the rough types, the wife-beaters you could hate. All that charm and power. Gentility could be disarming. Most dangerous of all were the accommodating ones who pretended not to care or even gave their assent, only to sabotage you behind your back, driving you crazy with double messages. Leo might prove to be one of those.

I clasped a morsel of fish between my chopsticks and, concentrating on the logistics of transport, lifted it to my mouth. When I looked up, Leo Stern was staring at my button.

"Women's Liberation? Is that what I heard you say?" A smirk was on his face, a smirk as arresting as the button at which he was now leering like a cat who has spotted a roach. "You're one of those?"

"Yes."

It disturbed me that Leo had heard of us but we hadn't penetrated to Rhoda, who probably had no time to read and no one to talk to.

"The liberation of *women?*" he repeated. "Women? My god! From what?"

From you! I wanted to say. Just keep talking, Leo; you're on my list. Every word you say from now on is going straight into my file. Keep talking, baby. You'll be learning from what soon enough!

But instead, I let the voice of reason prevail. ("Patience," said the *Debater's Manual*, "is one of the highest manifestations of will. In the midst of a mob, the man who can stand absolutely quiet and master it has the strongest will.")

"From serving men," I said calmly.

The smirk broadened to a sneer. How well I knew it. It was a look I'd been seeing all the years I'd been in New York but until recently had never really understood. It was the same intimidating look that had made me cower in fright in the Cafe Lucia, that had sent me reeling anxiously to the New York Public Library to read up on Trotsky, that had made me choose a husband half to escape, that had effectively kept me off the streets and even out of the peace movement.

Always before I had retreated in the face of it, turning soft, shy, affectionate, accommodating. This time, though, protected by the magic circle of the Third Street women, I knew I would stand up to it.

Leo dabbed at the corners of his mouth. "I've always been under the impression that it was men who serve women, not vice versa. But please, Zane, do tell us about it, this movement of yours."

Ricky seemed to shrink into his chair at Leo's invitation, but Rhoda watched us closely. Ashamed of all the erotic messages Leo and I had passed back and forth over the years in front of them in the guise of combat, I lowered my eyes, as Leo leaned on the table, spreading his authority.

That week I had read a brilliant thirty-two-page pamphlet denouncing love and sex, put out by a Boston group. The position paper, a tour-de-force, scathingly castigated male-female love as no less than collaboration with the enemy. The group concluded their presentation with a principled vow of celibacy, to be honored until the completion of the first stage of the revolution.

I doubted I could take such a vow myself. My position was precarious: I had a husband, children, a household, and other duties besides. But I admired the stand both for its motive and its goal. Purity and autonomy; an end to diversion. If love itself could yield before the onslaught of our will and the penetration of our analysis, then indeed nothing was sacred; there could be no quarter for the enemy, no thought or action above suspicion; nothing was even neutral.

"Well?" said Leo, the smirk now permanently affixed to his face.

"You're really interested?"

"Please."

And though I knew he could be interested only in the battle, not at all in the substance, for his views were as fixed as the solstice, I had such faith in the power of our idea that I proceeded to speak.

Across the table I paraded for Leo only the most glaring, indisputable inequities—politics, economics, education, law; not a word about those deeper aspects of our bondage, sex, power, dependency. With modest gesture, iron logic, and irrefutable statistics I launched a low-keyed presentation, putting all my skill and passion into it.

When I had finished, Leo still looked amused. "Maybe you have a point about women who work. But look at your own life, look at Rhoda's—you girls hardly have cause to complain."

Women who work? Once I would have followed Leo's lead and chastised myself for my dissatisfactions and vain desires. Now I had only to recall that morning's *Times*, remember how Ricky was unreachable in an emergency, think of the sox left on the floor, the anxiety, the years of isolation.

"Would you really trade your life for Rhoda's?" I asked.

Leo hesitated before clearing his throat to lie: "Well, yes, if I knew how to do the things she does. And if she could do my work. Why not?"

"The dishes Leo—surely you know how to wash dishes."

"Really, Zane—be serious."

Now it was my turn to jeer. "I bet Rhoda even types your manuscripts, doesn't she?" It was a safe guess. All those writers had wives for secretaries, whom they thanked on the acknowledgments page. (Such an acknowledgment appeared in a standard med school textbook currently circulating in the movement. In it the author-doctor thanked his wife for typing the manuscript and doing the index. But an index entry under B read: "Birds, for the, pp. 1–2574.")

"That's right! I do type his manuscripts!" said Rhoda.

"Come on now, Rhoda. What do you think my secretary does?" said Leo.

"I'm not talking about your office work, Leo. I mean your articles."

"When you offer to type them, yes. But when did I ever ask you to type for me? Never. Except maybe once."

Her eyes opened wide. "No, you don't ask me, it's true. You just leave your brown notebook on the kitchen table with the pages you want typed marked with paper clips. And you kiss me when I hand it back to you."

Leo turned his back to his wife to shut out her protest and addressed himself to Ricky. "I presume you've had something to do with this, Ricky. Suppose you tell us how you feel about your wife running around stirring up trouble among your friends and parading around in that ridiculous button." He tried to make light of our complaint. But I could tell he was rattled from the way he speared several shrimp with less delicacy than usual and popped them into his mouth.

I was rattled too. "What has Ricky got to do with it?" I cut in. "He's no authority on the subject of women. You know, Leo, you're never going to learn anything about it by listening to men. Why don't you listen to me?"

He stared at me incredulously. I had always been so ingratiating with him. Competitive, yes; but never offensive, never rude.

As though in protest to my outburst, Julie knocked over her tea, launching hot sugared jasmine across her tray and a frightened cry though the air.

I welcomed the interruption. What was the use of this argument? The hard-line separatist position the Third Street Circle had taken on male reporters at demonstrations had proven itself correct. Perhaps it ought to be extended to all unsympathetic males; Leo could only drain me of energy.

While I wiped up Julie's tea Leo trotted out the usual rebuttals. We were small-minded complainers, narcissists soured by envy and self-pity. If you don't like housework hire a maid. Let them eat cake.

But what were women to do? We could either "accept" our lot or fight it. Leo, of course, would have us accept it; what else could such charges as "discontent" and "self-pity" mean? But we had chosen to fight it.

"Envy, of course, I can understand," Leo was saying. "But your willingness to admit it, to elevate it to a principle, to organize a movement around it, to want everything—that, frankly, I find alarming."

He chewed chicken and continued. All groups, all movements, he considered suspect, regardless of their particular program. They lacked subtlety. What was an advocate after all, what was an arm-waver, a button-wearer, however sincere, but a person who had surrendered the power to think independently?—another sheep grazing on the range of the sloganeers—dogmatist, faddist, follower, fanatic.

A clever line, I pointed out, to denigrate groups. Because without solidarity we couldn't have any power, and without power, nothing could be changed.

On we went. Soon we were no longer calmly "discussing" the issue, waiting politely for the other to finish making a point, then nicely returning the volley, but were locked in boring debate with our premises the stakes. It was infuriating: When I called feminism a heresy he called it a fad; I spoke of injustice, he of ingratitude. I felt the blood rise to my cheeks as my anger quickened, felt the children grow restless and Ricky unsettled as we began repeating ourselves, but I kept going. Every question Leo raised could be explained by my theory, every fact I offered could be dismissed by his. I sensed we were probably beginning to tire even Rhoda.

In fact, we might never have stopped, though neither of us could possibly win, if the futility of the argument hadn't suddenly dawned on Leo. At a certain moment his face changed, he raised his index finger in the air and said, with what he must have thought withering triumph: "But if that's your position, my dear Mrs. Thompson" (I winced at the name), "you can prove anything you like. Your argument's a mere tautology. There's no way you can lose."

As though truth could be established by verbal skill, as though the world's insufferable injustice could be quibbled away or a vision be dismissed as "mere." "Where do correct ideas come from?" asked Chairman Mao. Not from the sky but from "social practice." Until that moment I too with my debater's head had believed in logic chopping despite the warnings of the Third Street Circle. But now I realized that our battle of words was useless.

We were enemies, Leo and I. Our struggle went deeper than words. He sat there thinking he had me because he'd established that logically I couldn't lose, but really I had him.

"That's right!" I cried, leaning forward over the table abandoning every debater's rule in my moment of passion, "I've lost all the arguments I'm going to lose, *Mistra* Stern. I'm through losing arguments!"

He blinked to get his bearings and then archly repeated with a pained expression intended to wound, "Mistra?"

But I didn't care. In that moment I was exulting in my new commitment: to win every battle, every argument, if it meant making an enemy of every male.

"Yes," I said, leaning back. "Why not? You call us Miss and Mrs.; we'll call you Mr. and Mistra."

Now certain that he had won, Leo expanded his smirk to an embarrassed giggle (embarrassed, no doubt, for me). But Rhoda liked my little barb and smiled a different smile. ("To be attacked by the enemy," said Mao, "is not a bad thing but a good thing.") Yes. The time had come for me to stop losing. The time had come to win.

"Tea?" said Rhoda again. She filled the cups, restoring harmony.

"Can we have fortune cookies now?" asked Sammy.

"In a little while," I said in my mother-voice.

"Please," whined Tina, who had long since finished.

"I'll try to get the waiter," offered Ricky.

Around the table the platters of food were passed again. By now they had been reduced to just that level of emptiness at which everyone must begin taking helpings by the morsel instead of by the portion in order to leave the last little bit for someone else, a potentially infinite regress.

"Does anyone want to finish up the shrimp?" asked Rhoda. "Who'll have a little more of the shredded beef? Come on. There's just a drop left. It's a shame to leave it."

No one answered.

"Well, if no one else wants it," she said, "I guess I'll finish it." She emptied the beef dish onto her own. I took the last spoonful of shrimp while Ricky and Leo vied for the last word. Sammy and Cliff returned to fencing with their chopsticks, Tina and Marcia resumed their punning, and I took a mental inventory of caps and jackets.

It was already after seven. We'd never get home for Julie's bedtime, which meant I'd be late for my orientation meeting. But maybe, I thought, my lateness was justified by my gains. Not the useless battle with Mistra Leo Stern or even the pitch to Rhoda, whom I'd be better off recruiting privately. My big gains were two insights I should probably have known for years.

The first even Ricky had known: that without a change in will a verbal win means nothing. The second came to me as a resolution. I lifted Julie to the floor and helped her into her jacket, all the time vowing over and over in my mind: *No more diversions.*

4 · TRASHING

Golda was driving the getaway car. I had bought the spray paint. Kitty had assembled the addresses and planned the route. Faith was the lookout, and the others were along to prove themselves.

Tonight's midnight raid was a fast zap action—not only to change consciousness but to seal our solidarity. It was a moonlit night, but I didn't care. The more danger, the better the proof of our commitment. Witches traditionally rode in the full moon.

Each of us had selected a target from our private enemies list—some bastion of misogyny that particularly riled. NBC (Faith's choice), the Electrical Workers' Local 3 (Golda's), the Archdiocese of New York (Marya's), the Playboy Club (Kitty's), and for me—there hadn't been a moment's doubt—the Harvard Club, with its diminutive Ladies' Entrance, the Harvard Club, where half the people on my list and some of the most powerful men in the land smugly congratulated one another.

"Okay," said Golda. "Half a block. Get ready, Zane. Your turn next."

I was ready. A few months before I couldn't have done it. A few months before I'd have been proud to shower the world with leaflets naming each antiwoman atrocity or plaster the subways with stickers proclaiming, THIS AD INSULTS WOMEN. But as our cause spread, our tactics escalated and now we wanted revenge.

We'd heard that a women's group in Chicago had lured into their headquarters and held captive for four days and nights an evil professor who preyed on his female students. In Minneapolis a radical women's group had formed an antirape squad that apprehended rapists and exposed them publicly. The California sisters were openly performing abortions. In Boston women were harassing pimps. Floridians were trashing porno stands. Everywhere: liberating buildings, preparing briefs, taking risks, getting strong. We in New York had our own style. Joining other groups in coalitions we had done everything from take over presses to pack legislative hearings and organize lawsuits, from desegregating the all-male bars and launching whistle-ins in Wall Street to posing as prostitutes and arresting johns. The whole city, with its vast insult to women, was one great target.

Since my eyes had adjusted to the new light, I saw the insult everywhere. In the playground, where women came like political prisoners to the prison yard, bringing their charges day after day. In the dimestore and supermarket, where, invariably, lowly, underpaid female clerks (softspoken, accepting) drudged under men. Always before I'd seen them simply as working people under bosses, poor under rich, never noticing (as the male Left still refused to notice, though it was as obvious as it was terrible) that they were female: women under men. Why, half the working class were women, and more than half the poor. Wealthy women were half as rich as men, but poor women were twice as poor. In the hamburger dives, those who served for tips were women while the cooks and managers and owners were all men. In the banks all those who touched money, even the lowly tellers, were white men: exploited, yes, but still a cut above the women. In the morning papers: men's names, men's pictures, men's news, men's filthy wars, men's pronouncements, men's fantasies leaped out page after page, day after day, to mock us. In all the offices men ruled while women served them. In all the ads women's bodies were harnessed for the sell. In the clinics harried women carried out doctors' orders. In the schools women were teachers while supervisors, superintendents, professors, principals were mostly men, lording it over them. In all the books I read to my children (my own children consumed their pernicious propaganda!) timid prissy girls stood by and cheered while boys leaped and ran and accomplished prodigies. . . . There was nowhere, not one place you could rest your eyes without seeing monsters or shadows of monsters, not a moment's relief from the all-embracing, coercive knowledge of the ubiquitous insult. Well, we would redress it. The more opposition we encountered, the more ardently we would fight. We would plant a partisan in every home, office, school, shop. We would build an army, a multitude. There'd be no stopping us: we were half the universe!

"Okay, make it fast," said Faith, her hand already on the door handle as we pulled up on West Forty-fourth Street before the august Harvard Club.

Faith crossed the street, looked carefully up and down the block, and motioned to me. She stayed near one corner while Kitty guarded the other side. Golda turned off the lights but kept the motor running, ready to fly at the first sign of trouble. Marya and I got out of the car with our spray cans and crossed the street.

"Here?" asked Marya, my partner.

"Yes," I said. "I'll do the top line and you do the bottom."

The Ladies' Entrance was small, painted, demeaning. I tried to fix it indelibly in my mind for a permanent before-and-after spread. Then we raised our cans and sprayed in bold black letters: DEATH TO MALE SUPREMACY.

"Beautiful," said Marya, admiring our handiwork. "Now let's go."

"One more sec," I said. My pulse was racing, but it was too good to let end. I ran to the next door, the imposing entrance reserved for men with its green canopy, its rosette-decorated posts, its polished granite stairs.

"Come on! We don't have time for that. Someone will see!"

"Get in the car," I said. "I'll be right there." I centered the spray can on one post beside the stairs. Pushing the button, I released a fine spray of black in a circle, then a line and a bar. One female symbol across the left pillar: for Ricky.

"Heads up," said Kitty, walking past. "Someone's coming up the next block."

Golda at a signal pulled the car up from across the street, opened the door and hissed, "Get in!" Everyone piled into the car but me.

Now I was before the other post. Again, I pressed the button until another female symbol appeared, dripping down the right pillar. That one was personally for Leo Stern. For a moment I was tempted to sign my initial, but individualism was out. Adventurism was bad enough.

"Christ, Zane—will you get in?" said Kitty in a frantic whisper. Faith was holding the door for me.

At last I jumped into the car as Faith made room and pulled the door closed after me. Golda stepped on the gas and we were gone.

At the corner we had to wait interminably for a red light. The pedestrian who'd been spotted waited across the street oblivious of us.

I looked back and admired my artistry. Black paint dripped down the pillar like blood, embellishing my message. Yes—crime was exalting!

"Death to Male Supremacy," boomed Faith in the deepest voice she could muster as we started into the intersection.

And I said: "Long live the power of women!"

"Long live the power of women!" echoed Golda and asked, "Where to next?"

Kitty was ready. "Go to the next corner and take a left."

5 · FAITH

Across the makeshift screen in Roxanne's living room passed stirring images from our stolen past. Anne Hutchinson, Abigail Adams, Harriet Tubman, Sarah and Angelina Grimké, Sojourner Truth, Victoria Woodhull, Susan B. Anthony, Elizabeth Cady Stanton, Lucy Stone, Emma Goldman, Mother Jones—and others too, French women who fought the king, George Sand, Russian women who went to the people, the German martyr Rosa Luxemburg, England's Pankhursts, brave Chinese women, Vietnamese fighting women. Women whose works were forgotten or misunderstood, whose achievements lay buried under the boots of men who derided them in their lifetimes and deleted them from history once they were dead. Women mocked like my Aunt Louise, scorned like Morgan Moore, women who might have served as our heroes if we had been permitted to admire them (better than the useless male heroes marked Reserved for Men), but who, it was shocking to admit, the fifteen feminists in the room including me had barely heard of before joining The History Project Collective.

Now we were changing that. Almost every day and night for five months we had worked to create this happening that Faith and I had thought up on a picket line. A happening of our own; not someone's put-on to witness and admire for $3.00 admission. In one two-hour multimedia vision we had produced a vast and moving spectacle of the hidden history of our sex. "Emotional and ethical proofs are integral parts of any debate," conceded the *Debater's Manual*. Maybe, I was coming to think, they were the only proofs. Using all the tricks and artistry we could invent or commandeer, we had drawn on the talents of an astonishing spread of women. Most of us had never met, much less worked together in a group, before Faith and I had sent out the call through the movement for "artists, scholars, writers, publicists, and whoever wants to retrieve our stolen history: women only"; but now, having given the best of ourselves, we completed one another like strings and bows. At last, three days before our deadline, in a fever of activity—scrutinizing each of the separate parts, polishing them, refining their politics to the end—we had assembled and finished the show. Finished! Tonight's first (and last) dress rehearsal—stark, ravishing, profound—exceeded my most extravagant hopes. Who, seeing our spectacle, would not be moved to change?

Sojourner Truth stared out of the screen while Lil Backrack from Newark, New Jersey, brought to a close her Ain't I a Woman speech (once famous, then forgotten, now soon to be famous again). "If the first woman God ever made was strong enough to turn the world upside down all alone, these women together ought to be able to turn it back, and get it right side up again! And now they is asking to do it, the men better let them. Obliged to you for hearing me, and now old Sojourner ain't got nothing more to say." End of Section Three.

There were only fifteen of us in the room—fifteen women whose consciousness had ripened in each other's care—but the applause that erupted reverberated as if we were a hundred.

Two tears of pride welled up in my eyes, defying my lashes to contain them, as the projector moved to that shocking still of women ravaged in Vietnam, signaling the opening of the final sequence that Faith and I had worked on together. I reached across the green sofa pillow between us for her hand.

These revolutionary women, of whom even the living had once been dead, would never be dead to me again. The past itself had been reborn in me: History, poetry, theory, art—all had been waiting to be rediscovered, relived. It was chilling to know that in only a few brief decades so much had been forgotten. Except for the new ideas about sexuality, it seemed that almost every idea we were now exploring in the movement, even the most outrageously radical, had been delved by our predecessors. Delved, some even embraced by millions—and then somehow murdered and forgotten. How had it happened? We would have to find out so it couldn't happen again. We would not let them die again.

"Here it comes," I whispered, as the music, perfectly matched to the stark images, changed tempo, the pictures speeded up, and Brigid, the graduate student from Hunter with the deep Dietrich voice, took over the narration of the words Faith and I had written.

Faith squeezed my hand, triggering a feeling of such pride and love—not only for the sisters on the screen, and the Collective, but for Faith herself—that the two tears broke loose and slipped down my cheeks. Pride, love, and that crowning thrill, achievement.

This was the first sustained, difficult work I had ever finished other than for family or for self, yet from it sprang my whole significance. Six months earlier there had been nothing, where now, after an enormous outpouring of thought and effort, there was something—something that might, in however small a way, as a direct result of our energy, affect the world. Not one of us could have done it alone; our Collective was the perfect model of that "leaderless" group that represented the current ideal of the Women's Liberation Movement, with all decisions by consensus and drudgery assigned by lot. But, equally, not one of us could be denied that sweet lingering taste of achievement, headier than cocaine, more gratifying than orgasm. Even if the backlash were to eclipse us as it had eclipsed all the earlier waves of feminism, we would still have had our recognition. When the next wave came (and they would keep coming, as they always had, as long as women lived—that much we'd learned on the History Project) they'd find us there in the microfilm records, in private collections, on library shelves, in feminist archives, a testament to our spirit. The world could drown in bigotry; still, every woman in this room knew each other's voices, knew them and respected them; that could never be undone. My mark was made. In the Collective, and beyond that in the movement, we were now of the world. Identifying ourselves only as a group, we remained individually anonymous; but we had made a difference to the world and we were known to each other.

The thought flashed through my mind, extravagant, maybe crazy, but true, that if I were suddenly to die, I would die fulfilled, knowing I had done one thing that mattered, knowing I'd made myself heard. (Not yet, my ego petitioned. Let me live till Saturday when we'd be presenting our History Project to the editors of every newspaper and magazine in the country with a circulation of ten thousand or more, every TV newsman, radio manager, and whoever else attended the plenary session of the American Media Association; let me stay long enough to see their stunned faces when the lights go on.)

Now I returned the pressure on Faith's hand. Let the academics, who had never spent a drop of ink on our history, scoff at our credentials; they'd soon be mining our work, as they mined every vanguard's, for dissertations and publications. Our work was rich enough to sustain industries, large beyond the sum of its parts. Even Lil, who had once had an article published, and throaty Brigid, only a thesis short of her Ph.D., both of whom had at first been skeptical about working with housewives and other unknowns, quickly agreed with the rest that working together we had each transcended our own capacities. A miracle, we thought, given the widespread splintering and growing debacles in the rest of the Left. But we had managed to submerge our differences in the collective pull, outdoing ourselves, until we had come to feel an almost mystic union.

Union and support: unexpected, delectable rewards after a life alone—especially, I thought, for me and Faith, who had dreamed it up and now sat hand in hand on the green sofa witnessing the child of our will alive and prancing across the screen, a new demon loose in the world. We had created a happening destined not for the back pages of the *Village Voice* but for history.

It was over. Faith lifted my hand. Then wild applause—for each other, for all women, for ourselves.

"Lights? Can somebody turn on the lights please?"

When the lights went on, fifteen proud, grinning women—women who half a year before had been isolated in their typing cubbies and kitchen cells—were hugging one another and weeping.

We had planned a half hour of criticism–self-criticism, but now it was clear that tonight there was room only for celebration. Even the grim mouth on Roxanne's Emma Goldman poster seemed to be turning up.

I looked over at Faith sitting beside me. Her long legs were folded under her like the petals of a closed flower. Her cheeks, puffed out in a smile, glistened with the same tears as mine from eyes filled with the same pride. In the sudden light our eyes met and held each other's. But not in the old way; in an absolutely new way I had never known before. In that rush of admiration and success something passed between us that had not passed before. There was no mistaking it: desire.

"Till Saturday, then," said Roxanne at the door. At last—everyone was leaving. "In the Hilton lobby half an hour early," I reminded Brigid and Lil and each departing friend. But all the time, I was waiting to be alone with Faith, to see if she felt what I felt. Every moment I was aware of exactly where she was in the room and what was ready to burst from my lips.

"You want to go out for some coffee with me?" I said anxiously when the group had thinned.

She held my eyes and nodded a new way.

Then she had felt it too! I rushed for our coats in the bedroom and held hers for her as she slipped it on. We had helped each other with our coats a dozen times, but now, touching Faith's shoulder, it felt like the first time. I could not believe the feelings coursing through me, could not believe what was happening.

We said goodbye to Roxanne as though nothing had changed, then stood silent among the others in the elevator, restrained ourselves from rushing out the door, endured more—endless!—goodbyes at the door before we could get away. We turned the first corner into Bleecker Street, and at last alone, clutched at each other's hands and made our declarations.

"You feel it?" I asked, my voice unsteady, yet somehow feeling no embarrassment.

Faith nodded. On her lips played that lovely reassuring smile that had welcomed me to my first meeting of the Third Street Circle. "I feel it."

"Now what?" I gulped, sensing the danger from Ricky and the world if I dared to push open this heavy door on all the shattering implications.

"Why not come home with me?"

Why not? Suddenly there were a hundred reasons why not. Because the plunge was said to be irrevocable. Because I was not prepared to undo my life. Because I was from Babylon. Because the price of deceit was guilt. Because I didn't know what would happen next. Because it would be impermissible to use against a sister the weapons with which I protected myself from men.

Yet somehow Faith's question was different from such an invitation from a man. From a man those very words would carry overtones of a thousand years of seduction and betrayal, to be met by suspicion and guile. But from Faith—I didn't know what they meant.

"Okay?" said Faith.

"Fine," I said, risking all.

We continued across Bleecker Street linking arms (acceptable) instead of hands (taboo)—only ten minutes in love but street-wise already. Sisters still, but more. Sisters and lovers.

What a paltry understanding of the sources of love must befuddle those who sneer and call us "gay." I can still hear their voices in the White Horse or the Cafe Lucia saying "faggot," "dyke," "fairy." The young men who now inhabit the Left—do they know what Trotsky said of Lenin?

> *He had a way of* falling in love [*Trotsky's emphasis*] *with people when they showed him a certain side of themselves. There was a touch of this being 'in love' in his excited attention* [*to me*]. *He listened eagerly to my stories about the front and kept sighing with satisfaction, almost blissfully. . . . Again I felt the same slightly bashful, all-enveloping glance of Ilyich . . . that special glance that seemed to reflect his pleasure that I had understood him.*

Understood. Outside the movement, who could *understand?* What man and woman could *understand* each other like Lenin and Trotsky, like me and Faith? What man and wife? What poet and beatnik? What mere lovers?

In case you think I'm preparing to detail for you a case history of True Love, think again. Even if I could, I wouldn't. This book is about changing the world at its roots, not isolated moments of poignancy. No matter how perfectly our wild extravagant movement seemed to seal us in our tower, obliterating the world of men (What, we were always asking one another, had we ever found to say to men?), I lived in both worlds. If I now take you upstairs to Faith's apartment in order to share with you several crucial insights I was lucky enough to discover in her bed, it's certainly not to suggest that happiness consists in finding the right lover. Hardly! As our Manifesto clearly states, *there are no personal solutions to political problems;* and besides, as Aunt Louise made clear, *some things are more important than happiness.*

Actually, even while I was walking rapidly across town toward East Third Street, arm linked in Faith's, I was still unprepared to fall in love with a woman. Like everyone in the movement in those days I'd thought about it abstractly, intellectually; had even sometimes desired it. The "gay-straight split," or what was now known in some circles as "the lesbian-separatist solution," was a question on which everyone was required to take a stand. It was always there, a fuse waiting to be lit, coming up when you least expected it, provoking our enemies, setting feminist against feminist, creating the first great schism in NOW, leaving no group unaffected. From the beginning, in every group I'd known, there had always been at least one or two gay women who, sometimes patiently, sometimes angrily, explained their resentments and fears to the rest of us, exposing for the group the scars of that special sexism that made lesbians pariahs. With secret shame I'd heard them out, each time recalling with horror my own aversion to Nina, worse, my dropping her for no other reason than that she made love to women. As our understanding of the intractable tangle of sex and power and misogyny quickened, as we began to see how our lives, our culture, our whole civilization was built on the degradation and rape of women, a new breed of lesbian began to come out. Self-styled "political lesbians" who, often as not, had yet to make love to their first woman but who, nevertheless, hungering for some self-respecting life which would enable them to repudiate men without repudiating love, proclaimed themselves gay. Bold, imaginative women, I thought, who refused to be corrupted or brutalized by consorting with the enemy.

But for me, the "lesbian solution" had been out. Not only had that carnal urge which rose up to muddy my connections with men never been openly stirred by a woman despite my best intentions; even if it had, my three children, who seemed to love their father despite his shortcomings, deserved all the parents they could get. It was fine for the childless and single to urge everyone to smash monogamy, refuse dependency, and proclaim the death of the family, but until they were ready to baby sit, make birthday cakes, take temperatures, and buy new shoes—until the revolution—I knew I'd have to do my best for the children myself. And my renouncing men would include their natural father, who, though imperfect, was the one they wanted. How the contradictions proliferated! Before the movement, when he came home from work so late the children barely knew him, I might have left him or banished him with impunity if I'd had the will. But since the Third Street Circle had emboldened me to require that Ricky act the father, it was unthinkable to leave him out of the reckoning. The fact was, now, two years after I'd begun to feel my strength, in some ways we were a closer family than before. Mine was only one voice in a chorus of five—the only one that knew the tune of the "lesbian solution."

But while I couldn't embrace separatism for myself, I'd wanted to make common cause with lesbian politics. "We define the best interests of women as the best interests of the poorest, most insulted, most despised, most abused women on earth," proclaimed the Principles of New York Radical Women—and that description embraced lesbians no less than sullen unpaid mothers in the playground, mutilated abortion casualties, waitresses, maids, the poorest prostitutes, victims of rape and betrayal—all the martyrs to male supremacy whose cause had given my life passion and purpose just in time. I'd tied a purple armband to my sleeve and marched up Christopher Street with my sisters for gay liberation; I'd applauded each new radical lesbian manifesto as it left the presses.

But my attraction had gone beyond sympathy, I had to admit. That newly proclaimed Lesbian Nation with its nerve and panache had appealed to all my fanatical yearnings. What other life was at once principled and seditious, dissident and moral (refusing to pander to the hateful Man), and, for those who could feel the erotic pull, fulfilling?

Yet, belief had not been feeling, the mind was not the heart. And now finding myself unexpectedly lit by Faith's touch, being—yes!—*in love,* I was as mystified and overwhelmed as a furclad eskimo suddenly dropped in the lushest of tropical rainforests.

At Faith's apartment, the setting was eerily like settings from my past. Lumpy mattress on the floor beside a whitewashed brick wall in the upper reaches of a heatless walkup. Posters on the wall in place of prints, cheap California wine, marijuana, stacks of precious books, and even an expensive hi-fi (the one invariable luxury marking the poverty as partly voluntary, decade after decade). And yet, how different this felt—how absolutely different! —from all the sordid romances of my bohemian youth.

For one thing, we were not adversaries but collaborators. For another thing, after we made love we began talking as no man and I had ever managed to talk. Not about "him" or even "us," but—

"You know, Faith," I said, tracing her delicate profile with my index finger, "you're probably the first lover in my life who hasn't said I think too much."

"I'm probably the first lover in your life who isn't afraid of what you might be thinking," said Faith laughing.

Intimate, understanding laughter kept bubbling up from the geyser of insight that had suddenly begun to spout and kept following each new revelation. They were coming like sparks in a fire now, like more faces and figures buried in a picture, until one by one all the old clichés about women loving women turned into their opposites and I found myself in on a vast, intricate joke, an in-joke I had never been able to get before. A joke not on *us,* it turned out, but on *them!*

True, Faith and I were both stoned, which frequently elevated the droll or amusing to hilarious revelation. But I knew our insights were going to survive this night.

"I'd always thought," I said, "that what would be different

about loving a woman was the passion. But the passion is what feels the same."

Faith laughed at my innocence. "Passion is passion," she said.

"But there is *something* absolutely different," I persisted.

"Oh, yes."

"What is it? The equality? Is it our starting out equal?"

Not starting out the same, of course. We had different lives and histories, different weaknesses and strengths. But for all our differences, we still started out equal in a way it was impossible for any man and woman, carrying within themselves all the weighty historical differences of the sexes, ever to be.

"I myself think it's the honesty," said Faith. "Not playing the game; not using tactics."

I thought about that. It was true, Faith and I would have had a hard time deceiving each other. Both of us, having lived as women in the world of men, both having gone all the way through marriage, would have recognized the tired tactics of the love-game in a minute. But was it impossible to be honest with a man the way it was impossible to be equal? "Haven't you ever been honest with a man?" I ventured.

"Yes; I suppose I have. But with a man, honesty itself is a tactic."

Honesty a tactic! There it was! Another figure that had been hidden in the picture all along, suddenly plainly revealed.

"You see," she continued, "for me with every man, no matter who, the time always comes when a small protective voice at the back of my mind starts warning me, 'Watch out—don't trust him!' Every man knows we're only women, so at bottom they can despise us. Unless we somehow impress them as exceptions. Which means dissembling, since we're not exceptions, and we know it."

"But none of that applies between us."

"Right. None of it," said Faith. "It would be ridiculous for us to pretend to be exceptions. Anyway, we can do much better than impress each other. We can know each other."

It seemed almost too rich to digest: all this insight at one meal. All the old facts were there, but in a new, enhancing light. They'd been there all along, so simple and clear, but not till this night had I understood them. Not all the lesbian manifestos, conferences, consciousness-raising sessions of the past years could yield the astonishing flashes of this single night. It was like the difference between reading music and hearing it; reading recipes and tasting them. Without feeling it there was no way to appreciate the amazing difference between loving a man and loving a woman. Faith called it honesty, but to me there was another difference that was even more basic, one to which all the others might possibly be reducible. And the difference was simply this: that between two women absolutely nothing was given. With every man I'd ever known, from the most casual stranger to my husband of many years, I could never escape the ubiquitous knowledge of our roles, given from birth by the mere fact that I was the woman and he the man. Nothing (except maybe dope) could free me from that absolutely pervasive awareness. With a man I could play the woman's part or defy it, amend it or rail against it, but I could never, ever escape it. Woman and man, man and woman. From the most trivial kindness to the weightiest sacrifice it was there, the burdensome consciousness of our sexes, carrying the import of millennia.

But with Faith, nothing at all was given. What did the "woman's part" even mean between us? You had to have a "man's part" to have a "woman's part." If we had roles we'd have to invent them and choose our parts ourselves. Of course one of us could assume a man's role if we wanted, but we didn't have to. Instead of dividing up the universe, we could share it. And far from my now loving "a woman" (as in the past I'd always had to have "a man") I was loving Faith Newman (Newoman, rather) —someone I'd known intimately and trusted as my comrade.

"You know what?" I said, snuggling up beside Faith.

"What?"

"For a while I'd begun to think there was something the matter with me—like being tone-deaf or frigid—because I'd never been in love with a woman. But now—I see I'm normal after all. What a relief to find out I'm normal!"

It was never too late to start again. That was the first big lesson of our movement. And once again, as old meanings were revealed as their opposites, we dissolved in a frolic of laughter that *they* would probably have called *defensive*, but I knew was, if anything, *offensive*.

"Absolutely everything is upside down," I said. "Normal, sick;

feminine, masculine. *They* think women who love women are either sick or 'masculine.' Or else that we can't get a man. As if a woman were second-best, a mere consolation prize."

"In a way we are," said Faith. "We can console each other for having to live in their world."

"No," I objected. "It's just that their egos can't take the truth."

"The truth?"

"That we *prefer* women to them," I said—already expert.

"That's right. They want to believe they're necessary to us," said Faith.

"Their egos. They want to think of themselves as perfect lovers, born knowing how to please a woman."

"Only women," said Faith, breaking once again into her glorious smile, "are born knowing that." And there we were again, sharing that intimate laughter that distinguished our love from theirs.

"*Vive la différence,*" I said, running my fingers over her smooth, mysterious belly. Another astonishment. Faith was soft as a rose petal. Her body, so like mine, ought to have felt as familiar as a hand, and yet it was strange and wonderful to my touch, as mysterious as an insect's delicate wing. Her hair was long and silken, her hip curved like a tea cup, her shoulder fit into my palm, she had no edges or angles or coarse fur or stubble.

"My god, Faith," I marveled, feeling her. "You're so lovely. Now I see what men love so much in women. You're so soft, so delicate."

And I, who had always been uneasy in my body, ashamed of my smells, preferring darkened rooms to light, unseeing men to perceptive ones, suddenly realized that if Faith was soft and sweet and delicate to touch, then so was I! If her taste and smell were delicious, then so were mine!

"What dupes we've been," I cried, "giving ourselves to them, saving nothing for ourselves. How lucky they are to have had us!"

"Not us," said Faith. "They haven't had me for a number of years."

"They won't have me, either," I said, "any more"—and then suddenly I remembered the world.

"Jesus. I forgot to call Ricky."

With a pained smile, Faith handed me the phone from the

floor beside her. I dialed my number and waited till Ricky's voice doused me with reality.

"Hi, Ricky. It's Zane."

"Where are you?"

"I'm at Faith's. The meeting's over but we still have a lot of unfinished business." I smiled at Faith as I said it. "Are the children asleep?"

"Of course," he said.

Did I detect resentment? A couple of years earlier I would have been full of apology. Thank you for putting the children to bed. Would you mind if I stay out late? Can you amuse yourself? Shall I bring you home something? But now, thanks to the movement, I needed to make no apologies. They were his children too, after all. And though I still didn't earn any money, with Julie home every morning and the others always out of school from illness or holidays that seemed never to overlap or spontaneous school closings the mayor proclaimed on a day's notice, I had work at least the equal of his.

"Will you be home late?" he asked.

"Probably. But I'll be here at Faith's. You can reach me if you need me."

How easy it was. I didn't even have to lie—for me to love a woman was that unthinkable.

"Well, all right," he grumbled, "I'll probably go to bed early. I'm exhausted."

As usual, I'd made them all dinner before I left for my meeting. As I did every night, I'd laid out the night clothes and helped Sammy with his homework. I couldn't feel guilty about Ricky's exhaustion.

In almost the same words Ricky had so often used on me, I said, "Don't bother waiting up for me, honey. I have a lot to do on my project."

"Any more errands?" asked Faith when I'd hung up.

"Not that I can think of. And that's another big difference," I said.

"Between women and men?" asked Faith.

"Yes."

"Do me a favor?"

"What?"

"Forget about men now."

She took me in her arms. And as our kisses stretched on I forgot about many things. About dominance and submission, winning and losing, concealing and exposing, protecting and sacrificing. Finally I forgot to wonder, what does he think of me? How long will it last? How long will it take? But sinking myself into the soft yielding pillow that was Faith's lovely body, so perfectly matched by mine, I let myself wallow in equality. And as my lover —my sister, my friend—admonished, for a while I forgot about men.

6 · THE WOMEN'S MARCH

Even on the very morning of the first August 26th Women's March—the fiftieth anniversary of the vote for women—we could not have told you whether we'd be the same old handful of zealots multiplied by ten or a hundred or a thousand. We knew there were more groups abroad than we could count. We knew our supporters were everywhere, for everywhere we took our message now we were treated like heroes almost as often as we were shouted down as devils. But we didn't know who was actually willing to take a stand. "What do you think? Do you think many women will show up?" Marya'd kept asking anxiously at our final meeting the previous night. I'd never seen her hesitant before; it was a bit unnerving. She'd always shown an uncanny instinct for what people were thinking; she was the weathervane of the Third Street Circle.

We knew what the police thought. They had refused the Parade Committee a permit to occupy more than one lane of Fifth Avenue. "The pigs?" scoffed Golda, putting a finishing flourish on the poster she intended to carry. "What do the pigs know? They're stupid."

"Stupid, stupid," echoed my Tina, drawing a magic-marker border on Marya's poster.

"Don't count on it," said Kitty. "It may be a smart tactic. If they can make sure we start out in confusion they may win the day."

It always pleased me to hear Kitty as savvy as the rest of the group—as it pleased me to see the group taking charge of Tina. I remembered when Kitty's only contact with the world of action was the radio, as the group's only contact with the world of children was memory. Everyone had changed.

For myself, I refused to predict—just hoped for the best. Full-time activists might still be few, but our ideas had spread with amazing speed. I'd watched the movement grow with each new action, contagious as laughter, as the unlikeliest-seeming people, people you'd never met before, turned up as allies. Even without speaking you could feel the affinity. On my way to a briefing in the sumptuous borrowed suite of an unsuspecting media man at the Hotel Pierre ("Imagine!" said Kitty, "a swanky hotel apartment for planning the takeover of one of the major channels of communication in this country. I love it!"), I'd recognized as one of us a woman standing in that de luxe lobby. The woman looked like half the other women in town between eighteen and thirty-six that year, with her straight center-parted hair (like mine), black pants and boots; but still, there was something about her. I'd felt so sure she was part of the feminist conspiracy that when we got into the elevator, instead of pushing the button for nine myself, I waited to see what she would push.

Nine!

"Nine twelve?" I asked, unable to resist.

She smiled and nodded. "I thought we might be going to the same place," I said, feeling that gratifying rush that we had already begun to label "sisterhood."

"I wonder what it means, though," I said as the elevator began to rise, "that we can just look at each other and know we're going to the same meeting. Maybe it means something awful, like that we're all pressed from the same mold." I remembered the fifties when those of us who wanted to be different had all dressed in a single style that made us interchangeable.

"Oh? Do you think so?" the woman asked. I was surprised to hear a heavy European accent, I couldn't tell which country. So we were not even from the same mill! "I think it is interesting," she continued, "but not awful. It is like the Freemasons in Europe. They can recognize each other across a room, I don't know how. There is a way they have to communicate. I think it is rather nice, myself. We have something in common."

"With the Freemasons?"

She laughed and shook her head. "Heavens no! Among ourselves. In Belgium, I'm told, the Freemasons have considerable power. Perhaps when we can recognize each other this way it means we will be having power too."

It was a nice idea. No doubt the movement was taking hold if strangers in lobbies could recognize each other without a word, even strangers from different countries. Perhaps it did have some thing to do with power. A massive march might prove it.

"Well, it's silly to speculate," said Faith, connecting two outrageous posters as a sandwich board. "We'll just have to wait till tomorrow and hope."

But by the time the women began to assemble in front of the Plaza Hotel at five o'clock the next evening, as they poured out of their offices up to Fifty-ninth Street and down on busses from Riverdale and Morningside Heights, it quickly became apparent that we would have a huge turnout and that nothing would be able to stop us from swarming across the whole width of the avenue with our banners and signs, leaflets and slogans, spreading from curb to curb, from coast to coast.

I came up on the subway with the children and a stroller a half hour early; an hour later it seemed as if all the women of New York City were determined to march triumphant down Fifth Avenue. The women who had smiled sweetly on MacDougal Street when I first saw them, the women who worked uptown, mothers with babies on their backs and toddlers in strollers, pretty young women in summer dresses. They came from work, from school, from home, from out of town, in groups, in families, by themselves.

Our turn now.

Sammy and Tina (now nine and seven—how fast they grew) agreed to walk beside me if I'd get them balloons, while five-year-old Julie rode in the stroller. Ricky had said he'd take them from me at Forty-third Street, near his office, when we got down there; but I wanted them with me for the march. Even if they forgot about it afterward (though I hoped they might remember), I'd tell them about it later, and they'd be able to tell their children that they were there. And their children's children.

It was a hot day in the middle of summer at the beginning of a new decade: August 26, 1970. Who could guess what might be coming next? The sixties, people said, had been the opening wedge. In the seventies maybe we'd complete our revolution.

The crowd was big, but the children were game—it was a parade, after all. We marched as a family with the rest of my group behind the red and black banner of the Third Street Circle, stretched between two broomsticks.

Only the antiwar groups carried worn banners; the rest, it seemed, were new.

All there. All the early groups who'd split off from each other in successive epiphanies, and new ones I'd never heard of: together for the first time. The National Organization for Women (NOW), who'd organized the march, and Betty Friedan, who'd called for a strike, led off with a carful of aged veteran suffragists, heroes from the first wave of feminism. Behind them came WITCH and BITCH and OWL (Older Women's Liberation) and Redstockings and The Feminists and New York Radical Feminists and us, all pioneers. Then Big Sisters and Black Women's Liberation and the National Coalition of American Nuns and RAT and Radicalesbians and Gay Activist Alliance and New Yorkers for Abortion Law Repeal and Women in Childcare and Newsreel Women's Caucus and Media Women and Women Artists in Revolution and the Third World Women's Alliance and Spanish American Feminists and Women Strike for Peace and Jeanette Rankin Rank and File and the YWCA and the Emma Goldman Brigade and the Alice Crimmins Brigade and the Stanton-Anthony Brigade and the League of Women Voters and High School Women's Coalition and the Lesbian Food Conspiracy and Betsy Ross Junior High Women's Liberation and Women in Publishing and SCEF Women and CORE Women and SNCC Women and SWP Women and the Young Socialist Alliance and International Socialist Women and Daughters of Bilitis and Half of Brooklyn and It's All Right to Be Woman Theater and Off Our Backs and Up from Under and It Ain't Me Babe and Aphra and Lilith and The Group and Multitudes to Obliterate Misogyny and Columbia-Barnard Women's Liberation and Queens College Women's Liberation and Brooklyn Women's Liberation and West-Side Women United and Westchester Women's Liberation and Bronx Feminists and Revolutionary

Childcare Collective and Youth Against War and Fascism (YAWF) and Women of the Venceramos Brigade and Sparticist Women and Maoist Women and National Welfare Rights Organization and Women *vs.* Connecticut and Professional Women's Caucus and Women for Bella Abzug and Women's International League for Peace and Freedom and the Joan Bird Bail Fund and Independent Radical Women's Caucus and hundreds of unidentified women wearing buttons of their own design and hundreds of unaffiliated women carrying signs and women without labels and Men for Women's Rights and a few independent men too.

On the sidewalks and from windows of buildings along the route people held up signs, unfurled banners, and cheered. DON'T COOK DINNER TONIGHT—STARVE A RAT TODAY. CLEAN THE STREETS OF RAPISTS AND SEX MURDERERS. LIBERTÉ, ÉGALITÉ, SORORITÉ. DON'T IRON WHILE THE STRIKE IS HOT. UPPITY WOMEN UNITE. FREE OUR SISTERS, FREE OURSELVES.

A few heckled and jeered, and a few others giggled, and many just stood and watched. But mostly, the people along the streets chanted and cheered. Men and women alike held up the clenched fist of solidarity or just grinned happy, supportive grins.

At Forty-third Street Ricky was waiting at the curb. We kissed like a couple; I handed over the children, and then he grinned too. Everyone, it seemed, even the uncommitted, perhaps even the resentful, were for us that afternoon.

"You going to stay for the speeches too?" asked Ricky, for some people were leaving, now that we had reached our destination in defiance of the police.

I laughed. "Of course I'm staying."

"How long?" he asked, like a wife.

"I don't know. Why?"

"I'd just like to know."

In Bryant Park, as many as could sat in the rows of folding chairs and hundreds were squeezed around the edges, on the steps, on the ground, and even in the bushes. I watched everyone pour into the space, watched for familiar faces and new faces, smiling at each other: the new women.

Marya, representing the Third Street Circle, one of the earliest groups, sat on the speaker's platform among the leaders of other early radical groups and influential women. She seemed smaller up there and nervous; but as she peered out over the crowd with her jubilant flashing eyes, again I saw that almost beatific glow I'd seen at my entry into the movement at Faith's two and a half years before, an expression that had immediately told me this woman would make history—and I wanted to be along when she made it.

Who would have guessed it could happen so soon? Thousands and thousands of women as far as you could see in every direction covering the park like clover. Women united, clamoring for change.

Our group tried to cluster around our banner in a corner of the park where Marya could hear us cheer her. But in the end, everyone wound up sitting wherever she could.

At last the program was called to order. "Shh," said Faith beside me as the speeches began.

It was a hot night, made hotter still by the bodies crowded together, and some of the speakers talked too long. But though people began to grow restless as speaker after speaker rose, hardly anyone in the audience left. Together for the first time in our lives—for the first time in generations—none of us could get enough of it.

Finally it was Marya's turn to speak. She rose slowly and walked to the mike, set too high for her. She raised her chin high, and I couldn't tell if it was for comfort or for pride. On us it was pride: our moment: we had all worked so hard for this.

She looked out over the huge crowd of sisters, the fulfillment of a dream. She looked out, saying nothing for a long time; for a moment I was afraid she might be too moved to give her speech. Then she adjusted the mike, cleared her throat, and said softly, simply: "Well, we did it. We really did it." She grinned and grinned. Her eyes glistened. And again she said, "We did it."

Afterward, she gave a short speech, beginning with a summary of the work of the Third Street Circle, ending with a sharp, brief program of what remained to be done. But all the time she was speaking, my eyes filled with tears as I kept hearing over and over in my mind, exactly as Marya had said it: *We did it.*

We did it. Without help, without money, without sympathy or government grants, in the face of ridicule and subterfuge, we did the impossible. We came together and created the miraculous beginnings of women's liberation. By will and work and vision we had altered the course of history, we had affected the consciousness of the world, and now no one in it, not one of us, would ever again be the same.

When the last speaker had spoken, Faith took my hand, and we sat there while the crowd thinned out. Then we stood up and I held her eyes with mine while before the world I pressed to her lips an unembarrassed kiss of love.

PART V

New Space

1 · NEW BEGINNINGS

I wish I could tell you that the decade you saw us launch at the end of the last chapter—those seventies we anticipated with such hope and glee that many of us committed rash acts on the basis of our glowing prognosis—had gone on to keep its promises. Oh, how I wish I could now give you that happy ending desired by every revolutionary author, an ending embodying some grand uplifting historical sweep.

Alas, I can't do it. Marx himself warned us not to "draw the magic cap down over eyes and ears as a make believe that there are no monsters" or to imagine that "tomorrow a miracle will happen." Miracles don't happen. I have been chastened, humbled. Never again will I allow myself to get so carried away by my blind desires as to make foolhardy predictions and take reckless stands. To have been stung more than once by unwarranted optimism, to have fallen for our own propaganda, is quite inexcusable. Not that I ever (thank god!) committed any of those irrevocable excesses like disowning my son or robbing a bank as some I know did. But still, indulging my fanatical tendencies as if one moment were forever I allowed myself to believe we had won when it was perfectly obvious we hadn't.

As Mao wrote in that common sense guide, *The Little Red Book:* "There are no straight roads in the world; we must be prepared to follow a road which twists and turns and not try to get things on the cheap. It must not be imagined that one fine morning all the reactionaries will go down on their knees of their own accord." Of their own accord, indeed! Others less experienced than I might be forgiven such youthful naïveté; but if there was one thing my whole life had conspired to teach me by that high summer of 1970, if there was one invariable law that all my study and experience should have drummed into my head, it was that history never lets up for a minute, that all things, as Hegel says, become their opposites, and there is no point in stopping at some arbitrary moment in time, however alluring, to say: *We did it!*

The fact is, many winters have passed since those high times when we had only to announce a Sunday organizing meeting on People's Radio or in the *Village Voice* a week in advance, maybe tack up a few fliers around Columbia and NYU, in order to double, even triple, our ranks. In one week we recruited hundreds of women, and not just students, either, but secretaries, waitresses, nurses, and housewives like me who might have been lost forever to revolution but for feminism.

Now, half a decade later, it is impossible to slip through a February on last year's gains. The winter gloom deepens; the boom has collapsed. Friends on tranquilizers are increasing their dosages. Once, we dreamed that if only every soul were pressed into a group, like helium in balloons, our spirit would expand and rise, leaving the old ways trailing behind. But now, most of the old groups are empty skins, names from the past; and what few are left hover limply near the ground, their spirit thin. Only a handful of old-timers show up any more at demonstrations. The potent ideas that carried us aloft have seeped out, diffusing through the air until now traces are everywhere but the pressure is gone; and in place of action there is a vast network of mailing lists. In the officially designated Year of the Woman we witnessed the Second International Women's Film Festival, the third Symposium on Women and the Arts, the fourth Conference on Marriage and Divorce; but instead of weekly meetings that concentrate our energies, people throw parties and receptions that dissipate them: a book launching, a new production of the Woman's Theater, "assertiveness training workshops." Instead of trying to change the world people seem content to change themselves.

No one knows exactly what happened—only that the Left sang a premature victory song (even before the war ended!) and then the whole movement quietly split apart. Those radicals who'd committed rash acts went underground (including that hellion, Nina Chase, one of the notorious Brookville Nine and the third woman on the Ten Most-Wanted List according to the *New York Times*). The dogmatists hardened their lines; the fickle followed the fads. But most of us had no choice except gradually to resume what we once contemptuously labeled "private life"—settling into jobs, making ends meet, questioning basics again, falling in love. What else were we to do without a movement to rally and sustain us? Not a few went West to meditate, and Faith now lives in Vermont on the Women's Farm.

How can one interpret these events? Though I have no doubt that in the end a clear meaning will emerge for all that happens to us, in the short run history is quite impossible to decipher, given its propensity to reverse itself. "How young the whole of human history still is, and how ridiculous it would be to attempt to ascribe any absolute validity to our present views," wrote Engels. "We must shun subjectivity, one-sidedness, and superficiality," wrote Mao. From now on I'll try to control my own tendency to leap to unwarranted conclusions as if the future could be known. It would be as mistaken to give up in defeat as it was to announce our victory prematurely. Action must only follow analysis.

Please bear with me, then, while I try again. Having reached the last section of my book I'll try to keep my balance, resisting excesses of both optimism and pessimism, though we are already deep in the throes of a new era. For while certain aspects of my life have turned out far better than I ever dreamed, these are still bad times for revolutionaries and my gains aren't everyone's. Even my greatest personal triumphs have their decidedly negative aspects.

Let me give you one example. It happened that several years ago I was invited as a "distinguished alumna" to address the graduating class of Middletown State Junior College. A dream come true, you'll have to agree; a classic triumph. No amount of genius could have led me to predict or even invent such a perfectly vindicating outcome to my life of revolt. Imagine me there, standing before a mike exhorting the young, on the very campus where I had once been deplored as a corrupter of youth; I, the "incorrigible," the "fanatic," with the peculiar costume of the misfit, whose worried parents had been repeatedly warned that their only daughter was on probation—now being honored to address the entire student body of my alma mater! Below me in the audience a Middletown *Sun* reporter (a former classmate from Babylon High) took notes on my speech.

Now, wouldn't you think my parents, faced with such an honor, would at last be satisfied? Isn't that half the point?

But no. Never! True, Mama sat smiling in the front row of the auditorium displaying on the lapel of her flowered navy blue dress a red clench-fisted feminist button, as proud of me, perhaps, as of the three scrubbed grandchildren surrounding her; she was able to make the same allowances for her wayward daughter as she made for my queer Manhattan children who didn't know how to ride bicycles or throw balls properly or speak without accents, who, though they were her own flesh and blood, somehow presented the same threat to Babylonians that every New Yorker had always presented. But I could sense—I knew!—she felt far more anxious than proud.

And my father, who had never been particularly diffident—my father, that man of logic and learning whose high standards had kept me always reaching beyond myself, the man for whose approval I'd struggled to transcend my lowly sex and make a mark—wouldn't you think he would for once allow himself to bask in the honor his only child had brought to the family (and from an institution of higher learning)?

Yet, as Daddy drove me and the children to the airport (for train service to Middletown had long since been discontinued) after my day of triumph, all he could do was knit his troubled brow, shake his silver head, and say: "I don't know, Zane. I think the trouble was we were always too easy on you. We let you get away with everything. Somehow you were always able to wind us around your little finger."

"Still, Daddy?" I cried.

How the sting of fury and failure burned against my eyes! How could he so wantonly misunderstand me? I was sure my supporter, Aunt Louise, would have been unstintingly proud of me. Permanently bedridden, however, she had been unable to attend the ceremony. Anyway, a parent can never serve the function of an aunt.

Again I cried, "Isn't there anything I can do to please you? Isn't anything enough?"

Now I am able to see that my poor daddy was at that moment as woefully misunderstood as I. It was unfair of me to attack him for simply expressing the same concern as always—worrying about my character, my future, as he'd done whenever I undertook something big or unpredictable: when I got in trouble at school, when I ran off to New York, when I married, when I divorced, and every time I "made a spectacle" of myself. And rightly, too, no doubt: who knows better than a parent that today's triumphs won't necessarily carry tomorrow? With my own children I can see this perfectly well. That they manage to get through one year without calamity is no guarantee they'll be able to survive the next.

But though I am now mother and daughter at once, it's not so easy to retain parental perspective while your father is sitting there shaking his head. To be able to hold on to two opposing ideas simultaneously—to be at once child and parent, to see past and present, to "shun one-sidedness" (Mao)—may be as difficult to pull off in maturity as in youth.

I am duty-bound to try. To give up because of setbacks or to expect miracles are equally irresponsible. Let armchair historians pronounce verdicts on the decades as they pass in procession; let graduate students write monographs pigeonholing the Third Street Circle and the "Generation of '68"; let disillusioned revolutionists like my neighbors the Rosens (who resigned from politics in 1939) sit out on their stoop every day reading the papers cover to cover trying to discover how "it will all turn out" (as if the future would one day arrive at the door headlined in the *Times*!). All I hope to do in the few remaining chapters of my book is let you in on our doings up till the very moment I have to turn in my manuscript.

Certainly amazing things have transpired since the decade began, but most of them are things none of us ever imagined. Don't expect any sweeping summaries or tidy conclusions from me. In fact, even as I tuck into my story the few raveling threads I am able to grasp, I have to warn you that they may all come loose again tomorrow and every trend be (temporarily) reversed.

2 · THE HAPPINESS QUESTION

Right here, before I go one more page, I have a ticklish confession to make. At this very moment, when it looks as though we blew our revolution, I find myself happier than I ever dreamed I could be. I am full of energy, confidence, little pleasures, big plans. To me these short, soiled February days with their slush and gloom that depress so many inspire visions of crocuses, asparagus, pink rhubarb stalks. If I hadn't perfected my dialectical approach I might even suspect this unaccountable joy to be another instance of that old contrary streak Daddy always called perverse which has kept me swimming all my life against the stream. How else explain the paradox that at the very moment of our failure I've reached this apex?

Of course, being a veteran, one who has watched the decades come and go, I know my happy state is probably temporary. In a poem by Brecht (a man, please note) that I keep posted on my wall, my fears are enshrined:

It is true: I earn my living
But, believe me, it is only an accident
Nothing that I do entitles me to eat my fill
By chance I was spared. (If my luck leaves me
I am lost.)

When Ricky left us we had to move to humbler quarters. But our luck held, for even in the new place if you stood on the toilet and peered dangerously out of the bathroom window you could still see the tips of the trees in Washington Square.

I know, too, that I ought to keep my satisfaction to myself; for to those who don't share it I'm afraid it must look like callous or mindless complacency. No matter that even such an unassailable rebel as the martyr Rosa Luxemburg could write from her prison cell, "the more the infamy and monstrosity of daily happenings surpasses all bounds, the more tranquil and more confident becomes my personal outlook. . . . I lie here alone and in silence, enveloped in the manifold black wrappings of darkness, tedium, unfreedom, and winter—and yet my heart beats with an immeasurable and incomprehensible inner joy." She is above suspicion. No matter that the large-souled Angelica Balabanoff should not hesitate to write (though her revolution, too, was betrayed): "I knew that I was a very fortunate person. [My] suffering and struggle . . . had meaning and dignity because they were linked to those of humanity. *Life lived in behalf of a great cause is robbed of its personal futility.*" (My italics.) No matter that the free-spirited Emma Goldman should insist: "I did not believe that a Cause which stood for a beautiful ideal, for anarchism . . .

should demand the denial of life and joy. . . . If it meant that I did not want it." These precedents can't vindicate me. Not only am I, unlike them, no martyr, but I suddenly find myself in the compromised position of having for the first time in my life almost everything I've ever desired, short of a different world. Having had the incredible luck to be on hand at almost the exact moment when the Third Street Circle was forming, I am now a veteran of the passion of my time—never again can my life be discounted. Some things, as Aunt Louise taught me, are indeed more important than happiness; but in my dogged pursuit of those "more important things," I have somehow wound up with happiness instead. For look: Though I have no degrees, I am a teacher now. Though their father left them, my three children have miraculously survived their first decade without disaster. Though my job is precarious, still, with my salary from the New School and my lecture fees (supplemented by Ricky's contribution to child support) I am for the moment self-supporting. And so full of passion and action are all my days (between meetings, debates, classes, conferences, and PTA I barely have time to read my mail!) that I shall never again be judged not to have lived.

Indeed, at the very moment I was counting my blessings, I was riding uptown on a Sixth Avenue bus to have an expense-account lunch with Leo Stern. After lunch I'd have to dash back to my afternoon class and use my traveling time to read the morning mail I'd hastily stuffed into my briefcase (because after school I'd have the children and that evening I'd promised to help draft a petition). But whereas a dense schedule had almost undone me when the children were small, now I felt blessed just to be able to keep on going at this pitch of intensity. And as our cross bus driver jerked the green monster past Herald Square and the dregs of another Christmas up Sixth Avenue through the rude traffic and poisonous air, "happy" seemed too mild a word to describe my state. Privileged or not, guilty or not, I felt nothing short of saved.

I'm not the only one to feel uneasy about the ironies of the present moment. Some time earlier, a former sister of the Third Street Circle back in town on a visit from California where she'd moved like so many around '72, called me to catch up on the East Coast news. (I'll call her Phyllis.) From the way a certain name kept thudding awkwardly into the conversation I could tell something was up.

"Are you in love with him?" I asked. ("We must destroy love," the Feminists, now disbanded, had boldly proclaimed in their earliest manifesto. "Love promotes vulnerability, dependence, possessiveness, susceptibility to pain, and prevents the full development of woman by directing all her energies outward in the interests of others.")

Phyllis hesitated.

"You can tell me, Phyllis," I reassured her. I was still brooding over my break-up with Faith and might have felt ashamed myself to be "in love" with a man that year, but I tried to be tolerant with my friends. Though I was half sorry to watch our old certainties slip away, I already knew you can't force certainty. So much we had rashly renounced in the sixties had been gradually resumed in the seventies that all the old pieties had to be rethought. For example: the Old Left mother who had been booed from the platform at a Motherhood Conference in '69 for prophesying the future maternity of her young audience might well get a different reception now. And in my own life too: though I had once seriously contemplated living outside the world of men, now that Sammy's voice had changed it was obviously out of the question.

Phyllis hesitated, then finally confessed, "Well, yes—actually I am in love. But please, Zane, for god's sake don't tell anyone. I'm afraid it doesn't look good."

"To whom?"

"You know. The movement."

The movement, the movement! Shades of the past when we cared only if the movement loved us. When inside the movement we found comfort and protection and outside a jungle of preying men. But things were no longer so simple as they'd once seemed. *The personal is political* had a larger meaning now.

I tried to reassure Phyllis. "Listen," I said, "Golda's in law school—should she feel guilty about it? We need lawyers, too." And then, summoning all my courage, I confessed with that honesty our Circle had once unleashed as our secret weapon: "And look at me, Phyllis."

"Are you in love too?" she asked eagerly.

"No, not in love; worse! I'm happy."

Into the silence that ensued I dropped my shameful secret. "I mean—here I am, teaching at the New School, traveling around giving speeches about what matters most to me, writing articles, debating—must I feel guilty?" Blurting out my list of sins, my satisfactions, the question sounded more like a plea for indulgence than the reassurance I'd intended; for in truth my voice was soft with guilt.

But just as I had laughed off Phyllis's precious compunctions about love, she immediately brushed aside my own qualms about happiness.

"But that's completely different, Zane. You can influence your students. You can sway your audiences."

"And you can influence your lover," I threw back.

"Love is different," she insisted.

"Why?" I asked. "Is he married?"

We laughed. "No. But seriously, don't you think falling in love is . . . backsliding?"

It was a question I might once have thought delicious, but these days it sounded a little daft. Lines had certainly hardened in recent years. For some sisters men had been eliminated from their lives altogether, while for others they'd gradually been resuming their place as the main attraction. For a long time I hadn't read a single book by a male, though I knew I was probably depriving myself of several excellent works. Then, gradually, I began readmitting select ones to my reading list and was considering even more. Backsliding? Without a sufficiently dialectical approach every deviation from the ideals of those early days could feel dangerously like backsliding; yet one had to adapt.

"The sixties are over, Phyllis," I reminded her. The second dialectical moment out of which our movement leaped had become the first dialectical moment of another stage—the negation, the transition, requiring different bearings. It was foolish, even arrogant, of us to have presumed the revolution would be won at precisely the moment when we arrived on the scene. You're born when you're born, you fight as well as you can—that's all. "Listen, Phyllis," I said, "it's not your fault we didn't bring it off. Even Mao predicts the revolution will take five hundred years."

"Mao is a man."

"People have to live."

"Well, still," said Phyllis, "I'll feel a lot better if no one knows about John."

Across the table Leo Stern was using all his old resources to reassert his power, plus a new solicitousness. Was it because we were alone together without Rhoda or Ricky, or was it simply a case of his wanting to "fuck the feminist"? He had shaved off his beard and decked himself out in an elegant three-piece suit out of deference to the new times, but I doubted that he'd really changed.

"All right, Zane," he said magnanimously, drawing on his pipe, "I'll admit there were some things I was really quite blind to back then, as I once failed to notice your black bishop. Everyone makes mistakes. But as you probably know, I've been making amends."

For failing to notice what? I wondered—injustice or the bishop? He raised his glass and sipped martini.

These days it was hard to fathom who had really changed. On the surface, at least, everyone had: rulers, liberals, and misogynists alike all claimed to have come around. Those who'd denied us our rights in the old days by saying we didn't need them could now deny us our rights by pretending we already had them. Every morning over coffee one could read in the *Times* about the "new equality" and "women's takeover of key positions." The whole world had gotten into the act. Some of the most fashionable new movies were about women's condition. And Leo himself had launched a new series of books called Women and Society, which used as its colophon an almost exact replica of the old button he had been so quick to denounce when he'd first confronted it on my shirt. For his foresight he'd been made a vice president, complete with his picture in the *Times* and a new, young wife.

"You'll remember," he continued, "even when I was, as you'd probably say, a 'male chauvinist,' I was always partial to women. I've always found them nicer than men; but lately they're more interesting too, now that they've finally come into their own."

Our own? It was too much. "A handful, Leo," I said, unable to restrain myself. "Tokens."

"Come now, Zane. Considering that you didn't go to college, you're doing pretty well for yourself, aren't you? Teaching courses at the New School."

Before we'd even finished our drink he'd managed to find my jugular, implying like Wolfe those years before that I was a sellout because I was "doing pretty well." No, I wasn't a typist any more, I wasn't on welfare; but it was unjust that every satisfaction a rebel might attain could be called a betrayal of the cause. My New School classes hardly brought me real power: They barely paid enough to keep me and could be dropped without notice.

I should have argued the principle, but instead I defended myself. "People can get a college degree in four years just by taking a survey of everything. Or a law degree in three. I've been reading one thing for five years, Leo. Who's better qualified than I am to teach the history of women, of revolutionary women?"

Of course, it was a mistake to respond defensively. Even the *Debater's Manual* warned against "evading the issue by defending the person" or by focusing "on minor contentions in the rebuttal." The few times I had managed to hold my own against Leo it had been by confidently pressing my advantage. Maybe happiness tended to make one soft, or maybe, as Mao said, victory brought "inertia, love of pleasure, distaste for continued hard living."

"Easy, easy," said Leo. "I never said I doubted your qualifications. As a matter of fact, I have a very high regard for you. The self-taught are often better educated than the rest of us. All I said, Zane, was that you were doing well."

"Am I supposed to give up my job to convince you that women are still oppressed?"

"Actually, I have a more constructive suggestion. That's why I invited you to lunch. If you can write without such barbarisms as 'oppressed,' how would you like to do a book for me?"

A book? I was stunned. Though I hadn't finished college, Leo Stern, smiling as though he had just presented me with a rare and fragrant camellia corsage, wanted me to write a book! He sat back and let the perfume of his offer fill the air between us.

Something warned me to leave the tempting flower lying in its Celluloid box, though it was all but irresistible. Falteringly, I asked, "What's the matter with 'oppressed'?"

Leo shrugged and wrinkled up his nose. "It's one of those dated propaganda words."

Propaganda? Dated? It seemed to me descriptive. If one thing had always been with us, it was oppression.

"You know—" he went on, "it smacks of the sixties, which are over, thank god."

If God were to be thanked for anything, it was for sending the waiter at that moment with our food. Because by the time he had finished serving us I'd thought enough about my discomfort and Leo's remark to get my bearings back.

The sixties—how different they'd been for women and men, anyway men like Leo. Of course *they* hated the sixties; of course *they* were glad to see them over. Naturally they called them "barbaric" and "chaotic"—I could see why. By the time the sixties were going strong *they*'d already wrapped up their degrees, their positions, their futures. But for us, who could so easily have spent the rest of our lives letting the men speak for us, the sixties were anything but chaotic. Not that we lived serenely in those years, but we took our first steps on our own. We learned organization, discipline, caring, concerted action—the opposite of chaos. With analysis guiding our deeds, with insight and understanding, in the sixties we learned how to be civilized. We stood up for each other, made community, tried to provide sympathy and support and something lasting for all of us and our children—what could be more civilized than that?

But the sixties were over, Leo was right; "oppression" was out; and the reaction had certainly come far if we had to rely on Leo Stern to champion women's liberation. (Or, as everyone was calling it nowadays, chucking it familiarly under the chin, "women's lib"—and us, "libbers," as painful a barb as "chick" or "baby" had ever been.)

"The book I have in mind," said Leo, "would be something of a popular history of the women's movement, maybe title it *The Book of Firsts*."

There was another one: the "women's movement," as he called it. No longer the Women's Liberation Movement, it was now just another nebulous movement with the fighting word eliminated. Words like "liberation," "struggle," "oppression," and, yes, "revolution" itself, were now embarrassments, "barbarisms" as Leo would say, dated. My own daughters complained that "women's lib" was passé:

"Old stuff, Mommy."

"Old! Half a dozen years ago it was nothing but a dangerous

idea. And now it's 'old stuff.' You're pretty lucky it is. Now at least abortions are legal." (They were on the verge of their teens; abortions should matter to them.) "Do you realize that only six years ago—"

"Six years is a long time, Mommy," said Tina, "it's as long as I can remember."

"Yeah," said Julie, "it's practically my whole life."

"I like the title, *The Book of Firsts,*" Leo said. "First woman astronaut, first woman cabinet member, first woman jockey, first woman fireman, with a bit of history and intimate portraits."

First hangwoman, I thought wickedly; first Pope.

"Not those bra-burning crazies, of course, but strong, serious, independent women, role models for our daughters. And if you didn't object—though of course it would be your book, Zane—I think it would be a good idea to include a couple of key men. Maybe that doctor—what's his name?—who pioneered the birth control pill, or the judge who first ruled on paternity leaves. The pioneers."

How quickly ideas were absorbed, distorted, and forgotten. In my briefcase with the rest of the mail I'd opened on the bus, I had a letter from a high school student in Austin, Texas, whose class had read a speech of mine in an anthology of movement readings. It had been an impassioned speech on the denigration of motherhood. I'd used all the *Debater's Manual* tricks and delivered it like a pro. But something had evidently got lost in the transcribing. "Your problem," offered the student helpfully, "was that you lived at the wrong time. Now women can do anything they like. We don't have to be simple-minded housewives any more. If we don't want to have children we can get abortions and use our true possessions, our minds. I'm writing this letter for credit in a class in Sex Roles. How do you feel about Equal Rights? If everyone including you could take a course like mine, people would see that women are as good as men and wouldn't have to be so bitter or make so much fuss."

"Of course," said Leo, "you'll want to get across to the readers that women like these, by becoming more worthwhile, self-fulfilled people, can actually enhance their attractiveness. You know what Henry Kissinger said? 'Power is the ultimate aphrodisiac,' and he ought to know. We want attractive women, achieving women, maybe show some of their families too—show that achievement doesn't necessarily interfere with family life. A book of positive images. What do you think?"

To hear Leo Stern ask me like that with real concern, *What do you think?* I would once have rented out my soul; and for the chance to do a book (a book!), I wouldn't have hesitated to throw my body in as well. But—surprise—even as I savored my fancy lunch, I knew I couldn't consider the offer now. Not because of the movement's one-time condemnation of individual authorship as elitist, opportunist individualism. That hard line that had once frightened some of us into silence and conformity, telling us where to work, how to dress, whom to love, how many children to bear, whether to breastfeed or bottlefeed, marry or not, till droves of converts fled for air, didn't work on me. Nor was it because Leo Stern was a man, one in the pay of an establishment publishing house owned by a multinational corporation that was the sworn enemy of our revolution. The list of works by true heroes of the revolution that were published and even commissioned by "the enemy" could stock a small library. No, if I rejected this latest inducement to sell out it was less to "combat self" (Mao) than because I now, miraculously, had integrity to defend and a community of sisters to answer to. There were students of mine who looked to me as I'd looked to Moore and whose disappointment if I let them down would crush me. We were an interconnected network. The new me had responsibilities. What student or comrade of mine wouldn't see instantly that Leo's *Book of Firsts* could as well be called a *Book of Lasts* or a *Book of Lies*? Those "positive images" he was so eager to peddle implied that women's liberation was in the bag, that oppression and struggle were passé, that there was little to get upset about any more.

Oh yes, I longed to write a book. I was my father's daughter, a lover of print, an autodidactical, irrepressible mouth-shooter who enjoyed making a spectacle of herself. I won't be so hypocritical as to deny my authorial ambitions. But if I were going to risk calling down the movement's curse and provoke that old green herring "sellout," it would be for my own book, thank you, not some flash-in-the-pan make-book to aggrandize Leo Stern. It would be for an honest book of analysis composed of our insights, however heretical; my passions, however perverse; my own hard-earned

Zanity. (I'd learned a few things over the years I'd have liked to see passed on in print.)

"Anyway," said Leo before I had spoken, "you don't have to decide right now. Take your time and think it over." He reached across the table and squeezed my hand. "Whatever you decide, I'm glad we had lunch together again. It's always a pleasure to be with you, Zane."

I agreed to consider his flattering proposal, to sniff at it overnight. But riding downtown on the Fifth Avenue bus to my afternoon class, opening the rest of that morning's mail, I knew I would send back the corsage. My community, though scattered, now sustained me as no book could. Each day greetings arrived from all over: postcards from sisters in Boston starting a press; Lolachild in Berkeley collecting documents; Miriam in Michigan with a personal crisis; Sally Battleaxe from L.A. on trial as a midwife; the Cynthiana Tennessee Health Collective newsletter; Vicky in Buffalo appealing for the Women's Prison Project. The sixties were over, yes, but some of us were still fighting our holding actions, keeping in precious touch. Though the Third Street Circle had popped and all that compressed passion had escaped, still I knew I'd never return to being the maid in the attic of someone else's movement, taking orders for their coffee and typing out their speeches or even authoring their books. I typed our speeches now, wrote my own outraged letters to the editor, attended planning meetings of our devising; so far, at least, I didn't need Leo Stern.

As the bus approached Twelfth Street I ripped open the last sealed envelope of the pile in my lap. Reading over the printed circular for a certain protest I had sponsored, I saw at the bottom of the page my new adopted name, Zane IndiAnna, printed side by side with Morgan Moore's.

It was the second time that month my name had been coupled with Moore's. There could no longer be any doubt that our paths, which had once run parallel for a little while, then had crossed long ago and diverged for so many years, were now converging again. My compass, so long out of whack, was working smoothly again, keeping my vessel in the wake of hers.

As the bus pulled up to the New School stop I stuffed the rest of my mail in my briefcase, then leaped over the melting slush to the dry curb. In two minutes my favorite class would begin—the one in Revolutionary Women; the text was Luxemburg's prison letters, on the question of Happiness.

Personally, I would never claim to feel, like Rosa Luxemburg, "as if I were the possessor of a charm which would enable me to transform all that is evil and tragical into serenity and happiness." To me happiness was a mysterious, delicate thing which might vanish like a snowflake if you tried to catch it. It wasn't solid like comfort, which you could sit on or wear or chew or grow used to or do without. It was like a delicate flower that unexpectedly blooms on a plant you've nurtured for its leaves: at once offshoot and seed. As with luck, you'd be foolish to pluck it; better simply to rejoice in it. It was a charm, as Luxemburg said, but only if you didn't count on it.

Still, at that moment, basking in the pride of having won one more draw from my old adversary Leo Stern, and holding in my hand a paper that linked me with Moore, I knew that if ever a teacher could be inspired, it would be I, that day.

3 · THE STUDENT

When class ended Tracy Blum, one of my best students, appeared at my desk.

"I wonder if I could talk to you? Do you have time for a cup of coffee, maybe?" She asked so shyly that the question was all but inaudible though her face was puckered with urgency.

I hated to say no. The semester was almost over, and this was the first time Tracy had approached me alone. Seeing how hard it was for her to ask, I didn't want to put her off. But after school on Mondays the children returned from their long weekend with Ricky and I had to be home when they arrived. "I'm afraid today is bad for me. What about Thursday, Tracy?"

Dejection crossed her pretty face like a shadow. And remembering my own vexing discomposure each time I had hoped but failed to establish contact with Morgan Moore, I said, "Look, my kids are coming home today, so I really have to leave now. But I live nearby. If you want to walk me home, maybe we can talk on the way."

As quickly as one slide can replace another on a screen, Tracy's face lit up in a radiant smile: the sign of a student crush. Though I'd been touched and quite astonished the first time I'd received this particular tribute from a student, remembering how I'd revered Moore it no longer surprised me to find that a radical feminist of thirty-five whose own husband saw fit to leave her might nevertheless be the object of youthful crushes.

"You have kids?" she asked surprised. "I didn't know that."

Despite our tireless propaganda, some people still seemed surprised to learn that radical feminists had kids.

"Yes. Three."

I gathered up my books and answered the parting questions of the other students clustered around my desk while Tracy waited near the door; then together we rode down in the elevator and walked out through the New School lobby.

At the entrance I eyed the large easel on which a poetry reading called "Beats and After," coming up in a month, was announced in tall black letters, but I made no mention of the fact that I had once lived with the featured poet, Marshall Braine. I relied on my own achievements nowadays, not Marshall's.

There'd been a long time, I was sorry to admit, when I'd felt a secret pride each time Marshall's name appeared in print. Not the respectful pleasure I took in Moore's work for its own sake, but the cheap pride of association. When his first collection of poems was published by an obscure local press I'd even hoped to find myself mentioned as a muse. Several of the poems he'd once "dedicated" to me were included, but not their dedications; and after that I settled for the vicarious kick of seeing Marshall's name alone. At first my shameful pleasures were rare: an occasional mention in a group review and one Off-Off-Broadway production that ran ten days in the warehouse district. Then finally, in 1967, my moment of glory came when Marshall's second book of poems received a substantial though guarded review in the *Times*, complete with quotes and a photo. ("I see your friend Marshall finally made it," said Ricky, presenting the paper, unaware of my still intimate secret involvement.)

Now, accompanying my student through the New School lobby, I did my best to ignore that name mocking me in letters half a foot high. If it were known, a past like mine could easily disgrace a teacher of Revolutionary Women. Trying to maintain a dignified professorial silence about the confusions and mistakes of my youth, I simply proceeded with my student Tracy into the yellow air of Twelfth Street, New York, 1975.

Life was different now. Tracy dogging me was nothing like the girls (myself included) who'd hung around Marshall the Poet. That groupie crush had meekly settled for reflected glory. But Tracy's crush on me was different. Like mine on Moore, it was ambitious, tinged with optimism and self-love. The goal was victory, not surrender, the object mentor, not patron: a different story entirely.

"We'll have about ten minutes to talk," I said encouragingly as we proceeded down Sixth Avenue toward Eighth Street. But Tracy said nothing. And as the troubled student at my elbow struggled vainly to speak, I remembered my own panic the one time, years before, I had managed to speak to Moore.

I remembered every agonizing detail. I'd followed her into an uptown gallery and blurted out her name—"Morgan Moore?"—and then had failed to produce another word. I had suddenly realized how ridiculous I was to chase after someone whom I'd practically invented and impose my fantasies on a witless stranger. How rude to intrude my passions into her private life. No wonder she'd looked frightened: Like other recipients of aggressive overtures she was a victim of assault. The tall, redhaired woman backing away from me probably shared with my mentor little more than a body, a by-line, and an address. In that painful moment I took a long look at her lush red hair, the carrot I'd pursued through so many dreams, and then—mortified by my folly—had simply turned around and fled.

By comparison, Tracy was now managing well enough. Though she too was momentarily tongue-tied, at least she had good reason to be walking beside me. "Do you live around here?" I asked lightly, trying to set her at ease.

"No. I live in Queens. But I plan to move to the city this summer if I can find the right job."

"What kind of a job?"

"I don't know exactly. Something worthwhile, even if it doesn't pay very much." She tossed her head in a manner disturbingly familiar—was it a gesture she'd learned from me?

Though she immediately lapsed back into shy silence, I knew

she couldn't possibly be feeling the same terror I had felt chasing Moore. We were student and teacher: legitimate. And though only a few brief years had passed since our movement had been launched, our students could now practically declare themselves. Already options had significantly multiplied. Tracy could insist on "worthwhile work" and take risks with me, whereas I, living a perfect double life, had been ashamed of my work and had slinked around for years, mooning at the window, spying on Moore from behind dark glasses, composing letters and declarations that never left my hands. A folder full of passionate protestations that never took wing still rested in the back of my desk drawer. Most of the pictures of Moore I had clipped over the years still lay concealed behind the children's drawings and valentines tacked up on my wall. Rumors of her forthcoming book, *Dialogues with Women,* the work that would make her one of us, had been circulating through the movement for months. But as the perpetual threat of "dyke" had once silenced me, now shyness or my sense of being unworthy kept me from speaking of her except to Kitty.

Tracy was already well beyond my starting point. Young feminists were not afraid of shackling fifties words like "dyke" or even seventies attacks like "man-hater." As for feeling unworthy, some of them made no secret of their belief that they had already superseded us.

At least, I thought, the silence I kept about Moore was more honorable than the noise I'd made over Marshall. Not that I'd ever gone seeking credit for his achievement; but when it was offered gratis I didn't rush to repudiate it, either. I remembered one of the mothers, who often waited at school with me for our kids to be dismissed, pointing to that picture of Marshall in the *Times* and asking, "Wasn't he your boyfriend?" (There he was in an exotic California tunic adorned with knotted ropes and beads and the very eyes that had once copulated with mine.)

"Who? Let me see," asked another mother, taking a look.

"Marshall Braine," replied the first proprietarily, for it was her paper.

"Yes," I said proudly.

"Oh, you know him?"

"Not any more, really. But I used to."

"Did you know him well?"

I allowed a suggestive smile to linger on my lips before I answered meaningfully, "*Very* well."

Later, after I'd turned my back in disgust on that whole vicarious world of men and discovered the fascination of women, I still found it hard to resist discussing Marshall whenever his name came up—and it came up surprisingly often. Sometimes, in fact, it seemed as if half the women in the movement, especially if they'd spent any time in California, had Marshall stories to swap for mine. Several women claimed to have returned to school under his inspiration; another had turned feminist in reaction to his cruelty ("He did that to you too? Well let me tell you what he did to me!"); another had sought him out in San Francisco because he was the only living poet, she said, who "combined politics, mysticism, and art"; another had taken him in when she'd heard he was homeless in Iowa; and one of my students always carried around a volume of his poems. ("The writer's pitch," Wolfe had called his line.)

Even Faith had had her turn with him. Every week for several months in 1966, it seemed, Marshall had gone to sit in the East Village bar where Faith waited on tables. "Marshall Braine was your first love?" she had asked me in a conversation I still remembered because in it she'd revealed one of her more fascinating theories. "That man sure does get around!"

"I had a high school crush first," I told her, "but of loves that really count, yes—Marshall was the first."

"How many have there been altogether?" she asked. "Loves that really count, I mean."

"I don't know—four or five."

"Ah! That confirms my theory."

"What theory?"

"That four or five is everyone's number, after a certain age. My number is five. It hasn't varied in years."

"Really? Who were the five?"

"Sarah first, then Bruce, Chris, Frankie, and you—or whoever it is I happen to be in love with at the time of the count."

We laughed, but even so the theory sounded plausible. My fifth love had been the movement.

At last, Tracy beside me managed to find her tongue. "Have you lived in the Village long?" she brought out brightly. Her discomfort barely showed.

"Seventeen years," I answered. Her whole life was probably not much longer than my New York residence.

"Seventeen years!" she repeated with awe.

She could never imagine what it had meant to me to have squatted here a spectator for so many years, waiting for my chance. Not that I knew history would call me if I stayed, but somehow I knew that if I left history wouldn't. And then to have heard the call.

"How lucky," sighed Tracy.

At the corner of Ninth Street where we stopped for a light Tracy turned to me with courage I had to admire and began her self-inflicted ordeal. "There's something very important I wanted to ask you about. But I thought we'd have more time. It's hard to ask you here, like this."

She spoke with the same shaky bravado I had affected myself at her age to disguise my jitters. I could see she was extremely agitated, clutching her books to her body, hiding her eyes under her lids. I wanted to ease her embarrassment (as Moore had never eased mine), to assure her that she could trust me, that I'd be careful with her confidence. "You want to say what it's about, anyway?" I asked as solicitously as I could.

"It's about"—she blurted it out at last, dissolving all her chagrin in a rush of trust—"my life!"

As her words splashed out I could almost hear her heart thumping. Just so had mine. Could Moore have been as disconcerted by my needy gaze as I was by Tracy's? Whenever Marshall had looked into the eyes of worshipful youth he had pressed on to seduction, feeling it the poet's right. He made five conquests per reading. But Moore had backed away from me as I stammered her name in that gallery—backed away like someone under attack—before I had turned quickly from her and fled.

I would neither conquer nor flee. Though I was nonplussed by Tracy's trust, I wanted to be worthy of it.

"I feel you're the one person I can talk to about it," said Tracy, "because I think I'm a lot like you. Your letter to the *Voice* last week? It said exactly what I tried to write myself. Of all the people I know, you seem to be the only one who's really in charge of your life."

What was I to say? With my life leading me by the nose as lives will do, I could hardly presume to advise anyone else about hers. I too was full of indecision. Not only had I always been afraid to speak to Moore, but the one time I'd seen Marshall in the New School cafeteria I'd slipped away before he could recognize me. Fear had overpowered curiosity as I imagined our conversation.

"You?" he'd say surprised, using those eyes on me. "What are *you* doing here?"—a perplexing question, given that I was the New Yorker now and he the visitor. "Don't tell me you're still taking courses at the New School."

"No," I'd answer with a little flurry of pride. "As a matter of fact—" (pausing for effect) "—I'm teaching them."

But of course, only my fantasies would give me a rejoinder like that. In real life, unless Marshall had profoundly changed, he'd have only to ask me what I taught and then he'd have me.

What did I teach? Revolutionary Women, Feminist Perspectives. "Ahh," he'd say with that familiar comprehending nod that discounted women's work. "Women's Studies."

Tracy, of course, knew very little about me—only what served her needs. She hadn't even known the crucial fact that I had three children. The one brief time when I'd had sure answers had long since passed, and I was far less secure than she imagined. But knowing she was ready to cling to my every word, I couldn't simply brush her aside. My new role carried responsibilities. To teach was to enlighten if not to convince. "To be among the masses and fail to conduct propaganda and agitation or speak at meetings," Mao warned, was the seventh type of that dangerous tendency he called "liberalism." I wondered how much sooner I might have stood up myself if I hadn't shrunk from meeting Moore?

"Listen, Tracy," I began, "I've made plenty of mistakes, believe me."

"Oh no," she said, laughing but adamant. "I've made a study of you."

"Maybe Thursday after class we can have coffee and a long talk," I offered as we walked across Eighth Street. "We'll go to the New Space Cafe—have you ever been there?"

But I don't think she even heard my question, for at that moment all her attention was concentrated on the difficult task of thrusting into my arms a large manila envelope.

"Here," she said, "I brought you these. I hope you don't mind. Please—only read them if you really want to. Don't feel you have to comment at all." And then she backed slowly toward the entrance to the Eighth Street Bookshop.

Embarrassed, I studied the envelope one long moment, already knowing what would be inside. They would be poems, of course, love poems; reflecting a rare kind of love. Anne Sexton explained it in a poem of her own:

A woman
who loves a woman
is forever young.
The mentor
and the student
feed off each other.

My response would require more than a little tact. Love poems from Tracy to me were not like comparable poems to or from a man, though it was possible that some day they might be. Now, Tracy's poems to me were likely to be declarations less of love than of hope, though she might not be aware of it herself.

"Tracy," I began, "I'll try to . . ."

But when I looked up Tracy was gone. Instead, from the corner of the bookstore window Morgan Moore peered out at me on the jacket of her newest book.

4 · NEW SPACE CAFE

I took Tracy to New Space on a dreary Thursday afternoon when snow streaked the windows and it was relatively empty. (Even so, Tracy became an immediate, devoted regular.) But I want you to see it on a Friday night half a year later—hot, crowded, and scintillating. The New Space Cafe ("NEW SPACE F♀R NEW W♀MEN," read the sign), off MacDougal Street, end of summer, three quarters of the way through the century.

It was one of those uncomfortably sticky nights when the Temperature-Humidity Index (the THI: a sophisticated measure invented to satisfy the New Yorker's urge to complicate) was high up in the seventies. Unfortunately, the two proprietors of New

Space, Sissy Smith and River Goforth, had not yet obtained either a liquor license or an air conditioner, though the cafe was about to celebrate its third birthday. That was okay; we made do by bringing our own wine and settling for whatever breeze the large ceiling fan could stir up; for there was absolutely no place like the New Space Cafe in the whole Village, air conditioned or otherwise.

In fact—has there ever before existed anywhere a place for women like this? All through history the intellectually stimulating public places, from the coffee houses of London that Charles II closed down as "seminaries of sedition" to the cafes of Paris where theories were advanced and movements born, excluded women. The few exceptions proved the rule. Though the first cafe was established in Paris in 1686, according to one authority, it wasn't until the 1890s that "women appeared in cafes not only on Sundays with their families but on weekdays too and alone."

(Women in cafes alone? I've read all about it: "*grisettes*" they were called; ornaments.)

No one labeled the young nihilist women of St. Petersburg during the reign of Alexander II "ornaments," though they flaunted their emancipation by smoking cigarettes, cropping their hair, wearing dark glasses and eccentric dress, and living in "fictitious marriages"; but neither did they have cafes to gather in. Sometimes they held meetings of their own on the "Woman Question" and other pressing matters—as, elsewhere, women excluded from male debate established exclusive clubs of their own. (The *Brittannica* reports that "even the prince of Wales was refused admittance when he called for the princess" at the Alexandria.) But a private club, a meeting, a secret organization, a salon is not a coffee house or cafe, where the endless quest for answers to the burning questions is open to the public.

As for the radical and bohemian cafes of New York of an earlier day, I have seen drawings and cartoons of the famous places and have read reports—of Pfaff's cellar where Poe and Whitman (and a lone token woman, Ada Clare, "the Bohemian Queen") held forth before the Civil War; of Sachs's Cafe where the anarchists gathered at the turn of the century; of the basement of the Brevoort, favorite of actors, playwrights, Eugene O'Neill, and Edna Millay; of Polly's Restaurant on Washington Square where Max Eastman and the whole *Masses* crowd savored the cooking of Hippolyte Havel and John Reed wrote *Ten Days That Shook the World;* of Chumley's, the speakeasy for the twenties literati (a tourist favorite still); of the San Remo, Rienzi's, the Figaro, the Gaslight, the White Horse, the Cafe Lucia, and all those places I remember on MacDougal Street where we came in the fifties on trains and busses searching for truth and significance. The smile displayed by the women in those prints is the same smile we wore.

But at New Space there was an entirely different atmosphere. You'd never see those accommodating smiles pasted on the faces of the listeners here. New Space was unlike all other cafes I've ever known.

In my head I can still hear the art talk of those bearded guardians on MacDougal Street who enforced their exclusive aesthetic by beating us down with their pricks, snatching away our pens and brushes, smirking at feeling, squeezing us out, calling us girls girls girls until we cried. But in New Space we set the aesthetic. Our jokes were the funny ones. (Those who think we lack a sense of humor just don't get them.) By definition, good conversation was our conversation, important concerns our concerns. The men who chose to venture inside New Space were suffered only on their good behavior. However hot or muggy it might sometimes get, the heat was comfort itself compared to that old icy freeze of exclusion.

No doubt this clean cafe, with its pale brick walls, well-tended plants in hand-thrown pots hanging in the windows from leather thongs, and the rotating displays of women's graphics, was not for everyone—though the proprietors made some effort to gather a diverse crowd. On Tuesday nights our poets read and Saturday afternoons our musicians played. But on every other night of the week, and especially on Fridays, the main attraction was the talk.

Talk. Provocative, stimulating conversation: that's what New Space offered. And what talk! Intellectual rhapsodies—the Purpose of Life (the old P of L), What Is to Be Done?—all the burning questions of our movement. Hour after hour we'd sit in the back and dig away, as if the outcome of our fervent talk could change the world.

Not that we all agreed or even knew each other. Remember—New Space was not a club; there was a varied clientele. There was usually a sprinkling of the curious, attracted by the publicity that came in spurts whenever some uptown journalist "discovered" our place anew, plus a few mixed couples off the street who saw the crowded tables inside and decided on impulse to try it out. But even among the feminists, there were many I didn't know, though I was a habitué.

Perhaps certain types did predominate: childless women in their twenties and thirties who had tentatively chosen to live alone and understandably sought the kind of good talk and companionship New Space offered at the end of a long day. Or family women like me who couldn't pass up a chance to go out at night once our kids were old enough to be left without sitters. Movement veterans, converts, young enthusiasts here on a pilgrimage, visiting feminists from as far away as Australia who always tried to save a night for New Space when they were passing through New York.

Still, our movement was no monolith. On the contrary, in recent years it had grown as many shoots as tassels in a cornfield. Now there were separatist feminists, cultural feminists, lesbian feminists, socialist feminists, anarchist feminists, Marxist feminists and their manifold sects, bourgeois feminists; there were feminists who wanted to run for Congress, start a magazine, learn mechanics, found a matriarchy, discover God, take over Vermont; there were women's study groups, theory groups, rock groups, therapy groups; there were man-hating feminists, child-rearing feminists, feminists out to smash monogamy or enforce monogamy, abolish housework or earn wages for housework, end motherhood or enshrine motherhood; feminist quilters, weavers, singers, dancers, vegetarians, soldiers, witches, poets; feminists beyond the finest categories of the FBI's wildest imaginings. But no matter how vehemently you might disagree with the party pontificating at the next table (our cafe already boasted two celebrated fistfights), no matter what your particular feminist bent, there was one thing practically everyone here had in common. We all knew where to go after a hard day's work for that precious feeling probably never before in history experienced in a cafe by any ordinary unaccompanied woman: belonging.

On this particular Friday night I arrived late. I had arranged to meet Faith, who was driving down from Vermont with her lover, Liz, but I knew she'd be late too. Not only because with the heat so fierce they'd likely have left late to avoid traffic; but because Faith had her own private system of reckoning time.

I'd learned about it through harsh experience. Of all the strains between us, time had been the worst. Not even my marriage, which Faith had tolerated as a necessary nuisance, had distressed us like time. I, mother-of-three, lived by clocks and compromises, while Faith, without a tie, lived by fancy and impulse. When she'd "had it" in the city she simply moved to the country; when she was lonely she joined a commune. (And people still say that love is everything!) We might have gone on loving if we'd had the time, but the parameters of our lives had been hopelessly incongruous. Our ways of freedom, which we each clung to fiercely and took great care to insure, were irreconcilable. I, the mother, the early riser, who depended for mine on tight schedules and judicious lists, exercised freedom by rising earlier, making arrangements, compressing my days more tightly than before. But Faith, lover of risk and uncertainty, found hers in improvisation. She worked only free-lance and part-time in order to be able at any moment's notice to pick up the suitcase she always kept packed and follow her impulse wherever it led. Why not? There was no one to stop her (except me). I was Time's master, she Time's renegade. And although we were now able to joke about our once terrible quarrels ("You're so uptight!"; "You're undependable!"; "Be impetuous!"; "Think of the children!"), they'd subdued and tempered us. Another revelation of this perplexing decade: Every solution entails its problems. In the end, the baffling enigma of love depended on the mystery of person, after all. How else explain that our passion, fueled on equality, finally foundered on one unsuspected difference?

We'd recovered soon enough. When passion toppled (as it will) trust remained. And something else as well: knowledge. For me, thanks to Faith, the world would always be more complex and less bifurcated than I'd imagined.

By the time I arrived at New Space, the conversation was well under way. Empty bottles, countless coffee cups and glasses, and several overflowing ashtrays covered the large table at the back where our little band sat deep in solemn discussion.

(Though times had changed, we were still earnestly trying to get to the bottom of things. Granted, our conversations did often fail to produce results; still, our talk mattered. Better to talk than act prematurely or without a plan. Indeed, maybe a case could be made that women talking politics without embarrassment or apology was itself a significant "act," given traditional misogyny. "Silence gives the proper grace to women," said men as far back as Sophocles. Samuel Johnson: "A woman preaching is like a dog's walking on his hind legs. It is not done well; but you are surprised to find it done at all." Nietzsche: "When a woman inclines to learning there is usually something wrong with her sex apparatus." Malcolm X: "To tell a woman not to talk too much was like telling Jesse James not to carry a gun, or telling a hen not to cackle. Can you imagine Jesse James without a gun, or a hen that didn't cackle?")

On this occasion everyone was discussing the latest revelations in the continuing scandal of the government's infiltration of our lives. New stories had broken in the newspapers all that week. Not only was the CIA keeping 7,200 "personality files" as well as an index of over 300,000 suspects—and local Red Squads all over the country, the military, Internal Revenue, and even the Post Office had been caught dipping their fingers into our privacy and compiling dossiers—but the FBI had been forced to reveal some of its most shocking operations. Besides compiling lists and dossiers of its own running into the high six figures, it kept a secret index of people to be rounded up for "detention" in case of a "national emergency"; it had a separate Operation Chaos for destroying the Left, and it seemed to place no limits on what its agents and paid informers were permitted to do to find us out. Bugging our phones, opening our mail, infiltrating our cells, manipulating our private lives, stealing our files, disrupting our meetings, diverting our energies, subverting our ideals. Our own guiding principle for a time had been *shock without terror* (with a potential ally in every home, what need had we to resort to terror?), but the "intelligence arms," as they were quaintly dubbed, seemed incapable of making use of such distinctions.

Golda Feldman, now a lawyer, was suggesting a tempting if temporary solution to our permanent Friday night quandary, What Is to Be Done? Simply by writing certain letters to specified bureaucrats in accordance with two unusual laws, it was now possible, she informed us, to force the spying eyes of government to cough up all the files with your name on them stored in their computers and reveal exactly what they had on you.

"Can anyone do it?" I asked quickly.

Golda nodded.

A hoarder of implications from my earliest debating days, I saw a new chance to prove myself. In that poem of Brecht's up on my wall occurred the lines:

There was little I could do. But without me
The rulers would have been more secure. That was my hope.

At the very least, my dossier would prove that without me the rulers would have been more secure.

Golda explained the procedure. "Actually," she said, "if you find any mistakes or slanders in your file, by law you can sue to get them corrected."

I suddenly imagined our family tree, with Uncle Herman circled in red and all the relatives demanding a correction. And while everyone else at our table was laughing at the latest instance of the triumph of bureaucratic absurdity, this fanatic was busily taking notes on how to send for my records.

My student Tracy Blum took a new bottle of California chablis from a brown paper bag (naturally, one of the brands that didn't violate the United Farm Workers' grape boycott we all scrupulously observed) and refilled our glasses in preparation for the debate that was clearly brewing at the table: Should we or should we not send for our files?

Everyone was voicing an opinion. Several people thought it the only correct thing to do—disruptive, impudent, and vindicating in these depressing times. But some considered it imprudent at best. "It's turning your name over to them like a criminal returning to the scene of the crime; probably just what they want us to do," said Roxanne Dubois, one of my old cohorts from the History Project. She had brought her daughter Sasha, who was listening wide-eyed. The zealous Marya called the project "important"; but Kitty struck the table with her fist so her wine spilled and declared the whole idea "dangerous." Golda, the lawyer, who'd studied the matter, was for it, though she warned with characteristic legal caution that if they didn't have anything on you to begin with, they'd have you after you wrote to them. "Your letter will become document number one in the new file in your name."

As with most questions of action in which you could only guess at the consequences, each side had its compelling reasons.

Years had passed since our tiny band, full of passion and hope, had known how to work together like a fist, folding into each other like five squeezed fingers to deliver a single well-aimed blow. Nowadays, instead, when we gathered to talk we spread ourselves wide as a hand and ticked off each finger as a separate point of view. But for me this question had only one answer. If prudence hadn't stopped me from doing the things that had probably landed my name in the government's computers in the first place, it couldn't stop me now from sending for my files. I could think of a dozen good reasons to do it—from sabotaging the enemy's schemes (one more bureaucrat copying out my records meant one less tapping a phone), to satisfying my curiosity. Never in all my life had I been able to resist knowing everything, the bad with the good. Eavesdropping from the top of the stairs to Mama and Aunt Louise discussing my future; intercepting notes in study hall; sneaking my records out of the principal's office; even keeping informed about Ricky's infidelities. But the one true reason was contained in those lines from Brecht. I knew I would do anything possible to prove I was not, as all our detractors insinuated, merely trivial or "paranoid" but on the contrary was sufficiently dangerous to the rulers to warrant an extensive dossier.

"I know for sure they have a file on me," said Sasha Dubois, "because since I was in China they've been systematically opening my mail."

I leaned close to Sasha. "You were in *China?* When? How did you ever manage that?"

"I started applying when I was in high school, and I finally got there for a month last spring with a group of student activists."

"But how?" When I was in high school my dream had been to get to New York; and here I was. But China! Getting there, I thought, would require a miracle.

"I always thought if there was any place in the world miracles could happen," said Sasha, reading my mind, "it would have to be China."

"So did I," I said, "but it never occurred to me that just anybody could go there. How do you apply? Doesn't it cost a fortune?"

Sasha was eager to answer my questions. No, not just anybody could get a visa; but if you had radical credentials and a group to sponsor you, you could probably swing it. Yes it was costly, because it was so far away; but when you considered what people usually spent their money on . . .

Aunt Louise had done it—had gone clear around the world. Why not I?

Right away I began figuring. Sasha'd had a small grant, but I could borrow the money from a bank if necessary, now that I had a salary. Three years earlier I'd have needed a husband to get me credit, but now, thanks to the movement, the banks could no longer refuse us if we made a fuss. And if I could get a visa (maybe my FBI dossier would serve for radical credentials, I thought mischievously) and find a group going over when school was out, and if Ricky would take the children—

Tunnels were funny things. You could dig and dig and never know how close to the end you were getting. You could give up two feet short of your destination and never even know it. But if you were really serious about getting through, maybe with enough tenacity and faith it was possible.

"If you go to China it'll change your whole life," said Sasha, beaming.

"Change your life?" snickered Kitty. "How can a four-week trip to China change your life?"

That kid Sasha accepted the challenge. "By letting you see with your own eyes how a whole society can really be completely transformed."

"Come on," continued Kitty. "Socialism never liberated women, not in Russia or Cuba or your precious China either. There isn't a place on earth where women are equal."

"Yes—how many women are in the Party?" asked Golda, joining in.

"A lot more than there are in the government here," said Marya, "and at least in China the government is committed to training women for leadership."

"Look," said Sasha, "it takes time to change a four-thousand-year-old culture. You can't write off a revolution for not producing a perfect Utopia in a mere twenty-five years."

"According to Mao—" began Roxanne.

"Mao!" cut in Kitty with a loud guffaw.

And now the whole table was getting into it, voices were rising, eyes gleaming: the excitement I thrived on. Can revolutionary socialism free women? Was optimism ever justified? What was the relation between sex and race and class? What were the pros and cons of marriage? The relation of freedom and equality? Psychology and politics? Work and motherhood? Commitment, orgasm, and love? It was one vast subject, interconnected and limitless, debated in Xerox skirmishes and international conferences as well as Friday nights at the back table in the New Space Cafe.

It was half the reason I was happy.

It was after midnight when a disheveled Faith and a breathless Liz finally arrived, waving an early morning *Times*. On their way down from Vermont they'd heard disturbing news on the car radio—news confirmed on the front page of the paper, with pictures and all.

Roxanne and Tracy, nearest to Faith, grabbed the newspaper.

"What is it?" asked Marya dryly. "More assassinations?"

This was an allusion to the recent historic *Times* front page—probably the first in the paper's history—in which every photograph on it was of a woman. Four photos in all, four women, and only one of them appearing as a wife. The wife had been the President's; but the other three women were his enemies: two independent presidential assassins (Sara Jane Moore and Lynette "Squeaky" Fromme) and the unfathomable Patty Hearst. An astonishing selection of women to be featured by the *Times*, one that had inspired a torrent of mocking commentary at our table. "At last we know what we have to do to get off the woman's page," Marya had summed up sardonically. And because we knew it would probably be years before we'd ever again see women take over the front page of the *New York Times*, we had spent the evening composing delicious tributes, musical and otherwise, to the sister assassins.

(Maybe that was the best thing about New Space—the way you could blaspheme freely with people who shared your blasphemies.)

"No, not an assassination," said Faith excitedly. "They've arrested one of the Brookville Nine in an all-women's house in Paterson, New Jersey. She's been underground for four years. They wanted her for trying to blow up a trainload of flamethrowers heading for Vietnam—remember? But listen to this. When they arrested her she made an impassioned defense of feminism and a plea for support from her sisters. Now for sure they'll start hounding the whole movement."

"Now?" said Marya. "They already are!"

"What's her name?" asked Kitty.

"She moved underground as Solotaire. But her real name is Nina Chase."

Nina! "Let me see!" I said, grabbing the paper. "She was a good friend of mine once."

"She's gonna need all the friends she can find now," said Marya.

It was Nina, all right, little, principled, pixie Nina, with her picture on the front page of the *Times*. It was awful to see her, of all people, the freedom nut, handcuffed to a fedoraed agent. She looked haggard; the mischief was gone from her eyes and her cupid's bow mouth was hard. But she looked proud too, I thought: tough as ever.

"She's in bad trouble," said Liz, shaking her head. "Seems they're going to charge her with half a dozen different felonies. According to the radio she could get thirty years."

Some of the Russian women revolutionaries had all but longed for prison, knowing the power of martyrdom; but here, now, what was the point? On went the Left: a time of arrests always followed a time of action, and then came a time of defense committees. Without a movement, Nina was in for it.

Then Faith and Liz told us the glum story of the latest grand jury hearings in the Boston area where the government was fishing for informers against the Left in the lesbian community; and River came out of the kitchen with fresh coffee, and we all sobered up to talk over the newest developments.

Some people, I knew, would have been impatient with all our talk. Some clamored for instant action—even though lately, it seemed, action as we'd once known it had been temporarily played out. Some—including several New Space regulars—might have dismissed our talk as mere bullshit. (Marx himself called certain talk the "learned pastime" and "theoretical bubble-blowing"—though he should talk!) But I ignored them all. Even if our talk produced nothing but pleasure, it would have been justified. (Rosa Luxemburg reached ecstasy watching birds; Emma Goldman was transported making love; Voltairine de Cleyre loved poetry above all else; Sojourner Truth, like Joan of Arc, grew happy listening to her private voices.) But it did more. For as we sat there into the night trying to figure out what to do next, I knew that even if we burned no brighter than a pilot flame keeping our ideas lit till the next historic moment came around, still, as long as we burned and went on burning, the movement would stay alive. It would live as long as we lived and keep going as long as we kept it going.

The very next morning while the children slept (for they had finally reached the age of sleeping late on weekends) I sat down and wrote three letters. My Documents of the Seventies. (Take note, those of you who dismiss all cafe rebels!)

The first, to the Director of the FBI, began: "In accordance with the provisions of the Freedom of Information Act . . ." as Golda had advised. The second, more thoughtfully composed, was a letter of inquiry to the U.S.-China People's Friendship Association, a group Dee-Dee Larson would call a "communist front." The third letter was a personal note to Carole Buxbaum, my one-time friend and Nina's former roommate, who for the past several years had been a regular news reporter for People's Radio. In it I asked her to put me in touch with Nina's defense committee if she knew of one because I wished to offer my services. If none existed, I said, I'd be honored to form one. "I have an old debt to pay," I said in closing my letter—and hoped Carole would understand.

5 · MEN

This is not, as you may have noticed, a book about men. Still, it would be misleading if I allowed you to leave the New Space Cafe thinking we never talked about sex and dishonest if you finished my book thinking I had renounced the other gender. Ricky, sadly, yes; Leo Stern, happily so; Marshall, maybe. But there were other men in the world, all kinds, including some who spoke directly to the heart. (And one in particular: a socialist with blue boyish eyes and a gentle voice who sat opposite me at a round-table panel on sex roles at a New School conference on Whither the State? Something about him reminded me of Faith—maybe the way he unhesitatingly came to my defense when a fatuous professor attacked me, maybe merely his eyes. We went out for coffee and exchanged addresses before he returned to Baltimore; when he comes back to New York we'll see each other.) Men were everywhere; they were half the human race; and since the movement I was no longer so afraid of them.

Not that men weren't as firmly entrenched in power as they'd ever been, with misogynists on top; but since I'd been moving around a bit and expanding my experience I'd discovered (sometimes in the most unlikely quarters) a number of men who deserved our sincerest regard. In fact, in the feminist notebook I now carried everywhere in place of my old New York one, I was keeping a list. No list of conquests—my key-collecting days were past—but a list of potential allies. On it were the names and numbers of half a dozen men whom I would personally guarantee we'd be able to count on when the roll call came. Not men free of sexism, as universal as sin, but men who'd committed themselves; and I had the names of as many more who were likelies. My list was shorter by half than my enemies list, which, if I chose to update it, might have to go on microfilm (for a man could as easily be threatened by us as moved); but it was a start. And other women were compiling lists of their own.

As for sex, the subject of some of our Circle's most fascinating conversations (which I certainly have no intention of revealing here), I'd undergone a small revolution of my own. Please don't think I fell into the habit of casual sex as soon as I began traveling around to conferences—it wasn't that kind of "sexual revolution." For no matter how extensive my opportunities I simply wasn't made like those free-wheeling men or women who could find satisfaction in casual adventures. Not for me the brief encounter, the *ménage à trois,* the conquest list, or groups. A fast-living, free-loving Elizabeth Gurley Flynn might pull off such stunts from time to time, or a passionate Emma Goldman ("to me anarchism was . . . a living influence to free us from inhibitions"), or an Alexandra Kollontai: tall, handsome, and sure of herself. Not I. Even divorced and experienced, I was always too insecure in my body, too chary of trust, to risk the exposure of sex without the reassurance of love. (Which isn't to say I question the testimony of those young women in our Circle, raised on the pill, who claim to want to keep sex free of emotionally taxing "complications"—women who are clearly puzzled when I speak of the "transcendence" of sex. My way isn't theirs; their way isn't mine.) After a few initial, understandable mistakes following Ricky's departure—mistakes I identified by my feelings of shame the morning after (for it still takes two to be "liberated")—I learned to protect myself with the old *no*. In less than a decade I'd gone from thinking sex unnatural for whole categories of people (me, fat people, bald people, people I admired, people over a certain age, mothers, the serious or accomplished), all in need of "liberation"; to recognizing that in fact everyone did it, every living soul had an ordinary set of organs between his or her legs to use or not without accruing any special credit; to regarding sex finally as a highly charged, misunderstood emotional connection hopelessly tainted by power. But sometimes, nevertheless, I felt that the right person might be trusted enough to love and the right answer be *yes*.

How am I to characterize those post-movement relationships? Though we've talked about them endlessly among ourselves, it's still difficult to explain. For all our analysis, love is still a vast mystery. All the factors are interconnected: trust and risk, risk and independence, independence and abandon, abandon and respect. All I can say with certainty is that with a movement to back me up I finally managed to say to a man I trusted, "there" and "here" and "don't stop now." It was a desire I'd felt often enough, but only after our movement did I dare to specify. Now that I was supplicant no longer, I was able to drop my guard and move my hips with abandon, knowing my movements were no more ridiculous than his.

One last word about marriage while I'm on the subject of men. Not that I mean to begin blabbing about Ricky just because our marriage is over. Like most rebel women on this subject, I will be brief. (Elizabeth Gurley Flynn, leaving her husband at twenty, said only: "I don't love him any more. Besides, he *bores* me." Vera Figner explains her failing marriage: "He was inclined to be conservative while I became ever more strongly attracted to the radical group"—and the next and last we hear of her husband they are formally separated. Even Mother Bloor, with four children to consider as she contemplated divorce, was reticent about her agony, restricting her remarks to a page: "My interests and activities were more and more leading me away from my husband. . . . My problem was to arrange a separation and at the same time keep his friendship and maintain his relation with the children. . . . The struggle was so severe I had a nervous breakdown." Of her next and lasting marriage, she said as little.) But having considered the subject from many sides, I want to pass on my interim conclusions.

Struggle, that first duty of the rebel, is usually the wife's undoing. How can you sip your discontent all day long and suddenly hide it in the oven when your husband walks through the door? Complacency is as unseemly in a rebel as is complaint in a wife. No, the virtuous wife suffers silently while the rebel, living always in opposition, must squawk, holler, fume, rail, and finally strike! Let a wife become a rebel or a rebel a wife and something has to give: either her spirit or his or the marriage. How they work it out depends on a lot of things, mainly the children. But a "solution"?

Kitty, in her fifteenth year of marriage to the father of her children, seemed to me to enjoy the best compromise of all, balancing family, work, and lover with grace and discretion. But not even a perfect balancing act is a "solution."

My own marriage had, I thought, evolved after a decade into a model of that particular accommodation that depends on space. We had an understanding. Between Ricky's late hours and my endless meetings, one of us was out almost every night while the other stayed home with the children. Though long empty of thrills, our arrangement was adequate as marriages go. Or so it seemed to me. It gave each of us and the children the necessary balance of freedom, support, security. Not the romantic union envisioned by the single or the "open" marriage touted by the new, but an arrangement which got the homework done, the skinned knees kissed, the terrors soothed, the victories applauded, meals enjoyed, rent paid.

Naturally now and then each of us mooned for perfection, even sometimes "falling in love" or confronting each other with the resentments of the long-married, though we each knew better. But while I, a dreamer, merely entertained vague fantasies of independence and perfection, imagining that Ricky would wake up one morning as an ardent feminist or else conveniently die in a car crash leaving enough insurance to take care of the children, he proceeded, lawyerwise, to conceive and execute a plan.

One night, after eleven years of marriage, I returned from a meeting to find Ricky waiting for me in a semidarkened living room (too formal, too calm) with "something I have to tell you, Zane."

I knew, of course, what it was. Those wavering, guilty eyes, that pained, impatient voice that brooked no conciliation or argument: What else could it mean but quits? After that: panic, war, divorce.

I'm not saying I was right and he was wrong, though I still think in other times we might possibly have worked things out. Who knows? By then it was too late, he already had another wife picked out. If time and luck hadn't left their scabs I'd still be bitter just thinking about the way he left without so much as a "may I?" to the children, forget about me. At the moment I read his face, our three babies were sleeping peacefully. My pulse raced ahead to the morning when they would wake up as usual and Ricky would be gone as usual but nothing else would be the same. As far as their father cared, they didn't even seem to merit a separate explanation. His reasons for leaving me were evidently broad enough to cover his leaving them too, enabling him to take upon himself the decision of who would be sacrificed for whose happiness. Undoubtedly, if we had taken a family vote at that moment, Ricky would have lost by 4 to 1, though I certainly had no more illusions about romance than he. No longer serious lovers, hardly even chums, it seemed to me we were still quite friendly enough to satisfy the children's needs. But where individualism is King and fulfillment is Queen, children's needs are dispensable, and justification for every sort of behavior can readily be found in any popular magazine, from the most radical to the most reactionary.

"Luckily we're both young enough to start again," said the wily Ricky, betraying a peculiar indifference to the interests of the youngest of all. "It's not too late to correct our errors"—as though the error of divorce didn't carry equally grave consequences as the error of marriage.

Expensive errors all. When they began to tell in the succeeding months—as Tina climbed into our bed on Sundays to soak her father's pillow with her tears; as moody Sammy socked the wall and kicked the floor; as little Julie, taking it worst or best (no knowing which), purged her Daddy's name from her now considerable vocabulary—he wasn't around to see. Safely removed from the scene, ensconced uptown with his next wife, Ricky could choose not to believe in the children's suffering. He could elevate their wounds to "reality training," as some shrink no doubt advised, dismissing my reports as manipulative. "Tell Tina I have tickets for the circus. Maybe that will cheer her up," he said sarcastically, buying his way out.

As long as he sent a regular check he had a world of supporters. Not only among other fathers, but, through one of those acrobatic flips by which history stands all our expectations on their heads, among women, too, who were also flaying the family in the name of freedom, confusing symptom with cause. Mostly, though not only, childless women, convinced that what's good for the parent is good for the kids, whom they somehow consider endlessly adaptable.

Adaptable? Yes—you adapt if you have to. We had to.

I can't say I'm sorry, either. Who can tell? My friends say I'm better off, and Ricky and I are even "friends." Not that I wouldn't prefer a whole family to a broken one and a secure life to a precarious one; but you can't have everything. Luckily I am not a person of regrets.

Whose fault was it? Now that it's all over and we've made our adjustments, so that it sometimes feels as though everything may have happened for the best, I can take a philosophic view and pull out an answer from the sage pages of Simone de Beauvoir:

> *It is useless to apportion blame and excuses: Justice can never be done in the midst of injustice. A colonial administrator has no possibility of acting rightly toward the natives, nor a general toward his soldiers; the only solution is to be neither colonist nor military chief; but a man could not prevent himself from being a man. So there he is, culpable in spite of himself and laboring under the effects of a fault he did not commit; and here she is, victim and shrew in spite of herself.*

Victim and shrew. Thesis and antithesis. The synthesis had yet to be worked out.

6 · CHINA

It was our last night in the People's Republic of China when Comrade Chu announced at dinner that she had that day received permission to take us as requested the following morning into the tunnels under Peking.

Two men in our group, who loved all matters military, whooped aloud and immediately downed their beers in one celebratory draft. I thrilled silently. Hadn't I dreamed in a hundred dreams of passing through a tunnel under China?

Our whole group had listened intrigued to the story, told us by three Swedish engineers we'd met in a hotel in the provincial city of Loyang, that underneath Peking lay an intricate web of tunnels, an entire underground city, with dining halls, conference rooms, piped music, dormitories, generators, first-aid stations—built according to Mao's odd formula for self-defense: "Dig tunnels deep and store grain."

The part about grain we'd noticed ourselves. Having arrived in China during a great June wheat harvest, we had no trouble believing the proud claim that, in accordance with Mao's edict, the people had finally achieved their goal of storing enough grain to feed the entire eight hundred million population (nearly a quarter of the people on earth!) for one full year. That in itself was a miracle, considering that almost every year for thousands of years until Liberation masses of peasants had died of starvation or been forced to sell their children and wives for lack of food to feed them. No more. Now children were not for sale, women belonged to themselves, and everywhere we went people were busily gathering in the wheat. Even in the larger cities it was not unusual to see a broad thoroughfare or one of the great public squares closed to traffic and turned into a threshing field. From our boat in the eight-hundred-year-old Peking park where we spent one Sunday, we watched cadres and youths threshing wheat beside a lake once dug for the pleasure of an emperor. Before Liberation, an admission ticket to that park, which housed the imperial Summer Palace, cost the price of a sack of flour; now it cost one hundredth as much. Inside the Summer Palace's Great Hall of Happiness and Longevity we stood in a room in which the Dowager Empress had been served 28-course meals that cost enough to feed

5,000 peasants every day, with thirty kinds of soup alone and many dishes meant only to be smelled, then thrown away.

But tunnels?

At our meeting that night in Loyang our group had voted unanimously to request the visit. We wanted to see. For though we'd all been intrigued by the tunnel story, at the same time we'd been skeptical. Despite the accomplishments we'd been witnessing for three weeks, skepticism was still our initial reaction to everything Chinese, from the painlessness of acupuncture to the collective transformation of agriculture. We were amazed Americans for whom China was unfathomable, still the other side of the world though it now lay directly beneath our feet.

I was no better in this than anyone in our group. Not until I had actually seen the needles protruding from my body—one between my thumb and index finger, another above my wrist, one in my forearm, another in my neck beneath my right ear—not till I felt the momentary sensation as of an itch while each needle penetrated my skin and then afterward felt nothing at all—did I abandon my own lingering doubts about the absence of pain. And though I swore to my comrades, "Really, it doesn't hurt a bit!" all the while the medic was twirling the needles in my flesh, I could see my testimony doubted. My comrades would continue to doubt until the moment they tried it themselves.

As for the transformation of agriculture, one visit to the once arid, now densely planted, terraced fields of the Tachai People's Commune, one day at the Beacon Production Brigade in Shensi Province, were as convincing as all the notes, quotes, and statistics I had recorded in my tiny script in four fat notebooks, margin to margin, cover to cover. For millennia, the Gin River had devastated the surrounding countryside (now the Beacon People's Commune), flooding it in spring, leaving it parched and barren the rest of the year. But after the land was collectivized, the peasants dug a new river channel, filled the old flood beds with soil carried from the surrounding mountains, built ditches and dams (and Leap Forward Village and new schools), planted trees, and turned the badland into fertile fields that stretched before us from horizon to horizon. "We used to say: 'The people must make way for the river.' Then we 'ordered the mountain to bow its head,' and now," said the leading member of the Brigade's Revolutionary Committee, breaking into a smile, "now the river makes way for the people."

During our very first dinner in China we had indulged our wicked skepticism, elaborating the thesis that (as one member of our group quipped) the five-year-olds of Peking's Municipal Kindergarten No. 9, who'd performed charming dances for us that afternoon, had "probably been rehearsing their stuff for ten years in order to impress the foreigners." "Dancing," added another, "is probably the only thing those poor kids will ever know how to do!" But once we had listened to enough schoolchildren reciting their lessons and presenting their music in every town we passed through, down to even the tiniest, remotest peasant village, the joke grew tiresome. Those children discussing ways to deepen their understanding of socialism were no less believable than "our" kids rattling off the batting averages and baseball scores of entire leagues. Twenty years earlier China was 90 percent illiterate; now the reverse was true and every peasant's child attended school. Seeing was believing.

Of course, there was always the possibility, someone suggested, that our entire trip was a communist plot. It was possible, offered someone else, that the schoolchildren who so enthusiastically discussed politics and the classics of Marxism-Leninism-Mao-Tse-Tung-Thought were not politicized at all but merely "brainwashed." As it was possible that the acupuncture subjects we kept encountering were not honest reporters but victims of mass hysteria or willful stoicism. It was possible too that all the peasants chatting among themselves in little groups in the fields whom we had been seeing from our bus windows for three weeks, like all the families gathered under the streetlights on the broad avenues of Sian playing cards, reading books, making music, or holding discussions when we strolled out in the evenings; like the well-fed textile workers we unexpectedly joined for lunch in a factory cafeteria; like the youngsters and old people doing their graceful Tai Chi exercises along the curbs or in the parks of Peking each morning after dawn; like the brigades of scrubbed, spirited schoolchildren with their backpacks and red flags marching off to the countryside to help in the wheat harvest; like the weekend park-goers or the occasional Sunday painter working at his easel in the communes we visited had all been planted there by the Communist Party or the army for our benefit and forced to perform their Happy Act for each busload of eager foreigners. It was even possible that the pretty pigtailed students at Chengchow University or the Foreign Language Institute or the May 7th Cadre School of whom we ceaselessly asked our American sex-obsessed questions ("What do you think about falling in love?" "What about premarital sex?" "What qualities do you dream of in a husband?") were uniformly lying when they answered that they were too young to think about such things, or had too much to learn first, or would choose a husband according to his "politics" when the time came. One wag among us even proposed that some secret mind-controlling Chinese herb had been slipped into the tea to make us so love what we saw. But as the days proceeded it became easier simply to accept the evidence of our senses: that acupuncture was indeed painless, that students really did want to "serve the people," that the Chinese masses were, probably for the first time in centuries, finally decently fed, housed, clothed, educated, inspired. In short, that the transformation of a huge society—a revolution—was possible, though it might take not years or decades but generations of intense devotion to achieve.

Of course, the revolution still had very far to go. And obviously, China's way would not be our way, as our interpreters repeatedly cautioned us, using the words of Mao: "In the fight for complete liberation, the oppressed people must rely first of all on their own struggle." And naturally, the problems of an enormous, ancient, developing Asian country were hardly those we faced at home. Still, at the end of our month-long trip most of us had come to believe that in one place at least revolutionary socialism "worked."

As for the tunnels, which were said to lie like a dream beneath every city, town, and commune in China, we would see.

I was the first one on our bus the next morning, the last day of a long journey. The others, their suitcases packed and passports checked, straggled on with cameras hanging from their sunburned necks and notebooks protruding from their bags and pockets, and at 7:45 we were rolling.

By eight, on schedule, twenty-two North American friends of China piled out of the yellow bus that now felt like home into a busy shopping street teeming with pedestrians and bicyclists in one of the older districts of Peking. As always, throngs of the curious surrounded and cheered us while we followed our guides into a small clothing store. We gathered before a counter displaying blue Mao jackets, caps, and white cotton shirts, and waited.

Our favorite interpreter, Comrade Chu, introduced the civil defense representative of the Shuan Wu District's Revolutionary Committee. Though it was the last day of our trip, once more I prepared to record verbatim in my notebook the speeches of welcome and background I had come to expect. For myself, I knew I would retain enough Chinese images to ponder for years to come, but I wanted to get down every word for Aunt Louise and the children.

But instead of presenting us with the usual detailed array of statistics (how many tons of earth had been removed from how many miles of tunnels dug with what tools by how many workers over what period of time in accordance with which goal of what committee), our host stepped abruptly back and with a dramatic flourish opened a curtain behind the display counter, smiled to the beaming onlookers, pressed a button on the wall—

Presto! Before our eyes the floor divides to reveal a hidden flight of stairs going down, down into the earth!

"Just like the movies, huh?" whispers the woman behind me. And from further back I hear: "They're never gonna believe this in Hoboken!"

"This way, please," says Comrade Chu, patiently gesturing us toward the stairs.

I half expect the terrifying dogs with eyes as big as saucers to block our passage, but there are none. Only our smiling hosts, who invite us to descend with them, two at a time, into the other China beneath the earth.

7 · THE DOSSIER

The fat document had arrived in the mail while I was off in China. As always, the FBI was a little behind.

    Subject: Zane Thompson, nee Bentwood, AKA
    Zane IndiAnna.

They insisted on calling me Thompson even though I'd been divorced since 1972. And at that they sometimes misspelled my name (Tompson, Tomson, Indiana). Henceforth I would call myself simply Zane.

> Pursuant to request made by [deleted] the following information is submitted to Headquarters.
>
> Zane Thompson was born on Jan. 31, 1940, in Babylon, Indiana, daughter of Ezekial Bentwood, high school teacher, now retired, who engaged in no known Communist activity.

Nothing on Uncle Herman; but why no mention of Mama? Didn't mothers count?

> Subject married Richard Thompson on Sept. 28, 1960. To date they have three children. They were divorced in 1972. The indices of the New York office contain no information concerning subject's husband.

Ricky would be glad to know about that!

> The following documents, however, reveal numerous Communist-front associations for subject, from 1960 on, when her known occupation was "housewife."

Here followed thirteen numbered documents, half of them riddled with deletions like the holes on a strafed wall. Some of the documents, in fact, had been so decimated by deletions that aside from prepositions, conjunctions, and articles, the only words remaining were "list" and my own name. I assumed these were statements and petitions I'd signed, sponsored by various proscribed organizations—which meant that Ricky had been right to be concerned.

They hadn't recorded my attendance at the Hanley Theater for those Russian movies or the 1959 meeting of the Trotskyists, and luckily I had escaped the night club raids, but they did have me down as "intimately associated" in 1960 with "a known Communist," then active on the Fair Play for Cuba Committee.

Who could it be? It was impossible to figure out. That was the year I'd tried sleeping around and also the year half of New York was in love with Fidel Castro, so it could have been almost anyone. I was more curious to find out how they'd got my name; but I knew I'd never find that out because they were fanatical about protecting their informers. In fact, the cover letter for my dossier said they'd held back two entire documents and made numerous "excisions" in order to protect their sources.

The next big item in my dossier, it seemed, was my Stop-the-Draft-Week arrest (`Subject was arrested Dec. 5, 1967, and charged with disorderly conduct in connection with the anti-Vietnam demonstrations in NYC`), for immediately afterward they stepped up their investigations.

> On [deleted] subject was seen carrying a large bundle into the building known as [deleted] W. 14th St. at about 7:50 p.m. On the third floor of that building [deleted] is conducted by [deleted]. At 10:20 p.m. subject emerged emptyhanded from [deleted] W. 14th St. and proceeded directly to her residence at [deleted].

So! They had actually followed me! I suddenly remembered the horrid little bearded man who'd hung around the park in plain view of my window week after week in the mad summer of '68. He had bad teeth, tiny black eyes, and an evil smile that had terrified me whenever I caught him watching me. He almost drove me crazy that summer, lounging against the park fence like an aging hippie, or lying on the grass disguised as a wino, and twice sauntering past in a ridiculous white cap carrying a ladder and pail trying to palm himself off as a house painter. A house painter in Washington Square! He didn't fool me! I was certain he'd been sent to watch me—I even saw him several times in the middle of the night. But in those days I was convinced he was a detective Ricky had hired, since his appearance coincided with my first love affair.

Now suddenly it seemed to me quite possible that he had been sent by the government to spy on me. Even back then the private detective theory had been flawed, since Ricky was so wrapped up in his own affairs at the time that he could hardly have cared about mine. It pained me to think that somewhere there might exist a complete record of the complicated means by which I slipped Victor in and out of my apartment while the children slept; maybe even of the foolish sounds we made in the throes of love; for sometimes when the mood and weather were just right we threw open that window to enable the wild music of the night people below to flow up and intensify our pleasure.

> [Deleted], who have knowledge of certain phases of Communist activity in the New York area, advised during Aug. 1968 that they had no information concerning subject.

Their big coup came a few months later when they discovered my membership in the Third Street Circle. That really got them going. From then on the reports come fast and thick. Not even their most experienced informers knew what to make of a movement that admitted to advocating total revolution at the same time that it railed against housework.

> On 10-6-68, [deleted] informed the New York office that subject was a leader of the Women's Liberation Front and a member of the Third Street Circle cell.
>
> Subject was one of about 60 agents of the WLF known to have participated in the disruption of the Miss America Pageant in Atlantic City, N.J., on 7-9-68.
>
> In a letter to the Village Voice of 3-5-69, subject took the position that a revolution on behalf of more than half the human race would be justified. Subject further stated that the U.S. Congress was a "bastion of male supremacy."
>
> In a 5-5-69 issue of Rise-Up subject was identified as one of eight persons alleged to have admitted at a public meeting at Columbia University to having undergone illegal abortions. These allegations are

under further investigation. New York office will be kept informed.

[Deleted] informed SAC that the subject participated in the April 15 "Hustle-In" in which demonstrators, impersonating prostitutes, solicited citizens in order to make citizen arrests. No arrests were made.

This item was a mistake on the deleted informer's part. For though I had helped plan this action, when the day came Tina was sick and I couldn't attend. Also, several arrests *were* made.

On 4-21-71, subject was one of three speakers at a conference on Violence Against Women.

On 5-28-71, subject was one of 18 members of a group calling themselves "Prostitutes Are The Victims," who disrupted Legislative Hearings on Victimless Crimes in the Municipal Hearing Room. After threatening violence to the legislators, subject was booked and subsequently released.

And so on, through some of my proudest moments. There we were all over again, demonstrating, organizing, speaking out, debating, writing letters, conducting workshops, protesting outrages, right up to the latest minute when I'd gone on the road for Nina's Defense Committee, attended a memorial for Trotsky (indicating that the WLF may be a domestic arm of the international Trotskyite conspiracy) and "admitted" on my passport application that I was planning a trip—possibly for subversive purposes—to "Communist China" (indicating, I guessed, that the WLF might be a Maoist arm as well).

Of course, Maoists and Trotskyists were enemies; and in addition to known housewives like me two Presidents, innumerable doctors, businessmen, movie stars, and fashion designers had planned trips to China too. But lacking training in dialectics the FBI was unable to focus on, much less reconcile, these contradictions.

It really gave me quite a lift to read over *My Life* like that, without the hesitations and vacillations, the cowardice and confusion, I would have had to admit to if I'd been writing it. The FBI made it read like snappy adventure fiction—direct, purposeful, even heroic. (A story always sounded more objective, too, in the third person.) I felt a little like Huck Finn at his own funeral, at last being openly appreciated.

Back when I'd first sent for my file, pursuing with my usual fanatical doggedness that latest of the rare but auspicious opportunities which had led me into the action of my time, I'd enjoyed speculating on what exactly the government might have on me and what, on the other side, I'd probably managed to put over on them. I admit I'd been frightened by the menacing letters written in officialese and typed by anonymous secretaries whose labors were not acknowledged by so much as their lower case initials in the bottom left-hand corner, letters encased in long official envelopes with intimidating return addresses (Office of the Director, Federal Bureau of Investigation, U.S. Department of Justice, Official Business, Penalty for Private Use) that began arriving. Though they were merely formal, they had the same effect on me as uniformed guards at the exits to department stores, compelling me as I passed before them to hold out my hands or open my coat to demonstrate I was concealing nothing. But my actual dossier here in my hands, despite the deletions and the errors, only filled me with pride.

Of course, the informers were ill-informed. They peddled air. With absolutely no discrimination they listed together events that had never happened alongside those that meant nothing to me and those that were the pride of my life. Our most subversive actions they evidently knew nothing about. The "intimate association" that had inspired them to open my case in '60 I could not even identify; my one night in jail had resulted from impure motives; the Hustle-In I'd missed entirely; my pilgrimage to China had left me with more questions than before; and the Trotskyist memorial to which they evidently attributed such weighty significance I'd actually attended only as a tribute to the passing of my favorite aunt. As for my true passion, they didn't know what to make of it. It was really outrageous that they had followed me around and checked out my love affairs and my travel plans, but I couldn't pretend I wasn't honored. Now no one would ever be able to accuse me of not having lived. Like an honorable discharge, my dossier was official, documentary proof that I had partaken of the passion and action of my time.

I was sorry my dossier hadn't come a few months sooner so I could have shown it to Aunt Louise. She would have been proud of me. In her last letter to me she said she had just helped found the Middletown Chapter of OWL (Older Women's Liberation), sick as she was by then. Then she had gone into a coma and never recovered.

Mama wrote me a long letter about the funeral. "I don't know if you remember that when Herman died Louise read from Trotsky at his funeral. You knew they believed in Trotsky? At the time it was a very brave thing to do. Well, at your aunt's funeral your father read the same passage from Trotsky's work. Before she died, Louise told me she wanted her books to go to you, Zane. They're now stored in boxes in our attic, but the next time you come home you can see what you'd like to take back with you."

When I saw the announcement for a Sunday meeting commemorating the thirty-sixth anniversary of Trotsky's death about a week after Mama's letter came, I took it for an omen and decided to attend in Louise's honor.

From the moment I walked into the large auditorium off Union Square, I had the feeling I had been there before. The high-ceilinged hall, the wooden folding chairs, the four speakers on the platform sitting impassive in their dark shirts and rumpled suits, the burly comrades guarding the doors—all seemed familiar. A replay of the meeting I'd attended in 1959 when I was fresh in New York? Even the audience had barely changed. Hair longer on some, sparser on others, but otherwise, the same earnest note-takers, pencils poised; the same young couples; the same few silver-haired old men dozing in their overcoats or trying to stifle their coughs.

"This is an historic meeting," began the chairman when the doors had been closed. "It is now thirty-six years since Leon Trotsky, the beloved founder of our movement, was ruthlessly murdered in Mexico. Yet the circumstances of that terrible crime, the crime of the century, have still to be determined."

Did I only imagine that the chairman, a small man, looked

exactly like my Uncle Herman? I'd been so young when Herman died and remembered so little that I couldn't be sure.

"There are those," continued the chairman, "who do not want this meeting to take place. It could not be otherwise. Trotsky's enemies are still at large. All the agents of imperialism, the capitalists, the CIA and the FBI, the Stalinists and the GPU"—he pronounced it gay-pay-oo—"and various revisionist tendencies . . ."

I was sure I had heard this very speech before, word for word. Had my aunt delivered it to Mama? Or had it been at that other meeting so many years before?

Two men began setting up a screen at the back of the stage for a brief film of Trotsky's life, and the chairman, wiping his brow with a large handkerchief, brought his speech to a close. "Trotsky's death is the most contemporary of questions because all the forces involved in the murder of Trotsky are alive in the world today. Titanic class struggles are on the agenda!" And as I thought of my aunt whose struggles were now over, whose agenda was now closed, the lights went out and onto the screen came Trotsky himself: young, vigorous, determined.

There was Trotsky, arriving in Leningrad in 1917. Trotsky organizing the Red Army. Trotsky reviewing troops on May Day. On the Polish Front: 1920. Addressing workers in Red Square. Wiping his nose (hair not yet gray). 1927: expelled from the Party; '29: expelled from his country; '30: in exile. "Ten more years to live," intoned the narrator. Trotsky at fifty with his wife and son. Last public speech (before I was born). In Copenhagen. In France. In Mexico City. Hair white now. Speaking in broken English in Mexico. Now at his villa: the bodyguards, the guns. And finally, suddenly—1940 (the year of my birth!): his corpse, his broken spectacles, his grave.

The lights went on. A few people clapped. Tears were sliding down my face. I rose quickly and headed for the door before the next speaker could begin and crying still put two dollars in the till for Aunt Louise and signed my name to the register.

How was one to think about the past? It was hardly dead if it could jolt me this way. ("We suffer not only from the living but from the dead," wrote Karl Marx.) Trotsky, Uncle Herman, now Aunt Louise—all dead before they'd finished. And yet, having thrown themselves into the action of their time they seemed less dead than some.

Rather than go straight home where the children, spurting life, would break my mood, I wandered down to Washington Square and stopped to sit awhile with my morbid thoughts. Though I needed no excuse for an hour in the park in this relaxed age, I reminded myself that it was high time for stock-taking. Since we'd moved I'd been unable to observe the changes from my window as I'd done in the past, though on they went anyway. And, frankly, I'd always been so caught up in life that I'd never given a moment's thought to death.

It was a glorious day—sunny, crisp, with that clear air New Yorkers see only on certain Sundays when the cars are resting in their garages and the wind in Jersey is blowing the other way. Joggers, unknown in an earlier age, loped past me, circling the park at regular intervals with their heads in the air. I'd heard that the park had turned dangerous lately because of the open commerce in drugs (as I'd heard that all the artists had moved to Soho and the best beards uptown); but except for the joggers and the vast increase in the canine population the park seemed hardly changed from the late fifties. The old jazz had resurfaced too—a sweet flute, a tenor sax, clarinet, bass for rhythm, with only guitar and wiring added to let you know the sixties had passed this way. And the Sunday rhythm was the same. There they were: the starry-eyed girls fresh from the provinces milling around the fountain, the boys in T-shirts throwing Frisbees, and the old people—the same. Even the old cafes were coming back. The Figaro, which had closed its doors in the sixties in deference to the (now defunct) East Village, had just reopened in its same old spot. It had died and sprung to life again. Indeed, with a new crop of young actresses donning aprons as before, forcing live steam through gleaming chrome spigots to yield three tablespoons of purest espresso, some people might not even know the Figaro had ever closed.

A long view had begun to possess me. When your baby grows up enough to play threesies and foursies (which you thought you had forgotten) suddenly the most striking changes seem negligible. Babies' phases fade into years. They stop sucking their thumbs, learn all about cruelty. James Agee's daughter's boyfriend baby sits, another sitter takes a Ph.D., before you know it the kids are old enough for day camp, you're past thirty, your husband leaves you for someone else, the babies grow breasts or their voices change, the rent goes up forcing you to move, the revolution you foolishly thought was moments away has slipped by once again—and watching the park pass through another spring, you begin to see the continuities you hadn't noticed before.

The war that started when my babies were little and ended when they were half grown—was it so different from the war of my own childhood, or the one before that? I was already an accomplished bicyclist the day our war ended, for I remember riding furiously with the older kids (just that once) down the hill to Middletown, where my aunt and uncle lived, to celebrate. My children, definitely city kids, marched on foot instead, shouting and carrying signs from the fountain in Washington Square all the way up to the Sheep Meadow in Central Park. But wasn't it essentially the same?

Would our rebellion mystify our children as the opaque Trotsky idea mystified me? Was each crack at justice doomed like True Love? "Contemporary history is running in high gear," wrote Trotsky. The Single Taxers, I suddenly remembered—what had happened to them? Or the Fenians? Would the force of feminism peter out again, as it had after the suffragists' success, leaving us once more buried in ridicule until we could be dug up again as doddering old women to ride in a triumphant twenty-first-century motorcade?

A lifetime, which had once seemed more than long enough, maybe wasn't so long after all. Louise was sixty-one when she died: not so very old. Why, I'd soon be catching up to her!

Louise had made admirable use of her limited time. She'd been the gutsiest woman in Middletown: radical organizer of her Welfare Union, sole picketer of the Board of Education hearings, irrepressible author of letters to the editor of the Middletown *Sun*, monthly reader of Shakespeare to the blind, co-leader of the library's Great Literature Study Group, Trotskyist, first female civilian in the world to ship out from Indiana up the new St. Lawrence Seaway and around the world on a freighter, co-founder of Middletown OWL, mentor to me.

To my consternation, I felt my eyes fill up again. It was foolish to be crying in public while a juggler tossed flaming pins only a few feet away and a brass band struck up a lively march at the fountain nearby; but what was I to do? A man on the bench opposite was staring at me.

I was too embarrassed to stay. The tears that had begun in moderation were now quite uncontrollably streaming down my cheeks in full view of everyone. Besides, time was pressing.

Supposing I lived as long as Louise had lived and used every remaining minute efficiently, there was still far more to be done than I had time for. Yesterday's acts didn't save me today. Half my life was over and the whole world remained to be changed. Nina was in jail awaiting trial; how could I sit idly in a park? ("So you've finally turned radical," she'd said mischievously when I'd visited her in jail. "And you've turned feminist, I hear," I'd parried. Then I gave her some macadamia nuts and we both laughed because we were in a cell instead of her old clubroom, and we were conspiring to get her acquitted instead of fired.) I got up to leave.

I remember noticing the man from the bench opposite following me out of the park. I assumed he was concerned about me (how many people, after all, suddenly burst into tears when a brass band starts playing?) or simply interested; it was not unusual to be followed in New York City. But as I got caught up again in my mourning and resolve, I forgot to notice how far he followed me.

Now, with hindsight, I wonder if I hadn't picked up a friend from the Red Squad at the Trotsky memorial or even an agent of the FBI? At the time I only half believed in them, but now it's clear there is more to be remembered than they have begun to disclose.

8 · WINNER'S LUCK

A big night was beginning at the New Space Cafe. No ordinary Friday night. I carried a gallon bottle of my favorite California chablis in a brown paper bag, Tracy was bringing some touted super-dope she'd got from a Guatemalan poet for later on; River was making four times the usual weekend number of her (justly) famous quiches; Olive had written a new song for the occasion; and Marya had prepared a little speech.

Three days earlier in Maryland Nina had been acquitted of all seven charges against her. (I'd been at the opening session of her trial, but then I'd had to get back to New York for the children, and Faith, who had rented a room across from the jail and dropped everything for the duration of the trial, had told me the happy verdict on the telephone.) Tonight—Friday—all the New York women who had worked on Nina's case were celebrating.

We'd invited half the movement to the party even though Nina would not be present. "I never want to see another blue coat," she'd said. "Faith and Liz are taking me to Vermont forever. Thanks anyway." And though it wouldn't be forever—even underground Nina hadn't been able to stay away from the city for more than a couple of months at a time, however risky—she'd gone off with Faith to the Women's Farm for at least a two-week recovery.

The aroma of melting cheese and onion signaling River's magic quiches caressed my nostrils as I pushed open the familiar door with my briefcase and entered the noisy welcome of New Space. It was more crowded than usual, even for a Friday; the network had done its work. New graphics adorned the walls and you could feel the celebration in the air.

"Back here, Zane!" shouted Kitty from a rear table ("our" table). I stopped to greet a couple of former students, then made my way toward the back and an empty chair beside Kitty.

"No, that chair's taken," said Kitty, hastily dropping her bag in the seat beside her. "Here. Move over, everybody, so Zane can squeeze in. Come on, there's room. Pull up another chair, that's it." Kitty was sparkling as she ordinarily did only for a curtain call.

I added my bottle to the others on the table, set my briefcase on the floor, and squeezed another chair in next to Kitty. "What's happening?" I asked.

"You'll see in a minute," said grinning Kitty.

"I've brought a little surprise," I announced, as out of my briefcase I pulled my FBI file, my latest round of ammunition, and waved it before the assembly.

"What is it?" asked Tracy across the table.

"My dossier," I answered proudly, "complete with deletions. My contribution to the festivities. Wait till you see!"

(In another crowd my crowing might have seemed vain or smug; but here we were all heroes.)

"What did they have on you?"

"Pass it around, Zane, come on."

"Oh! Let me see!"

My eager student Tracy, shyness long since reined, was reaching across the table, waving her arms. "Here," she cried, "here!"

"Wait, everybody, please. You have to keep the pages together and read them in order. It's not all that long, but it is my life. Just one person at a time."

One day, I thought, all our comrades would be heroes, and without requiring FBI certification. I'd been to China and knew how far people could follow a dream. Here in this country the female masses might be only beginning to awaken; our somnolent vision was still murky. But anything was possible given will and time. History was unstoppable. Two hundred years before, a woman named Zane (ancestor to Zane Grey) had risked her life dashing through heavy fire to reach a crucial cache of gunpowder during one of the last battles of the first American Revolution. Maybe this Zane would prove herself in the coming one.

Proudly I handed my file across to Tracy; and in that instant over her shoulder I suddenly saw emerge from the john Morgan Moore—tall, jacketed, alone—now hesitating uncertainly on the threshold of a room she didn't know (as I had always hesitated to enter the Figaro or the Cafe Lucia).

"Surprise!" whispered Kitty beside me, squeezing my arm, as Moore began walking toward our table.

Louise Michel returning to France after eight years in forced exile, Carrie Chapman Catt awaiting the final vote on the Nineteenth Amendment, Emma Goldman reunited with her lover after his fourteen-year imprisonment, Angela Davis or Nina Chase hearing of their acquittals, Marya facing her first mass audience could hardly have felt more feverish palpitations of apprehension and joy than I felt watching Moore approach our table with its single empty chair.

Kitty, that sweetheart, tried her best to make it easy for me, though she had known Moore herself for, at most, maybe ten minutes. "Morgan came over to help us celebrate," she said. "She's been following Nina's case." (I knew that. She'd sent a twenty-five-dollar check to the Defense Committee.)

"Yes," said Moore, in a voice much gentler than the one she used for the public. "I did want to celebrate. But actually I've been intending to stop in here for a long time now. I just never quite got around to it before."

"This is Zane IndiAnna, who chaired Solotaire's Defense Committee," said Kitty, trying to sound casual.

To which Moore replied with a statement that might have calmed someone else but, addressed to me, only increased my agitation. "I'm glad to meet you," she said. "I like the work you do."

I like the work you do. I was staggered. "You *know* the work I do?" I blurted out.

"I think so," she said, hesitating. "Didn't you used to talk on People's Radio sometimes? There was no other Zane in the Third Street Circle, was there?"

I'd been actively avoiding this meeting for the better part of eighteen years, and now here we were, talking like any pair of new acquaintances. Kitty reports that from the start I seemed reasonably composed. It's hard to believe: My own impression is that for the first five minutes I was unable to think of anything but the awful brazen letters I'd written to Moore (but, thank god!, had never mailed) after the publication of each of her books. "Dear Morgan Moore: For seven years I've followed your work from those early essays in the *Voice* to your new *Motive and Act* . . ." "Dear MM: All those years I trailed you around New York from a safely discreet distance I never dared approach you. But now, having read your new book . . ." "Dear Moore: I always knew, watching you from the front row of lecture halls and the back row of Intellectual Forums that it was only a matter of time until you embraced feminism. Now in your new *Dialogues with Women* . . ." I only prayed she wouldn't be able to know what I felt by merely looking at me, as I had learned to tell about my students.

"Zane's just back from China," said Kitty, making an easy opening for me.

"Really!" said Moore, leaning forward on her elbows, eager to hear. "When? How?"

Thank god for China, I thought, able at last to speak. In the moment before we'd sat down together, before either of us had said a word, I'd been intimidated by Moore's height. I'd jumped up to give her space to pull out her chair at our table and realized she towered over me by more than a head. Not that I hadn't known it before, but I'd never experienced it at such close range, and her stature was the one quality never conveyed in her jacket photos, no matter how stark or beautiful. A photo could reveal her classically regular features—large earnest eyes, straight nose, full mouth that often broke into flash smiles on the podium but was always serious for the camera, the high cheekbones. But the public that knew her only by her books had no more idea of her height than of her amazing hair, thick and red as Moroccan rugs and now, I saw, beginning here and there to gray. She was an imposingly tall and large-boned woman, with the stride of someone absolutely sure of herself. Evidently not even I, who had followed her through streets and jails, studying her in print and on podiums, had been prepared for the effect of standing face to face with her in New Space, separated by only inches of air.

But with China my prop, I was able to handle the conversation reasonably well. My voice worked normally, my hands were steady, my words intelligible, I didn't blow it by gushing or using fastspeak. We were in New Space, after all, where serious conversation headed the menu and everyone was accepted as more or less equal. In retrospect I think I can say it was actually a stimulating interchange. From China we went on to discuss Nina's case, and the movement, and the critical reaction to Moore's newest book. And though I saw I had eighteen years' worth of foolish preconceptions to undo, Moore had no reason to suspect that any of us had ever been anything but what we appeared at that moment: long-term, committed activists.

About half an hour later—after Kitty had gone to help River in the kitchen and I had begun to feel comfortable (for if there were three subjects I felt easy with they were China, the movement, and Morgan Moore's work, and the wine was by then probably having its effect, too); after I saw that Moore needed to be set at ease as much as I, for despite her celebrity she was the stranger here—our conversation took a slightly personal turn.

Moore had just answered some remark of mine by saying, "I've always been pretty lucky in my career." But then she immediately added, not without a note of bitterness, "It's just too bad there are always people around ready to hate me for it, and people who won't hesitate to use my luck against the movement."

I was surprised to hear her say so. Not that I didn't feel precisely the same way. Next to Moore herself, who knew better than I how people attacked her for being what she called "lucky," and through her attacked our movement? Had I not spent too many hours defending them both? Either people said she was an "exception," more deserving of respect than other women, or they said her success proved there was nothing stopping any woman of talent. Either way, she was pitted against the rest of us. But I didn't expect to hear her say it, and I certainly didn't expect the note of bitterness; she had always seemed to me above such feelings.

"That was one of the things I liked best in *Dialogues*," I said, hoping to be reassuring. "I thought you handled the whole question of exceptions and privileges really well. They won't be able to trot out that old argument against you so easily this time."

From a distant past I heard the charge of "Dyke!" and then Wolfe was saying, "I'll look after Zane if you want," and exchanging salacious grins with Marshall. The only model they could invoke for my regard for Moore had been the sexual one, for how else did any of them know women? But it was as inadequate to the feelings then—and now—surging through me as the romantic model was to marriage. What could they, men, have known of my ambitions, my fantasies—they, who had been free to dream what they wanted? It was a matter of admiration, of respect. "I like the work you do," she'd said. Respect, so easy for them to come by, was something I'd never got from a man till almost yesterday, something Wolfe and Marshall had probably never felt unequivocally for a woman in their entire lives. Respect could embrace sex, could include love, but it seldom went the other way around. How many men who loved women respected them too? Not till Faith had loved me had I found respect in love. Maybe a little from Ricky because he was naïve, but not nearly enough.

"Well, I hope you're right," said Moore. "I did try to deal with those charges in the last chapter, but to some people, I'm afraid, luck will always look sinister or corrupt."

"That's because we live under a corrupt system. They don't realize," I said, boldly indulging in an intimate allusion, "that in this world the winning player is always lucky."

The line, which had often puzzled me, was one I'd read more

than once in the pages of Moore. In fact, if I hadn't learned it already from my father, who'd often quoted it to me while teaching me chess, I might have picked it up from her.

Moore, startled to hear one of her pet lines on my lips, cocked her head and gave me a quizzical look. "Why, that's from Capablanca," she said.

"From Morgan Moore," I replied, grinning back at her, one champ to another. And for the first time I thought I understood Capablanca's conundrum.

Winner's luck was a funny thing. Though some of the people at our table pretended it wasn't luck but righteousness that brought us here on Fridays to drink coffee and wine and grieve together about the world, I knew we were riding on luck. ("One small twist of fate," wrote the black militant Angela Davis, "and I might have drowned in the muck of poverty and disease and illiteracy. That is why I never felt I had any right to look upon myself as being any different from my sisters and brothers.") Without each other our very insights were only visions and our luck could go at any moment. New Space could be closed on violations, we could lose our jobs, the country could plunge deeper into depression or back into war, our gains could be wiped out tomorrow—

Yet it was more than luck too. Skill, will, circumstance, history in some complex, mysterious balance had all combined with luck to land us here. How else explain that after half a lifetime of false starts I was now sitting equal and opposite Morgan Moore in an absolutely unprecedented New Space?

When Tracy produced the first joint, Moore, declining, shook each of our hands, wished us luck, and left. Not till hours later, while we were drinking our final toast to Nina with the last drop of chablis, did it strike me that I had once again leaped dangerously close to a conclusion. Sitting with Moore, I had allowed myself to be tempted by a momentary triumph into forgetting dialectics. As though the game were over and I the winner, when clearly the board was still changing with every move, pawns were slowly advancing, knights lay in ambush—would I never learn?

"I guess we ought to think about cleaning up," said Marya, yawning. "Big day tomorrow."

"Tomorrow?" said Kitty. "Tomorrow's dead. It's already after three. What an optimist you are!"

"And correctly," countered Golda. " 'Pessimism of intellect, optimism of will'—Gramsci's formula for a good revolutionary." Then with a glass in each hand she led the procession to the kitchen.

At that moment I had a vision. Pessimism of intellect, optimism of will—that was the winning combination, that was the meaning of winner's luck; if we held onto it we couldn't lose. (Somewhere I suspected Mao or someone had summarized my vision perfectly, but given the wine, the dope, and the hour, I was in no condition to search my memory.) I knew then how lucky we were to have been born at all, to have the gift of life, but especially to be women, here, now. Even the bad was good, for good would come of it. Ahead lay boundless opportunity. Now to make the most of it!

"Kitty? Listen. I've just understood the unity of opposites."

"Oh come on, Zane; enough. You're slurring your consonants. Tell me about it tomorrow, okay?"

But I was afraid to wait. By tomorrow the insight could be gone; I needed to preserve it tonight.

As we cleared off the tables I managed to entice Tracy and Marya, who were always game, back into debate. I was only hoping to find words with which to preserve my vision until morning, when I could look at it again. But while we were stacking the dishes in the sink, we got so wrapped up in the fascination of opposites and so involved in the burning questions that by the time we'd finished our self-assigned chore, River was making another pot of coffee, and it was clear there'd be no stopping us that night.

Dialectical Epilogue

Revolutionary memoirs usually end with an interim report on the general prospects for revolution. This is a tricky maneuver to pull off, for while tradition and logic demand that the final word inspire hope, if times were really ripe for revolution, if there were even a thriving revolutionary movement going, do you think any self-respecting activist would sequester herself in her study for the years it takes to write a book? Of course not! She would be out pounding down the palace doors, demanding concessions, leaping onto the barricades!

(As Lenin explained, postponing the completion of his own *State and Revolution* on the eve of the October Revolution: "The second part of this pamphlet . . . will probably have to be put off for a long time. It is more pleasant and useful to go through 'the experience of the revolution' than to write about it.")

The awkward fact is, most writing rebels have set down their histories in exile, in defeat, or in those unhappy times when optimism seemed least justified. This hardly boosts their credibility, and even when they write about events occurring right up to the last possible minute before the presses roll, their stories tend to look a little out of synch, anachronous, like those plumed hats and waxed mustaches slowly parading down MacDougal Street on Village characters in spring.

But really, if you think about it, this tendency too is fitting. What does it prove but that these rebels, even when they are at their tamest, quietly filling up notebooks in their studies, are deviants to the end, ever in opposition, straining against the times?

La Pasionaria, Mother Bloor, both hopefully name their final chapters "New Beginnings," though they end their stories in moments of terrible reaction and world catastrophe. ("The youth of Spain are our hope." "Out of this agony a new and better world will be born." Etc., etc.) Tragic Angelica Balabanoff, who must compose the last pages of her noble *Life* with a pen dipped in the knowledge that the glorious revolution to which she devoted her entire life has been betrayed, that tyrants are swarming over Europe, that her fellow revolutionaries spit upon her as a traitor—Comrade Balabanoff still confirms: "My belief has never been more complete than it is now." Facing likely death Trotsky confides to his diary: "If they consume me before the world revolution takes a new big step forward—and it does look that way—I shall still pass into nonexistence with an indestructible confidence in the victory of the cause I have served all my life."

But why pile up examples? They are all the same. Accentuate the positive. It is an old, honorable tradition, justified by dialectics, that I would not dream of violating. Every act has, as Hegel has shown, its positive and negative moments, and until the end of the world (still presumably some time off) the writer may choose which one to end on without feeling she has fudged the truth. Even my *Debater's Manual*, a partisan of partisans, concedes in a footnote: "There is no intellectual dishonesty in debating both sides of a proposition. There must be two sides or there is no debate. In championing either, recognize the existence of fundamental pros and cons." The joint is half-smoked or half-left, depending on how high you feel.

Now, remembering, as Mao says, that "New things always have to experience difficulties and setbacks as they grow," but "in times of difficulty we must not lose sight of our achievements," I'll sum up for you and take my chances that you may laugh at my plumed hat.

Some things were different because we passed this way.

Abortions were no longer illegal and for some people were cheaper and safer—which made a big difference for the young girls who still arrived in the Village every summer and fall seeking their destinies—though sterilization of the poor was alarmingly on the rise and the Supreme Court could not be counted on.

Child-battering and wife-beating, newly discussed crimes, were starting to scandalize the bureaucrats, thanks to us, though these outrages were rampant beyond anyone's expectations.

Nailing and jailing rapists had become easier than before we began to holler, but since, as statistics showed, rape was becoming an increasingly popular crime, we just couldn't seem to stay ahead of the game.

Similarly, though more women were out there working than in the past (so many, warned a presidential assistant, that they were going to destroy the economy and alter the face of the twenty-first century—much, I suppose, as Jews were once said to have laid waste the economy of Europe), somehow they just kept on earning less and less money than the men with every passing year. The *New York Times* continued to report these facts, but no longer on the front pages.

Some women, of course, were entering coveted professions—a Director or Partner here, a Governor there—but this was of little benefit to office workers, cleaning women, or nurse's aides; and it remained to be seen if those professions which did yield to women in any numbers wouldn't quickly (like the teaching and secretarial professions of several generations back) be deserted by the men who would grab their salaries and run.

Places of public accommodation were obliged to accommodate women. Bars opened their doors to us after court orders. Amid stormy battles, the Harvard Club finally locked off its separate Ladies' Entrance and admitted women to membership. But other power clubs remained exclusive. The U.S. Congress continued (you listening, FBI?) a bastion of white male supremacy.

Dorms and Yale were now co-ed. Some of the better public high schools were admitting girls, though not in Philadelphia. There was hanky-panky in the middle schools. Some texts contained a chapter, some schools an elective, on Women.

Marriage, divorce, the birth rate, the death rate were confounding the experts. Trends evolved and reversed. The Family was in a hopeless tangle. Some were for it, some against it, no one knew for sure.

But at least for some of us our lives had improved. We lucky ones spoke up now sometimes and fought back when they called us names—that was worth a lot. And some of the mothers were no longer all alone. Now when you lost your job, when they cut back your day-care or struck down your maternity benefits or took away your seniority or denied your appeal or phased out your function or negated their affirmative action, you were likelier than before to have someone understanding to talk to. If things got bad enough, you might seek refuge in a crisis center for rape victims, an abortion counselor on campus, a woman's commune for community, a neighborhood center for support, a halfway house for battered wives. Halfway but better than no way.

Not even love was hopeless. A few women still called it backsliding if your lover was a man, but for lots of us love between the sexes had definitely improved. Not only because it was possible to trust someone who respected you; nor because, uncloistered, we could now say yes or no with less shame than before; nor even because women were finally telling the world what they needed. (One member of our Circle who'd written an article on sex made sure prospective lovers read it; another came out with "three nonnegotiable conditions: plenty of dope, three hours minimum, and cunnilingus.") Part of the difference was possibly in the men. Could it be that some of them had really changed? Some of the new poets around the Village, though they hardly looked different than before with their beards and jeans and hiking boots, were, I thought, somewhat more softspoken, somewhat gentler, than I remembered, possibly even a little humble. More than ever before a few youths seemed genuinely interested in knowledgeable ("older") women. Though you still couldn't talk to them as you could to a woman (that would probably be the last thing to change), nowadays some of them found women worth talking to. A few wanted to learn. On top of that, they offered to baby sit, make the bed, do the shopping and dishes (including the silverware and the pots and pans); surely it couldn't *all* be show! Yes, some of them had definitely learned how to listen.

There was another generation coming up behind us to keep the pilot light lit. I don't mean only our natural children (of whom there were not, as yet, so many) or those smart "career women" just out for themselves, but the young women who came to New Space Cafe every Friday night like Tracy and Sasha full of high ideals, and the young office workers starting to organize and getting another chance, and the first girls ever to go to the free and demanding Stuyvesant High, and those who write letters in our defense and read our journals, and maybe a handful of men. Not many yet, but maybe enough to keep it going.

Even at New Space currently the hottest subject is whether or not to have a child. Surprised? But that's a pressing question for people approaching the critical age, especially in a sluggish time. Rosa Luxemburg herself, that most vigilant martyr, wrote to her lover: "Oh darling, will I never have my own baby?" Connection, we know, is all. The burning questions are always the same: how to live, how to be. (I'll be interested to see who will and who won't. If Sammy weren't almost a man and Tina and Julie half-grown, I might think of having one more child myself. Her father would be one of those fabled new types who would share equally in her upbringing and we'd name her Vera or Rosa or Hope.)

But is such optimism justified? That's the hardest question of all. I can't tell; some of my most tenaciously held beliefs have turned out to be mistaken. For example: After I got to know Morgan Moore (who comes to New Space Cafe now and then on Fridays, vastly preferring it, she says, to the crowded Figaro), she turned out to be not much like the person I'd always taken her for. Once you discounted the obvious similarities—our both being women, leftists, middle-class Midwesterners—we were not all that much alike. Our tastes—in music, films—were different; she never touched grass or drugs, though she had a ravenous sweet tooth that demanded chocolate; she had the high, calm outlook of a tall person, while I was essentially short and intense; she was the intellectual, I the activist; she had perfect teeth; and most basic difference of all, she had no children, while I had, would always have, a minimum of three. Though naturally I would always honor her with gratitude and respect, I sometimes wondered if, had it not been for the Dunhill holder, the nail-biting, and the chess, all of which she had long since given up, I would ever have thought us alike at all?

But in the end those weren't the facts that mattered. The significant ones were the intangibles. As Elizaveta Kovalskaia, one of the ardent Moscow Amazons, said during her underground work in Kiev where she kept coming upon traces of earlier revolutionaries:

> *Often when people try to sum up the activity of a group or individual and can point to no immediate, tangible results, they conclude that the activity was a failure. But how can you count all the circles made by a stone when you toss it into the water?*

Selected Bibliography

Balabanoff, Angelica. *My Life As a Rebel.* New York: Harper & Bros., 1938.

Beauvoir, Simone de. *The Second Sex.* New York: Alfred A. Knopf, 1953.

Bloor, Ella Reeve. *We Are Many.* New York International Publishers, 1940.

Chevigny, Bell Gale. *The Woman and the Myth: Margaret Fuller's Life and Writings.* Old Westbury, New York: The Feminist Press, 1976.

Cleyre, Voltairine de. *Selected Works.* Ed. by Alexander Berkman. New York: Mother Earth Publishing Assoc., 1914.

Davis, Angela. *An Autobiography.* New York: Random House, 1974.

Debater's Manual:

Behl, William A. *Discussion and Debate.* New York: Ronald Press, 1953.

Courtney, Luther, and Glenn Capp. *Practical Debating.* Chicago: Lippincott, 1949.

Ott, Edward Amherst. *How to Gesture.* New York: Hinds, Noble & Eldridge, 1892.

Engel, Barbara Alpern, and Clifford N. Rosenthal, ed. and tr. *Five Sisters: Women Against the Tsar.* New York: Alfred A. Knopf, 1975.

Figner, Vera. *Memoirs of a Revolutionist.* New York: International Publishers, 1927.

Flynn, Elizabeth Gurley. *The Rebel Girl: An Autobiography.* New York: International Publishers, 1955 and 1973.

Gilbert, Olive. *Narrative of Sojourner Truth*. New York: Arno Press, 1968.

Goldman, Emma. *Living My Life*. New York: Alfred A. Knopf, 1931.

Ibarruri, Delores. *They Shall Not Pass: The Autobiography of La Pasionaria*. New York: International Publishers, 1966.

Joan of Arc. *Joan of Arc: Self Portrait*. Compiled and translated by Willard Trask. New York: Collier Books, 1961.

Jones, Mary Harris. *Autobiography of Mother Jones*. Chicago: Charles H. Kerr & Co., 1925.

Kollontai, Alexandra. *Autobiography of a Sexually Emancipated Communist Woman*. New York: Herder and Herder, 1971.

Lenin, V. I. *What Is to Be Done? Burning Questions of Our Movement*. New York: International Publishers, 1929.

Luxemburg, Rosa. *Letters from Prison*. London: Bushey Mead Press, 1946.

Lynd, Robert S., and Helen Merrell. *Middletown*. New York: Harcourt Brace, 1929.

———. *Middletown in Transition*. New York: Harcourt Brace, 1937.

Mao Tse-tung. *Quotations from Chairman Mao Tse-tung* ("The Little Red Book"). Peking: Foreign Languages Press, 1972.

Marx, Karl, and Friedrich Engels. *Basic Writings on Politics and Philosophy*. Ed. by Lewis S. Feuer. New York: Doubleday Anchor Books, 1959.

Prima, Diane di. *Memoirs of a Beatnik*. New York: Olympia Press, 1969.

Thomas, Edith. *The Women Incendiaries (Les Pétroleuses)*. New York: George Braziller, 1966.

Trotsky, Leon. *My Life*. New York: Scribners, 1930.

———. *Trotsky's Diary in Exile: 1935*. Cambridge: Harvard University Press, 1958.

U.S. Senate Select Committee to Study Government Operations with Respect to Intelligence Activity. *Report of Hearings* (Vol. 6, F.B.I.). Washington, D.C.: U.S. Government Printing Office, 1976.

Zane. *My Life as a Rebel*. New York: New Space Press, 1977.

A Note on the Type

THE TEXT of this book is set in Electra, a typeface designed by W. A. Dwiggins for the Mergenthaler Linotype Company and first made available in 1935. Electra cannot be classified as either "modern" or "old style." It is not based on any historical model, and hence does not echo any particular period or style of type design. It avoids the extreme contrast between "thick" and "thin" elements that marks most modern faces, and is without eccentricities which catch the eye and interfere with reading. In general, Electra is a simple, readable typeface which attempts to give a feeling of fluidity, power, and speed.

Composed by Maryland Linotype Composition Company, Inc., Baltimore, Maryland. Printed and bound by American Book–Stratford Press, Inc., Saddle Brook, New Jersey

Typography and binding design by Virginia Tan